everywhere

and every way

ALSO BY JENNIFER PROBST

The Searching For Series

Searching for Someday

Searching for Perfect

Searching for You

Searching for Beautiful

Searching for Always

The Marriage to a Billionaire Series

The Marriage Bargain

The Marriage Trap

The Marriage Mistake

The Marriage Merger

everywhere
and every way

JENNIFER
PROBST

GALLERY BOOKS

New York   London   Toronto   Sydney   New Delhi

Gallery Books
An Imprint of Simon & Schuster, Inc.
1230 Avenue of the Americas
New York, NY 10020

First Gallery Books trade paperback edition May 2016

GALLERY BOOKS and colophon are registered trademarks of
Simon & Schuster, Inc.

For information about special discounts for bulk purchases, please
contact Simon & Schuster Special Sales at 1-866-506-1949 or
business@simonandschuster.com.

The Simon & Schuster Speakers Bureau can bring authors to your live event.
For more information or to book an event, contact the Simon & Schuster Speakers
Bureau at 1-866-248-3049 or visit our website at www.simonspeakers.com.

Manufactured in the United States of America

10 9 8 7 6 5 4 3 2 1

Library of Congress Cataloging-in-Publication Data

Names: Probst, Jennifer, author.
Title: Everywhere and every way / Jennifer Probst.
Description: First Gallery Books trade paperback edition. | New York : Gallery
Books, 2016. | Series: The billionaire builders ; 1
Identifiers: LCCN 2015042793
Subjects: LCSH: Man-woman relationships—Fiction. | GSAFD: Love stories.
Classification: LCC PS3616.R624 E94 2016 | DDC 813/.6—dc23 LC record
available at http://lccn.loc.gov/2015042793

ISBN 978-1-5011-2423-5
ISBN 978-1-5011-2424-2 (ebook)

It may be that the satisfaction I need depends on my going away, so that when I've gone and come back, I'll find it at home.

—RUMI

Houses are built to live in, and not to look on; therefore let use be preferred before uniformity.

—FRANCIS BACON

════════

In memory of my second "mom," Rochelle Penny Zwickel, who opened her heart and home to me and made the world a more special place. We miss you every day.

For those seeking their true home: you can search for it, build it, decorate it, change it, but I believe it is any safe place that brings comfort and peace.

And home is always sweeter
when it is shared with someone you love.

prologue

Caleb Pierce craved a cold beer, air-conditioning, his dogs, and maybe a pretty brunette to warm his bed.

Instead, he got lukewarm water, choking heat, his head in an earsplitting vise, and a raging bitch testing his temper.

And it was only eight a.m.

"I told you a thousand times I wanted the bedroom for my mother off the garage." Lucy Weatherspoon jabbed her French-manicured finger at the framing and back at the plans they'd changed twelve times. "I need her to have privacy and her own entrance. If this is the garage, why is the bedroom off the other side?"

He reminded himself again that running your own company had its challenges. One of them was clients who thought building a house was like shopping at the mall. Sure, he was used to difficult clients, but Lucy tested even his patience. She spoke to him as if he were a bit dim-witted just because he wore jeans with holes in them and battered work boots and had dust covering every inch of his body. His gut had told him to turn down the damn job of building her dream house, but his stubborn father overruled him, calling her congressman husband and telling him Pierce Brothers would be fucking *thrilled* to take on the project. His father always did have a soft spot for power. Probably figured the politician would owe him a favor.

Yeah, Cal would rather have a prostate exam than deal with Congressman Weatherspoon's wife.

He wiped the sweat off his brow, noting the slight wrinkle of her nose telling him he smelled. For fun, he deliberately took a step closer to her. "Mrs. Weatherspoon, we went over this several times, and I had you sign off. Remember? Your mother's bedroom has to be on the other side of the house because you decided you wanted the billiard room to be accessed from the garage. Of course, I can add it to the second floor with a private entry, but we'd need to deal with a staircase or elevator."

"No. I want it on the ground floor. I don't remember signing off on this. Are you telling me I need to choose between my mother and the pool table room?"

He tried hard not to gnash his teeth. He'd already lost too much of the enamel, and they'd just broken ground on this job. "No. I'm saying if we put the bedroom on the other side of the house, it won't break the architectural lines, and you can have everything you want. Just. Like. We. Discussed."

She tapped her nude high-heeled foot, studying him as if trying to decipher whether he was a sarcastic asshole or just didn't understand how to talk to the natives. He gave his best dumb look, and finally she sighed. "Fine. I'll bend on this."

Oh, goody.

"But I changed my mind on the multilevel deck. I found this picture on Houzz and want you to re-create it." She shoved a glossy printout of some Arizona-inspired massive patio that was surrounded by a desert. And yep, just as he figured, it was from a spa hotel that looked nothing like the lake-view property he was currently building on. Knowing it would look ridiculous on the elegant Colonial that rivaled a Southern plantation, he forced himself to nod and pretend to study the picture.

"Yes, we can definitely discuss this. Since the deck won't affect my current framing, let's revisit when we begin designing the outside."

That placated her enough to get her to smile stiffly. "Very well. Oh, I'd better go. I'm late for the charity breakfast. I'll check in with you later, Caleb."

"Great." He nodded as she picked her way carefully over the building site and watched her pull away in her shiny black Mercedes. Cal shook his head and gulped down a long drink of water, then wiped his mouth with the back of his hand. Next time, he'd get his architect Brady to deal with her. He was good at charming an endless array of women when they drew up plans, but was never around to handle the temper tantrums on the actual job.

Then again, Brady had always been smarter than him.

Cal did a walk-through to check on his team. The pounding sounds of classic Aerosmith blared from an ancient radio that had nothing on those fancy iPods. It had been on hundreds of jobs with him, covered in grime, soaked with water, battered by falls, and never stopped working. Sure, when he ran, he liked those wireless contraptions, but Cal always felt he had been born a few decades too late. To him, simple was better. Simple worked just fine, but the more houses he built, the more he was surrounded by requests for fancier equipment, for endless rooms that would never be used, and for him to clear land better left alone.

He nodded to Jason, who was currently finishing up the framing, and ran his hand over the wood, checking for stability and texture. His hands were an extension of all his senses, able to figure out weak spots hidden in rotted wood or irregular length. Of course, he wasn't as gifted as his youngest brother, Dalton, who'd been dubbed the Wood Whisperer. His middle brother, Tristan, only laughed and suggested *wood* be changed to *woody* to be more accurate. He'd always been the wiseass out of all of them.

Cal wiped the thought of his brothers out of his head, readjusted his hard hat, and continued his quick walk-through. In the past year, Pierce Brothers Construction had grown, but Cal refused to sacrifice quality over his father's constant need to be the biggest firm in the Northeast.

On cue, his phone shrieked, and he punched the button. "Yeah?"

"Cal? Something happened."

The usually calm voice of his assistant, Sydney, broke over the line. In that moment, he knew deep in his gut that everything would change, like the flash of knowledge before a car crash, or the sharp cut of pain before a loss penetrated the brain. Cal tightened his grip on the phone and waited. The heat of the morning pressed over him. The bright blue sky, streaked with clouds, blurred his vision. The sounds of Aerosmith, drills, and hammers filled his ears.

"Your father had a heart attack. He's at Harrington Memorial."

"Is he okay?"

Sydney paused. The silence told him everything he needed to know and dreaded to hear. "You need to get there quick."

"On my way."

Calling out quickly to his team, he ripped off his hat, jumped into his truck, and drove.

A mass of machines beeped, and Cal tried not to focus on the tubes running into his father's body in an attempt to keep him alive. They'd tried to keep him out by siccing Security on him and making a scene, but he refused to leave until they allowed him to stand beside his bed while they prepped him for surgery.

Christian Pierce was a hard, fierce man with a force that pushed through both opposition and people like a tank. At seventy years old, he'd only grown more grizzled, in both body and spirit, leaving fear and respect in his wake but little tenderness. Cal stared into his pale face while the machines moved up and down to keep breath in his lungs and reached out tentatively to take his father's hand.

"Get off me, for God's sake. I'm not dying. Not yet."

Cal jerked away. His father's eyes flew open. The familiar coffee-brown eyes held a hint of disdain at his son's weakness, even though they were red rimmed and weary. Cal shoved down the brief flare of pain and arranged his face to a neutral expression. "Good, because I want you to take over the Weatherspoons. They're a pain in my ass."

His father grunted. "I need some future political favors. Handle it." He practically spit at the nurse hovering and checking his vitals. "Stop poking me. When do I get out of here?"

The pretty blonde hesitated. Uh-oh. His father was the worst patient in the world, and he bit faster than a rattlesnake when cornered. Already he looked set to viciously tear her to verbal pieces while she seemed to be gathering the right words to say.

Cal saved her by answering. "You're not. Doctor said you need surgery to unblock some valves. They're sending you now."

His father grunted again. "Idiot doctor has been wanting me to go under the knife for years. He just wants to make money and shut me up. He's still bitching I overcharged him on materials for his house."

"You did."

"He can afford it."

Cal didn't argue. He knew the next five minutes before his father was wheeled into surgery were vital. He'd already been told by the serious-faced Dr. Wang that it wouldn't be an easy surgery. Not with his father's heart damage from the last attack and the way he'd treated his body the past few years. Christian liked his whiskey, his cigars, and his privacy. He thought eating healthy and walking on treadmills were for weaklings. When he was actually doing the construction part of the business, he'd been in better shape, but the last decade his father had faded to the office work and wheeling and dealing behind the scenes.

"I'm calling Tristan and Dalton. They need to know."

In seconds, his father raged at him in pure fury. "You will

not. Touch that fucking phone and I'll wipe you out of my will."

Cal gave him a hard stare, refusing to flinch. "Go ahead. Been looking to work at Starbucks anyway."

"Don't mock me. I don't want to deal with their guilt or bullshit. I'll be fine, and we both know it."

"Dad, they have a right to know."

"They walked out on me. They have a right to know nothing." A thin stream of drool trickled from his mouth. Cal studied the slow trek, embarrassed his father couldn't control it. Losing bodily functions would be worse than death for his father. He needed to come out of this surgery in one whole piece, or he didn't know what would happen.

Ah, shit, he needed to call his brothers. His father made a mule look yogic. They might have had a falling-out and not spoken for too long, but they were still family. The hell with it. He'd contact them as soon as his father went into surgery—it was the right thing to do.

Christian half rose from the pillow. "Don't even think about going behind my back, boy. I have ways of making your life hell beyond the grave, and if I wake up and they're here, I'll make sure you regret it."

Again that brief flare of pain he had no right to feel. How long had he wished his father would show him a sliver of softness? Any type of warmer emotion? Instead, he'd traded those feelings for becoming a drill sergeant with his boys, the total opposite of the way Mom had been. Not that he wanted to think of her anymore. It did no good, only scraping against raw wounds. Caleb wasn't a martyr, so he stuffed that shit back down for another lifetime.

"Whatever, old man. Save the fight for the surgery."

They were interrupted when Dr. Wang came in with an easy smile. "Okay, gentlemen, this is it. We gotta wheel him into surgery. Say your good-byes."

Caleb froze and stared into his father's familiar face. Took in the sharp, roughened features, leathery skin, bushy silver brows. Those brown eyes still held a fierce spark of life. In that moment, Caleb decided to take a chance. If something happened in surgery, he didn't want to regret it for the rest of his life.

He leaned down to kiss his father on the cheek.

Christian slapped him back with a growl. "Cut it out. Grow some balls. I'll see you later."

The tiny touch of emotion flickered out and left a cold, empty vastness inside his belly. So stupid. He felt so stupid. "Sure. Good luck, Dad."

"Don't need no damn luck. Make sure you do what I say. I don't want to see your brothers."

They were the last words Caleb heard as his father was wheeled into a surgery that took over five hours to perform.

The next morning Christian Pierce was dead.

And then the nightmare really began.

chapter one

Caleb sat in the fancy conference room of the lawyer's office. His brothers had arrived and taken seats at the gleaming mahogany table far away from one another, eliciting a raised brow from his father's lawyer. Yeah, the Pierce brothers had no love lost between them. Caleb had waited too long to make the call, and now there was another item to be checked off the Caleb-is-a-shit-brother list. He should've gone with his instincts and told them as soon as Christian was wheeled into surgery. Instead, he figured he'd wait a bit, not wanting them to hurry home to his father's nastiness. Caleb never doubted he'd make it through the surgery. It wasn't even a worry in his mind as he sat in the waiting room drinking bad coffee, answering texts, and watching CNN on the television. Of course, he'd been wrong, and now he was taking the heat. He'd ripped the choice out of Dalton's and Tristan's hands on whether they wanted to make the trip to see Dad, and when they showed up and looked at his body, something cold passed between them, stretching the distance by a few miles more.

He refused to feel a pang of pain. It did no good. There

was never going to be a tearful reunion around his father's casket anyway, and even during the wake they'd all stood separately, greeting people with a polite demeanor and only speaking when necessary.

Even now, Dalton's face held a permanent scowl. Didn't really go with the whole California-surfer vibe he had going on. His hair was caught back in a ponytail and had gone almost blond. The face that launched a thousand ships—his many girlfriends' tagline—now looked like he'd be happy kicking someone's ass. Probably Caleb's. He'd gotten the height in the family, so those long limbs were crossed at the ankles under the table like he was on lunch break at the beach rather than waiting to hear the will. He'd changed. Still the best-looking in the bunch and probably still a man whore, but there was a new determination his aura reflected that was never there before. At twenty-eight years old, he was the youngest and always seemed to be competing for his place. Of course, it had been over five years since Caleb had seen his brothers. After his mother's death in a horrific car accident, everything had splintered, shoving them into confrontation, and breaking underneath the strain. Both his brothers had walked out shortly after they lost her and never looked back. This time, the pang came and went without even an inward flinch. He'd gotten better under his father's tutelage to bury all that anger and discontent. Too bad Dalton hadn't received the same benefit.

Caleb flicked his gaze over to Tristan. The golden child. The peacemaker. Caleb always figured Tristan would be the one to run the family empire. Even now, his amber eyes held a steady light, and his manicured hands were calmly clasped on the smooth surface of the tabletop. His reddish-brown hair seemed perfectly tousled, and he wore some type of pricey customized suit that screamed *I'm important*. Guess property sales and renovating dumps was a decent living. Tristan refused to look him directly in the eye, which told Caleb how seriously pissed he was.

Samuel Dyken, lawyer extraordinaire, droned on as he read from lengthy paperwork and used legal jargon like a ninja used throwing stars. Finally he looked up and cleared his throat. Caleb caught a strange wariness in his gaze. A tingle began at the base of Caleb's spine, spreading outward and warning of something bad to come. Dyken neatened the stack of papers in front of him and took a deep breath. "Now I've come to the new agreement your father put in his will. It affects all of you in a rather large way."

Dalton rolled his eyes. "Whatever. I don't need anything of his anyway. I've been fine on my own."

Tristan nodded. "I think we all agree we want nothing to do with Pierce Brothers and will happily sign it all over to Caleb."

The words should've made Dyken happy, but he looked like someone had just overturned his winning verdict. He seemed to choose his words carefully. "Unfortunately, that won't be possible. There are new terms to the agreement of Caleb keeping Pierce Brothers."

The tingle got worse. He shifted in his chair. "What did the son of a bitch do now?"

Dyken winced. "He changed the terms of the will one year ago. The company originally would've been split among the three of you with an option to buy out the others' portions. There is no longer that option."

Dalton leaned forward with an impatient breath. "What are the options?"

"The company is not allowed to be split among the three of you. In order to inherit Pierce Brothers, all of you must run the company together as co-owners."

Caleb heard the words, but his brain had put up a barrier. Probably to protect him from losing his shit and going straight down to hell to kick his father's ass. It had to be a mistake. His brothers were staring at Dyken with comical half-opened mouths. Yeah, they'd been gone a long time. They weren't used to their father's tricks or viper meanness, even after death.

"What are the terms?" he asked briskly. "And how do we get out of it?"

Dyken held up his upturned palms. "The terms state all three of you must live in the house together and run Pierce Brothers for one year. If the company makes a profit—I have specifics on what he termed successful—you can all decide to sell your shares and leave. If the company is not profitable after a year, it gets dissolved without recourse."

"Guess we're going to court," Tristan said simply. "Dad must've been out of his mind when he wrote that."

Dyken spoke up. "Christian made sure every loophole was tight and would hold up in court. I've been over this with him countless times, and he was sane, logical, and determined. He wants all of his sons involved in the business or none at all. I'm sorry, gentlemen. I truly am."

Caleb stared at the shiny pen slowly rolling across the desk. Embossed with gold, with elegant scrolls over the black, it caught the light and gave him something to focus on while he tried to fight through the waves of emotion tugging at the lockbox, raging to escape.

He'd had a difficult relationship with his father. There

had been little warmth in Caleb's life after he lost his mother, and even less when his brothers split up and refused to talk to him. But there was one thing he'd been proud of for the past five years. His role in the company. Caleb had taken the reins and proved his worth, with every ounce of blood and sweat, and not an ounce of tears. His father pushed, demanded, insulted, but Caleb believed in his heart it was done to make him a better man. There was no one else to give the reins to and teach the business from the ground up. In a way, by staying to do his father's bidding, he'd allowed his brothers to carve out their own paths, and he rarely spent time on regrets. He loved building houses—creating a new home for someone ran thick in his blood. The company was Christian's favorite child, and everything was sacrificed for the greater good of Pierce Brothers. He'd believed he had earned his father's respect, which was more important than any familial love.

Now he knew that had been a lie, too.

Because his father had despised him so much, he'd give up his beloved company in order to dick around playing God. It was his last manipulation from the grave. A way to control each of them on his own terms, without care to their wants or individual paths.

Blessed numbness finally took hold. The pen dropped off the table and fell to the cushioned floor without a sound. Caleb looked up.

"If we refuse to live and work together for a year, the company is dissolved?"

Dyken nodded.

Tristan shook his head. "It doesn't make sense. It's been in the family for generations! The company is worth millions—Christian would never give up all that money."

"Yes, he would," Caleb said softly. His brothers turned to stare at him. "He's always wanted the final word. Now he's got it. If we don't play by his rules, we'll lose everything we've worked for."

Dalton groaned, rubbing his forehead. "This is insane. We haven't worked together in years. Tristan and I have our own stuff going on."

An uncomfortable silence settled around them. In minutes, his whole future had blown up. His identity and livelihood was tangled within the company, and the idea of losing it brought a faint rush of panic. How should he play it? His brothers had taken leave years ago and couldn't care less. They'd opened up their own businesses and left the past behind. He'd done everything right, followed in his father's footsteps, and gotten fucked.

"I guess we dissolve the company," Tristan finally said. "There seems to be no other choice. I'm sorry, Caleb. I have no other suggestions."

Caleb appreciated the gleam of regret in his brother's eyes, but it wasn't enough. He was the one with everything to lose, and it was up to him to convince them they could have it all. He leaned forward. "Hear me out. I know you're ready to call it quits. I know you're pissed off that I didn't call you about Dad and never had time to say good-bye. I made a big mistake, but I swear to God I didn't do it to hurt you."

He had their attention. Good. He'd have one shot at this, and he had to be good. "I invested everything in this company. I was promised Pierce Brothers as my future; I stayed by Dad's side, taking his shit, because I was the only one ready to protect the family business."

Dalton shot up out of his chair. "Are you kidding me right now? Dad never listened to anyone else but you! Don't act like you were doing us some big favor or sacrifice for staying. Do you know how many times we tried to get involved? We wanted to be a part of this, too."

"Bullshit," Caleb retorted. "You hated taking orders, and you wanted to do whatever you wanted. Instead of listening to a customer's specs, you'd focus on your current dream project, then get mad when they didn't want to pay for it!"

"I'm an artist and you never gave me a chance. You drove me out of here."

"I think sleeping with my fiancée drove you out of town, brother. Not me."

Caleb could tell that it still stung, but Dalton kept to the script he'd been repeating for years. "I didn't sleep with her! I just wanted to prove she wouldn't be faithful."

"Thanks. I was real grateful."

"Shut up," Tristan commanded. "Everyone calm down. Let's stick to the facts. We can't even stay in the same room together, let alone run a company. We have no other choice."

Caleb clenched his jaw. "There's always a choice. I'm asking you to help me. Years ago, you wanted to bring real estate and renovation to Pierce Brothers. You can do it now. Open up and run your own business as part of the company. No interference from me."

Tristan blew out a breath and began pacing. Dyken watched the whole scene with quiet interest. "Real convenient. When I brought it up to Dad, he nixed it, and you backed him up. Now that you want something, you're happy to give me what I'd been fighting for. It's too late."

"Dad was never gonna bend, Tristan. I knew that, and even though you saw it as a betrayal, I was trying to save you from a bunch of crap. We have the power now to run the company our way. I know we have to do it together, and we haven't had a real conversation in years, but we can do this. Hell, it'll be a lot easier than you think. With the senator's job, and the other projects I just finished, we'll make plenty of money to be called profitable. All we have to do is ride out the year."

Dyken cleared his throat with a loud emphasis. "Umm, you misunderstood, Caleb. Your father put in a specific clause that states profits begin the official day you begin working together. In other words, no previous projects or funding will be counted. You start with a clean slate."

The tiny flicker of hope smothered and died. He hated himself even more for the frustration that believed there could possibly be a way out. No. Christian would've made sure every loophole was closed in order to suffocate them properly.

Dalton gave a bitter laugh. "See! You're just as delusional as Dad. That means we'd start out with a big fat zero. You know why he set this up? To laugh at us and watch us fail. Don't you know that by now, Caleb? Are you that far gone that you still want Dad's approval and will sell your soul for it?"

Caleb flinched. Direct hit. But he had nothing left to lose and had to fight dirty. "Yeah, I know. Let's just say I'd rather succeed and give him a final fuck-you."

Tristan turned to Dyken. "Does the will outline whether we need to run the company in a certain way?"

Dyken shook his head. "No, you just need to turn a profit. You need to live in the house together, and you all need to have a part in the company. That takes care of all the obligations."

"I can't move back here!" Dalton said. "I'm in California with my own woodworking business."

"It's one year, Dalton. Bring the business here and offer your services as part of Pierce Brothers. I'm telling you it's possible this can work. I'll find you some ocean to surf."

"Fuck you!"

Tristan glared. "Caleb, your point is well-taken. It's not impossible, and we can do this." His eyes darkened. "But I don't want to. I like living in New York and doing what I want with no one to please but myself. I've got money I earned on my own, with no one barking orders at me. For God's sake, I'm thirty years old, and I've been digging out from Dad's shadow my whole life. I'm not going back."

"Me neither," Dalton said.

"Oh, you're rich, too, huh?" Caleb threw out. He knew his younger brother had perfectionism issues when dealing with woodcraft. He'd inherited his grandfather's skill, but had been well-known in the family to throw away profits in pursuit of product. Caleb guaranteed his brother was living paycheck to paycheck.

"I do fine," Dalton clipped out. The corner of his left lip twitched in his trademark confession of a lie. Some things never changed.

Caleb had one last shot. He hated how dirty he was willing to play, but it was his life, and he had no choice. Already his brothers seemed to gather themselves up and walk out the door, ready to give up Pierce Brothers. In a way, he couldn't blame them. But he needed to win.

"If you don't do this for me, I'll lose everything," he said quietly. "You probably don't care about that, and I accept it. But I'm asking you to do it for someone else."

"Dad?" Dalton sneered.

"Do it for Mom."

Tristan stilled. Dalton jerked back, raw pain carving into his face. A long stream of curses emitted from his little brother's mouth, stinging his ears. Tristan just stared at him like he'd enacted the biggest betrayal—worse than Fredo in *The Godfather*.

The words fell flat from Tristan's mouth. "Tell me you didn't just say that."

Caleb didn't back off. "This was Mom's company. She gave it to us from her great-great-grandfather and renamed it Pierce Brothers because she believed in all of us to keep it safe. Sure, Dad doubled the profits, but she always told us this was our legacy." His throat burned with something, but he refused to name it. "Mom was the one who told us at the kitchen table every damn day that blood is the only thing we can count on. That if we're not here for each other, nothing else matters. To watch this company, the only thing we have of her memory, dissolve would leave us with nothing."

Dalton looked like a ghost had walked into the room. "She left us," he said. "We have nothing anyway."

"We'll never know if she was going to come back," Caleb said softly. "Don't we owe it to her to give it one last try? We were close once. I'm not saying we can get back that same type of relationship, but there's gotta be a way we can live in the same house but still have separate lives. Tristan, you can run your businesses from here and incorporate some of the changes you always wanted to see in Pierce Brothers. Dalton can take over all the woodworking. Then we can all walk away at the end of the term and decide what we want from there. I'm asking you, as my brothers, for one year to try." His throat was choked, but he forced the final word out. "Please."

He heard his father's spirit roar and call him a pussy. He watched the faces of his brothers harden, trying to process emotions they'd refused to deal with for way too long. Caleb didn't care if he went to hell for it. He needed them to keep his company alive, and he'd do anything possible to convince them.

Finally Tristan spoke. "I need time to think about it."

Caleb nodded. "Understood."

"You all can take a few days," Dyken said. "Talk it over. Let me know your decision."

"I'll tell you within twenty-four hours," Tristan clipped out. He straightened his suit jacket, tugged at the Windsor knot on his bright red tie, and turned. "I'm going out for a while."

Dalton slowly followed, pausing with his hand on the knob.

"You're wrong," he murmured into the silence. "Mom was never coming back."

Then he left.

Dyken packed up his briefcase and left Caleb alone, staring at the closed door for a long, long time.

chapter two

"Don't look at me like that. I've had a shit day, and getting drunk is probably the best thing on my to-do list."

Two sets of big brown eyes stared back at him. Every one of his moves was measured and studied in shaking silence. He'd been stupid to put the bag of rawhide bones near his bottles of precious bourbon, not realizing that each time he'd get a drink, the goofball duo would assume they were getting treats.

"No way. One of you stole the leftover chicken, and I still haven't figured out who's lying."

Bodies finely tuned, ears pricked, tongues lolling in helpless excitement, these two were impossible to say no to. Caleb bit back a smile.

He'd found the two puppy mastiffs tied to a tree during a job. Abandoned, dehydrated, and starving, with sores on their bodies, they'd likely been out in the woods for a while. After a vet visit that saved their lives, Cal couldn't stand the idea of them going to the shelter. They refused to leave each other's sides, bonding from the horrific incident, so separating them wasn't an option.

His father hated dogs and probably would've left them in the woods, deeming animals an unnecessary burden in life. Cal let Christian win most battles, since it was easier. But not this one. He'd decided to foster until he got them both a home together, but after a few weeks, Cal faced the truth: he loved them. He decided they already had their home—with him.

Because Caleb had tumbled straight into love with the gentle giants, who had no manners, little attention, but huge hearts that reached out and soothed his own.

They'd torn up his house pretty good the first few months, but after they realized they were safe, they turned into big mushes. Towering to his chest, almost two hundred pounds each, they resembled intimidating, ferocious beasts until you looked into their faces and saw the joyous abandon in their gaze. Unfortunately, they sucked at commands and rarely controlled themselves when meeting strangers. Most dogs wouldn't have recovered from their trauma. But Gandalf and Balin had a zest for life no one could steal from them. They reminded Caleb of all the good things in the world worth fighting for.

Even his father had surrendered. Though he muttered about their sloppy behavior, Christian had loved the dogs with a passion Cal rarely saw him show toward anything other than work. Gandalf and Balin were known to flank his father and gaze at him in adoration while he watched CNN every night, sharing his popcorn and commenting on the sad state of the world. There weren't too many people who missed Christian Pierce, but Caleb's mastiffs still waited at the door as if his father would surprise them by coming through it one day.

Maybe there'd been hope for the old man, after all.

Cal shook his head, scooped out two rawhide bones, and held them out.

Gandalf could never seem to handle the stress, so he did the only trick he knew to get the bone in his mouth as quickly as possible. He fell to the ground and played dead. Paws stuck straight up in the air, head cocked at a sharp angle, he peeked through his eyelids to make sure he had an audience. It was the most ridiculous thing Cal had ever seen, but every time he did it, a laugh escaped his lips.

He threw the bone, and Gandalf came alive just in time to snatch it in his mouth.

Balin was a little more patient but tended to try to eat his hand along with the bone. Cal paused for three beats, then slowly offered the treat. Balin let out a whimper of distress, seeing it so close but not allowed to grab it. Finally Cal nodded, and Balin grasped the treat and raced toward his dog bed, where all food and toys were always hoarded.

And now it was Cal's turn.

He poured a few fingers of his favorite Kentucky bourbon and tried to ignore the silence in the house. His gaze flicked around the elaborate kitchen, where his mother had reigned as queen. Memories rushed past him in a succession of images he didn't want to see.

They'd gather around the horseshoe marble island for meals and lively discussions, the scent of fresh bread warming the air. The kitchen was equipped with all the state-of-the-art appliances, from the Wolf double oven and Sub-Zero refrigerator to the espresso maker, soda machine, and customized popcorn popper. God, how she loved cooking for them. Some of his best memories revolved around elaborate meals and her warm laugh, her patient tone when lecturing them on their wild ways, and the way she insisted none of her sons ever go to bed angry at the others.

His mother's presence still beat strong in the bright yellow walls, eclectic collection of dish towels, and cheery splashes of color that livened up the cold steel and elegant marble. Their house was always a showcase for new buyers, and Christian held it to the highest standard of materials and elegance. The floor-to-ceiling bay windows with their silver velvet drapes; the vaulted ceiling, which gave the rooms amazing space; and such expensive materials as pine, mahogany, marble, and Italian tile all brought the place a greatness and quality his father proudly boasted of.

But Diane Pierce had made it a true home.

Now the house was quiet except for the chomping of the dogs. Cal held back a weary sigh as he made his way toward the porch. His brothers had avoided him since the reading of the will, but he needed an answer soon. It was time they had a real talk and figured out if they could forgive enough to work together.

He opened the door to the porch and strode to his favorite drinking chair. The wicker rocker was old and worn, and the seat molded to his ass with perfect precision. He propped up his booted feet on the matching wicker table, faded now to a dirty white, smirking a bit when he remembered how Christian had hated having any wicker in his house. It was a material he frowned upon, and it looked out of place with the custom wood rockers and cedar porch. Maybe that was why Cal loved this set so much.

He sipped his whiskey and tried to relax. Darkness closed around him, the thick woods that surrounded the twenty-acre estate full of lively night action from the crickets and frogs, each trying to outsing the others. The intricately structured gazebo of latticed painted wood and peaked roof opened onto the infinity pool. A faint greenish glow and trickle of steam rose from the right, connecting to the main house via a bluestone pathway lined with natural rock formations. The lush manicured lawn tumbled into towering oaks and pines, snugly wrapping the house around them. It was a sight that always startled him with its beauty. How many times had he and his brothers played in those woods, pretending they were Hansel and Gretel and that a witch with a candy house would eventually snag them? Cal swore he heard raucous laughter drifting to his ears. Ghosts from the past swirled and caught him in its net.

Three young boys who ran together, climbed trees, and shared secrets in an old tree house. Three boys who believed in magic and a future so bright, no reality could ever dim it. Three young boys who had no idea one day it would be torn apart and they'd never find themselves going back to one another.

A swarm of gnats hovered around his head, and he batted them away, reminding himself to get a few more citronella candles out. Summer was upon them, and the bugs were a bitch. He used to wonder why his parents never built near the harbor, closer to the bustling town. It was a location most people sought out in Harrington. Then he realized that land was key. Owning numerous acres gave power, the more the better. Cal wondered if his parents had been happy for a brief time, when endless possibilities stretched before them. It was as if the bigger the business got, the more their family began to break at the foundation.

Cal knew from experience that the foundation everything was built on was key. It could rot like termites eating through bad wood and never truly recover.

Now, wasn't he thinking like a damn poet? But he was no Dylan Thomas. Better to shut off his thoughts and just drink.

"Still drinking that bourbon shit, brother?"

He jerked his head around. Dalton smirked and dropped into the rocker to the right. His fingers clasped loosely around the neck of an IPA. Cal took in his tired face, ripped tank, and denim shorts with the ragged hem. Dalton propped his feet up on the railing, which were now clad in frayed flip-flops.

Cal tipped his head in greeting. "Still drinking the drink of the commoner, Dalton? Or is that all you can afford lately?" That comment got him a snarl, but Cal gave a laugh. "Sorry, I'm only screwing with you. Been a long time since I got to needle you."

Dalton let out a disgusted breath. "Dude, at least I'm not the one still living with my parents. A thirty-two-year-old single man shacked up with his dad? Cree-eepy."

"He's got you there."

Another voice joined them, and Tristan stepped onto the porch, leaning one hip against the pillar. His drink of choice was a dark ruby-red wine that probably cost way too much to actually drink. His reddish-brown hair was perfectly tousled in that way females loved. He was dressed in khaki shorts, a clean white T-shirt, and some designer-type sneakers. Tristan had always had a thing for expensive food, wine, and women. Except when he dated Sydney, of course.

Cal rubbed his forehead and groaned. "Fuck, you're right. I lived with Dad. That's kind of embarrassing."

"Humiliating," Tristan added. "Pathetic."

"Loserville," Dalton said.

"All right, I get it. I don't know, we stayed out of each other's way, and I never had the time to look for another place."

"You don't get laid much, do you, man?" Dalton asked.

Cal refused to let his face get red. Refused. "Keeps the relationship chicks away," he retorted. "For God's sake, it's a mansion. You could get lost for a week without seeing someone in there."

Tristan grinned and took a sip of his girly wine. "Sure. We understand."

Cal gave them the middle finger.

They stared at the woods and drank in silence. The presence of his brothers was a blessing and a curse. He missed them and the relationship they used to have. Being with them now in their childhood home and knowing the distance was thick like fog made emotion claw up from his gut.

Tristan finally spoke. "We have to talk. Make our decision." He paused. "Go over why I don't think it will ever work."

Cal took a deep breath. It was time to open up some raw wounds if he was going to have a shot. "Maybe it's time to finally discuss why you really left."

He risked a glance at Tristan. Then was sorry he did. The tiger ripped open its cage doors and let loose with a roar.

"Was I the only one in that room who remembered when I gave Dad an ultimatum and he threw me out? Was I by myself when he called me a failure?" Tristan stabbed his finger through the air. "I needed you, and you said nothing! I got tired of begging to do things differently from the side-lines of my own fucking company. And Pierce Brothers is just as much mine as it is yours, brother!"

Cal jumped up from the wicker chair and met him head-on. "I know. You think that I don't go over that scene endlessly, wondering if I made the biggest mistake of my life? Tristan, you know how Dad was. He fought change and focused on the construction. You always saw the bigger picture—you were more a businessperson than Dad ever was. You saw property and renovation and how we could ex-pand, but Dad would have never let you do it! Don't you get it? I backed him up so you would get the hell out of Dodge and come into your own. Because if you stayed here, Dad would've eaten you up alive."

Tristan gazed at him in shock. "You trying to tell me your cowardice was a sacrifice for me? Don't go there, Cal. Just don't."

Cal winced. "I'm not trying to be a martyr; I'm trying to explain why I didn't fight for you. Every day I watched you die a bit more, not being able to do what you wanted."

Tristan shook his head. "It was always you. By Dad's side, building house by house. God, I worked there just as much as you. All of us did. Through high school and sum-mers and after college. I never felt valued. Well, I finally found my place, and I'm not about to leave it. You made your choice once. Now I'm making mine."

Cal fisted his hands and tried not to howl with frustration. "This is Mom's company, and you're telling me you'll walk away without a glance back? Don't give me that shit. Let's get real honest here. You always wanted this company, and this is your chance. The only rule we have is to make enough money in three hundred sixty-five days. I need you. I can't do this alone. And I swear, if you walk away, you'll regret it, Tristan. That's not some threat from me. It's just the truth, because I regret letting you walk away that day every fucking second."

Emotion pulsed and crackled between them like a summer storm. His words seemed to hit Tristan straight between the eyes. His brother jerked back, looking at him with new eyes. Cal was done with half-truths and pride. He needed his family to pull this off, and the only way to gain back trust was to get messy.

He fucking hated it. But he'd do it.

Tristan let out a string of curses and turned away.

Dalton cleared his throat. "Well. That could've been on an episode of *Dr. Phil*. I'm surprised Dad didn't rise from the grave in pissed-off fury for that type of sharing."

Cal shook his head. Leave it to his youngest brother to use humor to deflect too many feelings. "What about you, Dalton? What's your reason for leaving?"

Dalton drained his beer, rested his elbows on the arms of the rocker, and snorted. "Actually, I think I'll stay and help you out."

Tristan whirled around. Cal's mouth fell open.

Dalton shrugged. "Why not? Sure, I got a great wood-working business going on in California, but been having a bit of trouble keeping good workers. They're sloppy."

Oh, yeah. Cal knew right then and there his brother was dead broke. He was such a perfectionist, and his jobs usually took double the time due to his high standards. Cal bet he just couldn't take on enough clients to make a profit. But he kept his mouth shut. "Huh. Too bad."

"Yeah, and then I got a little female trouble going on. May be a good idea to leave town for a bit. Let things cool off."

Cal raised a brow. "She's not married, is she?"

Tristan snickered.

Dalton narrowed his gaze, eyes flaring with temper. "Hell no! I don't do that, okay? Things got intense. I think she used the L word, and when I pulled back a little, she got crazy. Started stalking me. An address change may be good for both of us. But I want my share of the profits, and the business, if I decide to help you out. Got it?"

Thank God. He'd give Dalton anything he wanted. Besides, his brother took after his grandfather and was famous for his furniture. He'd be a huge asset. "Got it. Thanks."

Cal turned to Tristan. His voice softened. "Are you in?"

Their gazes met. In those familiar amber eyes, he caught a mixture of anger, resentment, and something else.

Want.

Tristan wanted to put his own stamp on Pierce Brothers, and it was finally his opportunity. Cal held his breath and hoped it won out over pride and a desire for revenge.

"Fine. I'm in. But it's not going to be easy. We're not

used to working together, let alone living together. Let's hope we don't tear each other apart after the first week."

"Agreed." Cal raised his glass. "To Pierce Brothers."

Tristan hesitated, then finally raised his wine. "Pierce Brothers."

Dalton slowly got up from the rocker and lifted his empty beer bottle. He didn't say anything but clinked his container with theirs.

It was a start.

chapter three

Morgan Raines tightened her fingers around the steering wheel and stared up at the gorgeous sprawling house that could put a Southern mansion to shame. She was used to impressive houses, but this one had a unique blend of old-fashioned charm and classic breeding that made her want to sigh.

Of course, she'd be quite worried if the house wasn't up to par. If Pierce Brothers boasted to be one of the top customized builders in the Northeast, first impressions were important. Her gaze took in the stone Georgian with the perfectly placed fat columns and the sweeping circular upper deck. The mix of colored stone, terra-cotta, and blinding white gave an onlooker pause and a desire to stare longer. From the larger-than-normal arched windows and massive carved wood door to the wraparound porch and definitive bursts of rich green foliage against the backdrop of a sparkling turquoise pool that rivaled a lake, the effect was dazzling.

Good. She'd made the right choice.

Now she just had to convince Caleb Pierce to take the job.

She'd gone to the Pierce Brothers official office first, located just down the road, but when Caleb's assistant told her he was at the house, Morgan decided it was best to track him down here. She'd learned early to try to maneuver around the layer of protection in the form of savvy executive assistants and go direct to the source. This way, he couldn't force her to stay in the waiting room for hours or sneak out to lunch through the back door.

Morgan pulled down the sun visor and checked her lipstick in the mirror. After reapplying a fresh coat of poppy pink to her mouth, she smoothed the stray flyaway strands of hair and did a quick review of her appearance. Good. No smudges, hanging threads, or stickers she'd forgotten to rip off. Other than the bitch of a blister on her heel, she looked professional, competent, and sleek. Morgan grabbed her Chanel purse and slid out of the white BMW convertible. Reminding herself she had gotten her way with much tougher clients than a mere contractor, she marched to the front door, her nude heels clicking smartly over the smooth pavement. She rang the bell, took a calming breath, and waited.

And waited.

Voices echoed and rumbled from behind the massive hand-carved cherrywood door. Trying not to be impatient, she raised her hand to knock, and the door swung slowly open. Almost like it was welcoming her in.

Morgan hesitated. The voices grew louder.

"Hello?"

She waited a bit longer, then poked her head in. The foyer made her want to sink to her knees and praise the godlike interior designer who'd completed such work. Gleaming

marble, a curved staircase to rival Scarlett O'Hara's, perfectly cut thick crown molding lining the ceiling and walls
with intricate carvings she wanted time to study. Maybe the
doorbell didn't work, and the house was so huge, no one
could hear her. She took another tentative step in, glancing
around for any human activity, then froze.

Two massive dogs sat at the bottom of the steps, staring
at her.

Not regular dogs. No, these were Cujo-size dogs, gi-
gantic bodies and heads in a mottled brown color. Saliva
dripped from their mouths as they both panted, never taking
their gaze from her as if she were a delectable piece of meat
who'd wandered in for lunch.

She was going to die.

Fear strangled her. She fought it back, having read
something about dogs sensing the emotion, making them
even madder. Her throat dried up, and she stilled, trying not
to breathe or make a move.

Down the hallway, voices rose and fell in a conversation
that was definitely beginning to turn into a fight. Two men.
Lots of curse words. Morgan tried to dredge up some spit so
she could call out for rescue, but the dogs began to shake in
a strange way, looking at her with a need she'd never seen
before. Not that she had experience with dogs. Her parents
disliked animals of all types for their messiness and com-
plications and had instilled in her a healthy fear of strange
creatures great and small.

"Help," she called out. Her voice came out in a tiny
whisper, locked down from her terror. Dammit, now
she knew if she were trapped in a horror movie, she'd be
the too-stupid-to-live heroine who just stood there while

she got hacked up by the serial killer. Morgan tried again. "Help me."

The dogs got up.

A squeal broke from her lips, but her legs still wouldn't move. "Umm, good boys, good dogs, oh, God, please don't eat me, good, good dogs!"

The dogs leaped from their stance and fell upon her.

Her ankle turned as she tried to flee, and she collapsed on the slippery, polished marble, her cushy butt hitting the floor with a whoosh. As Morgan waited to die, she held up her hands, curving her fingers into claws, ready to fight to the death for her life.

Then got a whipping, lashing tongue bath.

The giants wriggled and squirmed in pleasure, licking her everywhere, wet noses and slobber dripping onto the bare skin of her legs. She fought them off, but they were stronger and more competent, until Morgan desperately crawled to her knees in an effort to escape.

She got smacked in the face by a wagging tail and kissed damply on the back of her neck, which almost made her burst into giggles, before finally scrambling to her feet. They could've eaten her in one gulp, and now they wanted to kill her with affection.

By now, the low rumblings from the hallway had grown to deep, enraged shouts.

"I told you to stay out of my way and I'd take care of the damn cabinets!"

"Are you kidding me? You switched the order on them, and now I have to step in and fix it!"

Crash. Bang. Was that glass shattering? The dogs, now

having bonded with her, kept bumping her from each side in a competition to see who she liked the most.

"I'm done with this shit! You lied—you still want to control me, just like Dad. You want a servant, not a partner."

Morgan imagined gritted teeth and pure fury from the deep growl. A shiver worked its way down her spine, but she eased closer. If someone was in danger, she had a responsibility to help. Funny, though, the dogs didn't seem to sense any danger, barely glancing over at the noises floating in the air. Cujo #1 tried to grab the heel of her shoe and pull it off her foot.

"Don't do that," she whispered. "My shoe. Leave me alone."

Cujo #2 gave her a sloppy grin and drooled on her ankle. Ugh. What type of animals were these? Didn't builders usually have well-trained Labs for pets, or was that just canine profiling?

"The client wanted pine cabinets. Pine, you moron! You have to go get fancy with your tigerwood and show off, and now we're behind schedule, and I'm still not sure they're gonna like it! I give you one lousy job, and you manage to screw it up."

"Yeah? I know what I'm doing, and pine would've looked awful. How about this? Screw you! I'm done."

Morgan jumped as a man covered in sawdust and wearing faded jeans came storming out and stopped before her. His long hair brushed his shoulders, and she caught the impression of toffee-colored strands, burning blue eyes, and swirling frustrated energy. Her mouth opened at his fierce scowl. The Cujos quickly left and swarmed around the man's feet in adoration. He snapped his fingers, but they just jumped higher in obvious disobedience. "Who are you?" he grunted.

Her fingers clasped her throat. "I'm—I'm, umm, here to see Caleb Pierce?"

The man jerked his dirty thumb toward the door he'd just exited. "In there. Tell the asshole I quit."

"Oh! I—I—"

He stomped out with the Cujos at his heels and left her alone. Morgan glanced at the half-open door. Low mutterings and tinkling glass drifted to her ears. This wasn't how she pictured their first meeting, but then again, she had a job to do. Did this bode well? Running a family business with crazy dogs and family feuds seemed a strange way to retain and grow a client base. She paused for a moment, gathering her thoughts and trying to straighten out her clothes. A streak of mud from dirty paws now marred the clean white fabric of her skirt. Her right ankle throbbed, and the blister burned on her left heel. Dog hair clung to her once-spotless white jacket. Sweat had definitely done a job on her flawless makeup. Nothing like the adrenaline rush of looking death in the eye to put a healthy glow on a woman's face.

Didn't matter. She had to get it together and make her pitch. Morgan's job was to make sure her clients were satisfied by getting the perfect house built to specs. Pierce was the best. She'd settle for no less. Steeling her posture ramrod straight, she walked through the door without hobbling and waited.

The man had his back to her. He had a somewhat filthy mouth, judging from the colorful curse words lighting up the room. Average height, but his shoulders were quite broad, with a plain white T-shirt stretched to the limit over a mass of bunched muscles. He seemed to be fumbling with a decanter, finally splashing amber liquid into the target, then shifting so that she caught his profile. The man brought the glass to his lips and tipped it back with one neat, smooth movement. Her belly did a slow flip-flop as those carved lips closed around the rim of the glass. The tanned, powerful column of his neck worked as he swallowed, and for some strange reason, she was fascinated by the almost pornographic images of the other things he could accomplish with such a mouth that were flaring to life in her mind. His hair was a mass of thick hazelnut strands that looked finger combed and a bit damp. Her gaze followed the line of his impressive back to his rear, and her blood suddenly heated.

Goodness gracious.

The man had a great ass. Full, defined, and filling out the seat of his jeans just perfectly. Morgan fought the instinctive blush that heated her cheeks, decided her moments of voyeurism were officially over, and gave a discreet cough.

The man whirled around.

Goodness gracious.

She stared into a pair of gunmetal-gray eyes that should've been cold and hard. Instead, they held smoky tones of a raw sensuality and confidence no man should hold. He had a large hooked nose and bushy brows, and his face was a mass of sharp, slashed lines that held together his features in an arresting way. Not classically handsome. Not pretty. But this was a man who knew what he wanted, took without apology, and never looked back.

Her thighs trembled and her panties dampened.

What on earth was happening?

"Who are you?" he demanded.

Who was she? Her brain clicked back on, and Morgan suddenly remembered. She had to tread carefully if she was going to leave with her goal accomplished. She gave him a warm, professional smile and made sure her voice was steady. "You must be Caleb Pierce. The, uh, gentleman outside said to come in. I'm Morgan Raines."

One brow shot up, and he rubbed a hand over his head, messing up his hair even more. "I don't know you. And if that was my asshole brother, you can tell him to grow up and stop acting like a toddler."

She refused to bend to his rudeness. "Funny, he used the same term when he spoke about you."

The man gave a humorless laugh and went back to his drink. "Yeah, we're a real tight-knit family. Welcome to the fun house. Can you close the door on the way out?"

She lifted her chin. Great. Already she realized working with Caleb Pierce was going to be a bit . . . difficult. Lucky for her, she didn't give up easily. "Mr. Pierce, I'm here on behalf of my clients, Mr. and Mrs. Slate Rosenthal. I contacted you a few weeks back about building a house for them in Harrington on a recently secured piece of property on the harbor."

She hoped the celebrity name-dropping would make him turn back around, but he either lived under a rock or didn't care. "Name sounds familiar. Wait, I do remember. I told you no. I'm dealing with some other shit now and can't take on a new job. Sorry. Close the door, please."

Her ankle had turned into a full-blown ache, but she refused to shift her position. A show of strength at the beginning of any encounter was key to setting up the dynamics of a business relationship. "Mr. Pierce, I'm here to change your mind. It's imperative to my clients your company be the one to build their house. I'd like to discuss the benefits and terms with you. I'm sure you'll change your mind."

He had another long sip from his glass. She waited. Finally he glanced back. "I don't change my mind, princess. Now, I'm sure you can find another company to get you what you need. My assistant can get you a list of names. Just leave your business card on the way out."

This time, he deliberately turned his back and walked away. He sat at his desk, put his drink on the blotter, and began clicking away at the keyboard like she was some type of lowly, annoying gnat he'd just batted away. *Princess?* Was he kidding?

Disappointment flowed. He was going to be a real prize to work with, but she'd better wrap her head around it and deal. Morgan shut the door with a decided click, noting he didn't even bother to look up to see if she'd left. His brother was correct: he was an asshole.

She walked back over to the desk and waited. After a few moments, he stopped typing and looked up. His brows snapped together in pure annoyance. "You're still here."

Morgan smiled. "Yes. I don't think you understand, Mr. Pierce. I'm not interested in any other companies. I want Pierce Brothers. I'm also going to need to go over the initial plans with your architect and make sure we can start immediately. The house must be done by the end of fall. Mr. and Mrs. Rosenthal need to be settled in Harrington on their estate in order to be ready for filming. I can imagine how full your schedule is, but once you see my proposal, I'm sure we'll be able to work something out."

He seemed to break out of his fog and realize she wasn't going away. Satisfaction cut through her, until that hard gaze began at the top of her head and raked over her figure all the way down to her peekaboo shoes that showed her tasteful pink polish matching her fingernails. Morgan also noticed he seemed to spend way too much time on the thrust of her breasts from her very proper blouse, and the length of her calves, since the white business suit stopped at the knee in a perfectly conservative way. Morgan prepared herself to feel harassed or bullied, but instead, her skin tingled with anticipation. So odd. She should be positively insulted and disgusted by his male behavior. What was it about his smoky eyes that stripped her clothes from her body, saw everything underneath, and made her feel like a sexual wanton? And why, oh, why did she like it?

Her brain misfired along with her hormones, but Morgan held tight to her stance and met his stare head-on. She'd learned men respected strength. She usually won her battles by keeping her stubborn silence, waiting them out, and presenting a professional front.

Too bad inside her clothes she felt all itchy, turned-on, and completely nonprofessional.

But Caleb Pierce never had to know.

Those full lips twitched in a half smirk. Almost as if he

guessed her thoughts and figured it might be fun to toy with her. Too bad for him she'd gone through tons of confrontations with arrogant billionaires, diva celebrities, and demanding teen pop stars who wanted their way and refused to compromise. Morgan had learned from the best. A simple contractor wouldn't get in her way.

"You have mud on your skirt."

She never lost a beat. "I encountered the two Cujos in your foyer and realized they wanted to kill me in a way I wasn't prepared for. We wrestled, and I won."

"Never heard Balin and Gandalf called Cujos before. You'd be in more danger of being licked to death."

"Tolkien fan, huh? Nice. Still, I wouldn't term them a great welcome committee for new clients."

"I don't want any new clients, so they work great for me."

"You won't need any other clients after you take the Rosenthal job. You'll be able to pick and choose to your liking."

"I'm in a bad mood, princess. Sure you want to take me on now?"

She tilted her head and regarded him thoughtfully. "Why don't you try me, Charming?"

His gaze narrowed. Oh, yeah, that got his attention. She tried not to get sucked into the depths of those amazing eyes, but she was fascinated at how quickly they could turn from smoke to cold steel. She wondered briefly what they'd look like when he was buried deep inside a woman. Whoa, what was that thought? Was she insane?

"What did you just call me?"

Morgan smiled at his slightly shocked tone. "Charming.

If I'm playing the passive princess, you can play the part of the stud with brawn but no brains. Personally, I think the horses were the most interesting part of those stories."

He shook his head. "Who the hell are you again?"

Morgan decided this was a great time to grab the chair opposite his desk and sit down. Both of her feet wept in relief. "Morgan Raines. I'm a personal interior design artist hired by the Rosenthals. In case you haven't seen a movie in the past five years, let me remind you they're the darlings of Hollywood, and Slate was nominated for an Academy Award last year. His wife is the face of Glimmer makeup. Maybe you've seen her in half a dozen commercials while you're watching the Kardashians?"

Was that the grinding of his teeth or just her imagination? Oh, she hoped it wasn't her imagination. "I've heard of them. Why is a design artist trying to hire me to build a house?"

Morgan went to cross her legs, felt his gaze drop to the exposed skin of her thighs, and remained still. She clasped her hands on her dirty white skirt and gave her spiel. "I'm much more than an interior designer, Mr. Pierce. My clients hire me to be their voice and vision and oversee the entire project of their dream home. I work with the contractors while the house is built and am the only one they deal with during the construction. I'm the one involved with every tiny detail, from the faucets and tile all the way to what type of doorknobs I want installed. I'm present every day and work closely with the builder on all aspects to completion."

He fell back into the chair and let out a humorless laugh. "You gotta be kidding me. Basically, your job is to babysit all the spoiled, wealthy clients so they can show up to a completed house built to spec."

It was so much more than that, but Morgan knew he wouldn't understand until they began their project. Better not to mention he wouldn't be able to breathe without her knowing. "Close enough."

"You pick out their throw pillows, too? What happens if they're the wrong color?"

The jab didn't bother her. Morgan was used to the critics, but with a long trail of success stories and a book full of celebrity clients, she could afford to be gracious. "Yes, I pick out the throw pillows. And I never make a wrong decision."

"Never?"

She calmly met his gaze and refused to veer off course, even though that strange breathlessness was seizing her lungs again. The man was so very . . . vital. "Never."

"Must be nice." He remained silent for a while, but she waited him out, her face smoothed out in a mask of endless patience. Morgan noticed he seemed to have no twitchy habits. She'd studied men in countless confrontation situations, and most of them slipped up, giving her a sign of how they dealt with emotion. Some paced. Others tapped an object or finger. Some shifted in their seats or crossed a leg over an ankle or beat a foot against the floor.

Caleb Pierce never moved. Didn't blink. Just kept a stillness of thought and body that both fascinated and impressed her. He would be a worthy opponent.

What would he be like as a lover?

Demanding. Patient. Hot.

How sad her career was so important, she'd forgotten to

take care of her sex life. Of course, the man was a raw specimen of primitive male, from his rock-hard body to those come-and-let-me-do-very-bad-things-to-you eyes. Wasn't her fault she hadn't enjoyed a lover for a long time. She was too busy. And most of the men she met were off-limits as her clients or not worth her energy. Morgan didn't think she was picky. She just wasn't one to scratch a physical itch and walk off in the morning, and with her job traveling all over the place, settling down wasn't in her immediate future. Her rambling thoughts got cut off by his sudden, terse words.

"As interesting as this conversation has been, I must end it. I'm sorry, Ms. Raines, but my original answer of no stands."

"Why? The pay is quite generous."

His brow rose in mockery. "Money is nice but not the deciding factor."

"Tell me what you want to take this job, and I'll get it for you."

His gaze heated. "I'm tempted to test your claim."

She barely managed not to roll her eyes. "Please be original, Mr. Pierce. I'm sure you have much higher demands than me."

Was that an expression of humor flicking over his face? No, just a shadow thrown by the window behind him. Morgan already figured he'd have a wretched sense of humor. He seemed way too intense and focused for a few light laughs or jokes. "I'm sure you're right. But you're not understanding me. You won't be able to meet my price, because I don't have one. Pierce Brothers is already overbooked, and I've just signed an important client I'll be involved with for the rest of the year. When I personally oversee a job, I never take another one. I like to concentrate on the one I'm with in all aspects."

The words drilled at her seemed filled with buckets of meaning, all leading to sex. But Morgan now accepted that Caleb Pierce turned her on, and she'd have to get over it. She had no time for silly weak bodily reactions just because she was hot for him. Their short conversation already confirmed she wasn't his type anyway.

Morgan sifted through his explanation, probing the holes and what she needed to do so that he'd change his mind. "Who's your client?" she asked.

"That's confidential."

"No, it's not. You just don't want to tell me."

"You have excellent instincts."

Morgan pursed her lips and thought hard. "You have a large team. You couldn't shift your assistants to take care of your other client? The Rosenthals will be quite grateful. They're known for calling in huge favors, so Pierce Brothers will be set up for a long, long time."

"I don't have that problem now," he pointed out. "We have more business than we know what to do with. I pick and choose what jobs I want to work on and don't have to deal with any horse heads in my bed."

His acerbic wit was almost fun. Almost. Her instincts screamed that he was lying to her. He wasn't booked up. He just didn't want the project. A faint smile coasted over her lips. "You knew from the first you wouldn't take on this job, didn't you? Why are you so against it?"

He shrugged. "Maybe I like building houses people will

actually want to live in and settle into? Houses they can actually love? I know what your clients really want. They want a cushy home to settle into rather than a cold hotel. They'll spend buckets of money, move in, and stay six months. Then the novelty will have worn off, and they'll move on to the next interesting location, and all my blood, sweat, and tears would've been for nothing. Sorry, not interested."

Fascinated, she leaned in, studying the distaste on his face. Goodness, he was more passionate about his work than she'd imagined. A faint pang of regret coursed through her. He was right. Her celebrity clients didn't really care about a home they could raise children and build a history with. It was a means to an end, and when the film wrapped up, they'd probably move back overseas to Europe or to sunny, perfect California.

Morgan hardened her heart against such silly emotions. Her job was simple. Only Pierce Brothers would be able to take on such a complicated project and do it perfectly. She'd done the research. In the Northeast, they were simply the best, their reputation spreading far and wide even after losing their father, who had been the patriarch and main force behind the company. Already time was ticking, and they needed to break ground soon to meet her deadline.

She needed to change Caleb Pierce's mind. Fast. All obstacles had to be removed so that he had no other choice but to take this job.

"Thank you for being honest with me, Mr. Pierce." Standing up, Morgan reached over the desk to offer her hand. He jerked a tiny bit in his chair, obviously surprised at her sudden change of tactic, then slowly held out his hand. "I'll be in touch."

His fingers closed over hers in a firm, warm grip. For a stunning second, Morgan felt completely caught up and surrounded by him, as if his very presence pressed down upon her, lighting up her nerve endings and at the same time soothing her.

Goodness gracious.

Morgan dropped her hand, startled. She'd never felt such a connection by a simple touch, man or woman. Usually she was even a bit reserved, preferring to use verbal rather than physical communication. Yet, in a matter of moments, Caleb Pierce made her crave more. Goose bumps broke out on her arms, which were thankfully covered by her proper suit jacket.

His gaze was laser sharp, taking in her reaction. Morgan quickly gathered her composure and made sure to keep her pace even and steady, ignoring the pain as her heels clicked smartly on the polished floor.

"Do you want to leave your card for other referrals?"

Her hand paused on the knob. "No need. I'm sure you'll change your mind by the end of the week and take the job. I'm staying at the Hilton. Penthouse."

Morgan shut the door before he had a chance to respond.

Take that, Charming.

Now she had to get to work.

Caleb stared at the closed door and wondered what the hell had just happened.

His head pounded from a crap day and the fight with his brother, so he fell back into the cushy leather chair and took another stinging sip of bourbon. She was a slip of a thing, all Southern proper, until she opened her mouth and turned into a little spitfire. He'd been dealing with so many various people in his career, Caleb believed there was little that surprised him anymore.

But she had.

He remembered her proposal, and her multiple follow-up calls he'd transferred immediately to Sydney, his assistant. Name-dropping didn't impress him like it had his father, and he intended to take on only the clients he wanted to for the future. Sure, the company was struggling, but he was sure it would come around. With Jet McCarthy on board, he'd finally get to sink his teeth into a meaty environmental construction project. As a huge proponent of Green properties, Cal intended to build a home completely eco-friendly, demanding all of his time and effort. The money was good, too, so it would go a long way to paying off the piled-up bills he hadn't seen coming after his father's death.

The will was a real bitch. In addition to having to run the company with his brothers, all previous jobs were yanked from contributing to the bottom line of profit. Basically, Cal was starting out with almost a brand-new business that he had to prove would make money in a year. Only a month had passed since his brothers had all moved in together, and they were sinking fast.

He swiveled around in his chair, stared out the window at the rolling acres of green grass, and brooded.

Problem was they didn't want to work together. Cal had been so damn hopeful after their conversation on the porch. But the moment they began working on a job, each of them wanted to do separate things under the umbrella of the company. Tristan focused on property and renovation, Dalton tried to fill each house with a staggering amount of expensive cabinetry and built-ins to show off his technique, and Cal just wanted to put up the houses. Old resentment still stirred in the air, so they tried to avoid each other, and when they were in the same room for too long, a damn fist-fight almost broke out.

Not a great foundation for making a business profitable. The news of Christian's death had also taken a chunk out of their clientele, with many who had been loyal to his father dropping out, thinking the company couldn't get the job done in time. Cal knew that, like anything in life, reputation was half the battle. If people believed Pierce Brothers was successful and dynamic, the clients lined up. The moment they caught the scent of failure, his competitors were laughing their asses off all the way to the bank.

His thoughts flicked back to the woman. Morgan. He loved her Southern accent, a rich, sensual twang that stroked his ears and other parts of his body. He'd tried not to smile at the proper way she stood before him, as if she were a female David to his Goliath, with her eyeliner smudged, mud on her skirt, and pieces of dog hair stuck all over her expensive jacket. Petite, but she packed a punch with all those gorgeous curves. He was so tired of stick figures on women, and as a rough lover, he enjoyed being able to grab, lift, and position them during sex without worrying about breaking them.

Huh. Where had that thought come from?

Her appearance screamed pampered Southern belle. Straight, silvery blond hair. Big china-blue eyes. Pretty pink mouth. But she'd managed to surprise him.

She'd called him Charming.

Damn, it had been hard not to laugh at that one. He deserved it, of course. He rarely talked down to anyone like that, but she'd caught him off guard and in a pissy mood. Even Sydney, who'd worked for him for years, would never have tried that. Morgan Raines didn't hold much fear of him—or, he suspected, most people. It had been a long time since he'd sparred verbally with a woman who was that intelligent, too.

But it didn't matter. He wasn't taking that fluff job, and he refused to be told what to do in his own company. Dealing with her on a daily basis would be the stuff nightmares were made of. She struck him as the stubborn type. Cal shook his head, imagining her fierce cat claws during negotiations and the challenges of picking out every feature on an endless search for perfection. All for a client he'd never really meet.

Why would she want that type of job, anyway?

He finished his drink and placed it back on the blotter. Had to be money. Probably liked working for famous people and being involved in the inner circle. She seemed to dress and act the part, with her conservative designer clothes and her polite drawl and her confident manner.

Charming.

Cal bit back a laugh, put her out of mind, and got back to work.

chapter four

I'm sorry, Cal. I decided to sign with someone else."

Caleb stared at Jet. This wasn't happening. He'd come over to Jet's, contract in hand, to finalize the deal that would take some of the strain off the business for the next few months. He kept calm, nodding, as if this happened all the time. "Look, Jet, this is a big project. I know I don't have the usual background in Green technology, but I'd never take the job if I had any doubts. My architect finished up the plans, and I know you're going to love them. Can we go inside and talk?"

Jet McCarthy was well-known for his work with environmental conservation and was a huge investor in multiple Manhattan properties. He liked to acquire land and build eco-friendly buildings, but this was for a personal home in Harrington. He wanted a home base to commute back and forth to, like so many of the residents in a town known to be Green in other ways. Cal figured Jet had just gotten spooked over the massive project, and he needed to be persuaded.

Even now, the older man rocked back on his heels, dark eyes peering over a trendy pair of black glasses. He kind of reminded Cal of Einstein, with his shock of crazy silver hair and compact build. When he got caught on a thought, he'd just check out of the conversation, and Cal never knew when he'd come back. The guy was a genius and was well respected.

Shit. Cal needed this job. Bad.

"I'm not hiring anyone local. Decided to bring in some people I know who've done some work with me on previous jobs."

Cal looked him dead in the eye. "You don't think I can handle it?"

Jet dropped his gaze, looking uncomfortable. "Actually, Cal, I thought you'd do a great job. I feel bad about this."

Caleb frowned. "I don't understand. What happened to change your mind?"

"I got a call. Morgan Raines. She explained how the Rosenthals needed you to build their house on a tight deadline, and we had a long conversation. I've been looking to get more celebrity awareness regarding environmental conservation, and they agreed to hold a large fund-raiser for me. It was a win-win. Besides, my guys have done this before, so it'll free you up to spend all your time with their project."

The burning hot poker of anger prodded him like a matador bent on torturing his bull. Caleb blinked through the red mist of his vision and tried to salvage the mess. He gave a fake laugh and nodded, as if he knew Morgan well and had been involved with the situation. "Oh, I think you misunderstood, Jet. I decided not to take on the Rosenthal job. They'll be working with another company, so no worries. I apologize for the misunderstanding."

Jet shook his head. "I already made the arrangements, Cal. My team arrives tomorrow morning. Besides, Morgan said you'd tell me that because you felt bad and were trying to take on too many jobs. I think it's best this way. You'll build them a tremendous house." Jet patted him on the back, and his eyes got the familiar distanced look. "I'd better go—got some work to do. Thanks again."

Cal opened his mouth, but Jet was already trudging away, lost in his thoughts of spectacular visions of clean energy and recycling and saving the earth.

Son of a bitch.

He was going to kill her.

Cal got back to his truck and drove, allowing his mind to contemplate all the ways he was going to make that woman pay. Unfortunately, he was afraid it was now too late to book the job. Jet had his mind made up. The only revenge he had left was to show Morgan Raines that her plan had backfired. Now he was more determined than ever not to take the damn job, under any circumstances.

His cell phone blasted on cue, and he hit the speaker button. "Yeah?"

Tristan's voice clipped out, "We got a problem."

Caleb barely managed not to grit his teeth. The last time he'd visited the dentist, he was told that if he didn't stop the stress habit, he'd have no enamel left. "Surprise, surprise. What is it?"

"Are you close to the house? Dalton's here with me."

"On my way."

Caleb hit the accelerator and drove through town, wondering what was going wrong now. He'd run Pierce

Brothers without a hitch for the past five years, other than dealing with his control-freak father. In a matter of one month since his brothers had returned, they'd lost clients, blasted through money, and averaged a fight a day if they happened to all meet in the same room. In a strange way, Cal had thought maybe being forced to be together would help them start rebuilding their relationship. Instead, close proximity made it worse. They'd always been an affectionate, roughhousing type of family, but after Mom died, everything changed. Now they seemed able to communicate only by yelling. Sydney and Brady usually played referee, and already they were claiming exhaustion, refusing to get involved in future epic battles. He bet his father was laughing his ass off up there.

Or down below.

He pulled up the driveway and got out of the pickup. Two flashes of monstrous fur whizzed by him, ready to pounce, and he barely managed to get out the command in time. "Stay!"

Gandalf and Balin froze in midair. Gandalf fell to the ground in his dead-man pose, and Balin managed to get half a butt to the ground, the other half wiggling madly. Okay, at least they hadn't tackled him today. That must mean he was making progress, right? He leaned over and scratched.

"Go play," he said, finding the sweet spots and grinning as their matching legs thumped up and down in ecstasy. "Stay out of the mud, though; I'm tired of using the hose on you every day."

Dismissed, they bounced away like they were two Chihuahuas rather than giants and disappeared. Cal walked into the house, snagged a bottle of water, then headed toward the office.

The faint pang of memory stirred. Other families went to baseball and football games on the weekend. Other families took exotic summer vacations.

But Cal learned early on that free time was to be spent at the building site with his brothers, learning the business from the ground up. They worked through high school, and after graduating college, each of them returned to run Pierce Brothers and take their rightful place. They'd never had a choice, but then again, they never questioned their future. And his mother instilled pride in who they were and what they could accomplish together, as a family.

Every morning, they'd hold a casual meeting in the kitchen over breakfast. Mom had insisted that bonding over a meal to start the day was critical to success. Bacon frying in the pan, coffee black and thick, they'd huddle around the high marble countertops arguing over ideas, laughing at his mother's bad jokes, listening in rapt attention to his father's booming voice always lecturing on contracts, profit, or potential clients.

The office was a place for cold, calculated business. The kitchen broke the barriers and turned them into a real family. He may have sensed his parents' distance between each other but never wanted to think about it much. Because when they were all together, he'd been happy. Normal. Part of something bigger, from the blood that ran in their veins to the future of a company that bore their name.

He pushed open the door to the office where his father had ruled as king. Yes, this is where they belonged now. In a room filled with intimidating leather, high bookcases, and framed awards battling for space. The sprawling desk held two computers and the faint scent of tobacco from Christian's cigars. The discreet bar held a variety of high-end liquor, but Cal still couldn't break his habit of stashing his favorite bourbon in the kitchen. Maybe that was his way of separating himself from his father.

His brothers stared at him. Not like they had years ago. Not anymore. Now it was about pure survival, with eleven months to go until they could disband and go back to not dealing with each other. So many old wounds simmered beneath the Band-Aids.

God, they were so fucked-up.

"What's wrong now?" he asked.

Tristan spoke. "I stopped by to see Sydney. She gave me the profits for the month."

"Yeah?"

"We made no profits, Cal. In fact, we're starting at a serious deficit."

Caleb plowed his fingers through his hair and grunted. "I'm handling it. Why are you having Sydney pull figures? Don't you trust me?"

Dalton made a rude noise from the leather couch. "More like you don't trust us. This is a bunch of bullshit, and you know it. At this point, no matter what we do, we'll end up losing the business. I'm thinking of pulling out, Cal. Maybe going someplace new. Start fresh."

"Convenient. Barely five weeks in, and you're running again."

Tristan held up his hand as Dalton let out a blistering curse. "This isn't helping. If we can't even get through a simple meeting, we're never going to make this work. We have to change our tactic." He yanked a fat folder open and held up a bunch of papers. "We lost three big clients last week."

Cal glowered at his youngest brother. "Ask Mr. Tiger-wood over there. They walked when they heard about the little go-around on the cabinets with their neighbors. We were putting in an addition, but they went to Farell's."

Tristan groaned. "Are you kidding me? Farell's Construction is the damn Walmart of the contracting business. Their quality sucks, and everyone knows it."

"But they don't argue, and they put up the shit fast. Some people don't like waiting for perfection."

"What about the deck for the Peabody restaurant? That'll get us cash quick."

"They decided to wait till next year. Their profits took a dive over the winter, and they're struggling."

"Other than finishing up the last two jobs, I haven't been able to book anything. I thought you said you were turning down jobs the past few years."

Caleb swore. "I was! Ever since Dad passed, people have gotten spooked. Gossip has been spreading about losing the business and us not able to get along. Even though no one knows about the will, people are suspicious."

Tristan studied the file as if it held all the answers. His brother liked numbers and order, so he'd inherited the job of inventory and helping Sydney with the accounting. Cal would rather be out with the guys putting up houses, so he was grateful, but having his middle brother worried about a business he'd been running for the past years made him itch to prove he didn't need him.

"I guess the McCarthy project will keep the wolves from the door a bit," Tristan grumbled.

Fuck.

"We don't have that job anymore."

Dalton and Tristan stared. "What do you mean? You went out to see him this morning, right?"

Caleb turned away, not wanting to admit failure. "He hired his own team to come in and build it. I just found out."

Silence filled the room.

"Well, then. Maybe we should have a serious conversation about letting Pierce Brothers go."

Cal shot a fierce glare at Dalton. "I'm not giving up until the year is up, and I won't let you, either. We talked about this. We committed. Why don't you get your ass out there and find some woodworking jobs?"

Dalton jumped up from the couch. "You think the type of work I do is built for cold-calling? I'm an artist. You're such an asshole. Just like Dad."

"This isn't helping," Tristan interrupted. "I'm tired of you boneheads. Cut the crap and let's figure out what we can do. I made some property sales and took on a renovation project. We still have the last payment coming in from the Weatherspoons. That'll count toward this year's profits. What about the senator? That's a fat payment due in three months, right?"

"The senator pulled out when Dad died. I tried to get him back, but he hired a bunch of his personal friends to take the job."

Tristan raised a brow. "Mob?"

Caleb shrugged. "Probably. Another reason I didn't want to touch it in the first place. Seems the crew gets a lot of lunch breaks."

Dalton laughed. "Remember how Dad used to screw with them when they tried to encroach on our territory?"

Tristan snapped his fingers. "Oh, yeah, that time he dipped the baseball bat in ketchup and left it at the site with a note?"

"'We're watching. Always watching,'" Caleb recited. "They got so paranoid, it was like being trapped in *The Godfather*."

"Or the time he hung up the dead deer skins?" Dalton jumped in. "They scurried out of here fast like the rats they were."

"They're definitely city boys," Tristan said. "Dad knew just how to spook them. He knew we'd never get completely rid of them, but they disappeared from many of the big jobs for a while."

Memories of his father haunted him. So many were bad that the few good ones they had were sacred, ready to be pulled out and dusted off with the only people who got it. His brothers. Damn, he wished things were different. Wished they could be closer instead of consistently battling this distance and simmering resentment.

Things had been strained between his family even before the car crash. His mother and father had grown even more distant with one another, barely speaking unless they were all together during a meal. Tristan butted heads with his father on real estate. Dalton tried to carve out his own specialty in woodworking against Christian's wishes. But once Mom was taken from them, it all went to shit. They held on for six months, but the grief tore them apart instead of bonding them together. Christian became a cold son of a bitch, and Caleb ended up rushing into marriage to try to fix something that was too broken. It was like the perfect storm broke and scattered them across the globe.

Tristan was still pissed about Cal's decision to cut him out of the business by taking Dad's side. Cal was pissed at Dalton for sleeping with his fiancée and denying it. Dalton was pissed at both of them for ignoring his part in the business and the fallout from their mom's death.

It was just one big pissed-off contest with no winner.

But Cal didn't know how to fix it anymore.

As if they followed his thoughts, the smiles died from their lips, and once again they were looking at each other as strangers.

"Then what's the new plan, Cal?" Tristan asked. "At this rate, we need a big job with a completion date of about eight months max. Where are we going to pull that from the magic hat?"

Ah, shit.

Every instinct he owned screamed and bitched in rebellion, but he knew there was no other choice. He needed to go visit Morgan Raines. After the stunt she'd pulled, he'd do anything to come up with another alternative, but he needed something fast, and this seemed to be the answer. His head pounded, and he held back a groan. He needed a flawless approach, so she didn't think he'd rolled over like his dogs and surrendered. He'd make sure his terms were met and Pierce Brothers had a shot at survival after he took his punishment.

And, boy, this would be some serious punishment.

Each word that fell from his lips was another push down the plank. "I may have a solution."

"Dissolve the company and let us go home?" Dalton asked.

"No. I'll take a recent job I was offered. A big job. Some celebrity clients—the Rosenthals—bought property in Harrington. Gonna film some big movie here or something. Anyway, this woman, Morgan, wants us to build the house for them. We have to deal directly with her, but from what I remember, it's a pretty big house. Lots of custom furnishings. The three of us can all work on it together, and we can ask any price we want."

Tristan nodded. "Nice. This sounds like what we need to keep afloat. If we all focus on this project, we can complete it and get paid in full within eleven months."

"They want it in six."

Dalton winced. "Damn, that's tight. Did you show Brady the plans yet? How is this Morgan to work with? Pain in the ass?"

Caleb let out a dry laugh. "Yep. Seems she never makes a mistake and thinks she's goddess of the builders' world. Brady will be on board; he's as invested in this company as the rest of us. I'll go see her tonight and close out the negotiations."

"Don't push too hard," Tristan warned. "We need the job."

"I'll take care of it. I just need to make sure if we take it, you're both with me. Since we moved in together, we've kept our jobs separate. I think it's been the wrong move. If we work together on each project, we can streamline our productivity and show a united front to the town." His brothers shared a look, but Caleb had reached the end of his pride and his patience. If this didn't work, he'd lose Pierce Brothers. He raised his arms in the air. "I know we're not comfortable with each other. I know sometimes I act like a dick. This one time, I'm asking to put aside our crap and build this house together like the old days. Do this for me, and I swear to God, I won't ask for anything else again."

He tried to keep his face reflecting a calm he didn't feel. His brothers were stubborn and did what they wanted. Funny, never before had he thought Dalton and Tristan would have the power over his business. After all the decisions he had made to keep it intact and push them away, they were the only ones who could save him.

"One last time," Tristan repeated. "We do this job and give it our all."

Caleb nodded. "Agreed. Dalton?"

His little brother took his time, but he finally gave a sharp jerk of his head. "Fine. But we're equal partners in this. You can be the main point of contact with Morgan, but our feedback needs to count. Got it?"

"Got it."

The deal had been struck. Relief coursed through him. The company was safe for now. He needed to get a contract signed that would give them the advantage and make sure this house was move-in ready within six months.

Yeah. No problem.

"I'll meet with Brady in the morning and go over the initial plans," Cal said. "For now, I'm going to pay Ms. Raines a visit."

"Hey, is that the blonde I saw in the hallway?" Dalton asked. "She's cute."

Cute? Morgan was so far from cute, it was ridiculous. Caleb doubted she had ever giggled in her life. She struck him as competent but a know-it-all. A Southern belle who got transferred into Yankee territory and intended to get her way with a charming smile and sexy little accent. Caleb had a hard time finding the right adjective to truly describe the woman. At least not in polite company.

"She's a manipulator, and we have to keep a sharp eye on her. I don't trust her, but right now, we need her."

His brothers agreed.

And Caleb headed out to see her.

Morgan refused to pace because it only showed weakness. Instead, she pulled her linen pants tight so they wouldn't wrinkle and settled on the sprawling sofa in her hotel suite. Soothing music piped in low through the Bluetooth. She sipped her glass of water with lemon. And pondered.

The others had been less stubborn. It didn't bode well for the future of the project, but she'd had no choice. She waited in her hotel room most of the day, but he hadn't come storming over. No text. Not even a scathing email. Nothing but silence.

He'd have to take the job. She'd done her homework. Called in her favors. Pierce Brothers needed her more than she needed them. After studying the client profile, Morgan knew immediately that Caleb Pierce was the only one to make this house work. The Rosenthals were her most demanding clients, and nothing less than perfection would be accepted. Her entire career had grown steadily, her reputation impeccable. She got the job done and never faltered. Soon, celebrity clients lined up so she could build their houses, allowing themselves to trust her with the most intimate of projects, but when the Rosenthals came knocking, Morgan knew it was a turning point.

If she did a good job, she would be the darling of Hollywood. People listened to the powerful couple, and even Brangelina were no longer the crowning glory. They had been officially replaced.

Morgan was used to flying all over the country at her clients' beck and call, but it was always nice to settle in a town for those few months and feel a part of something bigger. She missed her Southern roots and the closeness of the community, but her mother had encouraged her to follow the road to greatness. Her job might be a bit eclectic, but she'd come from a long line of well-established decorators in South Carolina, and she hadn't wanted to stick around to be overshadowed. Her mother hadn't wanted that, either, having already claimed the main role as queen. And of course, Daddy always followed her mother's lead.

She let out an impatient sigh, glanced at her tasteful silver-and-pearl watch, and decided to order room service.

A low buzz echoed in the air. She pressed the intercom button. "Yes?"

"Mr. Pierce here to see you, Ms. Raines."

"Send him up, please."

A smile fought for victory, but she just stood on her three-inch cream heels, smoothed down her hair, and waited for his knock.

She reminded herself not to enjoy the upcoming encounter too much.

She opened the door a few moments later. "Why, Mr. Pierce, how lovely to see you," she drawled. She waved him inside, her poppy-pink nails flashing in the air. "Come in."

He didn't budge. Just stared at her, his gaze stripping all her bullshit and veneer aside and probing underneath. Scruff darkened his jaw. Dirt marred his meaty biceps. There was a hole in his black T-shirt, and he had a rip in his faded jeans. He looked sulky. Pissed.

And hot as a summer day in Charleston.

She tried to swallow and found she had no spit. Desperate to get out of his close range, she went to the bar and poured him a glass of water, dropping a few cubes of ice in, and handed it to him. "Here you go. It's hot out there. Shall we talk?"

One brow shot up, but he took the glass and shut the door. "Damn, you got some nerve. Did you have fun with your criminal activities?"

She blinked. "What?"

"You know. Blackmail. Stealing my job, which I worked hard for, just so you can play the game of *I'm more important than you.* Is that how you roll?"

Heat rushed to her cheeks. Oh, she really didn't like him. He cut right to the bone at every opportunity. He needed a lesson on manners and civility. "Funny, if I was a man, right now you'd probably be thrilled to play a game of hardball. Is it because I'm a woman you don't respect that in business, sometimes you have to bend the rules to get what you want?"

He barked out a short laugh. "Got no problem with

strong women. Just ones who lie. I have the same problem with men, by the way."

She grabbed her own glass for something to cling to and raised her chin. "Aren't we being a tad dramatic here? A bit over-the-top? I'm offering you a valid job, and your client has what is called free will. How is this suddenly blamed on me?"

He shook his head and tunneled his fingers through his hair. She watched the nutty strands stand up and settle back in delicious messiness. There was still a slight flattened ring circling his head. From wearing a favorite ball cap? Funny, she'd never been so obsessed with a man's hair before. Maybe because it was streaked with blond and very thick, brushing low on his collar. But he had hat hair! How was that so damn yummy?

Her last comment must've pissed him off more, because then he started pacing like a wild animal in his circus cage. "Unbelievable. Did you take lessons on how to deflect responsibility? What did you have to promise Jet McCarthy to get him to dump me?"

She tapped a nail against the rim of her glass and regarded him steadily. "Not much. Which tells me he had doubts about you on the project. I just offered him a bit of extra funding, but nothing that would've made a huge difference if he really wanted you."

His mouth fell half open at her direct hit. "Lady, with you in my corner, I don't need enemies. Next time you want someone this bad to build your house, I have a great idea: be nice."

"I was. It didn't work."

They stared at each other, but Morgan didn't retreat. The foundation was being set. They circled around like boxers, trying out jabs, looking for weak spots, because they were complete strangers. She expected him to start yelling or zinging insults, but he surprised her again by letting out a laugh and shaking his head. "Now that we're all warm and fuzzy with preliminaries, why don't we talk business?"

Her skin tingled. Talking business was her favorite thing to do. It was like getting to play hard in a controlled environment. "Agreed. I'm hoping you decided to take the job?"

He nodded, allowing her to pretend it was a question rather than a statement. "On consensual terms."

"Of course." The word *consensual* was matched with a tiny smirk. She ignored the tickle of awareness in her lower half.

"Add thirty percent to your initial proposal in cost," he said.

Ouch. He'd gotten the first hit. "Absolutely not. That's criminal and insane. The original price stays because it's fair. We can incorporate bonuses for early completion, and scales for specialized supplies we require."

"Not good enough. You stole a job that would've given me more than just money. I could've built my reputation as an environmentally competent builder. Instead, I get stuck with a house that will hardly be lived in."

Her nail tapped faster against her glass. "You'll get exposure by publicity and a featured spread in *Home Style* magazine."

"In this town, everyone's going Green. It's the new thing. Not overpriced, oversize mansions on the water that scream *I'm better than you*. Welcome to the new century."

She seethed, more because he was right. Kind of. Green building techniques were blowing up everywhere, and she'd snatched that prize away from him. She wished the Rosenthals cared about social consciousness, but they didn't. They wanted a huge, ostentatious house that said they had arrived, without openly bragging. It was a fine line she had been hired to walk. Morgan hated feeling guilty, but a tiny bit seeped in. Pursing her lips, her brain clicked away at the percentages, the financial breakdown, and her cushion that she'd automatically thrown in.

"Twenty percent. I won't go higher."

"Done."

The smirk made her realize she'd been conned. He would've taken 10 percent. Damn, damn, damn. That mistake would never happen again. To make herself feel better, she snapped through the list of needs she'd memorized. "Completion must be in six months. Turn-key ready. My specs were clearly listed on the original plans and triple-checked with some of the best architects in the world."

He snorted. "Don't care until Brady says it's doable. We go by my architect or no one at all."

She knew that would be the case, and had already anticipated agreement. Again, she'd researched Brady Heart, and he was top-notch. "Fine. I have final say in all decisions. The Rosenthals trust me to bring them a home completed perfectly to their expectations, and the only way to deliver is to be on-site the entire time."

"You like white, huh?"

She looked up from the glass she'd been tapping. "Huh?"

He jerked a thumb toward her outfit. "White. Second

time I'm seeing you in that color. Not a great look for a site, you know."

Her gaze narrowed. "Mr. Pierce, I've been to over a dozen building sites and know exactly how to handle myself. And what to wear. This is my choice of outfit for business meetings and personal events only."

"Like hanging out at home? Were you just relaxing here or waiting for me to storm the gates of your castle?"

Oh, he saw too much. She'd need to be at her smartest to take him on. The sizzle of challenge flowed in her blood, making her feel alive and whole. It was pretty much the only time she felt like that. Negotiating. Dealing with obstacles. The moment before she revealed the house her clients had trusted her to complete. She loved the hit, wondering if there was anything in life more fun than her job.

So far, sex had come a distant second.

Then again, she didn't even have an item ranking third.

Morgan made herself smile easily. "Relaxing."

"Huh. In that? You look like you're ready to host a tea party for some stuffy churchgoers. And you're wearing shoes. High-heel shoes."

Confusion marred her brow. "And your point is?"

He grunted. "You hang out and kick back in a white linen suit with frickin' heels on your feet? Do you know what that says about a person?"

She gritted her teeth and kept her smile. "That she's well prepared for anything?"

"No. It screams you don't know how to let go." He paused and looked suspicious. "I bet you don't know how to have any fun, either."

Her mouth dropped open. "I know how to have plenty of fun! And you're not one to talk about letting go. Something tells me from first sight you're a bit of a control freak yourself."

His gaze raked her over, and he gave another disgusted snort. "Your clothes don't even have a wrinkle. Look, princess, we're stuck with each other. You forced me to take this job by playing dirty, so don't expect me to treat you with pristine white kid gloves. We're looking at six months for completion. This means overtired workers, a hundred decisions every hour, and stressed-out suppliers. You say you've done this before, but never like this, and never with me. Be warned—I'm going hard-core. Understood?"

Oh, she wanted to curl her fingers into fists and stomp the floor and hiss. He insulted her appearance and her personal life and made snap judgments that enraged her. But she sensed he wanted her to get mad. He'd give her that little smirk and feel as if he'd won.

Hard-core.

Morgan was taken aback by the sudden vivid image of his hard naked body slamming hers against the wall, rubbing up against her, and getting her very, very dirty.

Oh, no. Not with him. Not for any reason. He'd only respect her if she exhibited a professionalism and took everything he gave while she politely asked for another. Please.

Time to reverse the direction of his little game.

Morgan closed the distance between them. Her own gaze flicked over his body in analysis and a cool dismissal that she hoped stung. "Now let me warn you about something. I've built fifteen houses for some of the most demanding clients you've ever met. They make you look like a sweet little pussycat. I've gone days without sleep, camped out at the site for a week to catch the thief stealing our precious koa wood, won a catfight with one of our construction workers' wives who insisted we had had an affair, and dealt with more sexual harassment and discrimination than you can imagine. So, Charming, don't talk to me about being hard-core." She pursed her lips and dropped her final words. "I invented hard-core."

Ah, shit.

He wanted to kiss her.

When he first walked in, he'd been struck by the clean elegance of the hotel suite, with her as reigning queen. The penthouse was pure luxury, and damned if the carpet and furnishings weren't white and vanilla cream. She looked like she perfectly matched her surroundings. The linen suit, heels, and smart bob drove him crazy. Who the hell hung out looking like that? The only weakness he deciphered was the tiny black ink spot on the edge of her sleeve. Probably from holding a pen that leaked. Her other saving grace was the loss of one earring. When she moved her head, subtle pearls caught the light at her ears, but one was bare. Maybe she'd lost it sometime today and hadn't figured it out. The fact comforted him that she wasn't a robot but real. Even better was her temper and her sharp tongue.

It was kind of magnificent.

Caleb watched her pretty pink mouth curl upward in a sexy kitten growl and her pretty pink nails curl inward as if ready to pounce. He locked his muscles down tight and rode out the fierce firestorm of pure want battering his dick. Well, this was not expected. He liked his women rough, tumbled, and messy. Morgan probably had sex with the lights off, under expensive sheets, full makeup on, and a wet wipe handy for quick cleanups.

But damn, she was kind of hot.

He studied her closely, and sure enough, there was a gleam of heat lasering from those china-blue eyes. Her cheeks flushed, and her breath came a bit faster than normal. A tight, swirling energy buzzed around them, a mixture of arousal, temper, and hormones. Hmm, interesting. She definitely felt the same connection, but like him, seemed determined to ignore it. Much easier to hold on to the prickly dislike they had for each other. He never slept with anyone on a job. Mixing business and pleasure was disastrous. He'd had too many close calls with women who liked the side benefit of banging their contractor, but Caleb wasn't stupid. He knew when to use his big head rather than his little one. There were tons of other women willing and able, and not pissy enough to ruin the job over jealousy, possessiveness, or spite.

No. Nothing could happen between them, but it was kind of fun to push her limits.

Her pupils dilated when he suddenly leaned in real close. Their faces were inches apart. He caught her scent—a balanced mix of floral and citrus, clean and refreshing and completely addictive. Caleb barely managed not to take a huge sniff. Her lips parted, dewy and moist, and he clung to his iron-will control that had served him in all situations, including the time he'd been greeted by a new client with a welcoming smile and naked body. He'd tipped his head, told her they'd talk when she had clothes on, and left while she cursed his retreating back.

"I have one question for you."

Her body stiffened. Her voice came out a tad ragged. "What?"

He smiled real slow. Let her wait for it. "How'd you get your hands on the koa wood? Were you building in Hawaii?"

She blinked. Shook her head as if to clear it, then stepped back. "Umm, no. We were in Texas, and we had a contact that got us on a list to snag a large inventory. That's your question?"

He rocked back on his heels, satisfied. "Yep. Those contacts could come in handy, I assume?"

"Very."

"Good. Now that we've got our financials squared away and Brady's confirming the plans, why don't we meet at the office tomorrow? My brothers, Dalton and Tristan, will be just as involved, and I want to be sure we're all in agreement. We'll walk the property, go over supplies, and I'll assign my best team to begin Thursday."

"Agreed." Suspicion eked from her pores. "So, we understand each other, then? I won't have to deal with any condescending remarks about my place on the site?"

Caleb knew when to back off and admit he was wrong. He might not like having to babysit her through the building of this home, but she seemed prepared. Hell, she knew about koa wood. That gave her points right there. He made a note to tell Dalton. His brother had wet dreams over koa wood and ebony burl. "Can't promise we won't butt heads, but if you earn your place, you get my respect. And I apologize if my comments came off chauvinistic. That was kind of an asshole thing to say."

He almost laughed as her eyes popped out of her head. Oh, yeah, she had low expectations of him. Assumed he'd never apologize for anything. But Caleb was fair, and he had insulted her. Yes, she'd pissed him off, but it was a sucker punch. He enjoyed watching her gather her composure, reach up to smooth her hair again, and nod like she wasn't surprised at his apology. "Well . . . good. Very good. I'll see you tomorrow at nine?"

"Yep. See ya."

He didn't wait for a response. Just took his leave before the impulse to stay longer grew stronger. Best to keep personal stuff to a minimum with Morgan and keep his focus on the only thing in his life that he loved as much as his dogs and pain-in-the-ass brothers.

Work.

chapter five

At nine sharp, Morgan entered Pierce Brothers Construction and greeted the attractive redhead at the front desk. "Good morning. I'm Morgan Raines. I have an appointment with Mr. Pierce," she said.

The redhead looked up with a warm smile. Freckles dusted her white skin, and her whiskey-colored eyes seemed to dance with an innate mischief Morgan immediately liked. "Nice to meet you, Morgan. I'm Sydney. They're waiting for you in the conference room. I'll take you there." She jumped up from her seat and motioned toward the kitchen. "Oops, I forgot to offer you a beverage. Our receptionist called in sick today, so I'm on double duty. Can I get you water? Coffee? Tea?"

"No, thank you. I've maxed out my caffeine level for the day already."

Sydney laughed. "Been there. Coffeepot works so much overtime here, we go through a new machine every few months." With a natural grace, Sydney led her down the carpeted hall, tapped on the closed door, and pushed it open. "Good luck," she whispered.

Morgan frowned at the conspiratorial tone that was all female.

When she stepped inside the conference room and the four men stood up from the table, Morgan finally understood.

She was a bit . . . overwhelmed.

Morgan straightened to her wimpy five-foot-three height—thank goodness for heels—and tried to pretend standing in the doorway while four ridiculously gorgeous men focused their laser-like gazes on her was a common occurrence.

The powerful presence of sheer male command radiated around them in waves that would batter an onlooker. She pegged the three brothers right away. Their shared blood was obvious, sketched out in the same full lines of the mouth, sharp jaws, and intensity radiating from their almond-shaped eyes. But each held his own individual brand of heat. Morgan bet when these three walked out of a bar, there wasn't a woman left behind with dry panties. The final man must be Brady, the architect, since he was a few inches shorter and sported a dark Latino look to round out the ridiculous sexiness contained within four walls.

Morgan wished she'd taken the water Sydney had offered.

Caleb motioned her in. "Morgan, welcome. I want you to meet the team. This is Dalton, Tristan, and Brady."

Her silver bangles jingled as she shook each of their hands, trying to exhibit cool professionalism while her heart thundered in her chest like American Pharoah winning the Triple Crown. "Nice to meet you," she murmured to each of them before sliding gratefully into the oversize butter leather chair and gaining a bit of distance. "I'm looking forward to working with all of you."

Caleb sat next to her. "We're all excited about this project," he said smoothly. Was there a glint of amusement in his eyes or was it just a trick of the light? Did his brothers know she had kind of blackmailed him into taking the job?

The men remained silent, studying her face. Morgan refused to fidget and stared back, as quietly stubborn as they were. One of them had to speak first, or the initial rules would favor them as boss, not her. The clock ticked, and suddenly Brady let out a deep growl of laughter.

"I do respect a woman who can hold her tongue," he said. "I think I'm going to enjoy working with you."

"I hope so," she said. "A man who can wait for someone else to speak is a beautiful thing. This may be a fine partnership."

Ah, there it was. Dalton and Tristan relaxed a bit at her ability to hold her own and have a sense of humor. The job site was stressful, and usually everyone was worried about having a personality glitch. It made for a long, painful process. Brady laughed again. "Agreed. Morgan, I went over the plans and they're solid. Your initial architect did a great job. I had a few tweaks to suggest, going with staircase placement and the film room location."

He motioned toward the plans, which contained the original and the markups. She tapped the paper. "This won't be grand enough for the Rosenthals. They want a classic spiral splitting the foyer so it's the main focus when you enter the house."

Brady made faint pencil marks to the left of the oversize entranceway. "Yes, but many of the features in the house are a bit quirky. This isn't the standard luxury mansion, and your client may benefit from having the staircase completely shifted off center." He grabbed a scrap sheet of paper and began drawing. "We make it curve into one main horseshoe and do stone instead of wood." His pencil scratched furiously. "The dimensions can still work, but we open up the main living room for more space, put the chandelier here, and give it more of a wow factor. By using stone and wood, we give it a more majestic look. Then do a bigger hallway, which looks more like a floating loft."

Dalton leaned over to watch Brady sketch out the new staircase. "Bluestone is done for outside work, but for this short piece it may work. Combine it with a dark wood with some gray tones and you have the perfect dynamic."

Fascinated, she watched as the house transformed into something she'd never seen before. Excitement slithered through her blood as the new shape took place and her mind sifted through updated design ideas. "Can you make this actually work? I've never seen it done before."

Brady and Dalton shared a smug look. "Yep," Brady said. "More money, though."

Caleb lifted a brow. "Pity," he drawled.

Morgan shook her head. "This increase is worth it."

"I'd like to decrease the film room to make up some of the cost."

"Now, that I can't agree to."

"What if we keep the same size but build an actual balcony to offset? Honestly, how many people are really gonna be in the film room at one time? Is he going to have one hundred executives over to the house to watch a movie?"

"No. But he wants to feel like he can."

"Understood. We can create a wide-tipped balcony for extra seating but keep it more intimate. I see him more watching a movie with a few friends and his wife, even when he's shooting here."

They went over the revised plans and shot ideas back and forth, and Morgan found herself agreeing to both changes. Tristan and Dalton dropped suggestions on varying designs, and she scribbled a bunch of notes in her pad for future decorating ideas. By the end of the hour, she already had a better handle on the project and the skill set each of the men brought.

"I'll get in touch with my suppliers to see how fast we can get some of the orders placed and shipped."

"I have a long list of contacts if you run into trouble," she said firmly. "The most important part is timing. We cannot be late, due to the filming schedule."

"Never been late on a project yet. Don't intend to start now."

A shiver tingled down her spine at the sound of the sandpapery voice to her left.

Her gaze cut to his. Those heated gunmetal eyes did bad things to her body and equilibrium. Thank goodness she was sitting. His brothers and Brady were extremely attractive, but Caleb owned an elemental maleness that just did it for her. He was dressed more formally than usual, still in jeans, but a blue button-down shirt stretched over his wide shoulders and chest as if trying to contain him within the material. The image that seared her mind came as violently as a tsunami.

Her, crouched over that magnificent chest. Revealing each hard, carved muscle inch by inch, while she flicked open button after button with her teeth.

Lord have mercy.

Morgan jumped up from the chair in a fake flurry of activity. "Well, this has been quite productive! I'll sign off on the finalized plans and meet y'all back on-site."

Caleb stood up with a frown. "I want to walk the property with you first. We can drive over in my car."

"I'll take her."

Dalton also stood up. His manner was easygoing, with a charming smile curving his lips. But the moment the words left his mouth, the temperature in the room dropped like a faulty elevator. She glanced back and forth, but there was some silent communication going on that she had no clue about.

"No need. I'm sure you have some wood to take care of. Elsewhere."

Huh?

Dalton curled his lower lip in a sneer. "Actually, I don't. My schedule is wide-open. I'd be happy to accompany Ms. Raines."

Brady cleared his throat. "Umm, guys?"

Caleb leaned over the desk. "I think it would be better if I took her. You can work on another . . . project that needs your attention."

Tristan bowed his head and groaned. "Not now, okay? I have a headache."

Dalton groaned with disgust. "I never took your wood! I'm tired of repeating the same story over and over. I was trying to protect you. You picked the wrong wood."

Caleb bristled. "No, I didn't."

"The wood was faulty, but you were too stubborn to see it!"

"It was mine!"

Morgan's mouth dropped open. This was the strangest family business she'd ever been involved in, but it was too late, and she had to deal with what she got. The pseudo-symbolism was also off the charts, because it was obvious they were talking about some woman. With men, it always revolved around women and sex.

Tristan sent her a beseeching look of apology and stood with the rest of them. "Enough of the *Full House* repeats, okay? I'll escort Ms. Raines to the property. You two hot-heads cool off."

"Mind your own business, Tristan," Caleb growled.

"I'd like to, but since I'm stuck here when I'd rather be anywhere else, I think I get a say. At least this time."

Morgan briefly wished for Dr. Phil to help figure things out.

"Playing the blame game again? You win, Tristan. I failed you, like you consistently remind me. Can we move on?"

"I have, you egomaniac!" Tristan hissed.

Caught between horrified laughter and sympathy for the brothers, who were definitely not a unit, Morgan took a deep breath, ready to stop the brawl threatening to explode right in the fancy conference room. Until a booming voice that brooked no argument cut through the air.

"May I have everyone's attention?"

Everyone turned toward the curvy redhead framed in the doorway. Sydney pushed the no-nonsense gold glasses up the bridge of her nose and glared with the fierceness of a pissed-off mama bear ready to corral her naughty cubs. She jabbed a finger at them in time to her words. "I. Am. Sick. Of. This. Behavior. I told you before, if you want to take pot-shots at each other, do it at home, not in my office. It's my safe haven. Got it?"

Morgan watched the four strapping men meekly nod.

Sydney relaxed and gave her a dazzling smile. "Good. Now, let's apologize to Ms. Raines for the interruption and move onward. Caleb, can you please meet us outside in ten minutes to escort Ms. Raines—"

"Please, everyone, call me Morgan."

Sydney nodded. "—escort Morgan to the property. Dalton, you have an appointment in half an hour to talk to Ms. Ferguson about new cabinetry. Brady, let's get these revised plans finalized. Tristan, you have a ton of phone messages you refuse to return, and I'm running out of excuses. Let's get to work, gentlemen."

Morgan noticed how her voice seemed to trip over Tristan's name. She also averted her gaze slightly, as if looking full into his face was a problem. Interesting. Tristan shifted his feet and didn't look at her directly, either.

Unfortunately, she had no further time to delve deeper because Sydney motioned her out, and Morgan trailed behind her. She was led back down the hall and into a full kitchen that held all the standard appliances, a high black granite bar with red stools, and an array of foodie toys: a soda machine, an espresso maker, a juicer, and an old-fashioned popcorn maker. She grabbed a tall glass from the counter and poured from a pitcher of water infused with cucumbers and mint, then handed her the glass.

"Drink. You probably need it after that display. I apologize."

Morgan drank, smiling gratefully at the cool, clean flavors as the liquid slid down her throat. "Delicious. Thanks. Do they always act like that?"

Sydney wrinkled her pert nose and sighed. "Sometimes. They haven't worked together in a long time, so there's some growing pains. But don't worry, their bickering will never interfere with their work or effort. Pierce Brothers is the best you can get."

"Have you worked for them a long time?"

Sydney laughed. "You mean because I feel comfortable yelling at them? Guilty as charged. I lived right down the road, so I grew up with their family. Started working for them when I was eighteen and never stopped." A faint shadow darkened her face, and Morgan wondered at her obvious secrets. "They had a falling-out years ago, but after Christian passed, they decided to run the company together again. This project will be good for them, especially after meeting you."

"Why?"

Sydney laughed. "You won't take their crap. You also know exactly what you want, but you're willing to listen to other ideas."

Morgan cocked her head. "How do you know all this? Come to think of it, how did you hear everything in the conference room when it's all the way down the hall?"

The mischief lurking behind those amber eyes glinted to

life. "My office is over there." She pointed to the other side of the hallway. "I bugged the conference room."

Morgan choked on the next sip of water. "Excuse me?"

Sydney winked. "Trust me, it's better this way. They have huge hearts but can use a little looking after. They're also pretty brilliant, which you'll find out. I hope we get to spend some time together while you're here. Where are you staying?"

"The Hilton." Morgan smiled. "And yes, I'd really like that. Something tells me it'll be a huge advantage to have you in my corner."

They were both laughing when Caleb poked his head in, a fierce frown marking his brow. "Are we ready? Or do you want me to get you both a Disney teapot for tea time?"

Sydney rolled her eyes. "Only if you play Prince Charming."

The joke hit Morgan right in the funny bone. She burst into laughter at Caleb's astonished face, as if he suspected Morgan had confided in her assistant about his secret nickname. Without waiting for Sydney's questions, Caleb grumbled something under his breath and practically stomped out the door. Morgan followed, cramming her fist against her mouth to stifle her mirth.

Oh, yeah. She was going to like having a friend around here.

So, the little hellcat was amused, was she?

He'd need to make sure Sydney and Morgan didn't get buddy-buddy. God help them all if they hooked up, because they both had a bit of spitfire brewing beneath the polished surface. Together, they'd be worse than Thelma and Louise.

Still, her outbreak of giggles had done a funny thing to his chest. He usually hated that sound, but on her it was kind of charming. He never would have pegged the woman even *able* to giggle, she was so serious. She'd held herself like an expert at the meeting, pushing his respect for her knowledge even higher. It was rare to meet a woman who could talk wood, design, and property features without falling asleep. Sure, they all thought they were experts because they liked the HGTV channel, or those two brothers they all sighed over, but most couldn't handle the reality of the day-to-day. Soon he'd find out if she held the stamina.

"I like your team," she said, breaking the silence. "Am I going to have to worry about who has better wood?"

He spit out a laugh. Damn. How could such a reserved woman have a wicked sense of humor? It was a total contradiction. "No. I can't promise you there won't be outbreaks, but it won't affect the job. You have my word."

"I'll need more than that. I don't care if you beat each other up after work, just as long as we meet deadline and hold strict quality control."

Embarrassment rushed through him. He hated that she had to be a witness to their dirty laundry, but it was his fault for losing his temper. He'd literally flipped out when Dalton offered to drive her. It wasn't so much the words he said as it was the look of intention carved on his face. His brother loved to play, and females fell to their knees to worship him for some strange reason. Yeah, the guy was good-looking, but he went through women faster than those Hershey bars he was addicted to. Cal did not want him ruining this job by making a pass at Morgan just 'cause he was bored. She deserved more than that. Hell, if anyone was going to try to seduce her, he'd be first in line. At least he'd take more care than his brother. A lot of care. Preferably long, heated, naked hours spent in tangled sheets with a lot of screaming.

Not that he was interested in seducing her, of course.

He shoved the thought aside and concentrated on the road. "Trust me, it won't be a problem."

"Good."

He drove and studied her from the corner of his eye. He wondered how many outfits she owned that were white. This was more a buttercream, but close enough. Tailored slacks that looked silky soft. Sandals with three-inch kitten heels. A sleeveless knit sweater molded to her high, full breasts, and the tiny V dip giving a tempting glimpse of smooth, pale skin. A delicate pearl pendant hung in the hollow of her neck. The truck smelled of lemons and wildflowers. Way too girly for him. But nice. Really nice.

"Is there a reason why you don't get along with your brothers?"

Oh, yeah. Bucketloads. But he wasn't gonna tell her. "Yeah."

"What?"

"We got issues."

She shook her head, but her lips curved in a half smile. "I bet you do. Get in line."

He let out a bark of laughter. "At least we're both mysterious. Always hated an open book."

"You? Funny, I figured open books would be the only ones you wanted to read."

"Ah, you got the wood references, huh? Now we're using books for Freudian purposes? Cool. Let's just say easy reads are good for quick entertainment and temporary satisfaction. Nothing wrong with it. Our culture thrives on such *books*."

She straightened up in her seat as if getting ready to rise to his challenge. "Actually, I agree. I just think we enjoy those types of books while we search for a more complex, deeper read. Think Tolstoy."

He gave a fake shudder. "I'd rather bring James Patterson to bed than old Leo. More fun."

"Overdose on Patterson, and suddenly you can't recognize the quality and classic taste of other . . . *books*. Then you can be ruined for life."

He gave her a heavy-lidded sidelong glance. "Speak for yourself. Maybe I'm looking for a balance. A little of this, a little of that. A book that's interesting, but not soul sucking."

She crinkled her nose. "Like Shakespeare?"

He almost swerved off the road. "I'd rather get a root canal with no Novocain."

She gave a delicate snort. "Dramatic, much? Guess you're not a romantic."

"Sorry, princess, but Shakespeare was a pansy and prolific at bullshit. I like a writer who's more direct."

"Got it. You're looking for Stephen King."

Her words were filled with pure satisfaction, like she'd figured out all his secrets. He opened his mouth to contradict her, then closed it with a snap. Holy. Shit. She'd nailed it. He hated admitting it, but even Cal knew a fair win needed to be acknowledged.

"How the hell did you know that?"

Morgan crossed her arms in front of her chest, her face

smug. The motion pulled her jacket tight across her chest, outlining those full, plump breasts that had been on his mind way too much lately. He'd woken up last night wondering what color her nipples were. Dark peach? Pale pink? Or ruby red like a ripe strawberry? After that thought, it took him a long time to get back to sleep, and only after he'd taken care of business.

With her name on his lips as he came.

As if she sensed the subtle change in his thoughts, the sexual tension in the car suddenly crackled like a bowl of Rice Krispies. He heard a tiny pull of her breath, and just like that, he craved to pull the car over and slam his mouth over hers to swallow the sound whole.

Instead, he gripped the wheel tighter and focused his attention on the road.

Finally she answered. "King offers the perfect combination. He's direct, incorporates real-life situations tangled with enough interesting fiction to keep the reader arrested. He delves into the human soul and isn't afraid to go deep. He's entertaining and avoids being called a literary writer or a hack. He's everything you want in a . . . *book.*"

King was his favorite writer. And he'd never really thought about women relating to books, but suddenly all the pieces came together. Yeah, she was right. If he found a woman as good as a book from King, it would be all over for him. But of course, Morgan Raines didn't read King and . . . wait. How would she know all that if she never read him?

"You read King?"

She rolled her eyes. "Everyone does."

"But you're not looking for King in your own book, right? You're more of a Jane Austen babe."

"Of course."

He relaxed. Yeah, he was right about her. She might show breaks in her facade, but he still bet late at night, with her proper heels and white suit on, her pleasure reads contained stuffy, old-fashioned, and very proper characters who'd put him to sleep if he ever deigned to pick them up. "Just as I thought. So your perfect book would contain structural rules regarding relationships, neatness, and as few twists and turns as possible. Right?"

"Correct."

Now he was the one who felt smug. He knew her just as well. "What book are you reading at the moment?"

She jumped a bit and averted her gaze. Pulled at the hem of her white skirt. "It's a series of books called the Inn BoonsBoro. They focus on certain stories linked to a historic inn located in Boonsboro, Maryland. Quite interesting."

"Sounds it." Not. Sounded more like *B* for *boring*, but at least he had his hormones under control again. Nonfiction books other than those about construction were the worst. Dry, dry, dry. At least they confirmed what *books* they were both looking for. Of course, they were polar opposites. "We're here."

He pulled the truck off the road and down the isolated winding path up the hill that led to the prime piece of real estate overlooking the harbor. He cut the engine and stared at the sprawling acres in front of him.

The Rosenthals had picked well. Both solitary like a king overlooking from his throne and close enough to the bustle of the marina, where expensive, artsy shops, seafood restaurants, and cafés tempted pedestrians to lose their money and their time. Surrounded by rolling hills and sparkling water, and nestled snug in the center of town, where retired Wall Street bankers, celebrities, and old money mingled. Harrington was pure aristocrat, as sought-after as upcoming Chelsea in Manhattan, as pricey as Westchester County in New York, and as beautiful as the Hudson Valley.

But even more exclusive, if possible.

The land was shrinking, and opportunities were scarce. Having a zip code in Harrington meant something, and Caleb knew that was another reason for this pick. A part of him withered at throwing his blood, sweat, and tears into a property that wouldn't be loved on a permanent basis. But as his father used to say over and over, business was business and green was green. Money ruled, not emotions. In work, play, love, and family.

His mother had thought differently and fought to raise them with other values. She lost when she left. His father's victory was a total eradication of anything they'd had with their mother.

Pushing the thought aside, he concentrated on the job at hand. He grabbed the paint spray can, the initial plans, and a pen. "Let's go."

Initial markers had already been set, but Caleb wanted to inspect every inch before his team came in and broke ground. His brothers excelled at renovation, customization, and property. But he loved the process of building, one beam at a time, watching something beautiful come from nothing. It soothed his soul and quieted his mind. The smell of sawdust, the bang of a hammer, the whine of saw against wood. It was worth everything. Another reason he went from project to project without rest, without relaxing vacations or

EVERYWHERE AND EVERY WAY   91

torrid love affairs that eventually broke into pieces. This, out of everything in the world, was solid.

This lasted forever. Or as long as forever could get.

"They chose well," he murmured, his gaze sweeping the horizon. Birds screeched overhead, and the wind blew hot and heavy against his face. The spread of vivid green seemed to stretch endlessly, burning his eyes.

"I picked it out," she said quietly. "They wanted to be in the center of town next to the water, but I finally convinced them to build here."

He raised a brow. Yes, the town center had the highest, most exclusive properties, but Caleb agreed with Morgan. This had more potential and a quieter dignity you couldn't get from bordering the water. She had vision, too.

Caleb got down to business. They went over the markings, confirming where the deck and hot tub would be placed to guarantee both privacy and stellar views. Walking around the sketch lines, they talked porches and garage and isolated the garden areas where his landscapers would sweep in and make everything look like Martha Stewart lived here.

He caught the soft smile curving her lips and the dreamy look in her eyes as she gazed at the empty land, seeing something no one else could. "How'd you get into this business?" he asked abruptly. "It's kind of an odd job to get interested in."

She tilted her head as if considering. Her white-blond hair brushed her neck and cheek. His fingers itched to briefly reach out and confirm her skin was as soft as it looked. "It is, right? My mother is actually an interior designer, one of the best in Charleston. I grew up learning the right way to set up a room for both aesthetic and spatial purposes. I got in trouble when I was seven years old for trying to redecorate the classroom during my lunch hour. I couldn't concentrate until the bulletin board was perpendicular to the reading charts and we changed the wall colors to purple."

He quirked a brow. "OCD or control freak?"

She gave a long-suffering sigh. "Probably a combination. And too much knowledge of feng shui."

He laughed. "Okay, so you have this need to beautify the world. It's still different from building houses."

Her face lit up. "I think I'm stealing that tagline. Beautifying the world one house at a time. Marketing genius."

"You don't have to pay me royalties."

"Good. I never intended to. I became fascinated not only by structuring the inside but how the frame and design of a house fits with the type of person living in it. It's hard to explain, but I played these games as a kid to try to fit people with their perfect home. Instead of sketching out Barbie dolls or fashion outfits, I sketched mansions or quirky cottages. For graduation, I gave each of my friends a specialized design of the home I thought they'd love, along with furniture, color design, and room setup."

Fascinated, he studied her face. "You began your own business at eighteen years old. Pretty impressive."

She shrugged. "Fitting someone with their dream house is a rush for me. I began studying construction and design, but I never wanted to be the actual architect. I tried to set up a clientele list at home, but my mother had full reign and didn't approve of me trying to change things up. She'd locked up Charleston tight and had firm ideas of how she wanted the business to run. She wanted me to join as her assistant. She's a bit overprotective."

Caleb thought of his father and the way he had run Pierce Brothers with an iron fist. Caleb also remembered the many go-arounds and times he wanted to quit to pave his own way. He loved what he did but wondered many times if his brothers had taken the smart road. They got to carve out their own lives, even though the way it happened was painful. "Yeah, I can relate."

Their gazes locked, and a shimmer of understanding passed between them. Along with a deeper spark of something . . . more. "I bet. I decided to embark on a new type of business that HGTV inspired. I tried to find clients who were stressed about building or renovating their houses, and then be their consultant. We pick out what they want in a house, and I do the work to make their vision come true."

Caleb gave an agonized moan. "Those brothers again? I can't seem to get away from them."

She laughed. "I love *Property Brothers*! I binge-watched all of the shows, then started taking some local classes and studying up on construction and recognizing specialized materials for high-level jobs. I moved to New York to see if I could start something away from my mother's strict Southern influence. I got lucky when Jenna Forrester—you know the television actress that does all the sitcoms?"

"Yeah."

"She wanted to build a house in Westchester, since she hated traveling back and forth from California. We met, sketched out ideas, I looked at various properties, and she bought it. I was in charge of the entire project from start to finish, and I loved every moment. She moved in, and they wrote this big article in *Entertainment Weekly* and did a photo shoot in *House & Celebrity* magazine. Then *boom*—I exploded. I had no idea my career would take off like it did, or that I'd be the hot new commodity celebrities suddenly wanted. I ran with it and focused on famous clients who had the money and means to hire me, and I never looked back."

"So, you travel a lot."

She nodded. "Yes. My home base is wherever my client sends me."

"You have no need to settle down?"

"No. My career is at its peak, and I have no intention of sacrificing my opportunity at success."

He paused. Considered. "You're very ambitious."

She stiffened, and he got the feeling he'd misspoken. Her voice snapped back to the cool, formal tone he was used to. "Yes. And so are you. I happen to like my life the way it is, and I have no intention of changing it."

"Ouch. Didn't mean it as an insult. Just an observation."

Her shoulders relaxed slightly, but Caleb knew there was more to her reaction than he realized. There was a pain there, a bruise in her soul she didn't want to poke at. A vulnerability that called to him. He tamped down on the impulse to push a bit more, reminding himself there was no need to know the secrets of his temporary business partner. In six months, they'd never see each other again. Better to set up the rules now.

As if she echoed his thoughts, she smoothed down her

cream pants and pulled herself to full height, though it wasn't much. "Sorry. I have a lot on my mind. I'll be at the ground breaking and available anytime on my cell if you need anything."

He hesitated, wanting to say more, but ended up just nodding and driving her back to the office. As she climbed into her sleek white convertible, he noticed the back of her pants was streaked with some kind of black grease. Probably sat on something when she was in his truck. The flaw in her polished, perfect image gave him pause for a second. He wondered why he had the urge to dig deeper and mess around in the muck instead of accept what she wanted to show the world.

Then refused to think about it again.

chapter six

"You need to widen that archway. I ordered a stained-glass window, so the dimensions changed."

Cal turned. The look he shot her practically screamed male frustration. Perched up on the ladder, drill at his side, those brows snapped down in a scowl. Too bad he looked smoking hot even when pissed off. Cutoff denim jeans and a black tank top showed off miles of tanned muscles and left little to the imagination. His hair was mussed. Sweat dampened his shirt. Dirt smudged his arms. His tool belt hung low on his hips. Heaven help her, she hated when he was on the ladder. It was much too distracting. The man had some serious muscles and the greatest ass in male history.

"Why the hell would you put a stained-glass window in the kitchen? I already approved these measurements. If you change something, you have to let me know."

"I did. I had to move fast on my order, since it's being shipped direct from Italy. I approved it with Tristan."

The scowl deepened. "I don't have time to check on every damn detail you change. The flood last week put us back a few days. Next time you find a pretty trinket that changes dimensions, you may wanna run it past me."

She treated him to a matching scowl and blew out a breath. Since she knelt in a pile of sawdust, a dusty cloud rose up to block her view. "Next time you start cutting into the frame, you may want to check with your business partners to confirm the status. Maybe a conference call or meeting now and then could be helpful, so when I buy a new *trinket*, you stay on deadline."

A snicker drifted in the air. Jason gave her a huge grin, awarding her the point in this current round. Heaven knew, they'd both gotten in a few solid jabs these past weeks, but the trophy was still up for grabs. The men seemed to get off on their encounters, picking sides to win and even having a betting pool for the big ones.

As usual, Cal didn't go down easy. "We'll keep our deadline fine as long as you don't keep changing your mind. You signed off on those measurements."

She raised her chin up. Her voice dripped icicles. "And my change was approved by Tristan. And vetted through Brady to make sure it wouldn't affect the weight-bearing beam."

Tension tightened around them. Unfortunately, it also swirled with a strange sensual undertone she was still fighting off. "Anything else I don't know about, princess? Wanna add a pretty skylight in here? French doors? A private terrace?"

She cocked her head and studied him. "Are we cranky today, Charming?" she asked pleasantly. "Tell you what. Let's just stick with the stained-glass window, and if there's anything extra I want to throw in, I'll be sure to tell Tristan or Dalton."

A smothered laugh rang out.

She had to give him credit. Cal could take a jab as well as give one. He muttered something under his breath but backed off. "I need the measurements."

"Which I happen to have right here." She gave a sunny smile as if being hot, dirty, and sore was a daily occurrence. Her back protested when she unfurled herself from the awkward position and walked over. Grabbing her phone, she recited the numbers while Cal marked it off with the tape. He stretched out, and the soft denim stretched and clung to his ass like a gift from the gods.

Darn the man.

Morgan swore to hang on to her irritation and not let some hot male body ruin her right to be right. She'd discovered Cal did not share well with others. Though he was the head of the project, he was consistently yanking specific jobs from his brothers and refusing to check in. There was definitely an underlying tension in the family, and she gathered that the main problem was Cal's inability to step aside and let them do their job.

They were deep into framing, and she'd decided to take a day to work with the men. In her experience, respect was earned, and nothing worked faster than seeing a woman building beside the crew. Morgan was used to the stunned silence she usually received when first showing up, and today was no different.

She owned a custom-made pink hard hat with matching work boots. Her personal hammer was built for a smaller hand and was also pink. As much as she preferred white, pink showed less of the dirt kicked up on a job site.

When she marched past the crew and announced her intention to work the site, their mouths fell open like a school of guppies'. A few hours later, they shut up. She knew her stuff, never complained, and worked harder than they did.

The pounding strains of some heavy metal band blared over the speakers. Not again. If she had to hear one more screaming guitar solo, she'd lose it. Marching over to her Michael Kors backpack, she fished around and grabbed a CD. "Sorry, boys," she called out. "My turn."

A combined groan rose in the air. "I can't work to girly music!" Sam yelled. The foreman stopped hammering to give her a beseeching look. "Don't torture us, Morgan."

She gave an evil laugh and hit PLAY. "Y'all are seriously undereducated in music. Besides, I'm cramped up like a pretzel doing the trim, and I let you do the fun part. You owe me."

Cal climbed down the ladder and grabbed his water. A begrudging look of respect crossed the harsh lines of his face. "She's right. She gets her turn."

Taylor Swift belted out the strains of "Shake It Off," and Morgan ignored the crew's taunting remarks. "Keep it up. By the end, you'll be agreeing she has talent and you like her music. Trust me. You're not the first site I've converted to my way of thinking."

"Would be better if the song was called 'Take It Off'!" Mike yelled.

Everyone laughed.

"I gotta get something from the truck," Cal said. "Need anything?"

"A bucket of ice water. It's frickin' one hundred degrees today," Jason grumbled. "Why can't we build houses in Alaska?"

"Oh, yeah, ice huts. Fun," Mike quipped.

Cal rolled his eyes and replaced the tape in his tool belt. Took another slug of water. Then peeled off his shirt.

Morgan stared.

His gaze flicked to hers. "You need anything?" he asked.

She tried to answer. She really did. But nothing came out of her mouth—not even a squeak. Her vision was blurred by the perfect male specimen before her that was every female fantasy of a construction worker.

He was . . . perfect. Defined pecs and tight biceps. Endless toasty-brown skin gleaming with sweat. A perfect swirl of lighter hair dusting his chest and traveling down washboard abs. He had an actual eight-pack. Not six. Eight.

"Morgan?" he asked.

Her belly dropped to her toes. Her tongue came out to wet her very dry lips. Between her thighs, an arousal pounded in demand for the slide of his fingers over her wet core and the feel of those delicious lips over hers.

Suddenly those eyes lit to hot charcoal, as if he'd just realized why she'd gone voiceless. Sexual energy swarmed between them. Her nipples tingled. Morgan wondered what she'd do if they were alone and he stalked over to her. Wondered if she'd put up even a little fight if he hauled her up and drove his tongue into her mouth. Wondered if he'd be primitive enough to take her over the worktable without finesse or apology, just raw, hungry need.

Lord have mercy.

She dragged in a breath. "No," she finally croaked out. "I'm good."

The man was a Neanderthal. With a smug grin, he hooked his thumbs in his belt loops and cocked a hip. The motion emphasized his lean waist and powerful thighs. "Sure? You look like you . . . want something."

Oh, she really didn't like him. Morgan gathered her composure, desperately fighting a blush. Her gaze deliberately pulled away from his sweaty, hard body. "No, thank you. Nothing appeals to me at the moment."

The crew kept working, not realizing the sexual undertone of the ridiculous conversation. He tipped back his head with pure delight and grinned. "Could've fooled me."

Morgan wanted to give him a good retort, but her brain muscles had died with the surge of estrogen, so she kept quiet. His chuckle as he walked away burned through her. She donned her work gloves, grabbed her drill, and got to work.

Time passed. The sounds of hammers, drills, and country-turned-pop music filled the air. The sawdust pile grew, dirtying her clothes and burying under her fingernails. Her arms burned. Her skin turned sticky from the heat.

She loved every second.

The guys broke for lunch but she was too Zen and decided to keep working. Morgan fell into the meditative space of old-fashioned hard work. As with Cal, this was her favorite part. She adored the steps of decorating and furnishing because it called to her creative energy, but the physical work of building a house was an adrenaline rush. Installing the guts and mechanics, her fingers gripped a hammer, everything fell away, and Morgan was left with a clean purity in her soul.

The clatter of wood startled her out of her happy place. She blinked and looked up.

"I got it."

Dalton stood over her with a huge grin on his face. A beam of cedar lay before her, the beautiful reddish tinge flirting within the grains to wow an onlooker. Morgan took off her gloves and picked it up, stroking the smooth finish. "Where?" she demanded.

He puffed up like a well-tipped stripper from *Magic Mike*. "Private contacts. I'm not telling you, because I'm afraid you'll filch him from me when you're done with Pierce Brothers."

"I'm impressed. I most certainly would." Her mind swept over her vision for the massive, open kitchen. "But I told you we were going with pine. It'll go better with the visual. I already ordered it."

"You're gonna cancel the order, 'cause this is better."

She squinted at him. He didn't wait for her to rise to challenge him. Dalton dropped to the floor beside her and cradled the precious beam in his hand. His tawny hair was tied back, and his blue eyes looked a bit dreamy. Their knees touched as they faced each other on the sawdust floor.

"Convince me. I'd have to cancel the order with the West Coast and piss a lot of people off. The Rosenthals like a more organic look, and pine fits the bill. Gives the impression of a kitchen where you cook and gather."

"Will they cook?"

"No."

Dalton grinned. "Good, we're going with cedar. It's more natural, and I'll stain it twice for a deeper finish and more character. I'll build the cabinetry around the horseshoe countertops and pair it with a hand-carved bench to match."

She visualized the possibility. Hmm. "I could still do that with pine."

"It won't look as good." His voice held a stubborn tone. "This is a huge open space, with the kitchen and background as the main focus. Tristan said you picked out the Amalfi gold marble, but you wanted the burlesque gold instead."

Morgan sighed. They both grasped the cedar wood, not wanting to relinquish it. "I did, but it's too light."

"Exactly. Let me do the cedar, and the burlesque will blend perfectly. The red tints will pull from the cedar. I can also do matching stools with the bench. I'm telling you, Morgan, this is the way to go. But I have to pull the trigger on this right away. My contact gave me a few hours before he's pulling the order on me—there's a lineup."

God, the cedar was more rare. Pricey, but so very worth it, especially if she got to switch out the marble. "I don't know."

His voice was a whisper of sound, urgent and convincing. "Do it. I swear it will work better. I feel it in my bones."

A smile curved her lips. She loved working with people with an obvious passion for their craft. Their fingers interweaved together over the wood, two artists admiring a perfect tool. It was risky. She didn't have time to call the Rosenthals, so she'd need to go with her gut. Morgan took the leap.

"I'll do it."

"You won't regret it. I'll make it so good for you."

They smiled at each other, still holding the wood, locked in an artistic embrace.

"What the hell is going on here?"

They looked up. Cal stood over them, face tight with anger, a muscle ticking in his jaw as he stared down at their clasped hands. "What do you mean?" she asked.

"Get your hands off her."

Her mouth dropped open. Dalton shook his head and stood up. "Dude, you've gone off the deep end. Chill."

"This is a professional workplace, not a pickup joint." Cal looked as if he was reining himself in from grabbing Dalton's neck. "I don't need you hitting on her, man. We have a job to do here. Not flirting on long lunch breaks."

"Oh, hell no, you did not just say that to me." Morgan jumped to her feet and jabbed a finger in the air. She bristled with fury. "For your information, we were talking about wood. Specifically pine versus cedar for the kitchen cabinetry, not that it's your business."

"Things looked quite cozy to be talking about wood." Cal glowered at Dalton, but his younger brother seemed to take it in stride. What had happened between the two of them?

Dalton shrugged like he couldn't care less. "What can I say? We both like wood."

Morgan would've laughed if she wasn't so pissed. She'd never heard so many wood references in her life. "As Dalton said, this is a discussion between us. We're canceling the pine and going with cedar."

"If you're thinking of changing materials, I need to know about it. Sydney already authorized the invoices for the pine cabinets because that's what we discussed."

Dalton shook his head in disgust. "There you go again. I'm in charge of materials, and Tristan does the invoicing, Cal. We decided I'd spearhead all the cabinetry and custom furnishings. If Morgan and I agree to switch things up, it has nothing to do with you."

"This is my business. Everything has to do with me."

"Just like always. You want to control each damn thing, and it doesn't work."

"You think I don't have a good reason? We got fired from the last job because of your 'creative vision.' We can't afford artistic temperament on this job."

Morgan sighed. "Besides being a Neanderthal, you're stubborn and controlling. Each home has artistic qualities or it wouldn't be a home. How many jobs have you handled with no changes, Cal?"

His silence spoke volumes.

"Now, I'd say it's time to back off and let Dalton handle it. We're going with the cedar. I'll call the West Coast and take care of my supplier so he doesn't blacklist me. I want sketches on the new mock-up by tomorrow, Dalton, and please tell Sydney about the change."

"Got it."

"As for you." She glared at Cal, marched over, and stood on tiptoes in her pink work boots. The delicious scent of male sweat and musk rose to her nostrils. He gave off buckets of pheromones that called to her so intensely, she felt halfway drunk. Ignoring his eight-pack abs and gleaming tan muscles, Morgan focused on her temper. "I'd advise you get off your brother's case and let him do his job. You can't do it all, no matter how bad you want to. Believe me, I've dealt with this before and we need all people on this team. And next time you accuse me of flirting and taking long lunches on the job, I promise, you will sorely regret it."

His eyes widened slightly, but she gave him no time to respond.

She turned on her very smart, very pink heel and marched off the site.

Goodness gracious, the man was hot.

He'd screwed up.

Cal brooded and drank his beer. After a long, sweaty day, the guys had convinced Morgan to join them for a drink after work, which had turned into buffalo wings, Guinness, and a sharing of war stories. He had to give her credit. Though she'd passed on the beer and drank a sparkling seltzer, she held her own with their banter and upped the ante with disaster tales from the building site. How on earth did this slight Southern woman charm this crew of rowdy, crude blue-collar men?

Maybe it was her ability to work as hard as each of them. Sure, she was the boss, and she liked to walk around in those cute white Bermuda shorts with the bows on the side, and those ridiculous pink work boots. When the guys had gotten over their shock, they teased her mercilessly, but she just took it in stride and refused to bat an eyelash. And proved once again she could do anything they could do. Last week, in the flood, she'd shown up in thigh-high waterproof boots and with a white umbrella, then walked around the muddy site like she was at a tea party.

Morgan Raines carried around a clipboard 24/7 and quizzed him on progress at the end of every day. But she visited the site regularly and spent hours on the phone with endless distributors, trying to line up and pick tile, marble, appliances, flooring, and a dozen other materials that all went into the final product of a livable house. Somehow, as prissy and opinionated and controlling as she was, she'd become an integral part of the crew and today had solidified their complete loyalty, a gift they did not give easily.

It drove him nuts.

She drove him nuts. He was still irritated at her power play that had robbed him of his first Green job, and it still stuck in his throat that he was building a house that wouldn't be truly appreciated. But little by little, day by day, she gained more of his respect.

As if she'd heard his thoughts, she shot him a cool look and stood. "Time for me to go, gentlemen. See y'all tomorrow."

She left without a nod toward him, and he followed an impulse. Throwing a few bills on the table, he said good-bye and caught up with her. Slowing his stride to match hers, he walked beside her for a while, waiting for her to acknowledge him.

She didn't.

The fact made him laugh out loud and gained him a withering look. "What's so funny? And why are you stalking me?"

"Just being a gentleman and walking you to the car."

Her snort was as Southern as she was. Polite, but cutting. Also quite charming. "What's your real motivation, Charming? Wanna accuse me of flirting with the crew now?"

Cal winced. He'd gone a little mad when he caught her

with Dalton. He didn't want to dig far to find out why, but the sight of their hands wrapped together and the intimate way they bowed their heads close had set him off. A tiny voice inside sprang to life, growled ferociously, and bellowed out one word.

MINE.

Ridiculous, of course. He knew it was wrapped up in the bruises of his past. When he'd walked in to find Dalton kissing his fiancée, her body arched under his like a present she begged him to unwrap, something died within him. Watching Dalton try to put the moves on Morgan just brought up his trigger point. It was the only reasonable explanation, but he still owed her an apology.

"I was out of line."

"You think?"

She quickened her pace, but he stayed glued to her side. "I know. Dalton and I have some history, and he set me off. I wasn't trying to disrespect you."

Morgan suddenly stopped and looked up at him. The curtain of silvery blond hair swung past the gentle curve of her cheek. The streetlight bathed her in a glow that made her seem almost ethereal, with those big baby blues and the aristocratic slope of her nose and those lush, bubble-gum lips. "Apology accepted."

"That's it?"

She gave a delicate shrug. "I can accept a meaningful apology when you offer. Besides, I'm used to stress setting people off at the site. But I still think you need to give your brother a break. You can't do it all, Cal."

She was right, but he remained silent. He came off

as a dickhead sometimes, but it was so easy to just do it himself so he knew things would be right. Maybe he was more like his father than he realized. He shuddered at the thought.

They walked past the brightly lit harbor, watching the boats bob and the sprinkle of moonlight over the glossy surface. Cafés and seafood restaurants stayed open late in the summer months, and residents and tourists poured out of their houses to walk around the marina and enjoy an ice-cream cone or a late-night cocktail.

"It's beautiful here," Morgan said. "There's something elementally sophisticated yet charming about Harrington. I'm also addicted to the lobster."

Cal grinned. "Yeah, I like living close to the water. My father took us boating regularly when we were young. Winters are a little rough, but it's also nice when the tourists go home and everyone's barricaded in their homes. Many of the bars and shops close down. The firehouse becomes a big draw for poker and pasta nights. And it's not far into Manhattan if you get really desperate for stimulation."

"I can imagine."

"The Rosenthals looking to hole up for the whole year here? They'll have a nice house to hunker down with."

Morgan's face said it all. His heart gave a little pang at the waste of building a home for a couple who didn't want to live there. "I'm sure they'll make use of it when they can," she said carefully. "The filming will be extensive, so they'll have a level of comfort. I can see them hosting big parties and bringing some Hollywood glamour to the town."

"Glamour or drama?"

She wrinkled her nose. "Probably both. My car is over there."

He looked to the right, where her convertible was parked in the lot. Then to the left. The second impulse of the evening overtook him and he made the offer. "Wanna see something no one knows about? Follow me."

Her brow arched. "Is it good?"

"Real good."

She hesitated, but her curiosity saved him. She followed his lead as he walked down the main dock and cut through the edge of woods. "Watch your step." The path was overgrown now, but he followed it by memory, letting his instincts guide him as they grew farther away from the main crowd. Darkness closed in on them, and the moonlight guided his way.

"This has creepy written all over it," she piped up. He held back a branch so she could step around a wild bush. "Why am I disturbed you have something to show me back here where no one can hear you scream?"

He laughed but pushed on. "A little further. Trust me."

"Said every serial killer on the planet."

"Here." Satisfaction rushed through him. It was exactly as he remembered, even though it had been years since he hiked the trail. The harbor spilled into a separate private watering hole, an oasis broken from crowds or boats, with only the thick, shady trees to witness a person's secrets. "What do you think?"

"It's beautiful." She smiled, her gaze sweeping over the short dock leading into the water. "Reminds me of a few places down South. There was an isolated marsh area down by the Ashley River. My girlfriends and I used to sneak out after dinner and meet there when it got dark."

Cal leaned against a moss-covered oak and crossed his ankles. A wistful expression flickered over Morgan's face, as if she were reliving the memories of her childhood. "Yeah, my brothers and I would hang here when we wanted some alone time," he continued. "Sometimes we'd just lie on our backs and watch the stars after a swim. Sometimes we'd sneak in liquor and try to get girls to make out with us."

Her laugh was infectious. "I bet you did," she drawled. "Bet you did lots of bad things."

"Bet you didn't."

She stiffened. Her annoyed gaze snapped to his. "Excuse me? You don't know what I did or didn't do."

"Again, I have a feeling it was a lot of didn't." He threw up his hands in defense. "Don't mean to insult you, princess. It's just obvious you didn't cut loose a lot."

She gave a sexy growl. "Obvious how?"

Cal raked a gaze over her figure. Took in her cute little lace T-shirt, white shorts, and Keds-like sneakers. "Look at you. You drink seltzer. Your sneakers are so white, it's obvious you haven't walked anywhere interesting. You wear pearls and diamonds on a daily basis and high heels to relax. You're a prim, proper, polite Southern woman."

She straightened up to all of five foot three inches and stuck her aristocratic nose in the air. "You don't get to judge me. I've done plenty of bad things growing up and had a good time doing them."

"Like what?" he challenged.

"Excuse me?"

His lip twitched at her endless politeness. "Tell me one bad thing you've ever done."

Morgan blew out a breath and turned. "I have nothing to prove to you. I'm going home."

"One thing. Name me one thing, and I won't say another word."

She stopped and shot him an aggravated glare. "This is ridiculous."

"See, you can't do it."

"Fine. When I was seventeen years old, I snuck out of my bedroom to meet a boy I liked. He was having a party, and my parents said I couldn't go because there was no parental supervision, but I went anyway. Oh, and I got drunk."

She seemed so excited by her confession, Cal couldn't laugh. "Did you hook up?"

"No. I found him kissing slutty Megan Davis. I still hate her."

"What'd you drink?"

"Wine coolers."

He gave a disgusted humph. "You lose points for that, princess. Lame."

"You're not my judge and jury, Charming. Those things pack a punch."

He barked out a laugh. Damn, he loved her spitfire way under all those neutrals. The quiet closed around them. The mugginess of the night pressed down in a hot, invisible presence. Suddenly he wanted more. Wanted to push and see what else was beyond the surface. "Ever go skinny-dipping in that river of yours?" he asked lazily.

"No."

"A shame, really. Can't say you really did anything crazy until you can claim a good skinny-dip."

Morgan bristled. "There was never a good opportunity."

"There is now."

She stared at him. Suspicion glinted in her steely blue eyes. "You want to go skinny-dipping now?"

"Yep. Up for it?"

"No, thank you."

"Why? Can't swim?"

She looked at him like he was a bug she ached to crush. Damn, this was fun. "I can swim. I just don't enjoy making a public spectacle of myself. Call it a hang-up of mine."

He pushed himself away from the tree and stretched. She tried hard, but he felt her gaze touch on his chest and drop a tad lower. She hated being attracted to him, but it was there, a constant buzz between them like an annoying gnat. "No one can find us out here," he said. "You're perfectly safe. And it's hot as hell. A night swim will cool us off." He toed off his shoes, enjoying the crisp feel of the grass under his feet.

"Well, bless your heart. Why on earth would I want to skinny-dip with you?"

"Why not?" Cal tugged off his T-shirt and threw it on the ground. "I dare you."

She sputtered like a cat getting a bucket of water dumped on it. "Dare me? Do you think I'm five years old? A juvenile dare isn't going to get me out of my clothes, so I— What are you doing?"

He flicked open the button on his shorts and lowered the zipper. "Getting naked. I'm skinny-dipping."

She gulped for air. Even in the dark, he caught the red flush to her cheeks. "This is outrageous. I'm leaving."

He dropped his shorts. Kicked them away from his ankles. And stood before her in his black briefs. His massive erection told the truth of how their banter affected him. A little gasp broke from her lips as she caught sight of him, but instead of being embarrassed, her reaction only made him grow harder. Cal took a few steps forward, studying her still figure with challenge.

"Just as I thought. You're afraid of letting go and having some fun. When was the last time you did something crazy, just for the hell of it? Live a little, princess."

Cal figured he'd dive in for a swim and she'd sulk on the sidelines. Maybe even try to find her way home with her stubborn nature. He didn't expect the sudden burst of outrage from her petite figure.

"You think you're the wild bad boy of the town, Caleb Pierce?" She went on her tiptoes and got right in his face. "Think you're gonna shock my poor little Southern heart by standing here, half-naked, with an erection? Think I won't take your dare, Charming?" Her slow smile glittered and stopped his heart. "Think again."

The earth shook a bit beneath his feet, but it was no earthquake. No, this was all breathless anticipation and pure lust as Morgan Raines tossed her silvery hair like a wild filly and accepted his challenge.

She bent down and untied her shoelaces, neatly stacking her sneakers beside her. With graceful motions, her fingers slid in a no-nonsense way and unbuttoned her little white blouse. She shrugged the fabric off and Cal was slammed with a vision of full, ripe breasts barely constrained in a delicate lace camisole. As his dick grew so hard, it was pure discomfort, his vision hazed when she casually unbuttoned her white linen capri pants and wriggled them over her full hips.

Holy mother of God.

She was gorgeous.

His gaze tried to take in all that pure white flesh and the way the cream camisole skimmed over her body as if it were a wrapped treat, every lush curve emphasized. His fingers itched to reach out and touch her. His mouth ached to press against her pink lips. His body craved to know hers like a song he wanted to learn from beginning to end and never stop singing.

But she gave him no chance. With a wink, she pivoted on her bare heel and ran straight for the water. Then launched herself through the air in a perfect jump, sinking below the surface.

Holy shit. The woman had just taken off her clothes in front of him and dove into the water. His Southern magnolia was really a hothouse rose, and he loved every fucking moment.

Cal took off and did a cannonball, spraying water everywhere. Her laughter was witchlike, echoing in the wind like a siren call. With economical strokes, she swam around him, finally flipping onto her back to float, her silvery hair spread around her, palms open to the sky like a sacrifice to the moon gods. He watched her in the beautiful silence that spilled over the lake, and something odd shifted within.

"Cal?"

Did she feel it, too? Something shifting? "Yeah?"

"I think I want to add another level for the film room."

He blinked. "Huh?"

She never changed her posture, just floated past him like a goddess. "I know Brady said a smaller balcony is fine, but the Rosenthals will probably screen their movie and will want more room. If we do a double-tier balcony, it will look better."

Cal tried desperately to get his mind on business. "Brady is right: it will throw off the aesthetics. What about two smaller side balconies, almost like luxury boxes? They may like that."

"Yes. I could do it in red velvet like the old theaters. Set up an old-fashioned popcorn maker and candy machine. We can make it work?"

"Yeah, I'll make it work." She threw him off balance. Was he the only one with a raging desire to steal a kiss while they skinny-dipped in the moonlight? "You surprised me."

Morgan didn't move, just bobbed gently in the water. "So did you."

"How?"

"You managed a decent cannonball."

He laughed. She was so different from any woman he'd ever met, consistently throwing him off guard. "I like a woman who takes a dare."

"Bet you do. Were you able to trick your brothers into doing ridiculous things by double-daring them?"

"The triple dog dare usually did its trick. But Dalton was always the one to fall for it. Tristan got me back by pretending to be above my crap, then he'd wait for his time and cut me off at the knees. He's the more ruthless one."

"And Dalton is the creative genius?"

"Yep, takes after his grandfather. Called him the Wood Whisperer."

"And you? What's your title in this crew?"

He swam and watched her and thought. Families were built on expectations and profiling because it was easier. Even the order of birth told a lot about a person. Sure, he was the oldest and the one to shoulder the most responsibility. He was the leader.

Or was he? Was it just easier to do what he wanted without question or apology? Had he ever truly wanted to compromise and change Pierce Brothers into what his brothers wanted? Or deep inside, did he agree with his father and just didn't want to admit it?

"The grumpy one."

Her giggle charmed him. Cal swam closer. Her nipples were hard and strained against the damp lace in an effort to escape. The wet camisole outlined every flow and curve of her body, making him burn. He tried to concentrate on their conversation. "What about you? If you had to place a tag on yourself, what would it be?"

It was a while before she answered. Her voice was a whisper of sound. "A fighter."

Cal didn't have time for questions. She flipped over and swam to the edge, easily hitting the deck with both feet and walking back to her neat pile of clothes. He watched her get dressed from a distance and finally joined her on land. He quickly donned his clothes and they stood facing each other.

"Thanks for the swim," she said politely. "We'd better get back." She tucked her wet hair behind her ears. Her makeup was smudged. The scent of lemon and fresh daisies rose to his nostrils. Her skin looked dewy and soft. A roaring began in his head and moved lower, wiping out his rational thoughts. He didn't know what was going on. He didn't know why, but if he didn't kiss Morgan Raines tonight, he might regret it for the rest of his life.

"You're welcome. I didn't like you at first."

A smile touched her lips. She tugged at the hem of her shirt. "That's okay. I didn't like you, either." Morgan paused. "I'm still waiting to make up my mind."

He closed the distance between them. Was that his heart beating? Stupid. Of course not. He was a grown man, and he didn't get those feelings anymore. She tilted her head back, and he saw the slight tremble of her lips as she gazed back at him, refusing to look away.

"I like you now."

She cleared her throat. The pulse at the base of her neck and the dilation of her pupils gave her away. She felt it, too. His nostrils flared like a predator's on the hunt, but he moved slow, bending his head so his mouth was inches from hers, so he could feel the warm rush of her breath against him. So she had plenty of time to pull away and cry foul. Still, she rallied.

She spoke his name on a ragged whisper. "What are you doing, Cal?"

"I'm sorry."

She shuddered. His hands clasped her shoulders, and he breathed her in.

"For misjudging me? Calling me a coward? Or not liking me at first?"

He locked his gaze with hers to show her his intention. Paused. "For this."

Cal covered his mouth with hers.

The moment her lips yielded under his, Caleb realized Morgan Raines was more dangerous than he'd ever imagined.

She tasted like all the things he loved in his past—sugar cookies and bourbon-infused chocolate. Freshly squeezed orange juice and key lime pie. Deliciously sweet and tart and tasty. Everything he craved and couldn't get enough of, wrapped up in this one gorgeous female.

The kiss was slow and deep and oh so thorough. Cal kept his hands firmly on her shoulders, not trusting himself to be cool. Who would've thought Morgan Raines would inspire violent lust instead of lukewarm interest? His body shook with the effort to control his instincts. Instead, he teased her, gathering her taste with his tongue and capturing the sexy little moan that spilled from her throat. It was a kiss that introduced, welcomed, lingered. It was the hottest kiss he'd ever shared with a woman, and he didn't know what he was going to do about it.

Their lips slid apart, breaking contact. Her flavor danced on his tongue. They stared at each other, and for a brief moment, both acknowledged the shock of connection. Would she try to analyze the situation? Ask for more? Run away? Slap him? Cal waited, not really sure what he even wanted her to do. The crickets seemed deafening in the shattering silence.

"I think I want to change the molding in the formal dining room. We need more of a wow factor."

WTF?

She reached down and scooped up her purse. "I know we said crown, but there's an artist who creates gorgeous stenciled molding with a bigger base. It's doable. Right?"

Cal fought the strange rise of emotions battling within, then finally surrendered.

A deep laugh rose from his chest and burst out. "Yeah. It's doable."

Morgan smiled. "Good. Let's go."

She led the way out of the woods and back to civilized society, but Cal wondered if they'd crossed an invisible line that would change everything.

chapter seven

"Hi, Mama."

"Hey, baby. How are you?"

Morgan propped herself up against the overstuffed pewter pillows and relaxed. Her laptop was perched on her lap; a glass of white wine rested on the beautifully carved chest beside her. Living in a hotel on a consistent basis may not be every woman's dream, but the ornate surroundings of the penthouse, gourmet room service, spa, fitness room, superb cleaning crew, and twenty-four-hour dedicated concierge to her pleasure was nothing to complain about.

Actually, it was pretty darn sweet.

Her mother's face filled the screen and gave instant comfort. Her blond hair was loose today and framed her face in perfectly straight strands, the tips curling just under. Her features were as familiar as her own, since staring at her mama was like looking in a mirror. Crystal-blue eyes filled with warmth. Sharp chin, high cheekbones, and a nose that bespoke blue blood. Her daddy always said Ashley Raines could be the spokesperson for Olay or any big beauty company, since she never seemed to age and nothing was fake.

An ache to feel her arms around her settled in deep. Morgan could almost smell the sweet scent of lavender rising from her skin.

"I'm good. The project is moving at a decent pace. I've got a virtual meeting with the Rosenthals later this week to go over swatches and paint samples. Pierce Brothers is solid, and I think we'll have no problem making deadline."

"How do you like the town? Harrington, right?" Her mama's Southern drawl was heaven to her ears. She'd forgotten how long she'd been working in the Northeast. Goodness, soon she might even pick up a Yankee accent.

"Yes. I like it. It's built around a harbor, with lots of fresh seafood restaurants and quaint shops. I found a gorgeous watercolor you and Daddy may like. I'll have it shipped."

Her mama's smile lit up the screen. "You spoil me, baby. I wish you could fly home for a weekend. We miss you."

"Miss you, too, but I can't see myself taking any time until we deliver in the fall. I'm working around the clock. I haven't even been able to hit the spa yet."

A frown marred her delicate brow. "Morgan, you can't overwork yourself. Are you eating properly? Sleeping? You know what they say about stress and how it affects the body. Have you found a local doctor yet?"

Morgan sighed. She wished her mama's concerned tone was the reaction of a normal overprotective parent. Instead, memories of the past rushed between them, and her stomach twisted into a knot. No matter how many years went by and how many tests came back negative, her parents would never get over the scare. Neither would Morgan.

Cervical cancer wasn't the standard problem an

eighteen-year-old should have. When her Pap smear had returned positive, Morgan hadn't been worried. She was young and fit and healthy. No one got cancer at her age.

Except the second test proved her wrong.

Young people did get cancer.

Each time they met with the doctor, the prognosis got worse. She met with some of the best experts in the world. Morgan learned terms such as *trachelectomy*, a procedure that would save the uterus so she could possibly still have children. But her cancer wouldn't respond to chemotherapy. Her cancer spread, and there was no choice but the most aggressive one of all.

She underwent a complete hysterectomy before she even hit twenty years old.

The memory of that morning, waking up and realizing she'd never hold her baby in her arms, still haunted her. In some crazy way, she felt like she'd let her parents down. Besides getting sick, she'd never be able to give them grandchildren. Her Southern roots went deep, and the idea of big families was never questioned. Morgan had envisioned at least four children running around her big plantation while she worked side by side with her mama in her design business. She wasn't the type to wonder what her future would be like, because she'd always known.

Until that morning when her life suddenly changed.

Ashley Raines held her while she cried. And then she did what any good Southern mama would do.

She went hard-core.

Morgan wasn't able to wallow in her misery. Her mama had taken her immediately to the pediatric ward to engage with the children who were fighting their own battles. She became friends with Peter Ward, who had a 50 percent chance of living. She met Alice Monroe, who used to have pretty blond hair and a future in modeling. Her smile was bright and her eyes were fierce as she told Morgan she'd be getting a bone marrow transplant soon and she intended to go back to second grade. And Morgan learned something from those children that changed her path forever over those next few weeks as she dealt with her new life.

She learned she was a fighter. She learned she had a new life, but it was a good life. It held hope and love and endless possibilities, and Morgan decided she wouldn't squander a second of it. When she caught sight of a mother cradling her child, her womb still wept. But she had carved out a career she adored and led a glittering, big life that kept her engaged and happy. A different path, yes. But her path.

Her throat tightened. The hysterectomy had done its job, and every test for the past ten years had come back clean. But her mama still worried that the ghost of their past would suddenly come surging in and wreak havoc.

"Yes, I checked in with the local doctor, and they sent her my charts. Everything's good, Mama. Please don't worry."

"Of course I'll worry—it's my job. But I'll change the subject because I know you're capable of handling anything that comes your way. Let's talk about something fun. Have you met any boys?"

The image of kissing Cal slammed into her mind. The firm texture of his lips. The delicious thrust of his tongue. The spicy, masculine flavor that heated her blood and made her knees weak. It was the most erotic kiss of her life, and she'd panicked because she hadn't seen it coming. When he pulled away and looked at her in the moonlight, her instinct was to jump back in his arms, drag him to the ground, and engage in carnal, glorious, raw, dirty sex.

Instead, she'd talked about molding and pretended nothing had happened.

Her mama's laugh tinkled through the speaker. "I do declare, you're blushing, baby. Who is it? Is he cute?"

She sighed and surrendered. "Yes. He's hot and grumpy and talented and a pain in the butt. But he's also off-limits. He's the builder, Mama."

Ashley Raines winced. "Oh, my. That could get a bit sticky."

"I know. We kissed, but it was a onetime thing. He's probably forgotten about it already."

Her mama snickered. "He didn't forget. If you like him, maybe you can make it work."

"No, I can't risk the project for a weak moment of lust. He's professional, so if he pushes, I'll just let him know it's better to avoid anything personal. I've seen firsthand what a mess combining work and pleasure can be. Explosions on job sites, delays, fights." She shuddered at the thought of such messiness. "I need to keep things tight."

"Pity. You could use a delicious affair."

Morgan laughed. "You're bad, Mama. Daddy would freak."

"That's why we don't tell Daddy girl things. He still sees you in pink dresses with baby dolls in your hand."

"I prefer pink hammers now."

"That's my girl. Now, I have to tell you before you find out from someone else. Elias Baker is back in town. He's decided to settle in Charleston."

Morgan waited for the ache of pain to hit, but there was only a mild poke. Good. She'd finally gotten over the jerk. Her ex-fiancé came from old money and had told her he was madly in love with her. When he found out she couldn't carry his children, he told her it didn't matter. She decided to believe him, but a few months before the wedding, he admitted that he couldn't bear a future without his own children. The gossip had fueled the town for a long while, and Morgan once again struggled to find her way past the humiliation. "Married?" she clipped out.

"Yes."

"Three point five children?"

"Three with another on the way."

"Is his wife pretty?"

Her mama cocked her head and considered. "Five out of a ten. She's an outsider and talks in a horrible accent. Already the Woman's Design group decided she wouldn't be a good fit with us. Plus, they bought the old Magnolia mansion, so you know their taste is excruciating."

"Hmm, they're wannabes." The Magnolia mansion had been vacated by a popular reality-star couple who ended up in jail for tax evasion. Their taste ran the gamut of animal prints, Elvis trinkets, and lots of gold. Their home was famous in town for its history, bad taste, and central location. Morgan couldn't imagine stuffy Elias living there, but maybe his wife had convinced him. Or maybe they'd renovate.

"Did he get fat?"

Her mama sighed. "No. But he's almost bald."

Their gazes met and they burst into laughter. "Good enough for me."

"Just remember, baby, he was never good enough for you. Goodness gracious, he probably wouldn't have wanted you to work! Can you imagine being stuck doing nothing but charity benefits and hosting dinners for his boring clients?"

"I love you, Mama."

"Love you, too, baby. Get some sleep. Kiss more boys."

She blew kisses to the screen and clicked off.

Morgan changed into her soft cotton pj's, pulled on socks for her constantly cold feet, and snuggled under the luxurious Egyptian-cotton sheets. Elias had broken her heart. When he rejected her because she couldn't mother his children, it confirmed her worst fears. Men wouldn't want her. For the second time in her life, she struggled with feelings of inadequacy and not being a real woman for losing a part of her body that was essential.

Once again her mama had realized it was not a regular heartbreak but ran so much deeper. On her urging, Morgan found a great therapist and joined a support group where other women struggled with the same issues. And she rebuilt herself for the second time.

Now, at thirty years old, she looked at the world differently. She no longer thought of herself as less and knew the right man would love her for everything she was and nothing she wasn't. Elias had never been meant for her. And Morgan didn't waste time wondering where Mr. Right was. She was too busy living her life.

She picked up her Kindle. Now done with Nora Roberts,

she opened up her new BDSM erotic series and read for the next hour. Finally she clicked off the light and snuggled against the pillow. The clean scent of cotton rose to her nostrils, and an image of a shirtless Caleb Pierce drifted past her vision. Rock-hard muscles and tight abs. Eyes that glinted like charcoal and burned like fire. Strong hands that caressed with a leashed power able to break her. She imagined him as a delicious dom type, stripping her, laying her out on the bed, and fucking her hard. Her body shivered, and her pussy throbbed with need. His kiss told her the type of lover he'd be. Controlling but patient. Thorough but demanding. Raw and dirty yet tender. Her nipples peaked into hard points, and her skin grew hot and itchy with desire.

Morgan slid her hand down her body and under her panties. Already wet and needy, she closed her eyes and let her fingers bring her temporary relief while the fantasy of Caleb Pierce took her away.

And she came with his name on her lips.

chapter eight

"For God's sake, where is everybody?"

Cal tore off his hard hat and scratched his head. Sweat ran down his neck and back in tiny rivulets, so that his T-shirt clung to him. His jeans stuck to his legs, crusted with dried dirt, and he cursed as he stalked over to Jason, the only guy left on the job. Foo Fighters screamed from the boom box, and Caleb stopped in front of the ladder, motioning to Jason to stop hammering.

"Why are we the only ones here?" he yelled up at him.

Jason dragged his forearm across his brow. "Dude, the crew went out to Harry's last night for dinner. I think they got blasted."

Temper bit him like a rattlesnake. "I don't give a shit what they do on their time, but with this deadline, I can't lose four of my guys. We have to finish framing."

Jason shrugged. "I went home to get laid. Don't take it out on me."

He cursed again and grabbed his cell, punching in the numbers for Sam, his foreman. Son of a bitch. Morgan was due here soon, and his workers decide to tie one on and sleep in. It was nine o'clock and already hot as Hades. This was gonna be a bitch of a day.

"Why is your ass not here?" he growled into the phone when Sam picked up.

His usual dependable worker groaned. "I think I ate something bad, boss. I'm sick."

Caleb ground his teeth in tempo to the music. His dentist was gonna strangle him. "It's called a hangover. Morgan's coming this morning, framing is supposed to be done, and I only have Jason out here. Take some Midol and get your ass over here with the other bozos."

"Isn't that for PMS?"

Caleb hung up. He shoved the hat back on his head, maneuvered his way through the multiple beams, and dragged in a deep breath. With such a tight schedule, he'd left little room for error. It had been a miracle they hadn't hit major issues with the first stage. Sure, they'd gotten a shitload of rain, but he'd pulled in every favor in his arsenal and bought himself a huge team for site prep, pouring the foundation and dealing with the usual horror of setting up the sewer and drain lines.

The usual bitch of such a large job was depending on so many other people to get the work done. Tristan and Dalton had been key in moving this along, though they grumbled most of the time they were using their talent to grease wheels rather than do any hands-on building. Plenty of time for that later, though. Without his electricians, plumbers, excavator, and suppliers happy, work would ground to a halt.

Why the hell did he get involved in this business again?

It sure wasn't for the glory. Or the money. No, this was

high-stress, ass-kissing, physically draining work not meant for the weak of heart.

Yeah. He loved every fucking second.

Caleb thought of calling his brothers for backup, then remembered Dalton had another job and Tristan was in New York to meet with the textile supplier Morgan was hot for. He liked his guy right in town, but that had been another go-around he wasn't up for, so he stuck it on his brothers to solve. She reminded him of Dalton when he got crazed for a specific type of wood grain and refused to back down. Impossible to argue with. She was rising to the rank of the most annoying, frustrating woman he'd ever met. Too bad he couldn't stop thinking about kissing her again.

On cue, she climbed out of the car.

Yeah, he was in trouble. Lately all his spare thoughts had been focused on making her happy in ways that didn't concern work. It was getting harder not to get hard on a regular basis around her. Every time he tried to figure out what it was about her that fascinated him, he only got more pissed.

Because she had completely ignored the kiss.

Cal had a healthy ego, but the way she'd dismissed him both amused and outraged him. She hadn't even wanted to talk about it. After he'd followed her back through the woods to her car, she gave him a dismissive wave and drove away. That was two weeks ago, and they still never mentioned the encounter.

How'd he get to be the girl in this weird relationship? His father would've died. He actually wanted to *talk* about what the kiss meant. Which he knew the answer to, anyway.

Nothing. At least to her.

She strode over to him without a pause in her step. Who the hell wore those outfits on the job and got away with it?

Today's white shorts had a scroll-like design on the sides in pale pink. She wasn't working the site today, so low-heeled white sandals clad her feet. A white scooped-neck top that managed to look conservative and businesslike was tucked neatly in her waistband, which emphasized her curvy hips and butt. She walked with a graceful purpose and razor-sharp focus that turned him on. Hell, everything about the woman turned him on. She was bossy, nosy, opinionated, and cool as a cucumber. Her Southern drawl nearly brought him to his knees with its rich honeyed texture.

But he refused to surrender to his aching dick.

Yes, he'd liked the kiss. Hell, he'd loved the kiss. But after she dissed him, Cal decided it was a blessing in disguise. Just because she'd taken his dare and gone skinny-dipping didn't mean she wasn't a tight-ass conservative in every other part of her life. As tempting as a steamy affair with her would be, she'd probably kill him with minutiae, and after the orgasm, she'd drive him crazy.

Not gonna happen on his watch.

She wasn't the right *book* for him, and she sure as hell would never be the proper *wood*.

She reached him. Her gaze flicked over the site, which clearly showed a single man banging away at the roof to gritty music. Usually there was a full team with staggered breaks for lunch, especially when the end of framing was in sight. The little frown creasing her brow told him what was coming.

"Why is Jason the only one working on my house?"

He was used to the clipped, polite tone. "They were delayed. Sam is on his way with everyone now."

"I'm not man enough for you, Morgan?" a voice called down.

Caleb stiffened, used to Jason's humor but hating the flirtatious tone in his voice. Morgan gave him a wave and a sunny smile. "Don't flatter yourself, darlin'."

Jason hooted with laughter, then went back to hammering. Caleb had originally wondered how she handled herself with a bunch of testosterone-fueled, rough men, and now he had his answer. She walked the perfect balance of business-like command and biting humor. She also had thick skin and no trouble giving a tongue blistering if she felt like anyone was out of line. Basically, Morgan Raines gave as good as she got.

He wondered if she took that same kind of attitude in bed.

Aggravated with his thoughts, he chugged some water and wiped his mouth with the back of his hand. "Need anything from me today, or can I get back to work?"

Those wide eyes chilled to Arctic blue. "We're supposed to be done with framing. We're behind."

"It will be finished."

"I need to confirm inspection."

"Already done."

Frustration clung to her aura. Caleb hid a smile. He found giving her the answers she wanted with no backup explanation drove her nuts. She liked to know who had scheduled it and when but was too annoyed now to ask. Her clipboard was so much a part of her, he wondered if she took it to bed at night. "You're missing five guys. I cleared

Rich's schedule so those pipes can be run and we can get the HVAC system going."

He bit back a groan. "You called Rich again? For God's sake, leave the man alone. He knows what he needs to do."

She gave a haughty sniff. "Rich overbooks clients, and you know it. I refuse to let him try to sneak in a smaller job and throw us off. Oh, I need you to meet me at Blossom and Company tonight."

He held up a hand and shook his head. "Hell no. Take Tristan."

"I can't. He's in New York dealing with textiles, remember? You're the closest I got."

"It's not my job to look at lighting and pick out froufrou chandeliers. Take Dalton."

"He's busy; I already checked. Stop complaining. If I do it now, we won't have to deal with it later when things are even more complicated. You're coming." She hesitated, and he watched the flickering emotions in her blue eyes. Almost like she wasn't sure if she should utter her next words. "I'll buy you dinner."

He paused. The thought of having more alone time with her was intriguing. And pathetic. "You're paying?"

She let out a husky laugh, and his heart did a weird tumble. This was like opening the cage a few inches, tempting the beast to escape. He searched her face for any indication that her invitation meant something bigger, but he couldn't gauge her calm expression. Not that he'd take her up on the offer. "Yeah, I'm paying. Consider it your fee for the torture."

"Fine." Two trucks pulled in and kicked up a burst of gravel. "Here they are."

She turned, and they watched as five giant guys made

their way toward them. "About time you ladies rolled out of bed," Caleb barked. "What the hell happened last . . ." He trailed off. Damn, they must've been drinking shots of one hundred proof. They walked with slow, tentative steps, sunglasses shielding their eyes and a green tinge staining their skin. Tiny, pitiful groans escaped their lips, as if each step was pure pain.

"You look awful," Caleb said.

Sam stopped in front of him. His throat worked as if trying to speak. His voice was a threadbare sound. "We're real sick, boss. All of us."

His team swayed on their feet. "I think we ate a batch of bad oysters," Mike said. "We all ordered them last night."

Caleb cursed, then looked at Morgan. He wasn't a monster, but damned if he wouldn't be screwed by a loss of a whole day's work. "It's okay, Cal," Morgan said. She addressed his men. "If y'all don't feel well, please go home and rest up. We'll work something out."

Knowing it cost her a lot to say that, he turned to his team. "What'd you wash them down with?" he asked.

Yep. They all shared a guilty look. "Some tequila," Frank finally said.

Caleb gave them a hard look.

Sam spoke up. "Come on, guys, we can do this. Sorry, boss."

They slowly trudged in, each of them taking various spots and beginning to work. With every bang of the hammer, it looked as if they wanted to shriek in horror. Caleb shook his head. "That never happens on my watch. They must've been celebrating something."

"It's not the first time I've seen it happen," she said. Her eyes glinted with amusement. "I've celebrated with them, and they usually recover fine. You have a good team."

Pride rushed in. "Thanks. They've been with me a long time, and other than an occasional screwup, they're solid guys. Talented. And in this business, a lot more dependable than other teams I've been with."

The words were floating like a cartoon bubble out of his lips when it happened.

Above the screech of guitars and hammers, a familiar retching noise cut through the air. Tools clattered to the floor, and groans of disgust peppered his ears.

Oh. No.

Frank vomited all over the floor. Clutching his stomach, he rolled himself back and forth in an effort to stop, but it only made it worse. Seconds later, Sam followed, his retching sounding like a baby monster who'd eaten an animal that disagreed with him. Jason hurried down the ladder, backing up from the two men with his hands in front.

"Ah, stop it! I'm a sympathetic vomiter!" Jason shouted.

Morgan took a step back, and Caleb watched in horror as the short story from *Stand by Me*, one of his favorite King tales, came to life—the disgusting scene about a pie-eating contest gone horribly wrong.

"Help!" Jason bent over and let loose. Then it was game on.

Mike turned the color of avocado and puked from the top of the ladder, and the last two guys surrendered. The sound of retching and groaning and male misery rose to a crescendo, and all Caleb could do was watch the nightmare unfold.

Finally a terrible silence descended.

The song ended and the boom box clicked off.

Caleb turned from the horrific scene and sighed. "All of you. Get the hell out of here."

One by one, the men left, heads hung in misery. He stood for a while, thinking about the long, terrible day stretching ahead. Then she spoke.

"Well, I guess it's just you and me. Let's get to work."

Morgan quickly switched gears and walked back to her car. Popping the trunk, she took out her hard hat and work boots, setting her mind to the task at hand. Sure, they'd still be a bit delayed, but if they worked all day with few breaks, they might be able to make up some time. She donned her boots and hat and stood.

When she looked up, Cal was staring at her.

It was hard not to laugh at his expression. He was a dynamic, puzzling man who consistently surprised her. If he said something crappy, he apologized and looked directly into her eyes. And meant it. He gave her respect on the job and always made sure she was treated like a business partner, listening to every suggestion and not openly pacifying her like so many other crews before him. He worked harder than anyone on his team and seemed to give every part of his life to the job. And the man was so sexy, it was as if a fire burned below on a constant basis. One she desperately wanted to slake.

The image of pleasuring herself to the thought of his kiss brought a flush to her cheeks. She'd been cool and distant in the past two weeks, giving him a clear indication she needed to reset their relationship back to work only. He took her lead with grace, but sometimes she'd catch him studying her with a banked fire in his eyes. Her body practically wept with the need for him to make good, but so far she'd been able to keep herself tightly under control.

Right now, hip cocked, dust in his hair, jeans riding low on his hips, and the symbol of construction hotness—the tool belt—wrapped tight around his waist, he was stripper-worthy. His damp T-shirt clung to his chest from good old-fashioned sweat, outlining the mass of carved muscles. Looking from his corded arms and bunched biceps to the sexy stubble clinging to his jaw and smoky charcoal eyes burning into hers, she was, simply, toast.

She did her usual, though. Fought her dampening girly parts with the fierceness of a woman on the edge. And, of course, kept her defenses firmly up. Morgan made sure to present him with the person he believed she was. A woman who read Austen, had every part of her life ruthlessly organized, and never missed a beat. Yes, skinny-dipping and kissing him in the moonlight had given him a hint of what was beneath, but she'd built back his original impression of the woman he thought she was. A woman he could never be interested in for a delicious, sexy, naked tumble. Because she knew one tumble would lead to another, and the last thing they needed was a personal relationship mucking up a perfectly good business one.

On that rule, they both agreed.

Morgan dropped her clipboard into the backseat and marched over to him. "Why are you staring at me like I've turned into E.T.?"

He jerked a thumb toward her feet. "How the hell did you get pink work boots?"

She wrinkled her nose and gave a humph. "I can get rare Italian tapestry from Rome if a client wants it. Pink work boots are easy. And why do you suddenly care what color my boots are? You've seen them before. We're wasting time. Tell me what you want me to concentrate on. Roof?"

Irritation bristled from his frame. "Even your hard hat is pink."

"Yep. My hat and boots both meet the standard requirements to be on the job. My mother instilled one hard lesson: a woman can do any job yet still look her best. Now, come on, Charming. Time is ticking. Where do you want me?"

He blinked. Muttered something under his breath. Morgan wished he wasn't so damn adorable when he was pissy.

"You sure you're not gonna fall off a ladder and sue me?" he drawled.

Morgan grinned. "I happen to love heights. Much better than doing trim. Also love banging the crap out of something and imagining the nail to be . . . someone else."

He laughed out loud at that one. Her heart squeezed a bit from the sound, and she wished she could hear it again. And again.

"Okay, princess, take a quick look at those plans, grab a hammer, and get your ass up over there."

She wrinkled her nose at the foul smell. "First I'm hosing everything down. Thank God I didn't get the oysters this week."

She caught his eye roll, but it was done with exaggerated

patience. She hooked up the hose and washed down the site until it was to her satisfaction, then got her ass on the ladder.

They worked in silence other than old-school Van Halen blaring from the speakers. The sun beat with brutal waves down on her body, but she was Charleston born and bred, and nothing burned hotter than a Southern summer. She slipped into contractor mode, not having to worry about anything but the materials in front of her, and got into a steady rhythm. She hauled the lumber over her shoulder and climbed the ladder, making steady progress as morning drifted to afternoon.

Until her stomach growl beat out the solo guitar thrumming the airwaves.

Cal wiped the sweat off his brow and hit the STOP button on the boom box. "I heard that. Let's take ten minutes to eat."

She nodded, climbed down, and grabbed another bottle of water from the cooler. "I didn't bring anything."

"I'll split my sandwich with you. You like ham?"

"I'd weep if you offered me just a saltine right now."

"Ham it is." They collapsed onto two cinder blocks and tore in. The hero was full of good, unhealthy stuff like cheese, mayo, and pickles, and she tried not to moan in ecstasy as her tummy got filled. She washed it down with Coke—not Diet—and eyed the bag of chips. Crap. Her personal Kryptonite. Most women fell to their knees for chocolate, but she worshipped every chip she'd ever eaten. Her idea of heaven was being locked in the Lay's factory. She tried to distract herself. "Your website says Pierce Brothers has been a family-owned company for decades. Was it passed down through your father?"

"No, it was actually from my mother. It was originally built by my great-great-great-grandfather. They all had boys to pass the company down to until my mom kind of put things in a tailspin." A brief smile tugged at his lips. "She was the only girl."

"Uh-oh. Did they try to arrange a marriage or something?"

"Nope, she learned the business from the ground up. When she met and married my father, there were no conditions. She could have kept the company in her own name—Wingate Custom Builders—but decided to sign it over to my father when I was born. Changed the name to Pierce Brothers. Must've sensed there'd be another boy on the way."

Morgan studied his face. Those gunmetal eyes had grown a bit misty, as if he was trapped in a memory that gave him pleasure. "So, it was a true family business."

And just like that, the distance snapped back. "My father had a firm idea what he wanted, so we just had to follow the plan."

"Is your mother still involved in the company?"

"No. She's gone."

"I'm sorry, I didn't—"

"Not a problem, I just don't want to get all touchy-feely about it. You want a chip?"

He held out the bag like Satan tempting Eve, and her fingers grabbed it. "Yes. Thanks. Just one."

"How's the Hilton?"

The first crunch almost made her moan. Ah, dear God,

they were sour cream and onion! What did he say? "Nice. Luxurious. Of course, room service and eating out gets old, but I'm used to it."

He stretched out long jean-clad legs. "So, basically, you don't have any type of home base?"

"I thought about buying a condo or a studio in Manhattan, but it doesn't make sense. I average six months in a place, sometimes less, and I can't have a bunch of different properties scattered. Hotels are more convenient, and I only stay in the penthouse. Not much to complain about."

She felt his gaze on her, but she concentrated on the chips. "Do you miss having a home?"

The question was like a bowling ball demolishing all twelve pins in a strike. Her insides took the hit, but she refused to let the emotions show on her face. Her gut screamed the truth. Yes. She wanted a home of her own, a sanctuary that was hers alone. A place no one else could tell her what to do or how to do it. Someplace she could cook and watch TV in flannel pajamas and crank the music really loud and dance like no one watched, because no one could. But she didn't utter any of those words. There was no point. Morgan loved her career and what she'd accomplished, and certain things needed to be sacrificed. Her parents had given her a solid home base she hoped she'd have for her own one day, on her terms.

"How can I complain about never doing laundry, cleaning, or cooking? That would make me completely ungrateful and selfish."

"No," he said softly. "It would just make you human."

She stilled. His masculine presence pressed down around her like humid air, wrapping her up in a tight hug.

She realized his muscular leg was pressed against hers as they sat. His arm brushed hers. His scent filled her nostrils, musk and sweat and soap and skin. All male, all him, all real and raw. Her stomach did a slow flip, and her fingers tightened around the bag.

A dangerous hum of attraction hung between them. Afraid to look into his eyes and be trapped there forever, Morgan drew in a shaky breath, but the energy was too much, and she turned her head, ready to take the tumble.

Suddenly the bag was ripped away from her.

"You ate all the chips."

She blinked, and just like that the spell was broken. Morgan didn't know if she was relieved or annoyed. "I only ate a quarter," she pointed out. "You owe me at least five more."

He peered into the bag and looked at her outstretched hand. "Hell no. I'm bigger and need more salt content than you. Besides, I'm doing you a favor."

She lifted a brow. "How?"

He stuffed a bunch in his mouth and chewed without remorse. "Don't women complain of bloating and stuff when they eat chips?"

Her mouth dropped open. Oh, hell no. He hadn't gone there. Had he? "Did you just put the words *women* and *bloating* together in the same sentence and expect to live?"

He paused, looking a tiny bit wary. "Stop trying to scare me. I'm trying to be nice."

She gave a cackle and jumped to her feet. "I'd hate to see what you're like when you're mean, Charming. Oh, BTW, watch the love handles."

He spit out the chips and jerked his chin up. "What?"

Morgan slid her palms down to cup the famous part where the extra fat settled. Not that he had any, but damned if she'd let him off the hook. "Love handles. Right here. You know, that part a woman grabs when she's having sex with—"

"I know what love handles are, dammit! Are you saying I have them?"

She tamped down on her amusement and relied on her brutal, cold, businesslike efficiency to make her final jab. Her gaze fell upon Cal's tight stomach and swept over lean hips that had a lot less flab than hers. Oh well. She liked her body and her curves and rarely apologized. If any man wasn't turned on by her form, she happily told them to keep on trucking and find a skinny-assed model. Besides, he'd already seen her practically naked and seemed to like what was on display. She ignored the dip of her belly and how badly she wanted a rerun of that night. "Ummm, no. Of course not." With perfect delivery, she landed the knockout punch. "But I think you may be right. I'll skip the chips."

His blistering curse was the perfect backdrop.

She got back to work.

chapter nine

Cal stood in the middle of Blossom & Company, one of the customized lighting and accent stores in Harrington, known for its uniqueness, quality, and of course, price.

After a brutal workday, they'd taken an hour to change and regroup before heading into town. Cal wasn't a complainer, but shopping for home decor was so much more Tristan, who actually gave a shit if a lamp was placed in a certain room for atmosphere, style, and correct shadowing. Him? A lamp gave light, and that was good enough.

Still, after Morgan had gone and put in a longer day than one of his guys, he was keeping his mouth shut. They'd stopped for a lobster roll, and he'd followed her obediently into the home warehouse, planning to be helpful and polite and home in time to put the baseball game on.

That was two hours ago, and his original intention had gone AWOL.

Now? Yeah, he was just cranky and bored out of his mind.

"What do you think of this?" she asked. He wished the

damn store served alcohol rather than sparkling froufrou water. He took in the beaded, fringy thing that looked like it should be from the seventies.

"What is it?"

She sighed. "A lamp."

He crinkled his brow and poked at it. "Where does the bulb go?"

"You hang it upside down and it gives the impression of a chandelier. See, I'd like to get it for the bathroom but wanted to get your take. Is it possible to make it work?"

Cal blinked. "We usually install the fan in the bathroom. Won't this fabric part get moldy from the steam? And why would anyone want a weird green thing hanging in front of the toilet?"

Maybe that was the wrong thing to say. Seemed like she didn't want his advice on how the thing looked, just how it could be installed. "It's vintage. I'm going with an antique-looking type of bathroom. Claw-foot tub. Tapestry. This would be perfect, and no, I don't want a fan in the bathroom."

"Huh? What if it gets stinky in there?"

She gave a long-suffering groan. "It won't. It's a bath-room to look at, not really use."

Cal scratched his head. "Yeah, like that makes tons of sense. Will there be a toilet?"

"Of course! Why are you asking ridiculous questions?"

"Why are you forcing me to look at ridiculous shit?"

She glared and tapped her foot. Her comfortable clothes consisted of white linen shorts, a yellow tank top, and white sandals with little silver chains on them. Her hair was back to its perfect condition, the silvery strands swishing past her cheeks at a sharp angle. He bet she'd paid a fortune for that cut. She'd be even more pissed if he told her the truth.

She looked hotter with the strands sweaty, tousled, and pulled back in a clip.

It had been getting harder to resist the attraction. When she was banging away with that hammer, her clothes mussed and dirty, muttering mild Southern curses under her breath when something went wrong, Cal couldn't deny he wanted her.

In fact, it was getting more difficult the more time they spent together.

Even now, when she was aggravating him, he kept gazing at that pink, lush mouth and wondered what she'd do if he shut her up by kissing her. Again. This time without stopping. Of course, it was impossible. She'd already dissed him, and pushing her would be sexual harassment and a whole bunch of mess. Still didn't make the thought go away.

"Let's rehash the ground rules, okay? I pick the materials and furnishing and accessories and hardware. You tell me if you can make it work."

"Fine. The answer is yes. I can make the ugly green lamp work in the bathroom that will never be used."

She seethed with frustration, her teeth snapping together. "See? Was that so hard?"

"Yes, this is painful. I'm doing you a favor. I'm bored. I hate this shit. Can you buy the ugly lamp, contact Tristan in the morning, and get me the hell out of here?"

Cal prepped for a female temper tantrum, but she switched gears. Suddenly she let out a laugh filled with such genuine joy, he couldn't help but smile back. She was so damn pretty. Standing in the middle of the store with that atrocity in her hands, dressed in her flawless white clothes, with her perfect hair and nails, able to laugh at his grumbling.

"I'm sorry," she said. "I'm being kind of bitchy—we had a long day. I just wanted to get a jump start on some of the design because of our tight schedule."

He relaxed. "Nah, I'm being whiny. Let's go pay, and I'll buy you a wine. Or a champagne. Or whatever you nice Southern girls drink."

She looked interested. "A Chardonnay sounds perfect."

Yep, just as he thought. Another white type of drink. Who was the real Morgan Raines? The cool, collected executive who controlled every aspect of her life, read literary classics, and was always color coordinated? The mussed-up, sharp-humored spitfire who swung a mean hammer? Or the sexy, half-naked woman who had accepted his dare and kissed him with everything she got?

He followed her to the cashier. Definitely the first. He had to stop thinking of her outside the business realm. She wasn't his type. He liked women who kicked back, drank a beer, and didn't care if their makeup got smudged in the making-out process. He didn't like women who not only wore white but drank it.

And then he noticed her shoe.

The silvery chain thingy had broken off and trailed behind her. The white strap sadly dragged over the dirty tile and ruined her flawless appearance.

And just like that, Caleb decided he wanted to get Morgan Raines in his bed.

● ● ●

Something had changed.

Morgan sat at the Oyster Bank under a cheerful red umbrella and studied the man across from her with suspicion. The lamp was safely by her side—she'd bartered a bit and finally gotten a decent price. One moment he was all pissy and gorgeous, doing that alpha male thing because he didn't want to be stuck shopping, and the next he was staring at her like she was Gettysburg and he was Robert E. Lee.

Morgan really, really hoped she didn't lose this war.

Her skin prickled with awareness, so she kept up some inane chatter and drank her Chardonnay. The offer for a drink had seemed okay at the moment, but now there was so much tension in the air, she wished she'd declined. She should be back in her safe, boring hotel room and get a good night's sleep. She needed to stay far, far away from men like Caleb Pierce and sour cream and onion potato chips.

They were so good at first. Then they turned real bad.

So, here they sat, Cal staring at her with all that yummy seething sexiness she'd only read about, and Morgan doing a fine imitation of Scarlett O'Hara before the war and heartbreak made her more interesting. Ah, the hell with it.

"Why are you looking at me all googly-eyed?" she asked.

He choked on his beer. Morgan remained patient as he gathered his composure and narrowed his gaze. "You know, every time I think I have you figured out, you surprise me."

Normally his statement would be a high compliment, but she didn't trust his intentions. "Maybe you don't *have* to figure me out," she said.

"Can't help it. See, princess, you've got me intrigued."

She crossed her legs and shook her foot. "And why do I care again?"

He laughed. "Never give an inch, do you? Gonna tell me you haven't thought about that kiss?"

Oh, Lord. He'd really gone for it. Emotion rioted inside her, a crazy mixture of relief to have him voice the truth and anger because he voiced the truth. She'd been counting on his general dislike and touch of surliness to keep his distance. She'd bet her cool disregard for the whole scene would slam him in the male ego hard enough for him to forget the entire encounter. Now, after one damn lamp-shopping trip, he'd decided to eat the damn potato chips.

No. She refused to eat the chips. No regret for her. Things were perfect, and nothing was worth screwing it up.

Even one wild night with this man.

Morgan crossed her arms in front of her chest. She was going to have to play hard ball. Cool as a cucumber, but polite enough not to get him pissy. She kept her voice calm and even. "I wouldn't be human if I told you I never thought about it. So I won't lie. It was a good kiss. But I'm not going to sleep with you."

Oh, no. He looked delighted by her response. Was it that chase thing that was turning him on? "A great kiss," he corrected. "You said no lying."

"Fine. A great kiss."

"Why not? Aren't you curious?"

She lifted a brow. "I don't intermingle with my business partners. Ever. It's bad for me, you, and business."

"Intermingle, huh? I like that word. Very proper. Problem is, I'm not thinking very proper thoughts when I look at you. I keep thinking about messing you up. Getting dirty. Making you scream. Stuff like that."

Blistering heat scorched her veins and turned her blood to lava. Goodness gracious, he wasn't playing around when he wanted someone. Morgan knew he'd be the type of lover to put all her previous ones to shame. Caleb would refuse to let her put up walls or hide. He wouldn't have sex with the lights off, either. Why did that turn her on instead of scare her? Oh, no, don't eat the chips, don't eat the chips . . .

Her voice cranked out a bit rusty but passable. "Well. That was quite . . . descriptive. It's a lovely offer, but I'll have to say no, thank you."

Cal leaned over the table. "Fascinating," he murmured. "You turned down great sex like you would a tea party invite."

She blinked. "You're not going to get weird on me now, are you?"

He grinned and tipped his bottle back to take another pull of beer. "First thing I'll make clear. Our business is separate from this." He motioned back and forth with his fingers. "Nothing between us leaks onto the job, so it would be kept under wraps. Second, you can tell me straight-out if you're uncomfortable and want me to leave you alone. There's nothing that turns me off faster than an unwilling woman. Finally, this was my scenario. We have about five months ahead of us. We agree to some rules we're both comfortable with, and we enjoy each other while you're here."

Morgan tried to utter the magic words that would make him go away. *I'm. Not. Interested.* "I don't do casual sex," she said. "I can't get comfortable with someone who sleeps around."

His brows shot down. "We'd only be sleeping with each

other," he said. "I don't share, either. I'm talking about a monogamous relationship for five months."

Huh. She'd never been approached in this capacity. Most men she was attracted to on the job just wanted a quick one-nighter to try out the new girl. But Cal had set guidelines ready. She loved rules. No one could get hurt that way, right? Reality suddenly hit her. No, it never worked like it should on paper. Hadn't she seen enough Lifetime movies to know this? "It won't work," she insisted.

"Why not?"

A sigh escaped her lips. She took a sip of wine. "We could get tired of each other within the week. That conflict could spill over to the site, and suddenly we're both screwing up on the job. I can't risk it."

"You don't think we can handle this like two reasonable adults who lay out the terms?"

"There's too many liabilities in the plan," she pointed out. "What if you fall in love with me and I want to break up after a month?"

His eyes widened with shock. A laugh sputtered from his lips. "Damn, you're hard on a man's ego," he muttered. "Okay, I'm a big boy. Past high school hormones. I'd bury the hurt and pain and work through it."

"I don't know."

"What if you fall in love with me? Can you handle it?"

She waved a hand in the air. "Bless your heart. I'm not worried about that. We're way too different for long-term. But if you enrapture me, I'm also a big girl. I should be able to handle it."

"See, this could work. People mix business with pleasure all the time. The key is to be smart and lay the groundwork."

She shook her head slowly. "Still, too many variables. We'd fight."

His eyes glittered hot charcoal. "We'd make up later."

Morgan wanted to laugh but fell short. The way his gaze stripped away her clothes and laid her bare thrilled her. How addictive to become one of those women who was empowered by sex instead of always running away or trying to fit it into her busy schedule. How delicious to imagine her body taking over instead of her very rational, very proper mind. Still . . . Caleb Pierce was out of her comfort zone.

She finished her wine, blotted her mouth with the cocktail napkin, and folded her hands in her lap. Morgan opened her mouth to say thank you but no. Instead, strange words popped out. "I'll need to think about it."

Now, where on earth had that come from?

His carved lips kicked up in a satisfied grin. "Good enough for me, princess. Now, put your leg up here."

"Excuse me?"

"Damn, I'm gonna wonder if you're this polite when I make you come."

"What!"

He chuckled, leaned over, and grabbed her ankle. With one quick motion, he lifted her leg so her foot was propped on his jean-clad knee. Morgan gasped as his hands slid over her bare ankle, the steady throb between her legs begging him to make a detour up, up, and *Yes, just keep going, please*.

His muscles stiffened, almost like he caught her musky scent of arousal drifting on the breeze. Her cheeks flushed, and she was about to yank her foot back when he began wrapping the broken strap of her sandal once around her ankle, then neatly tucked the frayed end into the center. She looked dumbly at him, not knowing if she wanted to jump in his arms or punch him for allowing this new mixture of emotions out of the bottle.

So she did nothing.

"I didn't want you to trip," he said simply. His fingers lingered, pressing into her skin like little pinpricks of electricity. He growled low in his throat, seemingly torn about something before he gently placed her foot back on the ground. "All done."

She said nothing.

Cal narrowed his gaze. "This is the deal. I want you. I can tell from the kiss you want me, too. I'm not following my dick on an impulse decision. I've been thinking about you for a while now, and I think we'd enjoy each other very much. Not just the physical but also our conversations. Company during meals. A midnight skinny-dip. You've managed to get under my skin, Morgan Raines."

She smiled and he smiled back.

"Think about it. I won't push. But I won't go away, either."

"I'll think about it," she said. "But I may push back. And I'm not going anywhere, either."

His laughter pumped through the air and gave her way too much pleasure.

Morgan didn't get much sleep that night.

She hoped he didn't, either.

chapter ten

Morgan walked into Sydney's office and stood by the desk. She smiled as Sydney nodded for her to wait, talking crisply into her Bluetooth while sifting through a massive pile of papers on her desk with one hand and tapping out something on her keyboard with the other. These tasks were completed with a mixture of booming male voices echoing in the air. Seems there was a heated argument going on over an episode of *Game of Thrones* right outside the door.

Morgan took a seat, giving a sigh of relief at the temporary easing of her aching feet. The thought of the hotel hot tub was getting her through the day, but the past week she'd fallen asleep before room service had even delivered her meal. She was in crunch time, and Morgan tried to remind herself that she went through this at every job. Coordinating the massive amount of electricians, plumbers, and construction workers was a bitch to deal with. The skeleton was now firmly wrapped, the windows and doors were finally installed, and now they were at the delicate part of the project: the time when supplies went missing, workers never showed up, fights broke out, and general chaos was the order of the day.

Fun, fun, fun.

So far, though, Caleb had impressed her. His competence, no-nonsense manner, and self-deprecating humor made him a well-liked boss who everyone seemed to want to please. That level of respect was hard to reach, and Morgan was forced to put another check in the benefits column.

The benefits of having a short affair with Caleb.

Since that night, they seemed to dance around each other with the question being the oversize pink elephant in the room. Cal never pushed, but with every long stroke of his gaze over her body, he told her again and again what he wanted. At first, she was worried the crew would pick up on those looks, but he was careful to treat her with a friendly distance when they were around anyone.

Morgan finally admitted she was playing the denial game. She also wondered how long he'd wait until he pushed the issue. Or, more importantly, *if*.

God, she wanted him to. How screwed-up was that? An independent, financially secure, ambitious, kind of sexually experienced woman waiting breathlessly for the man to grab her fiercely and kiss her senseless, thereby ending her denial in the most pleasant of ways.

So. Embarrassing.

Sydney clicked off and got up from her desk. "Sorry, Morgan, it's been kind of hellish around here lately." She jerked her thumb toward the loud guffawing down the hall. "And they're not helping." Her gorgeous red hair streamed down her back, and she wore an apple-green suit that showed off her eyes. The freckles scattered over her face and warmly curving mouth softened her appearance enough so most women couldn't hate her for being so damn beautiful. In the time she'd spent here, her chats with Sydney were sometimes one of the highlights of her day.

Morgan grinned. "Well, you're not going to be happy with me. I'm adding to the hellish day." She opened her briefcase, slid out her famous clipboard—which she'd probably be buried with—and handed her a huge file. "Invoices, checklists, receipts, and a bunch of other nameless tasks."

Sydney sighed. "Not your fault. I'm so used to being buried in work, I probably wouldn't know what to do with myself if I had five minutes to think."

"Any possibility of hiring an assistant?"

Sydney wrinkled her nose. "Nah, I'm a control freak, anyway. Would spend all my time trying to tell him or her how to do things."

"From one control freak to another, I hear you. Can I use the conference room? I have a Skype appointment with my client, and then have to wait for a few calls from the West Coast."

"Of course."

Tristan walked through the door without knocking. Morgan got an impression of lean height, wavy chestnut hair, and graceful features that reminded her a bit of old-school Cary Grant. The man exuded smoothness, grace, and a banked intensity hidden behind a chiseled exterior. He intrigued Morgan, but she wasn't attracted to him the way she was to Caleb, who made her burn. Still, she appreciated the charcoal custom suit—complemented with a red silk tie and gold cuff links with his initials—that framed his very fit body.

"Where's the Anderson file?" he demanded, stopping in front of them. "Hi, Morgan."

"Hi, Tristan."

Sydney's mouth tightened. "In the file marked *Andersen*. And good afternoon to you, too. Thanks for knocking."

Did his cheeks flush, or was that her imagination? His words were clipped and deliberate. "Good afternoon, Sydney. And the file isn't there. I thought we finalized the final cost of the refurbishment and new deck. We need to close the account."

His leashed power seemed to throw women off, but Sydney just turned her cool gaze on him like he was an annoyance. "I took care of it already. And did you check under *Andersen* with an *e*? It's not spelled with an *o*."

Tristan looked frustrated, and an odd energy burned between them. Odd. "Fine. I'll look again. Are you going to lunch?"

"No time."

His lips flattened to a thin line. "It's past two. You need to eat. We pay you for lunch."

"Thanks, but I can take care of myself. Been doing that a long time."

Whoa. Tristan stubbornly refused to be dismissed, flicking his gaze back and forth between each of them as if trying to decide how to frame his response. Morgan cleared her throat. "Tristan, can I steal you for a few minutes? I need to confirm some final decisions on flooring."

He treated Sydney to one more heated look, then nodded. "Of course. I have some time now."

Sydney kept her face impassive. "Morgan, let me know

if you need anything." Then she turned her back on Tristan and left.

Tristan's face reflected frustration, but he didn't try to stop her. They walked into the conference room, and she began setting out her laptop, clipboard, and bulging files of paint chips, samples, and fabrics. "Dalton and I went over the fixtures and picked out the floor finishes, but the terrace materials need to be confirmed. Do we go with traditional pavers or flagstone? I'm thinking about a matching wall on the adjacent left corner of the property."

His long fingers tapped the table in a steady rhythm. His figure hummed with a quiet energy that hinted at his complete focus. "Bluestone," he finally said. "We skip the pavers and go for bluestone, then river rock to do a matching wall."

Excitement lit her blood. "Yes, but will the river rocks be too neutral?"

He continued tapping. "We can do rainbow rock to pick up the color of the bluestone."

"I love it. Can we get the stone in time?"

"I'll start working on it. Confirm with you tomorrow."

"Thanks. I'm speaking with the Rosenthals in a few, so I'll let you know if we need to incorporate any changes." Of course, Morgan rarely had to change her initial ideas. What made her so good at her job was her ability to transform a client's dreams and wishes into reality. She had an instinct that had never failed before, and she didn't intend it to now.

"You picked out a beautiful piece of property," Tristan commented. "Land is shrinking and becoming overvalued here. I just hope Pierce Brothers never runs out of places to build."

Morgan studied him. She knew he had an affinity for real estate and turning a piece of property around. "How come you're not flipping?"

A frown marred his brow. "Want to. I think we're missing out on a critical piece of profit in Harrington. Problem is, Cal is focused on the building, and Dalton is mesmerized by wood."

She smiled. It must be hard being not only the middle brother but also the business-oriented one. "Do you know that old farmhouse on Balance Street? The one with the crappy roof and shoe-box windows?"

"Yeah."

"It's for sale."

He cocked his head. Considered. "It's a crap house."

"Exactly. Imagine what you could flip that for, since it's on a dead-end street. A family with children would go nuts for that place."

Those blue-gray eyes flickered with interest. "Who told you it's up for sale?"

"Perry at the granite store. His sister's in real estate and said it was impossible to sell. Seems they're looking to dump it for a song."

Tap-tap-tap. Morgan enjoyed the transformation on his face. Purpose carved out his elegant features, and she imagined his brain was short-circuiting with ideas. "Let me check it out. It's small enough to renovate fast as long as the foundation and guts are still good. A project like that can funnel money easily into the business and open up new doors. I've been telling Cal this for a while now. Maybe it's time I make him listen."

Morgan didn't want to involve herself in family dynamics, but it was obvious Cal liked things the way they were. Tristan was wasting his talent doing accounting and running back and forth to suppliers. She'd been out with him a few times already, and his knowledge of what would work in an empty room was pure magic. If he knew property as well, Pierce Brothers was sitting on a gold mine and didn't even know it.

"Thanks, Morgan. I'll let you know on the bluestone."

"Great. Good luck."

She spent the next hour organizing her materials, then finally dialed the Rosenthals for their meeting. The screen shifted to reveal the glamorous couple sitting on a white-cushioned lounge. Ah, they must be on the yacht. Water sprayed from the rail. The sprawl of stark white houses scattered on a cliff under an azure sky filled the background. Petra's signature honeyed hair and bright red lips still managed to startle her. Morgan thought she could be termed the most beautiful woman in the world. Her eyes glowed almost violet, and her body was lean muscle without being unhealthy. At over six feet, she had legs that were insured at Lloyd's of London for millions. A white floppy hat perched on her head, and her French-manicured fingers held a tropical drink.

Her husband, Slate, had taken Hollywood by storm for his part in a famous gangster movie that earned him an Academy Award nomination. The film taking place in Harrington was his next project, and critics said it was crucial he excelled as a main lead. His dark hair and brooding Latin looks were the perfect complement to Petra's golden aura.

"Morgan, darling! I cannot wait to hear the updates on the house. It's like a big Christmas present I'm dying to unwrap."

Morgan smiled. "I'm confident you're going to love it. We're right on schedule, and I'd love to go over some samples."

Slate leaned over his wife and waved his hand in the air in dismissal. "We're on the Greek islands for the next few days. I'd like to spend as much time as possible with Petra before we begin shooting, so let's keep this short. Besides, that's why you're the best. You already know what we want."

Petra laughed. "Slate is afraid I'll become overwhelmed with such a project and ignore him. Silly man."

"Slate is right. There's no need for you to stress about anything. I guarantee you will love your new house," Morgan said confidently. She pushed the array of samples out of the way from the screen. "I'm moving ahead with no troubles. Just wanted to touch base to see if you had any questions or concerns."

"We're doing complementary shades of blue for the bank of guest suites, correct?" Petra asked.

Morgan paused. She'd picked out coordinating green for the three suites and had even placed orders. Blue? How had she missed that—she'd been sure green was Petra's signature color. "Yes, of course we're doing blue," she confirmed. Her stomach twisted. She'd never gotten a color palette wrong. It was one of her strongest skills. Okay, no need to panic. It was just one tiny error easily fixed.

"Wonderful. Oh, I attended a party at Anne Hathaway's friend's and went simply crazy over her entertainment room.

Minimalist decor. Red walls, sleek black furniture, clean sculpture. I'd love to reflect the tone but make it unique. Lord help me if she visited and discovered we tried to copy her! But you're probably doing something similar, right, darling? You know how I adore that type of sharp expression."

Her heart began to pound. She'd missed this, too. How? She'd done a complete and thorough profile on her clients, and that type of scheme wasn't even in her notes as a possibility? They were as far from minimalist as a hippie was from a CEO. Were they kidding? Sweat pricked her forehead. Her mind sifted through the design mock-ups and furniture she'd placed on hold. Maybe they'd just changed their mind after seeing someone else's house. Sometimes clients thought they wanted a look even though it didn't fit them to live with it long-term. She couldn't doubt herself now. They'd sense doubt and go in for the kill like a shark.

"I have it covered," she said smoothly.

Petra clapped. "Thank you, darling, I knew I didn't have to worry. I'll let you get back to work, and we'll check in next week. Kisses."

Morgan said her good-byes and clicked off.

She was in deep trouble. Her gut was so clear and visible for this project, yet they seemed to be going in a new direction. Should she scramble back and redo? Or keep with the original plan with the hope they'd adore it when they walked into the house?

Morgan pulled out her dossier and samples and got to work. Re-sifting through every decision made so far, she threw out the green color scheme and researched blue. The curtains would need to be reordered, of course, and the French antique side table would be too fussy for them. Minimalist?

She had a damn headache.

Morgan worked through the next few hours, placing calls and contacting her various suppliers. The sun sank and the light bled away. Everyone had probably gone home by now, but she still needed to wait for one more call. Stretching out her cramped muscles, she spotted the TV on the sliding shelf and checked her watch.

No one was around. No one would know.

Morgan grabbed the remote, turned to her favorite channel, and poured herself a glass of sparkling water.

Anticipation ramped up as the beginning credits rolled and she sank into the leather lounge with a happy sigh.

Her favorite guilty pleasure.

The Real Housewives of Orange County.

Or *New York.* Or *Atlanta.* Of course, *Jersey* was one of her favorites, but it didn't really matter. The drama and catfights and sleeping around was pure deliciousness. *Million Dollar Listing* was too close to work.

Oh, Lord have mercy, it was the reunion show, part two! How had she missed part one?

In gleeful amusement, Morgan let the arguments wash over her, loving the way Andy Cohen delicately balanced the job of host with his other job to score as much drama as possible from his cast. She was having such a good time, she didn't hear the knock on the door until it was too late.

"Morgan? I'm the last one out of here tonight, so I wanted— What are you watching?"

Morgan jumped up like she'd been caught in a sex scandal and blocked the TV. "Nothing! Just flipping through the channels while I wait for my final call. Goodness gracious, it's late. You should've left a while ago."

"I could say the same for you." Sydney tilted her head to peek at the TV while Morgan tried to fumble with the remote. "Oh, my God. Tell me you are not watching the trashiest show on television."

"No, of course not! I was looking for CNN, and—"

"I love the housewives!" Sydney squealed. "It's the reunion show! They're the absolute best, and Andy is brilliant. Can I join you?"

And just like that, Morgan realized she'd made a new friend.

"Yes. As long as you keep my secret."

Sydney dropped into the matching leather chair and slid off her shoes with a groan. "Are you kidding? The men in this place would crucify me. They call this a complete nonfeminist show, but I don't give a crap. I love it."

"Me too. I love when they host parties and we see the houses."

"Yeah, but you're actually creating one. You have the coolest job."

Morgan beamed. "Yeah, I kind of do."

They watched the whole show, and Morgan loved being able to chat and compare notes on her favorite vice. After an intense debate over who was the best character on the show, Andy signed off and they flipped off the TV.

Sydney sighed with pleasure. "I feel so much better now."

"Me too." She glanced at her phone and the incoming text. "My call was rescheduled, so I can head out with you."

"How's the hotel?"

"Good. First-class pampering."

"It must be nice having everything done for you," Sydney remarked. "You need it, with your work schedule. How are you settling into Harrington? Have you been able to explore the town and have some downtime?"

Morgan sighed. "By the time I get to the hotel, I'm exhausted. I've seen a lot of the shops, though, and been looking forward to using some pieces to decorate the house."

"Have you gone to the Barn?"

She shook her head. "No."

Sydney clapped her hands. "Oh, I have to take you. You'll go nuts. It's this huge old farmhouse converted into a place filled with antiques and unique finds."

Her heart picked up the pace. There was nothing she loved more than finding a shop that surprised her. Especially since their last conversation had her doubting her choices. Maybe browsing more would help. "I always research the area for local stores, but nothing came up with that name on my Google search. Can you tell me where it is?"

"That's because the Barn doesn't have a website. The owner is old-school. I'll do better. You need some girl time. Hell, so do I. It's located right on the edge of town, next to my favorite bar, called My Place. We'll shop, then grab a burger and a cocktail."

The idea of having a relaxing night out with a new friend was too intriguing to deny. She was getting tired of being the only female in the boys' club. "I'm in."

Sydney gave a squee. "Great! I can line up a sitter for Wednesday night, if that works?"

"Oh, I didn't realize you had kids."

A shadow crossed her usual sunny face. "I have one. A daughter."

"I bet your husband dotes on her." Morgan imagined a little red-haired girl like her mama. The pang hurt, but just for a moment, and when she smiled, it was genuine.

"No husband. I'm a single mom. Always was." She paused, and her chin lifted an inch. "Is that a problem?"

Morgan jerked back. "Oh, my goodness, no! She's welcome to join us, Sydney. We can do a girls' shopping trip and eat burgers. I'd love to meet your daughter."

Sydney relaxed and smiled back. "Sorry, sometimes in a small town where you've lived your whole life, people judge. Bad habit. Thanks for the invite, but she's four years old, so I think she'd have more fun with a sitter and a Disney movie."

"Then Wednesday is perfect. Thanks."

"Awesome! God, I haven't been out in ages. Now, let's get out of here before we turn into pumpkins."

They left, and Morgan drove to the hotel, looking forward to Wednesday night.

"I've died and gone to HGTV heaven."

Morgan looked around the massive space and swayed on her feet. A bit woozy from the excitement, she spun around, head back, smile on her face, and let herself revel in the glory of such a find. The Barn was a giant red farmhouse with creaky double doors and a tiny sagging sign at the end of a winding gravel path situated close to the woods. She'd been doubtful at first, feeling as if she were stepping onto the set of a horror movie.

Until she got inside.

The two-story loft was filled to the brim with furniture, mirrors, signs, rugs, and endless accent pieces. Some were antique, some seemed new, and every taste and design was represented. There seemed no organization to it, and paper tags were attached to each item with a handwritten cost. One battered desk held an old-fashioned cash register. The back room contained old wood and various pieces that needed to be refurbished. It was a complete gold mine.

Sydney laughed. "Now you're starting to scare me. It's just stuff."

"Glorious stuff. Stuff that may save my job, because I've been stuck on this one. I know the general look I want to achieve, but they threw me off during our last meeting. They're new Hollywood, not old money. The Rosenthals want people to come to their house and be impressed but not be able to explain why. It can't be about a room full of expensive furniture or antiques. It has to look effortless, like throwing on a shirt and jeans, yet the outfit is so perfect, everyone stares."

Sydney blinked. "Wow. You're good. I never thought furniture and decor could do all that."

"Oh, it can. You won't be bored, right? I think we're going to spend some time in here."

"I have a toddler at home. I go to the grocery store and have breakdowns in Target. I'm good."

"Okay. Let's do this."

Morgan fell into the place like a woman fell in lust. Violently hopeful, voraciously needy, and hungry for satisfaction. She found a chaise lounge set reminding her of old-time Hollywood, the graceful carved wooden legs and velvet texture worn and faded. Beaded pillows in jeweled colors and hand-stitched afghans. Beveled glass mirrors so heavy, she could barely lift them. A mahogany dresser and matching nightstand with peacocks hand-carved into the wood. A jewelry armoire with double doors and ripped burgundy interior. Vivid watercolor paintings on canvas with chipped frames, sculptures of Greek goddesses in marble, and rugs with golden tassels in rich, swirling patterns that reminded her of medieval castles.

Her head spun with possibilities. Between Dalton's, Tristan's, and her own expertise, she knew she could furnish a good chunk of the house with finds from the Barn. They needed love and renovation, and each piece told a story and would be the focus of the room.

Usually at every step she would question whether each pick would fit the personality and lifestyle of her client. But this time she seemed off. Maybe it was best to go with a different approach. Trust her gut instead of the couple's last feedback. What if she designed this home by allowing the furnishings to dictate the theme? One outstanding piece would pull the room together. Then she'd build the Rosenthals' flavor and style around the centerpiece.

She'd Tim Gunn it and make it work.

Morgan set up a revolving account with Mr. Reynolds, the owner and seemingly only worker at the place. She tagged her buys and made arrangements to come back later in the week to go through the rest of her list. Once she mentioned Caleb and his brothers, he relaxed and seemed willing to work with her on finding more pieces that might fit her vision.

When they finally reached the bar, Morgan slid onto her

chair, exhausted but replete with satisfaction. Sydney shook her head and laughed. "You look like you just had sex."

Morgan didn't even have the strength to blush. "I feel like it. Maybe this is why I love my job, too. I've become a professional shopper."

"Braggart."

Morgan grinned and looked around. This was definitely not the type of bar-restaurant boasted about in the village of Harrington. It was a massive open space with a huge potential for greatness, but it needed some TLC. The rustic raftered ceiling, scarred wood floors, and eclectic art pieces made of odd assortments of wood screamed vintage. The bar must've been impressive years ago, with a huge brick wall setting off the endless bottles and glasses displayed with pride. The old mahogany was stripped and dull, and the surface needed refinishing, but if it were ever restored, it would be a mighty presence. The shadowed interior kept things intimate, encouraging secrets to be shared. The pool table and dartboard in the back contributed to the atmosphere of casualness, and the booths and chairs were simple wood with red vinyl padding. Knickknacks exploded from shelves and corners: bobbleheads, festive shot glasses, pictures, and interestingly shaped mirrors. Two big-screen televisions took up the corners. The scents of burgers and fries drifted in the air, and an impressive line of drafts was set up to satisfy a range of beer tastes.

"Whatcha drinking, ladies?"

The bartender had long coal-black hair that curled wildly around her face, inky dark eyes, and a badass manner. A diamond glinted in the side of her nose, and her nails were long and scarlet red. She wore jeans and a leather-fringed tank top and had a tattoo on her shoulder of a knife glinting with blood at the tip. Fascinated, Morgan leaned in. "White wine. Chardonnay. I like your tat."

The woman gave her a hard stare, as if trying to decide if she was being mocked. Finally she nodded. "Thanks." She turned to Sydney. "You?"

"Harp."

Her movements were lightning quick and graceful, and in seconds, their glasses were in front of them. Sydney and Morgan shared an impressed look. Sydney spoke up. "You're new here, right? Heard they got a new owner."

The woman cocked a hip, crossed her arms in front of her chest, and scowled. "I'm the owner."

Sydney grinned. "Awesome. We needed some new blood in this place. Do the burgers still rock?"

"They're better." The woman paused, then seemed to make a decision. "I'm Raven."

"Sydney. This is Morgan—she's new in town, too."

Morgan nodded at her. She wondered if Raven was more Caleb's type. She definitely didn't wear white, or scream relationship, or seem like a control freak. The thought depressed her.

Raven pushed two menus over. "I updated some of the apps. Wanna switch to a booth or eat at the bar?"

"Here's good," Morgan said. There was something so deliciously decadent about eating in an informal setting. She remembered all those years of perfect china and place settings and crisp linen napkins from her parents' tutelage. It wasn't a bad thing to know, but how badly did she crave to eat in front of the television or with plastic cutlery for a change? Her mother would have a breakdown if she knew her only child now frequented drive-throughs and usually ate room service in front of the TV. Her Southern roots embraced big dining tables and proper eating utensils. Her rebellious years got wiped out when she got her diagnosis of cancer. While her friends partied and dealt with college romances, she'd been in a hospital and had a long recovery. Of course, she tried to make up for it later, but by that time she'd been involved with Elias, and he frowned on frequenting bars. Now she finally had a valid opportunity.

"You got it," Raven said. She lingered, her gaze touching on the white wine, then flicking back up to her face. "I stock a decent label, but I specialize in cocktails. I can make them whiskey based, rum, vodka, champagne . . . Wanna try one?"

Morgan looked down at her glass. The last time she drank anything but white wine was . . . well, it was . . . well, maybe never? She nibbled on her lip. "I'm not sure what I like," she finally said.

Raven gave a slow grin. "Can't have that. I need a virgin palette to test some brews. I'll get you a few samples on the house." She turned to Sydney. "You in?"

Sydney rubbed her palms together. "Hell yes."

Raven laughed. "Great. Excuse me." She went to serve two older guys who already seemed halfway bombed. She rolled her eyes at their literal come-ons but poured them a drink. After a great debate over the menu, Morgan decided on a veggie wrap with sweet potato fries.

"So, how's it really going?" Sydney asked. Her green eyes lit with curiosity. "Are you and Caleb getting along?"

Morgan called on all her power not to flush. She didn't want Sydney to know about her boss's intriguing offer. Business matters needed to be kept separate from personal, and my, this was personal. "I think we reached an excellent balance," she recited. "He runs his team with competence. They respect him. And he keeps a tight ship, which I admire. There should be no problem meeting our completion date."

A delighted grin curved her new friend's lips. "Oh, my God, you're hot for each other!"

Her fingers jerked around her glass. "What? I didn't say anything about that."

"I know, that was the sign. Every woman who meets any of the Pierce brothers can't help talking about how gorgeous they are, or hot, or asking questions if they're single. You? Nada. Classic denial and cover-up from a female perspective."

Morgan sighed. "Fine. He's hot. But this project means a lot to me, and I don't want an attraction to mess anything up. This is a small town, and I also don't need to be the center of gossip. Make sense?"

Sydney nodded. "Absolutely. Emotions run high on a job site, and I know your deadline is tight." She tilted her head in thought. "Cal is a good man, though. He's not a game player or a liar. It's been a long time since I've seen him in a relationship, because he focuses so much on work, but you couldn't pick better if you're interested. Of course, I also understand what you mean about small-town gossip. It can be hard." Her tone held just a hint of bitterness.

Raven swooped in, took their orders, and placed two

flutes on the bar. "Try a Sweet Hot Chris. It's champagne based. Flavors are lemon and orange, with aromatic bitters."

Morgan lifted the glass and took a sip. The crisp bubbly liquid danced in her mouth, and the sharp, citrusy flavors exploded on her tongue. Delicious. The best cocktail ever. "This is amazing," she finally said, taking another sip.

Sydney agreed. "Dear God, I could drink this every day."

"Good. Didn't want to waste this cocktail on my current crowd." The rowdy college students let out another roar as one of the guys began chugging his beer. "Drink it slow if you're not used to it."

"How'd you get the name?" Morgan asked curiously.

Raven winked. "I'm in lust with Chris."

"Husband? Boyfriend?" Sydney asked.

"Hell no. Pratt, Hemsworth, Pine, Evans. Get the picture?" She disappeared into the kitchen with a sway of her hips that was all natural and not an ounce of fakeness. Morgan sighed. Yep. She officially had her first girl crush.

Sydney shook her head. "What were we talking about again? The cocktail melted my brain cells. Too good."

Morgan laughed. "Small towns. Gossip. I know exactly what you mean. Some of the locals in Charleston spread the news even before things happened, almost as if they sensed it coming." She took another sip of champagne and probed gently. "It must be difficult being a single mom in a small town."

Shadows crossed her new friend's face. Morgan sensed there were secrets buried deeper than the marshes where people buried bodies never to be found. "Yes, but worth it. Every time I look into my daughter's face, filled with joy and mischief, I remind myself I wouldn't have my life any other way. Caleb helped a lot. He gave me time off, kick-ass medical benefits, and flex Fridays. Becca is a happy little girl. That's all that matters."

She wasn't surprised Caleb was good to his employees. His attractiveness only rose in her eyes each time she watched him deal with his team, lending a firm hand, a good joke, or a supportive ear. He cared, and that was rare in this business. Too often people were treated as projects, as if ranked by percentage of return on investment instead of as human beings.

Yeah. Morgan wanted him. His delicious proposition danced in her mind nonstop. Other than a few boyfriends and Elias, it had been a while since a man intrigued her. Was that a sign to take a risk? She pushed away the tempting thought and refocused on their conversation.

"I'd love to meet Becca," Morgan offered. "Maybe a girls' night in with Disney and popcorn?"

Sydney smiled. "She'd love that."

They fell into easy conversation, and by the time their plates were cleared and Sydney left to go to the bathroom, Morgan was relaxed by her two amazing cocktails and some belly laughs. She didn't notice the man sliding onto the stool next to her until he leaned over and spoke. "Enjoying your night?"

She glanced over. Average height. Nice brown hair, dark eyes, and gold-rimmed glasses. The business suit and clean fingernails bespoke a businessman stopping on his way home for a drink. Morgan judged him completely harmless. "Yes, thank you."

He nodded. "How was your day?"

How nice. Most men she met would never ask such a question, especially in a bar. Not that she'd ever spoken to men in bars. Bars were places for women who made mistakes. Morgan never made mistakes.

"Good. How about yours?"

He gave a long sigh. "Bad. Lost a client. Stressed to the max. I'm looking for something to help me relax."

She clucked in sympathy. "Workaholic?"

"Absolutely. You?"

"Absolutely." What a nice glow humming within her. Thank goodness Sydney was driving or she'd need to take a cab. "Maybe we both need to find ways to have more fun."

"That would be nice. My name is Robert."

"Hi, Robert. I'm Morgan. What do you do?"

"I work in finance. Stocks. High profit equals high intensity. You?"

"I build houses for people."

He leaned forward, his brown eyes gleaming with interest behind the frames. "Interesting. *House* is your code word, huh?"

Puzzled by his question, and the secret game he seemed to be engaged in, she nodded. "Sure, if you say so. What's *your* code word?"

He grinned. "Oh, I love the word *house*. Great choice."

Uh, okay. Morgan figured he'd had a liquid lunch, but what the hell, he'd had a bad day. "You like helping others? Making them happy?" he asked.

Morgan smiled. "I never thought about it like that, but, yes, I like making people happy."

"By . . . building *houses*?"

"Mostly. I like to match up a client with their fantasy house. Their satisfaction is the most important."

"That's good. Satisfaction is very, very good for a client." He touched her hand gently, as if emphasizing his point. "These fantasy . . . *houses*. Are they expensive?"

"Definitely."

"So, if I asked you to build me a *house*, how much would you charge an hour?"

She scrunched up her face and thought. "Usually I don't charge by the hour. More like the entire project, depending on what you like, what you don't, and what I can provide."

"A real businesswoman, huh?"

"I guess."

"If you were forced to break down your fees, though, into an hourly wage, how much?"

This conversation was getting way too weird for her. She decided to just throw a figure at him. "A lot. I guess maybe around two hundred per hour."

The guy whistled. "That's a fancy house. What if I'm not happy after paying so much?"

She hiccuped. Put down her Rumba Martini and figured she'd order some water before leaving. What a lightweight. She bet Sydney and Raven could double her two glasses and never even sway on their feet. What had this man asked? Oh, satisfaction. "I've never had a client complain. I give you the best of everything in service and satisfaction. Trust me, you'll never have a better builder."

Robert gave a little laugh. "Boy, you're good at this. Okay, you sold me. Build me a house."

Oh, yeah, he was way drunk. Still, she felt sorry for him.

Poor man probably had no one to talk to. "You want me to build you a house, huh? When?" she teased.

His voice dropped. "Tonight. Right now. You in?"

Where the heck was Sydney? She looked around the bar. Raven was at the far end, trying to deal with the rowdy crew, and Sydney was nowhere to be found. She kind of wanted to leave and get away from this guy. "How long do I get to build it?"

"I'll give you the night. What the hell."

Morgan forced a laugh. "Build you a house in a night, huh? Yeah, sure. Why not?"

"Will five hundred do it?"

Morgan waved her hand in the air and finally got Raven's attention. Raven nodded and made a motion to bring over the bill. "Five hundred is fine."

"So, you're saying clearly we have a deal, Morgan? I pay you five hundred dollars, and you stay with me for the night?"

What had he said? Raven reached her and slid over the bill. Morgan fumbled for her purse, desperate to get some distance. No wonder her mother didn't want her to hang out in bars. Weird men frequented them. "Whatever you say, Robert. We have a deal."

As if. Morgan tossed some cash for Raven's tip on the bar and took out her Visa card.

"I'm glad you've been so accommodating. Made my job a hell of a lot easier."

His words still made no sense, so she basically ignored him. The click of Sydney's heels echoed over the plank floors and relief flooded through her. "Oh, there you are. I got the bill, and I'm ready to get out of here."

"I bet you are," Robert stated. "But you won't be building any houses tonight, sweetheart."

She cocked her head. "I'm afraid I still don't understand you."

Robert grinned and stood up. Opening up his suit jacket, he took out a pair of handcuffs and some black machine that looked like a recorder. Uh-oh. Was he going to try to blow up the bar? Oh, my God, he was a terrorist. Morgan thought furiously about her next move, but it was too late. He'd grabbed her wrist and locked a cuff around it. Cold satisfaction carved out his nondescript face. "You're under arrest."

Her mouth gaped open. Sydney shrieked. "Arrest? For *what*?" Morgan managed to yelp.

"Prostitution."

Raven whistled. "Dude, I had no idea. That's not cool in my bar."

Her mind spun, and she felt as if she'd stepped into a sci-fi movie that had gone straight to DVD. "I'm not a prostitute!" she yelled. "I build houses!"

"Sure you do. Let's go. I'm taking you to the station."

Sydney jumped in front of him. "You made a huge mistake, Officer. Let her go unless you want a lawsuit on your hands!"

The cop frowned and jerked his head at Sydney. "Wanna come, too? Just say the word."

Sydney gulped.

"Thought so."

As Morgan was dragged out of the bar, Sydney's voice echoed loudly behind her. "Don't worry, Morgan, I'll meet you at the police station—I'll fix this!"

Oh, this was very, very bad. The fake man named Robert settled her in the backseat, turned on the flashing lights, and drove. How was she going to explain this if anyone found out? Her mama would freak. The Rosenthals.

And Caleb Pierce.

chapter eleven

Caleb pulled up to the curb, got out of the truck, and watched her walk toward him.

Oh, she was pissed.

Royally pissed. Once again, he'd been wrong. Morgan Raines did have a temper, and it was a glorious thing to watch. Of course, if he'd been picked up for prostitution in error and dragged to a jail cell in front of Sydney and the whole bar, he'd be a bit cranky, too. But anger wasn't as sexy on him.

On her? Oh, yeah.

Her vanilla-colored skirt and matching lacy tank were a wrinkled mess. Caleb bet her hair had originally been up in some sleek hairstyle, but now it fell around her face in disheveled strands. She looked like she'd had a wild night of sex and rolled out of bed. Those baby blues were lasering firearms as she stalked toward him on ridiculously high heels, her lush bubble-gum lips twisted in a half sneer. Her fingers were curled into tight fists. Steam seemed to rise from her pores. Her normally pale skin was flushed a gorgeous pink, the same exact color he hoped she got when aroused. In those few seconds, he was hard and ready to go, and he was standing in front of a damn police station.

"What are you doing here?" she demanded. Damned if she didn't handle herself like the queen of England even fresh from the slammer. "I have a cab coming. Who told you?"

"Sydney called me. She wanted to come herself but had to get back to her daughter, so I told her I'd handle it. Are you okay?" He kept his voice soothing and low. For the first time, he didn't know what to expect from her. It was exciting as hell.

She hissed like a cat ready for a full-blown fight. "No, I'm not okay," she snapped. "I've been humiliated and called a whore! I kept telling him I built houses, for God's sake, and this idiot said I was using it as a code word for sex!"

He pressed his lips tight together. If he laughed, or even gave a tiny indication of humor, she might belt him. Southern women were not to be crossed at certain times, and this was one of them. "I'm sorry, I really am, but I spoke with the chief and the whole thing is being thrown out. It was a new guy on the force who wanted to prove himself, and he got carried away."

"Do I look like a whore to you, Caleb? Look at my outfit! I was having dinner with Sydney, minding my own business, and the next thing I know, I'm in a jail cell for telling him I'd build him a house for five hundred dollars!"

Her accent deepened when she got riled up. His lip twitched. Uh-oh. She stopped her rant, knitted her brows together, and nailed him with her gaze. "Do you think this is funny?" she whispered.

Caleb shook his head. Hard. "No, of course it's not funny. I'm still in shock. When Sydney called, I thought she was pulling a prank. It took her a while to finally convince me."

She jammed her finger into the middle of his chest. "If this leaks out, I'm going to have someone's ass in a sling. Does anyone else know?"

Was it possible he got even harder at her hint of violence? Man, he was messed up. Who knew so much fire burned underneath all that white? "No, it's not going in the blotter, and Sydney already called the bar owner to explain what happened. The chief reamed out Robert."

"I'm gonna sue the whole lot of them," she declared. "Why the hell wouldn't they listen to me? I told them I was working with Pierce Brothers."

He tried not to wince. "They thought you were lying. Robert was under the impression high-class call girls try to blend in and look conservative. He came from Kansas. Guess he doesn't know how it works out here."

She blew an aggravated breath between her teeth. "I'm calling my lawyer tomorrow. Right now, I need to get the hell out of here. I have the stink of prison on me. Let's go."

God, she was magnificent. How had he missed such layers before this? This woman was fierce.

She got into his truck and he drove. It was only after a few miles that he noticed her solid veneer hid a hairline fracture.

Small white teeth clamped down on her very bitable lower lip. Tiny tremors wracked her delicate shoulders, and her fingers twisted in her lap. Oh, yeah, she was about to crash. The night probably wrung her dry from the extreme ups and downs. He didn't want her to be alone in the hotel. He wondered if he could convince her to stay at his house. As far as he knew, other than Sydney, she had no friends in Harrington. No family. Of course, with her stubbornness, she'd fight him like a banshee, but he was gonna try.

Even though it was warm, he cranked up the heat and tried to make light conversation. "Did you have a nice dinner with Sydney?"

"Before my arrest? Yes. It was very nice."

Hmm, maybe normal conversation wouldn't work. Still, he tried again. "My brothers used to hang out at that bar you went to. Made the best burgers in the state. Closed down for a number of years. I was glad to see someone finally bought it. You didn't happen to have a burger, did you?"

She tossed him a suffering look of pure impatience. "Sydney had the burger. Personally, I don't think I'll be going back there again whether they put the Big Mac out of business. Maybe it's the whole prostitute thing, I don't know."

Ouch. Maybe he'd shut up until she realized he'd kind of kidnapped her. They spent the next fifteen minutes being quiet, and then her head spun back around. "Where are we?"

"My house."

"I don't see the Hilton."

Her acerbic wit cut right into him. "I thought you could crash here tonight in the guest room. Hang out with me for a bit. My place is so much better than a hotel."

"Do you have a concierge, cook, and maid service? Spa tub, steam shower, and private balcony?"

"No."

"Your brothers live here with you, too, right?"

He gave a sigh. "Yeah, but we never see each other. We have eight guest rooms."

She seemed to struggle with her decision. Damn, she looked tired, but as usual, her stubbornness won. "Better pass. I'll be fine."

He could argue and try to make her stay. Hell, he craved a good fight with her and hoped the experience led to making up in bed. He imagined Morgan naked and writhing beneath him while he punished her for tormenting him. But tonight she needed something he doubted she saw too much of. Gentleness.

He reached out slowly and cupped her jaw. Running a thumb over her bitten lip, he watched her pupils dilate with surprise and something much more interesting. Something he knew he needed to explore further. "I'm not trying to be an asshole. I know you'll be fine. But you had a hell of a night, and I don't want you to be alone. I'm asking for me, Morgan. I won't touch you. You can get a good night's sleep, and I promise to make you a great breakfast in the morning. Deal?"

She studied him for a while with those baby blues. Caleb ached to bend his head and finally taste her, but it wasn't the time or the place. "What if people talk?"

He grinned. "Princess, no one's gonna talk. I promise you, I'll take care of it."

She considered. Cal knew if she insisted on going back to the hotel, he'd obey and just sleep outside her door. Finally she nodded. "I guess. Okay. I like French toast."

"Cut out the French part and replace it with butter. Then I got you covered."

She grinned. He led her inside, keeping the door half-shut to block the brigade about to run her down. "Remember not to panic. They're all bark and no bite." Then he stepped inside.

The joyous howl hit his ear right before two strong bodies were upon him. He tried desperately to stave off the disaster. "Gandalf, Balin, down! Down!"

Their paws skidded on the slick floors inches before him, but it was too late. They slid full force, and he jerked back with a *hmmph*. The dogs took that for approval, and then it was a free-for-all, with lashing tongues and eager head butts. He repeated the "Down!" command a few more times until finally they both managed to get off him.

Damn. They'd already flunked out of obedience school. Should he try again?

Morgan peeked around the doorframe. "Is it safe?"

He grabbed on to their collars. "Never, but come on in."

She walked over to them with such tentative curiosity, he knew she'd never been around animals. She stuck out both hands in an awkward greeting. Balin and Gandalf recognized her scent and tried to bolt toward her. Caleb hung on for dear life. "Just pet their heads or something. They're dying to say hello."

She smiled and rubbed their ears, murmuring softly. They calmed down at her touch, and he was able to let go. Her face gentled, and a glowing warmth seemed to emanate from her as she wrapped herself in their canine presence. "They're so sweet," she said. Balin bumped her nose and gave her a hearty lick. Was that a giggle, or had he heard incorrectly? "Are they always so loving?"

"Yeah, they pretty much live for affection. My father hated dogs, but once I found these two goofballs I knew they were meant for me. Christian never admitted it, but I think they even ended up charming him. I caught him once with Balin's head in his lap. Let me take them outside first, and then I'll show you where you can sleep tonight."

He kept the potty visit short and refused to let Gandalf investigate a crackle in the woods. His obsession with squirrels was a definite problem. Finally, Cal took her upstairs.

He decided to give her the gold room. It seemed to fit her, with its warm tapestries balanced with earthy creams. A bit vintage, with an antique brass bed, French spindled furniture, and delicate lace curtains. The matching master bath held a claw-foot tub plus a steam shower. He pointed to the dresser. "There's a mishmash of clothes in there. I'm sure you can find a T-shirt in your size." He motioned toward the bath. "Its fully stocked with anything you need. We keep a few rooms ready for guests."

"This is amazing," she said, her gaze sweeping over the room. "Who designed this house?"

"My mom," he clipped out. "She had good taste. I'll be down in the kitchen for a while if you need anything."

"Thanks, Caleb."

Their gazes met and locked. His chest tightened, so he cleared his throat and broke contact. "Welcome."

Caleb left her alone, retreated to the kitchen, and refilled the dogs' water bowls. What was her real story? The more time he spent with her, the more he wanted to know. There seemed to be a richness behind her facade that he craved to explore, from her cool control, to her hot temper, to her gentle heart. She'd befriended Sydney. Loved his dogs. Held the respect and affection of his brothers and crew. Yet, she had no real home of her own. No lover. No long-term friends. Why? Did she hold secrets or a dark past? Or was she simply career-driven and enjoyed having no ties? Either way, he respected and admired her.

Now, though, he wanted to know her.

Caleb collected a few dirty mugs and Hershey wrappers, cursing Dalton's messiness. Then he moved Tristan's laptops from the countertop to the table. The guy had about four of them, and they cluttered every room. He shared a roof with his brothers but didn't see them much. He'd thought after their long talk on the porch they would spend more time together, but it seemed they were on different schedules. Last time they actually sat together was to watch a baseball game on a rare empty Sunday afternoon.

A faded memory sprung to life.

Junior league. He'd been damn good at baseball, racking up some trophies and acquiring a nice curveball and sinker as a relief pitcher. Decent at bat, too. He'd been hanging with his friends to check out Dalton's game, which was a few hours after his. Cal remembered the taste of hot dogs and Coke, the sting of the sun on the bleachers, the solid smack of the ball against the bat.

When Dalton got up to bat, they were losing by two in the final inning, down to the last out. Cal surged to his feet with Tristan, and they cheered him on. The intensity and pride on Dalton's face told him how important it was to be the game winner. To finally be able to go home to their father and say he was good at something.

Dalton struck out, and they lost the game.

Cal had a date that night. Tristan had plans with his friends. They cut out on both promises and stayed home with Dalton. That night, his mother cooked a huge meal and baked fresh apple pie. She got out the old photo albums, and they spent the night sifting through memories, eating pie, and sharing laughs.

He remembered that night she sat on the edge of his bed and spoke words he'd never forgotten, almost as if she knew one day they'd be battling to get back to one another.

There is nothing more important in this world than blood. Your brothers are part of you, and your soul won't be complete without them. Make sure you take care of each other, but more important, make sure you forgive each other . . .

"Caleb?"

He spun around. She shifted her bare feet, tugging down the oversize navy T-shirt that held the Pierce Brothers logo. It was so long, she'd chosen not to put on any bottoms, and her legs remained bare. She'd scrubbed her face clean, and he spotted the faint freckles scattered over her nose, the natural pink of her lips, the soft gleam of white skin under the kitchen light. Lust hit him fast and hard, taking him down faster than Mayweather could punch. An overwhelming primitive need to growl and pin her beneath his body blasted him in waves. Holy crap, he'd never felt this intense before. Especially when a woman stood in front of him with no trappings, looking a bit vulnerable from the evening's chaos. Caleb tamped down on his inner beast and tried to keep his hands busy.

"Good, you found something to put on. Are you hungry? Thirsty?"

A ghost of a smile slid over her lips. "You're such a proper host. No, I'm good. I just wanted to thank you."

He lifted a brow. "Can I record this?"

She gave a deep sigh. He tried really hard not to stare at her breasts straining against the faded shirt. "No, I mean it. It was very sweet of you to offer your house. I just hate to be a bother. I can take care of myself."

He nodded. "I never doubted that, Morgan. But sometimes it's okay to lean on people, too. I know we had our ups and downs, but you're part of the team. We look out for each other."

"Like your brothers?"

"Yeah." He thought about the tangled mess he and his brothers had made of their relationship. He wondered how to fix it. Wondered if it could ever be fixed.

Maybe he needed to step up and try again. A meal shared might go a long way toward them having some fun together. God knows they used to make him laugh, from Tristan's dry wit to Dalton's rowdy pranks. Sure, they'd fight, but before the epic falling-out, they'd been close most of the time.

Curiosity filled her voice. "Why don't you and your brothers get along?"

A personal question, but he gave her points for trying. Funny, he realized he was rarely alone with Morgan. Other than the night he kissed her, they were always surrounded by workers and teams and salespeople. For now, in his mother's kitchen, late at night, he relaxed a bit. Caleb never spoke about his personal business or family history. But damned if the craziest stuff didn't pour out of his mouth like he was one of the fucking real housewives and loved to gossip. "Dalton slept with my fiancée. Tristan hates me because he thinks I froze him out of the business and forced him to leave."

Her tiny gasp hit the mark. She wanted honesty? Fine. There. He just hoped she could deal with it.

He watched the emotions flicker over her face. She took her time responding, but when she spoke, she sounded calm. "Did he really sleep with your fiancée? Did he fall in love with her?"

"Nah, he wanted to prove a point."

"Did you love her?"

He stiffened. Holy crap, this was getting deep. Did he love Felicia? Ever? Yes, in his own way. As a boy, not a man. Not that he'd ever admit it to Dalton. "Yes, I did. But looking back, it wasn't the kind of love that could last. It wasn't the real kind."

"What's the real kind like?"

Energy swirled between them. He began loading the dishwasher to distract himself from his raging hard-on. "I don't know. I guess the kind that grows as you age. The kind that can handle daily stress, and kids, and work schedules. Felicia was excited about marrying into the family business. I think she liked the fact that I'm successful rather than who I really am."

A dark cloud passed over her face. He'd hit a nerve somehow but wasn't sure what it was. "Do you know who you really are?" Morgan asked.

"I think so. I'm not the kind of man who will ever like big parties, kissing people's asses to make a buck, and anything with fancy frills or empty meaning. I like building houses, having a few beers with friends, and hanging with my dogs. I have a temper, but I don't think I'm unfair. I can apologize. I don't like to lie. I don't like to waste time. I'm boring."

Her lower lip trembled. She took a tentative step forward. "*Boring* would never be a word I'd use to describe you," she said softly. "Felicia was an idiot."

He laughed then. Damn, he liked her style. "Dalton said he wanted to prove that exact point. Still wish he'd done it another way."

"Did you really drive Tristan away or was it a misunderstanding?"

Caleb thought about it. He'd gone over and over the scene a million times before, always seeing the truth to his side of the story. But right now he wondered if Tristan had seen it completely differently no matter how many times he'd tried to explain. "I didn't think so at the time. But he did."

That was all he really wanted to give her. His ears burned red. He'd never told a woman the real truth about his family's past, let alone a woman who drove him nuts and knew how to sneak past his defenses. Maybe he'd truly gone around the crazy bend.

She bowed her head as she studied the Italian tile floor. "I don't have any siblings," she finally offered. "So I can't judge or give advice. I do know many times I wished for siblings to bring more messes into my life. Blood is blood. Kind of like land. They're not making any more of it, so you have to deal with what's out there already."

Her analysis startled him on a level deeper than he had time to ponder. Right now, he craved more knowledge about her. "How about your parents? Are you close?"

A soft smile lit her face. His heart did a slow flip-flop, then settled. "Yes. We're very close, and they've always supported me. Through good and bad."

"Yet you didn't want to stay in Charleston?"

"No. Once, I thought everything I wanted was in Charleston. I had my path perfectly planned out. But then I realized I had to create something different, so I left."

"What happened to keep you from staying?"

"Life," she said simply. "Things changed. So I changed, too. And I have no regrets."

They fell silent. The kitchen clock ticked. The dogs whimpered.

Cal nodded. "Then I guess you know yourself, too."

Morgan looked up. He gazed into her eyes, and suddenly he was choking with more than lust. No, deep in those blue depths he found a raw emotion and heat that sucked him in. Made him want to take her in his arms and protect her from hurt. She made him want to be her conqueror of all evil and injustice in the world, and damned if that didn't scare him worse than the Beelzebub himself.

Balin and Gandalf bumped his hip with their heads. Their faces reflected impatience for their nighttime treat. He cleared his throat, closed the dishwasher, and wiped his hands. "Okay, guys. Treat time?"

They did their ridiculous dance of canine ecstasy. Morgan laughed. "Can I give it to them?"

"Sure." He reached into the canister and handed her two biscuits. "Balin gets a little eager, so make sure he's sitting completely before you give it to him."

Lips curved in an excited smile, she turned to the dogs. "Sit."

Then it happened.

He'd forgotten to warn her.

Gandalf dropped to the ground with a soft thud. Head back, tongue hanging out of his mouth, he played dead in the ridiculous way he always did to get his treat. Problem was, Cal was so used to his fake death, he recognized the game.

Not Morgan.

With a heartfelt cry, she watched the dog fall onto the tile. "Oh, my God, he fainted! I hurt him!" She flung herself on top of Gandalf's body and clutched at tufts of fur, trying to rouse him. Balin wanted in on the game, so he jumped on Morgan, tumbling her back in a tangle of limbs as she fought for purchase, until she was surrounded in a wriggling blanket of fur.

Cal cursed at the ridiculousness of the situation. "Gandalf, dammit, treat! Get up!"

Gandalf opened one eye, delighted at Morgan's reaction, and came back to life in time to snap up the treat as Cal tossed it in the air.

Morgan gasped as the dog reared back up, his tail thumping her in the face, and Cal dragged them both off her.

He dropped to his knees on the floor beside her. "It's just a game. Gandalf likes to play dead to get a treat. I forgot to tell you."

Her gaze narrowed. Sparks shot from her blue eyes. She sat, legs sprawled out, arms braced behind her, T-shirt riding up her thighs and exposing a pair of cream-colored lace panties. He was getting attached to the color white, and the sight of the virginal fabric made him ache to do very bad things. He tried to focus on her face. "Are you okay?"

She reached out and fisted a handful of his shirt. Her pink lips curled. "You forgot to tell me your dog likes to drop to the floor and play dead? I thought he had a heart attack."

Humor struck. For the second time that night, Caleb figured it would not be wise to laugh. Balin got tired of waiting for his turn and snatched up the second treat that had fallen onto the floor. The two sensed a change in the air and trotted out of the kitchen, satisfied at the outcome of the evening.

He tamped down his mirth. He'd laugh later. "I forgot you weren't used to animals. My bad."

She ground her teeth so loud, she gave him some competition. His shirt crumpled tighter under her grip. "Your bad? You know what, Caleb Pierce? I think you found this whole thing amusing. I think you've been silently laughing at me this whole time under the guise of trying to help. I think you did this on purpose!"

His gaze narrowed. "Now, why the hell would I do that?" he growled. "Think that's a smart way to get you in my bed, or do you really think I'm an idiot?"

She panted hard, and he leaned in. Their breath mingled, and he caught the scent of clean peppermint, the tightening of her nipples against the thin fabric, the way her pupils dilated when she was turned on. And yeah, she was turned on, and this time he didn't have the strength to back off and make proper conversation or polite excuses.

Game on.

"You are an idiot if you think by heaven or hell you'd get me into bed. Look at us! We're totally different. We'd kill each other."

"Nah, we'd be too busy fucking each other."

Her sharp intake of breath was sexy as hell. He'd pushed, but so had she, and it was time to sample what he'd been fantasizing about for a while. Her lower lip trembled, and she practically hissed with catlike spite, but Caleb sensed the arousal underneath and her desperate need to not think anymore. The pink flush of her skin, her hard nipples, the trembling of her hands, the musky scent between her thighs. Had she ever had a man just take what he wanted from her? Or was she so used to proper, she'd forgotten how much fun it was to be uncivilized?

"You—you—you're so crude!"

He laughed low and tangled his fingers in her hair. Twisting firmly, he held her head and tugged back. "That the best you got?" he asked. He pressed a kiss to her temple, teasing, then one to her cheek. Her skin burned, telling him she liked it.

"You—you—you're a Neanderthal!"

He nipped the sensitive curve of her neck, tugged on her earlobe. The whole time she shook underneath him, not pushing him away, telling him she needed this dominance for a moment to get out of her head. "Not much better. We've both been thinking about this for a long time, sweetheart, ever since we kissed. I know you had a bad night, but I can make it better."

She sucked in her breath, and a moan caught in her

throat as he pressed light, teasing kisses over her cheek. "That's a terrible line. Awful. I deserve better."

God, he loved that prim and proper tone. Having her say dirty things to him in that voice was his secret fantasy. But the time for fun and games was over, because he had to taste her again. Now.

"I promised I wouldn't touch you."

She stilled under his hands. Tension crackled in the air. He waited a beat.

"I lied."

With one firm pull, he drew her head back and crushed his lips to hers.

Cal never had a chance. She engulfed him with her scent and touch and flavor, and he surrendered to the experience without a fight. Opening her lips without hesitation, she took each thrust of his tongue with heat and passion and gave it all back. Being devoured like he was every fantasy she had, his head spun at her honest, raw reaction to his kiss. Her arms wrapped tight around his back, holding him to her; he made a primitive moan and released her head to grip her hips, pulling her hard against his erection.

She went crazy under him, rocking her hips, digging her nails into his upper shoulders, and kissing him back with a seething hunger he'd never experienced, as if she were drowning and he was the one to save her, making him feel like the fucking hero of every comic book out there.

God, he wanted more.

Swallowing her whimpers, he slid one hand under her T-shirt and hit bare skin. Thanking heaven above for the gift, he stroked her breast, tweaking a hard nipple with his thumb, cupping the glorious weight in his palm. Like he was plugged into a generator, she lit up under his touch, arching beneath every stroke until he pushed her down to the floor to lie flat, with every intention of ripping off her shirt, tugging down her panties, and taking her right here, right now, until neither of them remembered their names.

"Ah, shit! Sorry!"

The familiar male voice rang out, but it took a while for Cal to process. He was too deep in the moment, with a head stuffed with cotton and a raging erection from the woman beneath him. Nothing mattered except his readiness to dive deep and forget about anything else but claiming her for his.

But Morgan stiffened beneath him, going so still, he wondered if she'd become a statue. And then it hit him.

Son of a bitch. Tristan was home.

Slowly, he tugged down her shirt, removed his hand, and shifted so he covered most of the view. "It's past midnight. Why are you here?"

Tristan slapped his hand over his eyes and backed away from the counter. "I'm not here. Go back to what you were doing, I didn't see a thing. Hi, Morgan."

Her voice came out strangled. "Hi, Tristan."

"I came for my wine. Umm, is there leftover peach pie?"

Cal let out an irritated breath. "I ate it."

"Dude, I only had a piece."

"Dalton ate most of it. There's a bag of Ruffles in the pantry. Take that instead, then go."

His brother ducked his head to grab the bag of chips, keeping his eyes covered the whole time. This was ridiculous. The mood was completely broken, and he was screwed in an entirely new way. The bad way. Not the good way.

"Is there dip?"

"Tristan!"

"Sorry, I'm sorry, I'm gone. Carry on."

His brother disappeared with the chips and a bottle of very expensive red. Okay, how was he gonna save this situation? "Sweetheart, let me—"

She threw her hand up in the air, halting him midsentence. "No, Cal, don't. I've gotten arrested for prostitution, thought I hurt a dog, made out with my business partner on the kitchen floor, and found myself half-naked in a compromising position by your brother. I'm exhausted, embarrassed, confused, and still turned on from one of the best kisses I've ever had. I'm going to bed. Alone. See you in the morning."

Pivoting on her bare heel, head held high like Queen Elizabeth, she stalked out and left him alone.

Cal grinned. Best kiss ever, huh?

Oh, yeah. Morgan Raines was gonna be a hell of a lot of trouble. But also a hell of a lot of fun.

chapter twelve

Morgan dragged in a deep breath and climbed out of the car. Gripping her clipboard way too tight, she tried to calm her galloping heart. With each step toward Caleb, the events of that night roared in her memory in vivid, blasting neon.

His body pinning hers. Legs tangled, mouths fused, that delicious pounding heat between her legs that drowned out every reasonable thought. She'd wanted to give him anything and everything, everywhere and every way. When was the last time she'd ever felt so needed? Like she was the only thing in the world that would slake his hunger? That type of power was addictive. And it had only been a kiss. If he took her to bed, would she lose not only her body but her mind? Soul? And, God forbid, her heart?

She shivered in the blast of sun. She'd played with the idea of engaging in an affair, but after that kiss, Morgan changed her mind. It was too complicated. She wasn't a gambler with her love life. How bad she craved to be one of those kick-ass, fearless women who could take her pleasure and walk away in a few months unscarred.

But she wasn't. She couldn't lie to herself. If she took Cal as her lover, he'd end up sneaking past her defenses, and they'd both end up hurt. The project would eventually suffer—how could it not? Regret flooded her but there was no other way to protect herself. Better to know and accept her limitations than leap for something that would only cause pain. Her job forced her to live like a nomad, and she liked it. At the end of the project, what if she got attached to Cal? How would she handle it? Even worse, the possibility that she'd fall for him and he'd walk away without a backward glance sliced deep. No, the gamble held bad odds. She had four months left to build this house and needed to focus. Involving herself in a fling with a man who could snatch her heart wasn't wise.

She reached the site. Her mouth dried up as she watched him swipe his forehead and stride toward her. Strands of umber hair fell messily over his forehead and stuck up in odd places. His navy-blue T-shirt was damp with sweat, his muscles solid and tanned from the endless sun. Worn jeans hugged every hard curve with loving efficiency. Now she knew how good those thighs felt pressing her body to the hard ground. His gunmetal eyes glowed fierce and hot, touching her with their gaze, reminding her of every hidden place his fingers had stroked.

He stopped in front of her and scowled. Those full lips turned down. "You snuck out. Didn't even let me make you breakfast."

Morgan tried nonchalance. "I had a lot to do."

"How'd you get home?"

She blinked. "Cab."

He leaned in. His jaw tightened. "I got worried. I would've driven you home."

She loved his masculine code of chivalry, but she was used to taking care of herself. She'd freaked out a bit over the kiss. It was as if they'd formed a tight bond that went beyond a simple make-out session. The hotel seemed a much better place to wake up in. "Worried I didn't get to sample your five-star French toast breakfast?"

He studied her face, then shook his head. Muttered under his breath something about stubborn women. "I'm sorry about my brother. Sorry if I pushed too far. I lose my head around you."

Fascinated, she tilted her head to study his gorgeous face. No man had ever said anything like that to her before. She wasn't a woman to inspire mad lust or impulsive kitchen-floor sex. "Is that a line?"

"I'll prove it tonight. I'm cooking you dinner."

She jerked back. "Tonight doesn't work. I'm busy."

His lower lip tugged. "No, you aren't. Six p.m. We need to talk about some things."

"I'm not sleeping with you," she burst out. Then clapped her hand over her mouth. No, she hadn't said it aloud. Had she? Was she insane?

He looked delighted at the outburst. "Fine. But you're eating with me."

She squirmed. God, she wanted to. God, she didn't. "Can you actually cook?"

"Yes. Don't worry, I'll satisfy you."

Morgan frowned. "What an awful innuendo. I expected better of you."

His tiny grin widened. "When I'm ready to prove that, there won't be any innuendo involved, princess. Just action."

Her stomach dropped to her toes. "Says you."

He laughed out loud then, shaking his head. "Don't take on a challenge you're fated to lose. Oh, I have something for you."

Curious, she watched him head to where he'd dropped his bag with his lunch pail and fish around in it. Finally he drew out a familiar green-and-white bag that held the very essence of her own Kryptonite.

Sour cream and onion potato chips.

Her heart galloped in her chest. Her palms sweat. He walked back and handed her the evil gift. "Here you go. Figured you could have it with your lunch today and won't need to fight me for them."

Morgan swallowed hard. Stared at the bag. "You shouldn't have," she choked out.

He frowned. "What's the matter? Thought you loved chips."

Oh, God, she did. So much. Her mantra rose in her head and crashed over her. *Don't eat the chips . . . Don't eat the chips . . .*

How could she say no? It would be rude. She'd just hold them and think about eating them. She didn't *have* to eat them. The gesture of the gift told her what type of man Caleb Pierce was. He paid attention. He liked to please, even as much as he liked to fight with her. It was an intoxicating combination.

"Morgan?"

She fought off the voices and slowly took the bag. Her

fingers trembled slightly, and a rustling sound filled the air. "Thank you," she managed. "That was very . . . nice of you."

"I can be nice." His eyes darkened. "Very, very nice."

She fought the blush. Hard. It was time to steer this conversation away from chips and sex. "Maybe we should get back to the business at hand? Are we ready for the inspector?"

His amusement should've pissed her off. Somehow it didn't. The confidence of this primitive male trying to secure a date with her pleased her way too much. "We're ready. Drywall is set to go, and we're working on insulation."

"Good." Excitement shimmered as she looked at the shell before her. Already the main guts of her new baby was done. They'd gotten through the electrical and plumbing inspections, and now the house was fully wrapped with the roofing, shingles, sewer lines, and main plumbing completed. Sure, it had been a bit of a scare when the HVAC unit hadn't worked and they'd lost a day reinstalling and tearing it apart. And the stones they originally ordered to replace the shingles had been lost and wouldn't be delivered on time. The three days of pouring rain had caused some minor flooding, forcing them to slow down, and the blistering argument with Tristan and the tile supplier over gouging prices and wrong deliveries had been a challenge. But they were finally moving forward and had made up precious time. Once the framing inspection cleared, the house she imagined in her dreams would be a step closer to reality. The skeleton before her was just that—bones and organs that made up the heart of the house. The flesh emerged slowly, as if a drawing where hair and clothes and body shape came into view and the onlooker saw the full beauty of the completion. Her blood warmed, and a surge of adrenaline grabbed her in its delicious grip, confirming once again this job she had chosen was more than just work—it was a part of her soul. Trusting her to make such an individual vision a reality was a humbling gift, and she never forgot it.

Cal smiled as if he knew how the house affected her, and tugged on her hand. "Come on. Zach's here."

They went to greet Zach Griffin, a grizzled, booming bear of a man with crooked teeth, short black hair, and staggering height. Built like a quarterback, he was sharp, relentless, and honest. Morgan knew Cal respected him for refusing to take payoffs in his job and for making some very unpopular decisions. He was adored by the majority of the town and loathed by the rest. Another research tip she'd unearthed when making her decision to choose a builder. A bad relationship with the inspector was like rolling the dice at roulette. Morgan didn't like playing that way.

"Hey, Zach. Good to see you."

Morgan watched the inspector's face harden. His usual relaxed demeanor had been replaced by a hard, accusatory light in his sea-green eyes. Huh. Weird: supposedly he and Cal had always had a tight relationship. He nodded curtly. "Cal."

Instead of spending a few seconds bullshitting, Zach stalked past them and inside the house, beginning the walk-through and making notes on his paper. An odd tension vibrated in the air, and she shot Cal a worried look. Catching it, Cal cleared his throat and tried to make conversation.

"Busy this season, huh? Any time for vacation?"

Zach didn't answer. Just grunted and scribbled, occasionally touching the frames, checking sealants around the windows and doors, getting on his knees by the front foyer stairs and pulling out a measuring tape.

Uh-oh. This was serious.

Morgan had been through hundreds of inspections and knew there was sometimes a game involved. If the inspector wanted to be a hard-ass, he or she could insist items be redone to meet code, but there was a large gray area to be played with. Fortunately, Pierce Brothers didn't cut corners, and Morgan had been personally impressed with the amount of effort and time Cal put into every inch of the house, insisting on starting over on certain things even when it cost them time.

Zach stopped by the upper loft entryway Brady had convinced her to change for a more startling look. "Where's the beam for support here?" he snapped out. Shuffling through his plans and mass of papers, he shook his head.

Cal gave him a puzzled look. "No beam needed here, Zach. Brady changed the original plans, they were approved, and we moved this wall so we wouldn't need a beam here. See?" Cal motioned to her, and Morgan slipped the finalized copy into his hands so he could hand it to Zach.

Zach ignored him. "Not in my copies. Needs a beam."

Sweat prickled on her forehead. No. This wasn't happening.

"It's an open loft. Here, look." He shoved the paper at Zach.

The man barely glanced at it, then shut his folder. Zach's gaze held disgust as he looked up. "Never had an issue with your work before, Cal, but since your father died and those brothers of yours came back, work's getting sloppy. Put in a beam or get me new plans to approve and I'll come back."

Morgan stepped forward with a smile. "I'm sure it's just a paperwork snafu, Mr. Griffin," she offered. "I can call the office right now and fix it."

"Sorry, I'm done here."

Cal moved toward the door to block his exit. "Zach, is something else going on? First off, you know my work and reputation. It's obvious to both of us no beam is needed, and if I put it in, we'd block up the room for no reason. Here, let's go over it."

"I don't need to go over it, Cal. You'll have to call my office and schedule another inspection before you move any further."

Morgan tried to keep calm, furiously running over the schedule in her head. "Okay, I'm sure we can have you back out tomorrow to fix this."

His smile was pure mean. "Going on vacation for two weeks, so my office is closed. Maybe the first of the month I can get here."

Cal shook his head. "Zach, we can't lose that much time. I'm asking you to do me a favor here and work with me. Let me get Julie on the phone to find out what happened."

"My assistant won't be able to help. As for favors, keep them. Your brother has already done enough."

Warning bells clanged loudly, but Cal was already ahead of her. "My brother? Who?"

The man struck as quick as a seagull snatching food. "Dalton. Seems he took a liking to my youngest daughter,

Ashley. Also seems he's a lying, cheating scumbag who promised her a relationship and took advantage. Does he think he's too good for her? Maybe he gets away with that crap in California, but it doesn't work in my town." He threw his head back and glared. "Ashley's a good girl. Spent all night crying her eyes out because she thought she was in a relationship. Makes me sick. Is that the type of man your brother's become? If so, you can tell him to stay away from her or I'll beat him to a pulp."

Morgan gasped as the inspector marched past Cal and out the door.

"Zach, I'll talk to him. I swear I knew nothing about it. I'll set him straight. Don't take his mistakes out on me or this project. It's important."

Zach grunted. "I like you, Cal. I always did. And I know the trouble you've been in since Christian's death. But your company is called Pierce Brothers. He's part of it now, and it's time to take responsibility."

"I can get another inspector," Cal threw out.

"Good luck. I put in a few calls, and seems they're all out on vacations, too."

Zach left, leaving a shattering silence behind him.

Morgan was used to dealing with a variety of disasters on- and off-site, but for the first time, she didn't kick into fix-it-now-or-die mode. Instead, she watched the emotions flicker over Cal's face, slowly walked over to him, and tentatively laid a hand on his muscled arm. He flinched under her touch. "Are you okay?"

He let out a shuddering breath. "Yeah. I'm going to fix this."

"I know. Do you need any help?"

A grim smile curved his lips. "Kicking my brother's ass? Nah, I got this one."

He reached for the cell phone.

The familiar smells of varnish, wood, and sawdust hit his nostrils. The music rose to his ears, his brother's favorite wussy pop rock tunes Cal couldn't stand, and he stood studying Dalton in the woodshed he'd converted into his own personal castle. The workbench was set up nearby with an elaborate console table, currently stripped down to the grain. He had watched his brother work many times before, and always held a respect for the way he was able to coax wood into something like high art, a beautiful piece for a person to treasure and pass down for generations. Dalton's fingers danced over the flat surfaces, scraping the material down with a rhythmic precision that matched the tune. Dear God, was that One Direction? Cal winced with embarrassment for both of them. His father would've called him out for humiliation if he ever heard. They'd all had their turns under Christian's blistering tongue, but Dalton would take it the hardest. The resentment in his gaze had slowly grown to epic proportions, until only their mother was able to soothe the angry beast. Now all they had was each other, and Cal doubted they'd ever mend fences with no peacemaker in sight.

Cal turned off the music and waited. His brother stopped his sanding motions and turned his head. Messy blond waves framed his face, giving him an angelic look that always startled an onlooker, especially women, urging them to trust his charming words and lopsided grin.

"You just couldn't keep your dick in your pants, could you?"

Dalton unfurled himself from his kneeling position, stretching his arms over his head with a lazy lion's grace. Wariness crossed his features, but he showed no weakness. Another lesson well taught under their father's tutelage. "My dick in trouble again, bro? What'd I do now?"

Rage flicked at his nerve endings, but Cal swore he'd be an adult. He would not punch his brother today. He would be calm, and controlled, and not act out on the need to communicate in a physical manner. "I had a meeting with Zach Griffin today."

"Yeah. For the framing, right?"

"Right. He said we need a structural beam for the main living area."

Dalton frowned. "I thought Brady redesigned the plans. Sydney filed them with the inspector's office. No beam is needed."

"That's what I said. Imagine my surprise when Zach told me about his daughter Ashley and her so-called relationship with you."

The light went on in his brother's blue-gray eyes. Oh, yeah, the bastard knew what the real problem was. "Ashley? The pretty blonde with the curves? That's his daughter?"

"Yep. Not that you waited to know much about her or her family when you tumbled her for a night, then dumped her."

Dalton threw his hands up. "Slow down, dude. Ashley

and I met at the tavern and hit it off. I never promised her anything long-term."

"Funny, 'cause she thinks you did. Unless her idea of long-term is an actual date, and you ditched her after you got into her pants."

Dalton crossed his arms. "Why are you so obsessed with my sex life? I like women. Women like me. When I take one to bed, she knows exactly what the deal is, and most of the time comes back for more. Ashley and I met at the tavern, hit it off, and went back to her place. I told her I'd call but didn't say when. How was I supposed to know her father would get involved? Besides, that's unprofessional. Get another inspector."

Cal ground his teeth. "There is no one else. Zach made sure of it. And if you paid attention to anything but wood and women, you'd know to keep your damn hands off anyone related to my business!"

"Our business. Pierce Brothers. My personal life has nothing to do with work."

"Oh, yes it does. When it affects this project and causes problems with our deadline, your personal life is very much my business. If we don't get Zach back out here pronto and make him feel better about this situation, we'll lose two weeks, which we can't afford. God, when are you gonna grow up, Dalton?"

Fury leaped into his brother's eyes. Like a pissed-off stallion, he practically reared up and snarled, getting in his face. "When I'm treated like a partner and not some annoyance. When I'm finally respected and asked questions rather than told by a fucking drill sergeant when my projects are due. When I'm invited to business meetings instead of to the bar after work."

"You don't think I want that?" Cal tunneled his fingers through his hair and held on to his temper. "Dude, that's my dream. I don't want to do this alone. I thought we were going to be a team, but Tristan is still off tinkering with real estate, and you're taking on odd jobs to work on cabinets, and I'm stuck building this house that we only have four months left on. I'm going to lose everything if this house isn't done. I've been waiting for you to step up, but if I keep waiting, hell's not just gonna freeze over, it's gonna turn into the Arctic!"

Dalton began to pace the woodshed, his body vibrating with tension. "*We'll* lose everything, Cal! Not you—us. I may not want to be here, but this is Mom's company, and no way do I want to lose it. I'm tired of asking you to treat me like a full partner. You're so used to doing everything alone, I don't know if you're truly capable of letting us help anymore. You block us at every turn."

Cal glowered. "What are you talking about?"

"Tristan and I both tried a bunch of times to be on the site. You tie him up with suppliers and accounting, then double-check everything he does. When Morgan and I decide on aspects of the cabinetry, you want to sign off on it first. We know how to build, Cal. Instead, you depleted your team and have us doing errands to suppliers a competent office assistant can handle. You give us this big lecture about being a family and helping each other, but you're still a one-man show."

No way. His brother was wrong. "Bull. You like to pick

and choose what parts of this company you want to be involved in. I'm sorry, some jobs just aren't that glamorous."

Dalton glared. "Tristan and I can also grow this company, but you refuse to listen. You don't get it. Maybe you'll never get it. Or maybe you're just exactly like Dad."

Cal stiffened. The hurt cut as nasty as a paper cut, except through his heart rather than flesh. Never. He'd die before he became another Christian Pierce. Coldness replaced the hurt until he was able to gaze back at his brother in complete control. "And maybe you'd just be a big disappointment to Mom."

Dalton sucked in a breath. Guilt punched through Cal. Everyone knew Dalton had been Mom's favorite. She'd doted on the baby of the family, especially since Christian treated Dalton like a screwup. It was as if they'd been a team against their father, protecting each other from his scorpion sting.

Learning that Mom had packed her bags to leave Christian on that fateful day she was killed haunted them all. Something died in his brother along with Mom, like his foundation cracked and could never be repaired. He'd stuck around for Cal's engagement, but when Cal discovered his brother's betrayal, Dalton had quickly left along with Tristan. In one swoop, Cal had lost his mother, fiancée, and two brothers.

Dammit, he hadn't wanted this. He didn't want to go another round with his brother. Why couldn't he find that bond they'd had when they were young? When each of them could finish the other's sentences and long nights were spent sharing dreams and secrets. His brothers had been his world, his safety net, the only thing that made sense to him. Now he looked upon strangers, and he hated every second of it.

"Dalton, I'm sorry. I didn't mean it."

Dalton refused to meet his gaze. "Yeah, you did. Whatever. Mom's gone, and she's not coming back. You want me to be your trained seal for the next few months and build your house? Fine. Just tell me what you want and when you want it. I'll show up and be a good boy. But don't pretend we're something we're not. Don't pretend we mean more to you than the company, or that you want us to stay. Because we both know the truth."

Misery settled on his shoulders. How had this all gone so wrong? He'd been in the right, and now Dalton was twisting everything to get out of trouble. Cal tightened his lips and refused to back down. "What are you going to do about the mess you made?"

Dalton yanked the power cord from the saw, grabbed his baseball hat from the rung, and headed toward the door. "I'll fix it."

"How? More lies? Gonna promise to marry her until after the inspection comes through? That'll really help us."

His brother spun around. "I said I'd fix it. From now on, keep your damn nose out of my business and my sex life. Get your own." He gave a snort. "Interesting, though, you lecturing me on combining work with pleasure while you're hot for Morgan Raines. How about that as a potential disaster, dude?"

His ears buzzed with pure rage. "Did you touch her?" he asked softly. Deadly. His hands trembled with the urge to beat his brother senseless for taking another woman he was interested in. The image of that fateful night rose up before him in full, mocking imagery.

Excited about his upcoming wedding, he'd been tipsy as he stumbled into the house, making his way toward his bedroom. The room spun, but he was happy. He loved Felicia with the ardor of a man who had a future full of bright vision and endless fortune on the horizon. He had a plan, and finally all his hard work was paying off. He'd get out from under his father's thumb, make his own way at Pierce Brothers, have a big family, and be happy. God knew, he craved a slice of happy after his mother's death. Until the door swung open and he caught his brother with his future wife wrapped in his arms, her head tilted back, lips curved in a soft, intimate smile telling him they'd done this many times before. Dalton whispered something in her ear, and she gave the familiar giggle he associated with her happiness, but this time it wasn't for him. He stood and watched his brother hold his fiancée, and a strange numbness overcame him. Was he enraged? Brokenhearted? Ripped to pieces? He should be. Cal remembered thinking in that moment that he should go apeshit crazy. Instead, he felt . . . disappointed. Such a lukewarm emotion for a man who watched the woman he thought he loved and adored in his brother's arms.

The rest was a blur. The accusations. The tears. His brother's defense. Cal walked away, and the strong bond between them was splintered into a thousand pieces. It was more hurtful than losing his future wife. Losing his brother had been far, far worse.

Dalton shook his head in disgust. "Touch her? No. Give

me a little respect. And unlike you, if you want to go for it, I won't be getting in your way."

He and Dalton had always seen women in a very clear way. Tristan had been different, a bit of the artistic, emotional type they used to make fun of. He was the kind to write poetry and think deep thoughts in the woods. He'd been smitten with Sydney for years, and they'd had some secret love affair when they were kids. Dalton and Cal had joined forces to torture him. But the night Dalton took his woman away, Cal realized they'd never be able to repair their relationship. It was too . . . broken. Too far gone.

"Why'd you have to do it?" he asked bitterly. "I trusted you."

The demons swirled in the room between them, and Dalton swore viciously. "What do you want from me, Cal?" he asked. "Another apology? Another vow I never fucked Felicia? I didn't. I never would. She came on to me, and I knew if you got married she'd cheat. You wouldn't listen to me, so I decided to prove you'd be making a mistake. Instead, I made the mistake, and I've paid for it for years. I'm tired of paying for something I did because I loved you. I'm done. With all of it."

The door slammed behind him. The sound echoed in the silence, and Cal squeezed his eyes shut, trying to find his balance in a world that was beginning to sway beneath his feet. An odd need to forgive and delve deeper into Dalton's explanation pulled at him. But he fought it back, because in a way, he agreed with Dalton.

Cal was done with it, too. All of it.

chapter thirteen

Morgan twisted her fingers nervously and paused at the massive front door. Maybe she should turn around. After all, Cal and Dalton had some issues to work out, and it probably wasn't a good time to intrude. Besides, she wasn't good at this stuff. The bottle of champagne she'd brought suddenly felt obnoxious, and the banana cream pie purchased from Eddy's Gourmet Bakery in town seemed pushy. Oh, why hadn't she stayed in her hotel and ordered room service? The Greek salad was quite delicious, and she'd built relationships with the kitchen and waitstaff who anticipated her every order and knew she tipped well.

What was she doing here?

Morgan turned on her heel to flee.

The door swung open.

Trapped in midflight, she turned her head and caught Cal's knowing grin. He reached out to snag the presents, amusement dancing in those smoky gray eyes. "A woman who's on time is my favorite kind. Is this pie from Eddy's? I've died and gone to heaven. Come in."

Too late. The door slammed behind her, and she was

greeted by the enthusiastic moaning and wriggling fur bodies she was beginning to adore. Scratching their heads and trying to keep clear of their thumping tails, Morgan allowed herself to bask in the overabundant pure emotion of animals who just loved and welcomed her to their home. The pang of wanting something that made no sense hit but quickly dissipated. Morgan grew up in a solid home with loving parents and was well taken care of. She was grateful. What was she missing, then?

After her diagnosis and the disastrous breakup with Elias, she'd made sure she focused on ambition and career success. It was a good thing. She was used to relationships that were . . . clean. Built on mutual favors, similarities, and secure walls to keep out messiness. But these dogs gave her a glimpse of something else, something that was so deliciously blissful and pure and decadent. A sloppy, all-consuming affection and focus that made her feel like the most important person on the planet.

Like Caleb did.

Even now, his attention never wavered from her. Dressed in a pair of worn denim cutoffs and a black tank and sporting bare feet, he was completely droolworthy. His arms were corded with muscle that had nothing to do with the gym, and his jeans cupped his hard thighs and ass in loving abandon. Her heart picked up the pace at his sexy half grin, curving those luscious lips and making her burn for another taste. His look promised her he'd treat her better than the dogs, and Morgan had no doubts he was right. Her body already craved to melt her clothes off and offer itself up to all of his ministrations. She knew it would be perfect between them. The sex, that is. But Morgan had already made her decision that she couldn't sleep with him. He was way too dangerous. She hadn't trusted her body to fight, though, and knew her mind was iffy when it came to saying no to such pleasure. So Morgan had done the only logical thing women did to keep themselves from falling into bed with a man.

She hadn't shaved her legs.

Under her proper white pants and lemon chiffon blouse, she had a dirty secret. In the tub, soaking from the day's stressful activities, she'd picked up the razor, then promptly put it back. Knowing her stubble would keep her firmly chaste, she decided to forgo the feminine ritual. That would guarantee that if they shared a kiss and it began to get too far, she'd stop it. No way would she allow a man to see her naked for the first time and not stubble-free. That would be so humiliating, her brain would eventually kick in and stop all fun activities. Morgan kept the knowledge firmly wrapped around her like a security blanket. At least she could bask in his company, admire his gorgeous body, eat a good meal, and go home safe.

"I appreciate the invite," she said politely. "Will your brothers be joining us?"

He snorted and led her into the kitchen. With graceful, economical motions, he untwisted the cork and popped it off the champagne bottle. It flinched in his grip and gave a soft *whoosh*. "Hell no. And I apologize for the interruption the other night. Tristan is spending the night in Manhattan, and Dalton won't be coming home."

She slid onto one of the kitchen stools and put her

purse down. The dogs settled happily by her feet. "It's fine. Probably better that Tristan stopped us when he did before things went too far. Were you able to talk to Dalton about the inspection?"

His face darkened. Curiosity simmered regarding their past. Had Dalton really slept with his fiancée? The idea of Cal engaged to another woman made her tummy lurch with nerves. What type of woman did he really want? She burned with a thousand questions but doubted one would get answered. Cal seemed to guard his past as well as she did hers. One recognized the other well. It was so much easier to keep things light. The moment the closet door swung open, too many bones burst out, and shoving them back in was a real bitch of a chore.

"Yeah, I talked to him. Said he could fix it. If not, I have a contact who'll help me. He owes me a favor."

She raised a brow. "Why does that line make me nervous?"

Cal poured champagne into two flutes and slid one over to her. "No mob, I promise. Just a good friend who gave me one rabbit in the hat to pull. I say this situation calls for the pull."

"Dalton may fix it, and you won't need to use your only favor."

"We'll see. When it comes to my youngest brother, *trust* is not a word I use lightly."

"Because of your ex-fiancée?" The words tumbled out before she was able to catch them. Heat burned her cheeks. Hadn't she just given herself a mental pep talk about keeping things light?

He regarded her for a while before lifting the glass to his lips and taking a sip. He never took his hot gaze off her face. "Probably. It broke the trust. Then afterward he refused to tell me the truth."

"How do you know he wasn't telling the truth?"

"My brother is a master at putting moves on women. He'd been jealous of getting pushed aside in the business, and this was his way of getting even. It coincided with a huge fight we had. Guess he got the last laugh after all."

"I see." He'd finally answered one of her important questions. Cal had been so blinded by love, he'd chosen to believe his brother was the liar rather than face the truth that he'd been played. Much easier to turn all that disgust and anger toward a sibling. The closest people in life usually got the worst of the emotional carnage. What if Dalton really had been trying to tell his brother a hard truth Cal hadn't wanted to hear? "Did you ever sit and get the full story?"

"No need. Besides, it's the past, and we're both tired of dredging it up. How about you? Any broken love affairs to share?"

She flinched and took a sip of champagne. The bubbles danced in her throat. Tit for tat? Morgan kept her voice light, trying to give him information without the truth. "Ex-fiancé. Elias. He was the proper Southern gentleman ready to offer me a proper Southern life. It worked well for a while until life got a bit messy."

His gaze narrowed. How was it those light gray eyes could turn to smoky charcoal when he got all intense? "He didn't want to stick?"

She drank more champagne and gave a tiny laugh. "Yep. He did me a favor. I would've been bored and stuck in a role that wasn't for me. Now he's married with kids and has the perfect life he dreamed of. Hurtful, but not traumatic."

"Liar."

Her fingers jerked over the glass. A thin trickle of champagne fell on her hand. "What?"

Cal leaned forward. "I called you a liar. It was traumatic to you for some reason. Why did he leave you?"

She forced a laugh. "I couldn't give him something he wanted." The words were painful to utter.

"Tell me."

Irritation simmered. Why did he suddenly want to go deep? This was just dinner. He'd offered sex. Nothing more, nothing less. His delving into her personal life shouldn't leave her feeling so vulnerable. "Something important to him. I really don't want to get into it."

His gaze settled on her mouth with raw intensity. Her skin tingled as the reminder of his lips sliding over hers hit her memory and her body. "Fair enough." He paused. "Do relationships scare you?"

Startled, she struggled to answer. Her defenses slammed up. "Doesn't it scare you?" she shot back.

To her surprise, he gave a half smile, refusing to retreat. "Maybe. Maybe not if I found the right woman. I'm not scared of love, Morgan. I'm scared of screwing up again with someone who doesn't feel the same way."

Her heart skittered in her chest, barely able to keep up her breathing. His words held a truth and an intimacy she hadn't expected from tonight, especially so early. As if he sensed her hovering on the brink, he reached out and pushed her over.

"I'll tell you this: he was an asshole if he wanted anything more than he wanted you."

The words struck deep and healed her heart. The air charged with lit sexual tension. They stared at one another, gripped in a swirling cycle of need and want for connection, and Morgan ached to bury her head against his strong chest and let him hold her. Instead, she fought to get back on neutral footing.

"I had no idea we'd engage in dual therapy before dinner," she said. "What are we having?"

After a tense moment, her breath released. He drew back, following her lead. "Porterhouse steak with a balsamic glaze. Roasted potatoes. Asparagus."

She choked on her champagne. "Did you order out or really know how to cook this?"

Cal grinned. The boyish charm on such a masculine body was a killer combination. "I'm a good cook when I want to be. I've prepped most of it. Think you can help me cut up the asparagus while I check on the meat?"

"I think I can manage." She couldn't remember the last time she'd cooked or helped someone in the kitchen. The domestic scene wrapped around her with warmth. Instead of fighting it, Morgan swore to enjoy the evening.

He dropped a bag of asparagus, a cutting board, and a knife on the marble island. "Good. Oh, and on another note, I completely disagree."

She slid the tools over to her side and began washing her hands in the prep sink. "On what?"

"Tristan interrupting us. You said it was good he stopped

us from going too far." A wolfish gleam entered his eyes. "I disagree. We haven't gone far enough." His voice dropped to a husky growl. "But I intend to correct that problem. Later."

She stared at him, unable to form a word. He practically bristled with confidence and a sexual predatory scent that intoxicated her. Morgan should warn him off now. Remind him this was just about dinner and had nothing to do with dessert. Instead, she kept mute and heard his chuckle echo through the air. "Don't worry about it now, princess. That asparagus needs your full attention."

And with that, he stalked out of the kitchen.

Damn the man.

Yeah, he wanted her.

Bad.

Cal studied Morgan from across the table. He enjoyed watching her eat. Each movement was graceful and economical, from the way she cut her meat into perfect squares to the smooth arc of her fork lifting and disappearing into that delectable mouth.

His shorts were already way too tight. Cal shifted in his seat, trying not to focus on the way her tongue slid over her plump bottom lip in an effort to soak up the last of the juice. Crap, when had a woman eating made him want to come in his pants like a teen?

His words definitely put her on edge. Her conversation was deliberately light and stayed far away from any deep topics, including physical intimacy. He should've been frustrated. Instead, he was filled with an anticipation that rivaled Christmas mornings when he'd discovered numerous gaily wrapped presents under the tree, begging to be torn open. She was so damn . . . pretty. With her silvery blond hair curled just right to flip at the curve of her jaw and those wide blue eyes he wanted to see fogged with hunger. For him. Silver hoops caught the light as she neatly tucked a few stray strands behind her ear. Her scent danced in his nostrils. No musk or smoky perfume for her. Just the freshness of soap and cucumber and female skin, sexier than a bottle of opium. Her lemon-colored blouse kept sliding over her shoulder, exposing white, unblemished skin and the delicate strap of a cream-colored bra. He couldn't seem to take his gaze off that glimpse of exposed flesh. With unconscious motions, she kept shrugging it back, only to let it slowly fall again until the top curve of her full breast peeked at him.

The game of hide-and-seek was driving him crazy. Cal knew she wanted him. It was in the wariness gleaming in her eyes, the slight trembling of her fingers, the rapidly beating pulse at the base of her neck. He had no need to scare her with any outrageous remarks or bold moves. He enjoyed the subtle game of male to female—the chase, the capture, and the reward.

No need to hurry his pleasure.

Thing was, it was more than physical for him. He wanted this particular woman in his bed. He craved her particular smell and touch and kiss. He wanted to hear his name dragged from her lips. He wanted to make Morgan Raines come hard wrapped up in his arms. It had happened so gradually, working side by side, his initial irritation turning into amusement, and then fascination. The woman had gotten under his skin. The past few years, he'd only experienced brief, shallow relationships. Agreement on both sides, of course, because building houses came first, and most women were honest enough to admit they wanted something more from him. It wasn't that he was spooked by the prospect of a more permanent relationship. It was simply that no woman had tempted him to want more.

Until now.

"This meal is superb," she said, dabbing her mouth with the napkin. "I have to admit I doubted you."

"Thought the meal would be amateur, huh?" he teased.

"Kind of. You just don't strike me as the cooking sort."

"More like the takeout type?"

He enjoyed the slight flush to her skin. "I didn't mean it as an insult. Your schedule is like mine, and I'm sure there's not a lot of time to prepare a meal every night." She gave a delicate shrug. "Plus, when you're cooking only for one, it just doesn't seem worth it."

"My mother taught all of us to cook for survival. She also said it impressed women, and she didn't want any of her sons thinking his wife would be a maid."

Her lips curved. "I think I would've loved your mom."

Cal fought off the ghosts and nodded. "Yeah. I think it would've been mutual."

"I'm sorry she died," she said softly.

He wavered on telling her the truth of the circumstances but didn't want to ruin his time with her talking about things that couldn't be changed or made him sad. "So am I." She laid down her utensils with precision, and he stood. "How is it going with the Rosenthals?" He began gathering plates and napkins. "Tell me a bit more how it works. Do you check with them at various stages or is this all your show?"

She gave a sigh. "I work differently with each of my clients, and the Rosenthals are quite hands-off. Usually that's exciting, but I've been wrong a few times, and I'm not sure what's happened." Frustration curled into her Southern accent. "I Skyped with them and got a few items completely wrong. I'm worried about the furnishings and decor. I loved the Barn, but I don't have the time to shop like I need. Normally I'd fly to Paris or scour Manhattan for impulse buys, but this schedule is too tight."

Cal considered her problem. "Hmm. You know, I may be able to help."

"Gonna hand-deliver me a warehouse to pick from?"

"I'm gonna show you something. A surprise."

"A surprise, huh?" Was it her imagination or did her gaze sweep downward to his crotch? Yep. A guilty blush bloomed on her cheeks. Kind of hot and adorable at the same time. He kept his grin hidden. "Don't tell me. It's in the bedroom."

He chuckled. "Actually, it's outside. Think I just wanted to lure you to my lair?"

"No."

He winked. "Then you're giving me too much credit. You'd look good in my lair."

Morgan rolled her eyes and gathered some plates. "The wolf and Little Red Riding Hood, huh? Do you know that fairy tale was specifically instructed to warn young females not to get any big ideas of independence? Veer off the path from what people tell you and get punished. Always pissed me off."

They walked to the kitchen, and he began loading the dishwasher. "Had no idea fairy tales could be so politically incorrect. But something tells me you'd be the one to kill the wolf—not the woodcutter."

She tilted her head in thought. "Yeah, I would. No one's messing with my granny. Or getting my damn cookies."

He laughed. "Warning taken." She gave a cheeky grin, and they cleaned up together in comfortable silence. "Come on, guys. We're going out." He snagged her hand and led her to the porch while Gandalf and Balin bounded around them with joyful abandon.

The night was balmy and full of nocturnal insects partying. He switched on his iPhone flashlight and led her down the winding path behind the house, heading to the brink of the woods. She stopped short. "Uh, now I kind of feel like Red. I don't want to go in there. It's creepy."

He tightened his grip on her hand. "We have the dogs. They won't let any wolves hurt you. Neither will I."

As if they sensed her unease, Gandalf and Balin planted themselves on both sides of her like trained guard dogs. Their upturned faces vowed endless protection and love. Morgan patted their heads, then gazed at the shadowy private path that disappeared into a thicket of trees. "Okay, but I'm more worried about Jason or Freddy."

He pressed his lips together and firmly led her forward. She jumped when some owl-type screech cut through the air, but Gandalf's warning growl seemed to calm her. Balin led the way, stopping now and then to make sure they were still following, and her hand squeezed his harder. Hell, he was having fun on their outdoor adventure. Cal enjoyed the way she pressed close to his side. He rarely saw her afraid of anything, so knowing the dark spooked her made him want to protect her. Finally the large storage shed came into view.

"We came out here for this?" she squeaked. Her body trembled a bit, and she kept glancing back and forth at each noise. Cal unlocked the rickety double doors and flicked on the light.

"Surprise."

Morgan gasped. Filled to the rafters, the shed epitomized one motto.

One person's junk was another one's treasure.

She moved through the piles of furniture and trinkets stacked in haphazard piles. Cal knew the famous shed rivaled the antique Barn store, but Cal's family was the only one who knew about it. Since he wasn't into the restoration like his brothers, he saw the old shed as more of a junkfest but was always amazed at some of the pieces that were revamped from the items here.

Morgan stroked the surfaces of remnants of ebony pearl wood, shuddered over the frame of a pink marble headboard, and gave a sexy moan over a box containing a mishmash of knobs ranging from pure brass to crystal. "How did you get all this?" Her hushed voice reminded him of being in church. He bet Morgan thought the shed was even more holy.

"My father started collecting remnants of all our jobs and scrap material to put into future projects. Soon, it became more of an assortment of interesting items we didn't want to get rid of. This used to be Dalton's favorite place. Tristan's too."

The memories of him and his brothers hiding out in the shed to escape their father's constant demands flowed past. They set up their own private fort under a massive cherry-wood desk and pretended they were in a spaceship. Gathered late at night to tell ghost stories and munch on packs of Oreos, free from the eyes of parents, bonded by blood and circumstance and a friendship that got him through the days. He shook off the images, his throat tight, and watched Morgan's face. Delight and a sense of adventurous joy gleamed in her eyes. She picked her way through the piles, pulling items out, discarding some, running her fingers over sharp edges and broken wood, seeing something beautiful in each part.

An intense shock vibrated through him. For such a practical female, she held an inner sense of wonder that intrigued him. He liked the way she saw the potential in failure, the whole in the broken. Cal wondered what she saw in him.

"This is better than the Barn," she said. "My God, Cal, can I buy things? There are so many possibilities. I've decided to build each room around one special object, connecting a theme that resonates throughout the entire house. I think the Rosenthals can appreciate the concept." Her touch was almost reverent to a half-shattered grandfather clock with calligraphy replacing the numbers to spell out the family name of the one who had owned it years ago. Her nose wrinkled, and her brows lowered in a frown. "I'm worried if it's too subtle, they'll be concerned about not making an overwhelming visual impression on guests. They've always been a bit more ostentatious than some of my other clients. Well, at least I thought so before they threw me a curveball, suddenly embracing the minimalist look."

He crossed his arms in front of his chest, studying the slight frown on her brow. She was passionate about her job, and Cal knew she refused to settle for merely an acceptable house. Morgan intended to deliver the very best, every time. Frustration emanated from her petite frame. "You can buy anything that pleases you. Look, the Rosenthals hired you for a reason. That's why you're successful. Go with your gut. Instead of being limited by their own viewpoint, take them in a new direction."

"If I fail, and they dislike the new direction, it will be a disaster."

"You won't fail," he said. Oddly, he meant it. He had confidence in her abilities just by seeing her day to day on the job. She balanced a wicked work ethic with a creative energy and a vision of the goal. Not many people had the talent or the patience. "Have you ever let yourself go on a project and do what *you* want?"

She shook her head. "Too dangerous. The moment you disregard the client and his or her specific taste, you can veer off course."

Cal gave half a shrug. "The side roads are usually more interesting than the highway," he offered. "Maybe it's time you took a leap. With Dalton and Tristan to help, this house could be your masterpiece. Almost like your signature stamp."

"Maybe. I'd love to have more personal input. It's just so . . . unpredictable."

Her teeth pulled in her bottom lip and sucked. His

dick wept and ached to be part of the gesture. He caught a glimpse of sheer hunger on her face, but unfortunately it wasn't for him. No, this house held her in thrall, and she wanted to take it to the limit. He couldn't imagine building house after house without inputting part of his own identity. Wasn't she tired of limiting her creative vision? She needed more unpredictability in her life. And what would she be like if she put all that energy into sex?

Time to find out.

Cal barely restrained himself from licking his chops like the Big Bad Wolf. His body pounded with sexual energy, though he tried to leash it in. "Why don't we discuss it over dessert?"

Morgan stilled. Scenting danger in the air, she ducked her head and pretended to study a dusty beveled glass mirror. "It's late. I should go."

His nostrils flared with the thrill of pursuit. "Not without helping me eat some banana cream pie. I'll put on coffee, too."

His tone brooked no argument. She hesitated, dragging her feet, then seemed to give herself a mental pep talk. "Okay. A tiny slice. It's late."

"Yes, you said that." He didn't try to take her hand this time, allowing her the space. The dogs danced around them, occasionally stopping to investigate a scent or sound, making sure their temporary mistress was safe from Jason or Freddy. Morgan seemed to tense a notch tighter with every step. When was the last time he had to work to seduce a woman?

Hmm. That would be never. It was more fun than he ever imagined.

Cal busied himself in the kitchen cutting pie and pouring two cups of coffee. She perched on the stool at the marble island with one foot dangling toward the floor, as if planning a quick escape. He smothered a grin and forked up some fresh cream and ripe fruit. It was pure sugar heaven in his veins.

"I love pie," he managed in between bites. "How'd you know?"

She smiled and looked as happy as he was. "Didn't. Good guess. You seem like a pie sort of guy."

"All-American?"

She tilted her head. "Yeah, I think so."

"Why?"

Her shoulders lifted in a delicate shrug. Her blouse slid slowly down, giving him a great view. "You have all the trappings. Dogs. A successful family business. You build things instead of making a living pushing paper. You have the American flag in front of your house. And you talk well about your mom."

He licked the fork and considered. "Sounds solid. Must mean I'm trustworthy."

"Yes." The word came out with a touch of wariness.

He propped his elbows on the counter and leaned in. "And that means I always get the girl."

She pursed her lips and slid her plate away. "Not necessarily. It means you have patience, take your time, and are always a gentleman."

"Two out of three ain't bad," he drawled.

Her eyes widened, but she rallied. "Oh, I forgot the last quality. You're *nice*."

Cal chuckled. The way she emphasized the word was a direct challenge. "I heard nice guys finish last. I like to come in first."

"That ridiculous philosophy was constructed by a bunch of popular teenage girls who got obsessed with the bad-boy phenomenon. They weren't mature enough to see that emotional torture and pain does not reflect success in relationships. Nice guys get the real women because they have staying power."

"You date a lot of nice guys, Morgan?"

Her gaze dropped as if she needed distance. "Sure."

"Any of them finish first with you?"

She jerked back. A flash of temper lit her eyes. "Yes," she snapped. "In fact, I only date nice men. I'm past my experimental, yes-sir-may-I-have-another phase. I don't like games or cheaters or liars. I don't like men who have a Peter Pan syndrome or men who just want another notch in their bedpost."

"Doesn't leave much territory open, does it?"

She tightened her lips and stared at him hard. "Making fun of me?"

"Never."

"Good. I think it's time I say good night. Thank you for cooking. Thank you for the lovely evening."

She was so proper and adorable, he couldn't stop her. Yet. "You're welcome."

Morgan slid off the stool, took her plate and fork to the sink, and rinsed her hands. "Will you let me know what happened with the inspector tomorrow after speaking with Dalton?"

"Absolutely."

She nodded and spun on her very smart kitten heel, making her way to the foyer. The dogs leaped from their beds to give her a hearty send-off. She knelt down, hugging each of them with an open affection that made him smile. This was a woman who needed more in her life. More friends. More animals.

More . . . sex.

Her smile was nervous and forced. "Thanks again."

"Morgan?"

Her hand paused on the knob. "Yes?"

"What about my kiss?"

A tiny gasp burst from her lips. Cal straightened to his full height, slowly moving forward to close the distance between them. Her hand fell away from the door, and her back pressed against the hard frame. Stealing her space, he bracketed her body with his thighs, feet braced, hands on each side of her head so she was trapped. The leashed sexual tension between them whipped to life, and Cal soaked in the waves of old-fashioned lust and hunger between man and woman. An ancient dance that would never go extinct. His dick swelled, and his skin grew hot and tight, and Cal scented the heady smell of female arousal. Oh, yeah. Morgan Raines was not feeling very *nice* herself at this moment.

"What are you doing?"

He ran one finger down her smooth cheek. Her lower lip trembled slightly, but her chin tilted in pure stubbornness. Amusement touched his voice. "What do you think I'm doing?"

"Trying to take payment for dinner, Charming? Aren't we past that?"

She was trying to needle him, but it wouldn't work

tonight. He wanted her sweetness and light and honesty tonight. His senses screamed it was time to take what he wanted. "I don't want to play games with you, Morgan. I want to kiss you."

"I don't think that's a good idea. It's complicated. I already explained this."

Cal pressed a kiss to her temple. Smoothed back the silkiness of her silvery hair, which smelled like wildflowers. Her body shook so slightly, if he wasn't close, he would've never caught it. Her muscles tightened in a grip that told him she was trying to fight her body's natural response to him.

"I think it's quite simple. This is separate from our business contract. We can keep this private if you'd like or scream we're together from the rafters. I'm still going to be a hard-ass, and you'll still be a pain in the butt. But I swear to God, Morgan Raines, if I don't kiss you now and take you to bed, it may become the biggest regret of my life. And I've had enough of them to last me a lifetime." He lowered his head. His gaze locked with hers. Her breath came in choppy gasps, and as if she couldn't fight it, her fingers clasped his shoulders and hung on. Satisfaction shot through him, and the need to claim her for his raged in his blood, dulling every other thought.

"I don't know," she whispered.

He cupped her cheeks, his thumb pressed against her lush pink lips. "I do. Now open your mouth for me, baby, and let me in."

His mouth took hers.

chapter fourteen

Goodness gracious.

Morgan knew the kiss was coming. She prepared herself for the sensual assault like bracing her body for a war, ready for the pleasure but focused on keeping enough control to feel safe. A good-night kiss wasn't a terrible thing. Besides, she'd been dying to experience his mouth on hers once more. Even their banter seemed like foreplay, all roads leading to this one kiss. Morgan could handle it.

His body and spicy scent surrounded her. A little moan escaped her throat as she hung on, allowing the complete possession of her mouth and shuddering with pleasure. Strong white teeth nipped at her bottom lip, demanding entry, and his tongue slid home with no hesitation or apology.

She frickin' loved it.

There was nothing to think about or plan when Cal kissed her. The only thing Morgan needed to do was give him what he wanted, and she was rewarded. Rough, capable hands stroked her cheeks, controlling the angle and thrust of his tongue, sipping every last drop from her like the sweetest whiskey he'd ever tasted. Morgan arched up to the demand, her breasts tight and tingly from the delicious pressure of his chest dragging against her nipples. The thickness of his erection notched tight between her thighs, causing her clit to throb and ache for better pressure. She craved the feel of his fingers sliding inside her slick folds, his hot tongue against her breasts. As if he caught her unspoken thoughts, the kiss turned a bit wild, a bit savage, and instead of pulling back to reclaim control, Morgan surrendered without a regret, letting her body take the lead.

With a low growl of triumph, he picked her up and held her against the door. Her legs wrapped around his hips and she thrust all ten fingers into his already messy hair, holding him still and drowning in his kiss. His hips rocked back and forth, teasing her with what was to come, until she lost it and clamped her teeth down in a savage bite, arching her hips for more.

His head shot up. Charcoal eyes simmered with banked fire. "Did you just bite me?" he growled against her lips, lifting her up a few inches only to control her slow movement downward. Frustrated already, she wriggled her hips for more pressure.

"You deserved it," she shot back.

Pure lust glittered on his carved features, sending a jolt through her bloodstream. "I damn well knew there was a hellcat under all that white. There'll be payback for that. For now, hang on."

"I already am—oh!"

He slung her over his shoulder like a real caveman and stalked up the stairs as if she were the weight of a feather.

Morgan knew she had a healthy body with curves, and the idea that he took her size with no hesitation or care made her feel feminine, delicate, and very, very wanted.

She caught a flash of tigerwood floors and the scent of lemon polish and got dumped in the middle of a king-size bed. Morgan sank into a ton of fluffy pillows and fought her way to a half-sitting position to give him a piece of her mind.

Then stopped.

He'd taken off his shirt. *Ripped off* was a better term, since the material barely survived his savage striptease. Morgan looked at the mass of bunched muscles defining his pecs, the washboard abs from hard, sweaty work instead of a climate-controlled gym. Skin baked brown from the sun, a light dusting of gold-brown hair scattered over his chest and narrowed to a mouthwatering line disappearing past his waistband. One snap of his fingers released the button on his denim cutoffs. Never taking his gaze from her face, he approached the bed, studying her as if going over his plan to ravish her.

In that moment, Morgan melted like hot lava, helpless to prevent anything and everything he wanted to do with her. Those eyes gleamed with raw satisfaction, catching her innate surrender as she knelt on the bed and made no move to stop him. No move to escape.

"Do you know how many bad things I want to do to you?"

She shuddered. Licked her lips. "Then do them."

A vicious curse escaped his lips. And he was upon her.

Morgan never had a chance. This was no slow, step-by-step seduction plan. It was as if the moment they touched, only instinct survived, a desperate need to connect in every primitive, physical form. Her blouse vanished in seconds, her bra was flicked open, and then his soft lips closed over her nipple, tugging, licking, sucking. She writhed underneath him and pulled down the zipper of his shorts, shoving her fingers into the opening with little finesse to stroke and cup the hard, thick length of his cock.

He uttered her name like a prayer, but instead of getting naked fast, he kept his solid attention on her breasts. Tugging her nipples in a rhythm to his own private melody, he teased and tortured until her breasts were so sensitive, a cry trapped in the back of her throat. Pain and pleasure blurred into a fine line. "You're so damn pretty," he said, watching her reaction as he licked the tight tips. "You taste like coconut cream pie." She hissed as he worked his mouth lower, swiping his tongue over the curve of her belly, fingers curled around the band of her proper linen pants. "I can't wait to taste you. Make you come. Fuck you so hard, you'll never remember another man's name."

Arousal trickled down her thigh. Already poised on the edge of orgasm just from his words, Morgan panted, fighting for sanity. "I can't take much more."

"Neither can I. Lift up."

Her hips rose, and as he wriggled her pants down her hips, her mind suddenly sprung to awareness, reminding her of the final desperate measure she'd taken to make sure she didn't sleep with Caleb Pierce tonight.

"Wait! Oh, my God, please wait!"

Morgan shot up. Cal tilted his head back. Pupils

dilated with lust, mouth damp from kissing her, his gorgeous hair mussed up from her fingers raking through the strands, he was sex incarnate and every woman's fantasy. "You okay, baby?" he asked roughly. His breath came in ragged pants, but he held himself under control, gauging if she was about to tell him she had changed her mind or wanted him to stop.

"No," she moaned. His fingers tangled with hers, and he waited patiently. In that moment, her respect and trust for this man flooded her in waves. Even with a throbbing erection and a brain probably fogged by arousal, he stopped. He pushed when it was right, yet was man enough to back off at the first cry of no. He'd never do anything she didn't want, and that made Morgan ache for him even more.

"Did you change your mind? I want you, Morgan, but only if you want me just as bad. I'd never hurt you."

"I know!" she sobbed. "But I did something because I didn't want to sleep with you tonight because I got spooked and thought it would be better to keep my distance but I don't know how to tell you and I'm so embarrassed!"

He cocked his head, his gaze drilling into hers. "Talk to me. Good, bad, I want to hear you. What you want, what you don't, what you're scared of, what makes you feel good. I want to hear it all."

The heat from his skin wrapped around her. His scent was pure primal mating, and here she was with hairy legs, dying to part her thighs and take everything he had to give. Shaking with need, she burst out the truth before she lost her nerve. "I didn't shave my legs!"

Morgan shut her eyes, refusing to look at him. She'd

reached the height of humiliation. She was the spiller of female secrets, and the population would never forgive her.

"Baby, open your eyes. Look at me."

She groaned but slowly peeked at him. Pure amusement danced in his eyes, tugged at his lips. But he looked straight at her when he spoke. "You thought that not shaving would keep you safe from me?"

Misery leaked into her voice. "Yes."

Suddenly, with one strong motion, he ripped the pants off her, yanked her legs apart, and knelt between them. Shock and lust warred for dominance. His face reflected a determination that caused shivers to race down her spine. "That is the sexiest damn thing I've ever heard in my life."

She wriggled desperately to get away from him, even though she wanted his mouth between her thighs more than she wanted her next breath. "No! This isn't good. Let me use the bathroom and I'll clean up and we'll continue where we left off. Oh!" He gripped her thighs to keep her still and lowered his head. His openmouthed kiss against the thin fabric of her white lace panties caused her hips to shoot off the bed.

"You're not going anywhere. I don't want you clean and neat and proper. I want you messy and dirty and wet." His fingers played with the elastic edges of her panties, dipping inside to tease her. "And you're very wet right now."

Her head thrashed back and forth on the bed, fighting between her need for this man and her feminine pride. "I have stubble!"

"And I fucking love it. Nothing could keep me from worshipping your body tonight, Morgan. I intend to gorge on every part of you, and I'm gonna start right here. Now, stop thinking."

His tongue ran down the center of the damp fabric, slowly licking her, all the while his fingers played along the edge of the band. Between the strokes of his hand and the nibbling, licking motions of his mouth, her body straightened like a bow, completely under his command. His tongue pressed hard against her throbbing clit, then the edges of his teeth raked over her swollen flesh.

"Caleb! That feels too good."

"No such thing, baby. God, you're so responsive. So hot." His fingers hooked under the elastic, brushed against her wet lips, and dove deep.

It was too much. It wasn't enough. It was hell. It was heaven. The orgasm shimmered right there, so close, until a helpless whimper rose to her lips and he sensed right then what she needed. He cursed, added his second finger, and pumped in and out of her channel with light strokes. At the same time, he closed his teeth over the throbbing nub of her clit through the soaked fabric of her panties and bit gently.

She came.

The excruciating pleasure rolled over her in waves, and her body rode it out with wild abandon. He didn't remove his fingers or stop his tongue's delicious movements until every last ounce of that orgasm was done and she was wrung out. Finally he lifted his head, a satisfied crooked grin on his mouth.

"What's your name?" he asked.

She blinked. "I'm not sure."

"Much better. Now you're not thinking."

A shudder ran through her. "I'm sorry."

His brow lifted. "For what?"

Her cheeks flushed. "I guess I couldn't wait. That's never happened before. My underwear wasn't even off."

His laugh was rich and deep and very masculine. "Good. You're kind of magnificent, princess. I think you need to do that again."

Cal worked her panties down her hips, then leaned over. The drawer opened and a condom was in his grip. She watched with hungry eyes as he stripped off his boxers and fit himself with the condom. Raising her legs, he hooked her ankles over his shoulders and paused at her dripping entrance. Breath held, she shut her eyes and waited for him to take her. A trickle of fear hit. How long had it been since she'd been this intimate with a man? The sheer vulnerability of this moment overwhelmed her, but she wanted him too badly to pull back. He pushed in a few inches. Paused.

"Open your eyes."

The low rasp startled her, so she obeyed. Cal poised above her, held in a muscle lock she didn't understand. Was he afraid he'd hurt her? Sweat gleamed on his brow. "How do you like it? Slow and easy? Fast and hard?"

Morgan didn't know, because it had been two years since she'd had sex. Hating to admit her inexperience, she said the only words that came to mind. "I like it every way."

His jaw clenched. "Crap, you're gonna kill me. So tight and wet. Don't hide from me. I want to see your face when I make you come again."

Oh, my. Morgan had never engaged in dirty talk during sex, but his words were like a live wire to her body. The filthier he talked, the crazier she got, her body softening and opening up to any bad thing he wanted to do. Instead of surging forward, Cal began to stroke his cock against her swollen folds, rubbing against her sensitive clit until she was right there again, at the precipice of orgasm. She writhed beneath him, digging her nails deep into his shoulders, but he ignored her cues and kept up the maddening, slow, torturous pace until her sanity shattered into tiny pieces.

"For God's sake, Cal, fuck me! Please, take me now!"

"Good girl."

He plunged his cock deep inside, burying himself completely. She cried out and hung on, the sheer width and length of him making her squirm from the hot, stretching sensation. Morgan gasped. He completely filled her, allowing no room for anything but the primitive demand to surrender to him. She tried to fight it—her mind gave a good fight—but then he started to move and she gave up and gave in.

Cal gave her no time to shore up her defenses. With every stroke, he claimed her. She hung on to his shoulders while he drove inside her over and over, rocking his hips, putting just the perfect amount of pressure on her clit to keep her from tumbling over but maintaining the sharp edge. She cried his name. She begged. And with one perfect deep thrust, something in her belly shimmered with staggering heat, and she shot apart.

Brutal pleasure flooded through her, turning her boneless. His dim shout told her he had followed her over. Tiny convulsions wracked her body as she drifted down to reality. Helpless to move or make sense out of what had happened, she had one brief moment of clarity in her spent state and wondered if she should politely excuse herself. Maybe he wasn't the sleepover type. Maybe he hated women sharing his bed or trying to spoon. Maybe—

"Go to sleep, baby." He wrapped her in his arms and cuddled her against his damp chest. "I'm not done with you yet."

Morgan closed her eyes.

God, she'd eaten the chips. Every single last one of them, and it was just as she feared.

It had been a mind-blowing experience. And she wanted more.

"Hmm, that's nice."

The massage on his bare feet was a bit ticklish, but the warm, wet motions dragged him from a heavy sleep and allowed him to finally surface. Who would've thought she'd have a foot fetish? Of course, she'd surprised him in all sorts of wonderful ways last night. But this was—

"Ugh!" He jumped up from the bed and found a delighted Balin by his feet, tongue hanging out. Gross. Gandalf was by the side of the bed, patiently waiting for him to open his eyes, and all that doggy intensity went haywire when Cal finally sat up.

"Shhh, don't wake Morgan," he warned. They wriggled and shook with the need to get up on the bed and treat Morgan to a good tongue bath. Overnight guests weren't expected, so the dogs probably thought it was snuggle time.

Holding back a smile, he swung his legs around and threw on a pair of sweats. Cal studied Morgan's sleeping form with fierce satisfaction. He'd made sure there'd be no sneaking out in the middle of the night this time. No distance or politeness or walls up. Last night had changed everything, and he didn't intend to go back.

Now he just had to convince Morgan he was right.

Even in sleep, she kept to herself, as if not used to sharing her bed or her life with someone. Curled up in the fetal position, face smoothed free of worries, silvery hair spilled messily over her cheek, she looked open and vulnerable. Cal withstood the rush of possessiveness that roared in his head and his dick. This was his woman now. Somehow, someway, she'd dug herself under his skin and stuck.

He led the dogs out of the bedroom and out the front door. Watching them bound around the lawn, frolicking, his mind went over his odd thoughts. He'd never felt this good the morning after. The need for her was strong. But so soon? After one night of great sex? It made no sense. He wasn't the type to get lovey-dovey or attached. He hadn't been looking for anything, yet here she was. Just strolled into his life with a haughty, demanding attitude and a rockin' body, and he fell in one quick swoop.

The dogs finished up, and he headed into the kitchen to give them food and water. While they munched on breakfast, he started up the mega stainless steel coffeemaker and waited for it to finish brewing. How would she react this morning? Would she be cool and distant? Would she want to continue their relationship or term it a one-night occurrence?

He sensed their connection went beyond the physical. The way she'd opened herself up to him last night, and begged so sweetly. The way she stroked him like he was the only one to feed her hunger. The way she worried about protocol before falling asleep wrapped tight in his arms. He'd woken her up three times like an addict needing a hit, and she fell on him with a fervor that matched his own.

Cal waited for his coffee and pondered. The sun spilled through the window and lit up the kitchen. Damn, this felt good. *He* felt good. Even with Felicia, he was always trying to plan for what she needed next. He'd been besotted, and in lust. He'd envisioned a bright future with her, but he'd never looked into her eyes and knew who she really was. They'd been too young, and not meant for each other.

The moment he slid into Morgan's body and watched her shatter beneath him, something shifted. It was like coming home after years of searching for something.

Holy shit, he was waxing poetic after one night with her. This was definitely uncharted territory.

Shaking his head at his thoughts, he glanced at his watch. He'd let her sleep for a bit longer. They had a long day ahead, and he'd kept her up most of the night. Humming under his breath, he poured out a mug of steaming coffee and shared some toast and butter with the dogs. Hopefully, Dalton had fixed the problem with the inspector and he could get him on the schedule to start the drywall.

He mentally sifted through the rest of the schedule. It was tight but still doable. Sure, they'd had some setbacks, but that was part of the building process. Cal had to admit that, even though the deadline sucked, he'd had more fun building this house than he'd had in a long time. Working with Morgan brought a freshness and creativity to the site, along with a hard-core work ethic he respected. He looked forward to seeing her every day in her white khakis and pink work boots. She wasn't above doing a coffee run for the crew, and she handled the masculine environment with ease. He liked seeing her in the office with Sydney or bantering with his brothers.

And they had four months left.

"Hey."

He turned at the soft greeting and smiled. Morgan's hair was damp from her shower, and she wore one of his T-shirts with her white pants. Her face was scrubbed free of makeup. He had a moment of regret that he couldn't tumble her one last time before the day started, but he doubted he'd be able to get out of bed if he tasted her one more time. The dogs shot over to her, pressing against her in competitive ecstasy for the first belly scratch. She grinned and gave them what they wanted, using both hands until they were satisfied they'd gotten enough morning love. Cal wished he could get some, too.

"Hey. I figured I'd wake you in a bit. You needed the sleep."

Her blush was adorable and sexy. She tugged at the hem of his shirt. "I have to get home and change. My blouse got ripped, so I can't wear it."

The image of him tearing off her blouse to reveal her gorgeous full breasts shot straight to his dick. In seconds, he was at full mast and uncomfortable as hell. "I remember." His voice dropped. "My only regret right now is I didn't rip the pants, too."

Morgan gulped, then swiftly looked away. "Then I wouldn't have anything to wear."

Cal laughed. Oh, this was too good. She'd had her mouth all over him and there hadn't been a trace of shyness. Seems the morning light changed her back into a very proper lady. He refused to let her hide, though. He stalked forward and closed the distance between them. "Exactly."

"I have to go."

"We have fifteen minutes."

Her eyes widened with his insinuation. Cal kept the laughter from his expression. "Umm, we have the inspector problem and the drywall delivery and a meeting with Sydney and lots of stuff."

"God, you're sweet." He cupped her cheeks and tilted her head back. "A proper lady in the parlor and a—"

"Don't you dare say a whore in the bedroom or I'll give you a black eye."

His lips twitched. "I was going to say a hellcat. A goddess. A sensual, gorgeous woman I'm currently so hard for, I can't see straight." He pressed against her. "Want to help me out here?" he murmured.

She gave a sexy little moan. Already her body softened and her musky arousal drifted to his nostrils. "See, this is why sex and business is a dangerous combination. I can't think when I'm around you. I want to cancel all of our appointments and stay in bed with you until you're out of my system."

"Oh, baby, you can't say that stuff to me and escape unscathed." His mouth covered hers in a deep, drugging kiss, until she stood on tiptoes and wrapped her arms around him, clinging tight. He thrust his tongue in the delicious, wet cave of her mouth, drunk on her taste and her smell, wanting nothing more than to bury himself inside her again and again. Their dance of intimacy last night raged to life, and their clothes suddenly drifted off, and he lowered her to the kitchen floor, where they had shared their first kiss.

"I just showered," she said breathlessly. "I used your razor. I hope that's okay."

"No. From now on, razors are banned. I loved the rough scratch of your legs rubbing my ass as I fucked you. So hot."

"Oh!" Her cheeks colored. "You shouldn't—you shouldn't talk like that!"

He loved her obvious arousal and shy demeanor that fell away under his touch. "Then shut me up." He captured a throaty moan when he kissed her, his tongue diving deep and gathering her heady taste.

"We shouldn't do this," Morgan murmured, her teeth clamping down on his bottom lip. "I'm late. And we're on the floor again. What if your brothers come in?" But she didn't pause, curling her hot fingers around his hard length, squeezing mercilessly until he almost came in her hand. Oh, God, she was naked and so perfect. Tight rosy-red nipples and white skin. Full curves and sloping planes he couldn't wait to explore again. Damp golden curls hiding her sweet pussy. His fingers danced over her swollen clit, parted her slick lips, and tested her readiness. She cried out his name, sounding sweeter than a symphony.

"My brothers will not be interrupting us this morning."

Her hips arched off the floor. "This is not good."

"How does that feel?"

"So good. Don't stop, yes, oh, God, right there!"

He dragged her legs wider apart. His thumb flicked

over her hard bud while he took possession of her mouth, swallowing her sounds. He was ready to plunge and claim her like a wild thing, when his brain dully latched onto a thought. "Condom," he ground out. "I need a condom. In my pants. Reach back."

Her arm frantically searched around, and finally her fingers closed around the fabric. He got out the packet, ripped it with his teeth, sheathed himself, and dove home.

Her body gripped him like a hot vise, squeezing him so damn good, he could've fucking wept. She bucked under him with her own needs, and gripping her hips, he took her hard and fast, pushing her into climax without pause, drinking in her satisfied screams and the look of shattering pleasure on her face. His balls tightened, and Cal let himself go, emptying his seed with a hoarse shout of satisfaction, pumping his hips to the very last second until he was completely drained.

Rolling to his side so he didn't crush her, he leaned over and kissed her. She kissed him back with a sweetness he was already addicted to. "Did I hurt you?"

Morgan gave a half laugh. "God, no. But you might have some explaining to do." She motioned to the right. When he glanced over, Balin and Gandalf were sitting side by side, watching the scene with pure doggy sadness. "I suddenly feel like an exhibitionist."

He laughed. As if it was the signal everything was now okay, the dogs jumped up and began licking his back. A wet nose by his ass sent him stumbling up with a yell, and when Morgan fell into a fit of giggles, he grabbed her and tickled her relentlessly as punishment.

"Uncle, uncle!" she screamed, her naked body writhing in his lap. He finally relented and she slumped on top of him. Cal wrapped his arms around her back and cradled her. His hands stroked her soft skin. Her breath drifted over his cheek. The scent of their lovemaking hung heavily in the air. He clung to that perfect moment, with everything he valued surrounding him, and a quietness in his soul he rarely experienced. His original plan to keep things cool crumbled like ash.

"I want you," he said softly.

She sighed against him. "You had me."

"I want more of you. I don't want to push or have a big analytical discussion that freaks you out. I don't want promises of what happens after the house is built. I just want to spend time with you. We have four months. Will you give me that and see what happens?"

Cal held his breath and hoped he wouldn't regret the move. Instead of bluffing, he'd laid out all his chips and called her out. Half of him wondered if she'd retreat behind her wall and he'd spend another few weeks trying to scale past her defenses. There was something bigger than her fear of mixing business with pleasure. There was a secret behind her eyes that she protected at all costs. Cal respected secrets, but he couldn't let her give up this connection. It was too rare to throw away without delving deeper.

He watched the emotions flicker over her face. Her eyes darkened. "Do you want to tell anyone?"

"As long as you're with me, we can play it any way. Whatever you're more comfortable with. Though I think it will be easier to just tell the truth. I have no doubt you can handle any bullshit with aplomb. Or I can just beat them up."

A smile touched her swollen lips. "Four months. As boyfriend and girlfriend?"

He groaned. "That's awful. How about a monogamous affair?"

"You're so sophisticated."

He grinned. She wasn't leaping off him and racing out the door. For now, it was enough for him. "We have a deal?"

She wrinkled her nose. "Now, that's awful. We gonna shake on it?"

"No."

Slowly realization dawned, and she looked down. "Oh, my. How do you do that so fast? We can't. We're really late. I need clothes and to wash up and to—oh, God, yes."

Cal covered her body with his, took her mouth, and finalized the deal.

chapter fifteen

Morgan walked into a house that was beginning to resemble a real home. For the past few weeks, progress had raced forward with few disruptions. Dalton created a miracle by soothing the inspector's daughter and didn't even have to promise her a ring. Liquid insulation and drywall were done, and exterior finishes were almost complete. The mix of brick and stone gave the house a luxurious feel, using an almost crisscross effect to impress onlookers.

Her low heels echoed in the silence as she took in the sweeping archways, circular staircase, and open hallway floating over the main living area. Once again she gave Brady props for seeing something no one else could. He had a vision she'd love to work with again on other projects. She made her way upstairs, stepping around power tools, varnish tables, and a mess of equipment. Cal liked a clean site at the end of the day, but since they were pulling a long weekend to work on trim and cabinetry, he'd allowed the crew to be a bit more casual, especially since the actual owners weren't here.

Morgan floated through each room, relishing the quiet

while the sun slowly sank. Usually she thrived in chaos, from the loud music, hammering, mingling voices, and endless array of strangers in and out on a daily basis. But now was when the magic began. Her gaze swept over the empty space, picturing design and moldings, furnishings and layout. Each room told its own story, depending on the patron or the guest. She'd never failed before. She didn't intend to start now.

A prickle of worry poked at her. Between the Barn and Cal's secret shed of treasures, she'd been working with Dalton to finish some items and pick out her centerpieces. Morgan stepped into the master bedroom. This would be her masterpiece. She'd scored a vintage brass headboard for the king-size bed, seeing the Rosenthal's private oasis as a luxurious intimate space. With the blackberry back walls, lace curtains, vintage French furniture, and velvet fainting couch in the coolest of silvers already in place, Morgan intended to interweave shades of violet with silver and give the room a pampered feel with just a touch of masculinity to keep it from being too girly.

High ceilings screamed for a chandelier dripping with crystals. The doors leading out to the private rooftop balcony would slide rather than open like French doors, allowing only a whisper of sound and shadowed silk screens. She peeked into the bath, which would have a fireplace, remote controls, and a spa shower, but her crown jewel was the claw-foot tub perched high on a pedestal of rose quartz, along with the green lamp Cal still hated.

At first, she'd been set on keeping a more modern feel. The Hollywood couple liked their toys and conveniences, but the bedroom could be their own oasis, so she'd gone for old-style glamour. The Pinterest board and multiple texts from Petra showed a more edgy feel, with sleek metals, blacks, reds, whites, and staggering art sculptures to rival Michelangelo's. Worry nagged at her belly from her client's sudden taste turn. This was the first time her gut instincts warred with the Rosenthals' wants and needs, but Cal kept telling her to trust her skills.

Morgan stilled. Just his name spilling through her mind caused her body to light up, readying her for his touch. His kiss. His smart-ass remarks and his intriguing possessiveness and the way he never allowed her to hide either her body or her mind from him. He was a demanding lover, yet instead of pulling away and craving distance, she was doing the opposite.

Getting closer. Falling harder. Losing more of herself.

She shivered in the blistering heat. It didn't have to be complicated. In fact, Cal had made it easy for her. They averaged four nights per week together, and he treated her no differently at work. Of course, the moment she arrived at his place he ravished her completely, allowing her to dress only so they could share dinner. Occasionally Tristan and Dalton stopped in for a quick bite, and Morgan enjoyed their clever banter, finding herself drawn to the pull of a sibling bond they still struggled with. It was obvious they loved each other, but the iron-fisted way Cal ran Pierce Brothers was tearing them apart. Morgan squirmed but tried to be neutral, holding back from explaining to Cal how he was alienating them.

A smile curved her lips. It was wonderful to be able to

share her workday and passion for building with him. Her initial fears that they wouldn't be able to have both drifted away in the heat of his arms and the joy of his presence. But each day was like a ticking time bomb, moving her closer to the only ending they had.

When the job was completed, she would leave. And she'd never see him again.

Morgan laid her hand flat on her belly. Raw longing licked at her nerve endings. For the first time in her life, she was beginning to want more. But she didn't want to think of the future or what would happen right now. She intended to take every second with Caleb Pierce and wring it dry. Instead of holding back, Morgan decided to surrender to the relationship and see where it led them both. Her cards had been dealt, and it was up to her how she played them.

With a deep breath, Morgan finished her walk-through, taking in the energy of the house and its future occupants, making mental notes of finishes and details that would create a stunning debut and keep her at the top of her game.

Then she went home to Cal.

"We're going out."

He didn't let her respond, pulling her hard into his embrace and kissing her senseless. The dogs whined, waiting for their turn, but they already knew their master had first dibs. The spicy, masculine scent of him always had her ready for him. How had she become such a slut? In a good way. A delicious, naughty way. He made her hot and ready with just a blistering look. Or a dirty command. He refused to let her hide from her sexuality, and for the first time in her life, Morgan reveled in her feminine power, in her curves and her ability to bring this powerful man to his knees just by taking off her clothes.

He eased away, nipped at her bottom lip, then licked away the sting. She tried to remember what he said. "What?"

He gave her a smug grin. "We're going out. How about My Place?"

She shuddered with the memory of her call girl arrest. "No, thanks. I'm happy never to go there again."

"Understood. Let's do Italian. We'll hit Cena. Sound good?"

"Pasta sounds heavenly." She broke from his embrace and knelt down. "Come get me, guys!"

Balin and Gandalf attacked, pushing her off balance and licking her madly. Pure love shot through her for the canine goofballs she'd become so attached to. After a lovefest, they headed to the small Italian café, which boasted homemade ravioli and had a wait list every day of the week. Of course, Cal led her right in, the owners immediately recognizing such a valued customer and setting them up toward the back in a cozy booth. He ordered a Chardonnay for her and a Peroni for him, then attacked the bread basket with gusto. "How did the walk-through go? Dalton seems to have things under control for once, and we're on target. Catch any issues?"

She battled and lost the war with carbohydrates. Swiping the crusty Italian bread in olive oil, she moaned in delight. "No, things are tight. Once the cabinetry is installed, we can get started on the finishes. The mahogany crown molding will look amazing in the library, and the doors will need staining. We're still ready to hit our completion date." She ducked her head, not wanting to think about when their time would be done. Each night spent in his bed made leaving it that much more agonizing. She shook off the thought and refocused. "How are you getting along with Dalton?"

He shrugged. "Same. He fixed the problem with Ashley, but he's not really talking to me. He thinks I'm being a bully."

She shifted in her seat and kept her voice light. "Are you?"

"I'm responsible for the business. If he goes in the wrong direction, I have to pull him back."

"Maybe not. Maybe he needs to do exactly what he wants and is good at. Did you ever think you've never given him a true chance?"

A frown creased his brow. His gray eyes flickered with impatience. "Why are you defending Dalton? Yes, he's a genius at woodworking, but he needs constant supervision."

Morgan sighed. "I'm defending Dalton because I think he's fully capable of handling his share and more. You yank things away from him before he can try. You do the same thing with Tristan."

"Tristan is obsessed with flipping property. We need to build houses, not buy them. We have no time for real estate. I don't know why my brothers insist on playing around with our future."

Why did there seem to be more to the story? When she watched the brothers intermingle, there was a sense of loss that beat through each of their encounters. As if they were desperately trying to find their way back to each other but were blocked. She bet it was even harder to transcend the past without parents to hold them together. Morgan knew the brothers had a painful history, but she ached to help them all find their way back to each other.

Morgan studied him in the dim light. "I encouraged him."

Cal cocked his head and studied her. "What are you talking about?"

She dragged in a breath. "I told him about a house that needed renovation and said he should buy it. I agreed with him, Cal. I felt as if his strengths weren't being used to his advantage. He seems to have a gift with redesigning and conversion."

Cal cursed under his breath. "Morgan, you don't know what's going on. He needs to keep his focus on projects that make money fast."

"Dalton and Tristan have different interests, which should make Pierce Brothers stronger as a whole. Not every job needs to have a short-term profit. They're thinking on a grander scale, and they're back to help you. I think it's wonderful they wanted to come home and try again to be part of the business. I'm sure they were devastated by your father's death."

He averted his gaze, and her Spidey sense tingled. Why did he suddenly look guilty? The waiter came by with their ravioli, and Cal concentrated on his bowl like it held all the answers. She was missing another part of the puzzle but didn't want to push. Did they even have that type of relationship? Should she respect his space and privacy, even though she ached to share every last secret claiming this man's past?

Suddenly he spoke. "They don't want to be here with me, Morgan. I never told you about my father's will."

She reached across the table and grasped his hand. The hard lines of his face hurt her heart. "Tell me," she said softly.

His fingers squeezed hers. "My father put conditions on retaining ownership of Pierce Brothers. We have to live together and run it at a profit for one full year."

She nodded. "Okay. I know living together is a challenge, but, Cal, I rarely see your brothers at home. We only ate with them a few times; it's almost like your house is a ghost town. It's not like you're all stuck in a close space."

"True."

"Plus, you're already running the company at a profit. That won't be a problem."

His wince told her differently. "We started at ground zero. Meaning that all profits before the will went into effect were void. It's like starting a new business from scratch."

The full situation finally struck her. His original reluctance to build the house for her. His visit to her hotel to bargain for terms she thought was like a game. This project was much more than a healthy dose of money in their account or a way to build clientele. If they didn't hit the projected deadline and deliver, Pierce Brothers would fail. She'd forced his hand by removing all of his other clients so he'd be forced to work with her. And if he didn't succeed, Cal would lose Pierce Brothers.

And it all hinged on her.

She leaned back, removing her hand, and tried to process. Her pulse skyrocketed in a bit of a panic. She didn't want this. Didn't want an emotional stake in a business deal that was supposed to be cut-and-dried. Dammit, that was the reason she avoided relationships on the job—the stakes were way too high.

"You're getting spooked again," he said drily, taking a sip of beer. "This has nothing to do with you, Morgan. This is about me."

A mess of emotions roiled and rose. "How can you say that? I had no idea this house was a make-or-break deal. Oh, my God, and I put pressure on Jet McCarthy to decline your bid! I played a game to win, not realizing what was going on. I'm sorry."

Sparks shot from his eyes. His jaw clenched, and he lowered his voice to a commanding tone that still gave her shivers. "Stop it. Don't you put this crap on yourself. You protected your clients to get the best deal, and that's your job."

Guilt tinged her tone. "I know, but I was ruthless about getting what I wanted."

His lips twitched. "Tell me the truth. Even if you'd known about the will and I declined your project, would you have played your hand differently?"

She thought about it hard. And as much as she hated to admit it, Morgan realized she would've done the same exact thing. "No," she said miserably. "I still would've bribed Jet and forced you to build my house."

He grinned. "Good. That's the right answer. There's no blame here, Morgan. I told you for a different reason."

"Why?"

"Because I wanted to tell the truth to someone who gives a shit." He gave her raw honesty without flinching or sugarcoating it. "Because you mean something to me, and I don't want to hide stuff from you. That's all. I don't want pity or rage or for you to solve the problem. I just wanted you to listen."

In that moment, something shifted within her. A need to give him everything and anything he wanted surged inside, crashing through her like a tsunami until she closed her eyes, fighting to keep control. He was a proud man. A good man. A strong man. Sharing the details of the will allowed her entry into his secrets and his motivation behind the tension with his brothers. They chose to stay for Cal, but the resentment still beat in their blood. She didn't know how it would end with them. Would they stay? Move on without a glance back? Make peace with each other?

Only one fact revealed itself like a flawless oyster pulled from the sea.

Her link with Cal was so much more than sex. They were building their own relationship with each swing of the hammer. Already the thought of leaving him tore her apart, but when it was time, there would be no choice.

Right?

Morgan hesitated. She ached to tell him her own truth. But if she told him she couldn't have children, would Cal break it off immediately? Would he care? Was he falling for her as fast and hard, or was this just a satisfying fling? The questions swirled in her brain and gave her a headache. She hadn't thought this far, but things were changing, and she'd have to make a decision soon.

Not tonight. She needed more time. Time with nothing holding them back. No guilt or responsibility. She just wanted Cal to want her for herself.

"I understand," she finally said.

The tension between them eased. He nodded and gave a half smile. "Thank you."

"No, thank you." She cleared her throat. "For trusting me. I don't know what your brothers will choose to do at the end of this project. They love you, Cal. I see it when you're together, but it's like you're all trying to find each other again." She paused, wanting to show him how much he meant to her. The lines had already been crossed. The best she could do at this point was help them both succeed. "I promise you this: I will do everything in my power to make sure we both win and get what we need. At all costs."

His eyes darkened. Heat blasted from his gaze, wrapping her in sizzling warmth. "You already did, baby. You already did."

Words failed her, so Morgan looked into his eyes. Smiled.

And prayed he was right.

chapter sixteen

I t's gorgeous," she breathed, stepping back to admire the richness of the cabinetry and marble. "This kitchen is a stunner."

Dalton unfurled himself from his position on the floor and wiped his brow. Thank God the central air was cranking. The late-summer weather had been brutally humid, and working with power tools wasn't the best way to cool off. "Thanks. I've always liked a Tuscan type of kitchen, but the way you created a circular pattern opens it up." He motioned to the lighting fixtures that dangled from the ceiling. "And these pendants are unique. I've never seen anything like it."

Morgan grinned. "It's a small lighting place back in Charleston that does all my work."

He raised a brow. "Is that why you got into a war with Tristan about not purchasing it at his place?"

Morgan shook her head, grabbed a clean cloth, and began wiping off the thick layer of dust that had settled on every surface. "Tristan is too stubborn, so we made a bet. He ordered his lighting, I ordered mine, and we'd decide who was right."

Dalton laughed, grabbing his bottle of Dasani. "I'm gonna assume his shipment went back?"

"Damn right. He also owes me a statement."

"What type of statement? Didn't he get his money back?"

She shot him a wicked grin. "I made him write up a formal apology acknowledging me as a better design artist than he is."

Dalton burst out laughing. "Holy shit! That's so childish. I'm surprised at you."

"Childish, yet effective. He'll never question me again."

"I like you, Morgan Raines."

"I like you, too, Dalton Pierce. Even if you do cause havoc with the females on-site."

Over the past weeks, she'd grown closer to Cal's younger brothers. Once Dalton stopped flirting and realized she belonged to Cal, they fell into an easy camaraderie, almost like siblings. Their shared love for woodworking and transforming old junk into treasures built a mutual respect. With his surfer hair, his stunning blue eyes, and the artistic ink scrolling over both biceps, the man seemed able to mesmerize the female species. He was also charming enough to actually get women to forgive his many indiscretions, which fascinated her. He was dating Ashley again and another lady from the textile store. Thank goodness she'd already gotten her deliveries and installation before Dalton could break another heart. The time frame for him to gain forgiveness was way too tight to handle.

"Hey, I've been a good boy, according to Cal. No more catastrophes. Still on schedule. What could we possibly have to worry about?"

And right on cue, Tristan came stomping through the door.

Uh-oh.

Dressed in a smart charcoal suit, red tie, and silver cuff links, he cut an impressive figure. His Italian loafers squeaked as he marched toward them, his elegant features twisted in a pissed-off grimace. Giving her a polite nod, he turned full force on his brother. "Did you have a fight with Sandy Harper's father?"

Uh-oh.

Dalton stretched like he didn't give a care in the world. "Who's Sandy Harper?"

"She's the real estate agent over at the Sand Acre mall. Her father is Jack. He hired us to redo his deck. Remember that job?"

Dalton scratched his head. "Oh, yeah. What a nightmare. I kept telling him we needed to do redwood maple, but he was stuck on some cheap Trex imitation wood. Does he think we're, like, fucking Home Depot or something? Of course, I refused until he agreed to let me show him how the redwood would look."

Tristan ground his teeth, reminding her of Cal's habit. He practically hissed the words out. "You can't refuse a client because you don't like their choices! I was just negotiating a property and ready to close with a huge profit margin. Until Sandy Harper walked in and said her client refused. When I asked why, she said her father has a pile of wood and no deck and she didn't trust me. What the hell did you do, Dalton?"

Dalton narrowed his gaze. "I ordered the sample so I

could show him how it would look. He's gonna love it and book me for the job. I planned to go out there tomorrow. I'll handle it."

Tristan raked his fingers through his hair. The strands fell back in perfect precision. So different from Cal's, who always had hat head or looked like he had rolled right out of bed. Of course, it made him look so sexy, she hid his combs. "You always say you'll handle it," Tristan said bitterly. "You're not Michelangelo, and sometimes you need to suck it up and do what the client wants."

"Even if it's wrong? If I didn't think he'd go for the redwood, I would've shut my mouth and given him the Trex. He doesn't want the Trex. He wants to be impressed and in love with his new deck. When did that become wrong? I do my job with pride."

"I'd rather you do your job and get paid."

Dalton shook his head in disgust. "Why are you buying property anyway, dude? That's not your role here. Your ass should be in this house with Morgan and me to get this done in time. Instead, you're playing real estate games, and you're no *Million Dollar Listing* agent. You're not even half as good-looking and you have a hell of a lot less money."

Morgan bit her lip and tried to step in. "Umm, guys, how about we talk about this later? We're tired, it's hot, and it's been a long day."

"Are you kidding me? That show is a joke. I could outsell any of those agents, because I know how to redo a property. I pull my weight on this project every day. Is it wrong that I'm the only one who can see the future? Securing this property means we'll be renovating the project, then we can sell it for a huge profit. Sticking with only building is a mistake."

"We're not even gonna be here next year, dude!" Dalton yelled. "I thought the plan was we get in and get out. Cal wants this company, not us."

"Cal isn't capable of running this company the way I can. He's not Dad. I've been thinking about this problem for a long time and finally came to a decision." His jaw clenched. "I want to run Pierce Brothers. I think it's time for a change around here."

The silence was deafening. Dalton stared in shock at his brother. "You never wanted Pierce Brothers."

Tristan's eyes turned cold. "Yes, I did. I was pushed out and decided not to fight. But this time I'm not giving up. The company needs a visionary, and Cal isn't ready to make the changes."

Dalton took a step back. "You'd turn on him?" he asked. "On me?"

"I'm not turning on anyone. I'm just claiming what's been mine all along."

"Is that how you see it, little brother?"

The familiar voice rang through the air. Cal stood framed by the doorway, his gaze expressionless as he took in the exchange. Dalton muttered a curse. Emotions swirled and crested in the room, and raw masculine energy pressed down upon Morgan. This was a testosterone battle way out of her league. Still, she needed to try.

Pasting a smile on her face, she stepped forward. "Cal, I just think things got a bit out of control. Maybe we can take a break. Regroup. Let's quit for the day."

"I appreciate your trying to help, Morgan. I really do. But I think it's best if you leave now."

She glanced back and forth between the three of them. Half of her stubbornly refused to leave him, but this was a family crisis they needed to solve themselves. There must be a way for them to find each other again. Maybe if she left, the fight would turn and they'd make up. Maybe they could be a family once more.

"Will you be all right?"

Another man might have mocked her or beat his chest in masculine outrage at such a question. Cal only smiled, the last bit of warmth in the room. "Yes. I'll call you as soon as I'm done."

"Okay." She paused. "I know you have issues. I know it's not my business. But family is special. You don't choose blood, so it's not supposed to be easy. You understand each other in ways no one else could. Just . . . give each other a chance. For all of your sakes."

Morgan walked out and left them alone.

Cal heard her words, and his gut lurched. She sounded just like Mom. Always trying to stop the bickering and remind them of what was important. Yet, here he stood, listening to his middle brother plan to cut him out and leave him behind. Had it really come to this?

Especially this week. God, not this week.

Six years and it still felt like yesterday. Six years ago, his mother had died in that car crash and changed everything. His brothers were finally together, yet so far apart, they hadn't even mentioned the date to one another. Grief beat in his bones, and he desperately fought back. Not now. The anniversary was always painful, but this year all the memories were close to the surface, ready to draw blood. He just had to keep it together a little while longer.

Cal dragged in a breath and faced his own personal firing squad.

Tristan, never one to hide, met his gaze head-on. A crazy flash of respect trickled through Cal. Even now, pitted against each other, he managed to be proud of who Tristan had grown up to be. A man who had carved out his own future. Still, there was a darkness in Tristan that bothered him. A sad place he couldn't seem to reach, as if the best parts of his life were already behind him and he'd accepted it without a fight. "I don't want to make this a TV drama of the week, Cal. I was going to talk to you anyway."

Cal walked into the shell of a house that wasn't his and leaned against the new island Dalton had finished. "Seems like a good time now."

Tristan shifted his stance. Dalton glanced from one to the other. "Tristan thinks he's smarter than both of us," Dalton said. "Guess he's gonna save the business by his own hand."

Tristan shook his head. "What do you care? You just want to build your own projects without consequences and go back to California."

"Maybe. Maybe not. Pierce Brothers is mine just as much as yours. If we work together as a team, maybe we can build something even better."

"I'll believe it when I see it."

"Cut it out," Cal interrupted. "Do you really think I'll just step back and let you take over what I built, T? You have great ideas. I want to hear them and implement them, but we have to get through this project and the next few months before we can start experimenting."

Tristan made a rude noise. "Right. You'll never give me validation, Cal. You and Dad were alike and never enjoyed having anyone question your decisions. You don't want input—never did. It's happening all over again, but this time I'm not going to run away. This time I'm fighting for what I want."

"You want me out?" he asked calmly. He tamped down on the slight panic. His own brother seemed like a stranger. There was no trace of the boy he'd grown up with. Going on adventures in the woods, and sharing details of their first kisses, and facing down Dad as a team, always a team. All of the memories drifted in front of him, but Tristan saw nothing. Just what he thought he wanted.

"Of course not," Tristan said politely. "I want to work with you. But the dynamics need to change. I want you to take a step back and let me spearhead Pierce Brothers. I do have some ideas I'd like to implement, and of course you'd continue as the main builder, but this company needs more than you can give. It needs a new direction you're not able to take it in. I can."

A humorless laugh escaped Cal's lips. "Oh, boy, this is good. You run off and leave me with Dad and the mess left behind, refusing to come home for five years. Now you want to ride in on your perfect white horse and make it yours? Life doesn't work like that, bro. I'm the one who's stuck around, taking the daily crap. The problem you've always had was tunnel vision. I'm fine if you want to incorporate real estate and redesign. Hell, I think it's great. But we're builders first. Pierce Brothers Construction. If we lose sight of our main goal, we're going to forget who we are."

Tristan shook his head. "You're wrong. My tunnel vision is being able to see the future. I just bought two properties and plan to flip them for a huge profit. If we keep being afraid to branch out, Pierce Brothers will wither and die. You're afraid to grow. You think like Dad. Hell, you're still taking his orders from the grave, just like a damn lackey."

Rage shot through Cal. His fingers curled into fists. "And you're a damn coward. Instead of fighting for what you wanted, you slunk away. Now you want to come back here and take the company because you think it's easy. You know nothing about this company."

Tristan raised his voice. "I know when I asked for your backup, you screwed me. You watched me walk without a glance back. I'll never forgive you for that."

"It wasn't the right time!" Cal yelled. "I begged you to wait. Instead, you got bullheaded and pushed too hard, too fast. I had no choice, especially once Dalton followed you. One of us had to stay."

Dalton threw up his hands. "I'm tired of both of you. Whine and bitch when you always had more than me. Dad treated me like crap."

"He recognized you had a gift," Cal said. "He treated all of us like crap. I just took it instead of heading out."

Tristan glared. "Don't get all high and mighty, Cal. You probably planned it that way. You always wanted what was mine."

"It was all of ours to take or leave," Cal said. "You made your choice."

"Well, I'm making another one. This time I'm fighting for Pierce Brothers. Whether you like it or not."

They stared at each other. The tension crackled like a live wire between them, ready for a drop of water to fully explode.

"There will be nothing to fight for if we don't deliver this house," Cal finally said. "We have three months left."

Tristan's face reflected cold civility. "I'll do what needs to be done. But once the terms are met, things are going to change. Whether you like it or not."

Tristan left.

Dalton cursed and gave the worktable a vicious kick. "His ego is out of control. He needs to get laid."

Cal groaned and rubbed his temples. "I don't know who he is anymore."

Dalton cocked his head and studied him. "Maybe you never knew either of us," he said softly. "Maybe you saw exactly what you wanted to."

Cal jerked back. "What the hell does that mean?"

Dalton picked up his tool case. "Nothing. Never mind. I'm outta here."

Cal watched his brother walk away. The house fell quiet except for the soft creak of wood settling and the hum of crickets. Each time he hoped they were growing a tad closer, they had a blowout. Now Tristan wanted to yank away control of Pierce Brothers, and Dalton spouted confusing philosophical statements he probably didn't even understand himself. All Cal wanted to do was finish the house and present the lawyer with the profit margin. The rest he'd deal with later. If he thought about trying to build a relationship with his brothers and finishing the house and trying to figure out his relationship with Morgan all at the same time, his head would frickin' explode.

Cal left the house, thoughts of his brothers and broken family following him home.

chapter seventeen

Morgan poked her head into Sydney's office and waved. The redhead was chatting on the phone while typing furiously on the computer, several files open in front of her. Sydney smiled back, motioning with her head to wait.

Since that fateful night of Morgan's arrest, Sydney had become a close friend. The woman had a wonderful sense of humor, as well as a sharp directness Morgan appreciated, and made sure a fun female event was scheduled once a week. For the first time, she'd discovered the value of hanging with another strong woman who had her own challenges, yet faced them with her chin up and a positive attitude. She'd finally met Becca and enjoyed a Disneyfest of princess movies and popcorn. The little girl looked exactly like Sydney and had a wicked sense of mischief that charmed her immediately. Morgan was already half in love with her and was looking forward to spending more time with the dynamic female duo.

Sydney clicked off the phone and rolled her eyes. "Please tell me we're going out tonight. This place has exploded, and I swear, all I can think about is wine."

Morgan laughed. "Sure, tonight is good."

"Good. Becca has been begging for our babysitter to come over and play, so I have no guilt. Sometimes she orders me to go out, almost like she senses I need adult time. Four years old, and she's already brilliant, with a stubborn streak. Lord help me with the teenage years."

Brady came out of the conference room with a harried look on his face. "I gotta get out of here," he muttered. Dark hair caught back in a ponytail, his usual polished demeanor held a touch of the desperation. "Sydney, if anyone calls, tell them I'm working from home. This is like a pit of pythons, and I'm not getting swallowed whole today. How are you, Morgan?"

"Good. Client issues?" Morgan asked.

Brady gave a theatrical sigh. "Pierce issues. Meaning these three are going to put me in an early grave. Have you seen them yet today?"

Morgan shook her head. "I had some earlier appointments but wanted to stop and see Cal. Did something happen?"

Brady and Sydney shared a look. Something passed between them but it was obviously private. "Nah, just a bad day. Syd, keep an eye out and call if you need me. See you ladies later."

Morgan watched his retreating back and frowned. Last night, she'd tried to get Cal to talk about the confrontation between his brothers, but he refused. He smiled and held her and promised there was nothing to worry about, but a dark cloud she didn't understand seemed to hover around him. Almost like a brewing storm that she had no clue how to avoid. Her heart ached for him. "Is Cal in the back?" Morgan asked.

Sydney sighed and grabbed the ringing phone, motioning her to head to his office. Morgan walked down the carpeted hallway and found the door halfway open. She pushed it back and ducked her head in. "Got a minute?"

Cal looked up and gave her a tired smile. "For you? Always." He stood up, and she walked into his arms without hesitation. Warmth and strength closed around her, and she rested her head on his shoulder, enjoying his presence. The delicious spicy scent of him surrounded her. She lay quiet for a few moments, breathing him in. It shouldn't be this comfortable, or easy, at such an early point. At least, that's what her mind barked at her when the voice of doom clicked on and gleefully listed the million reasons a long-term relationship would never work with them.

But her body was currently making her mind her bitch, and Morgan loved every second.

"What's up?" he asked.

"Dalton's finishing up cabinetry and laying the flooring. Tristan is working on finishes and handling the appliance delivery. I'm heading out to check on things soon. Stuck with paperwork?"

She knew Cal hated being in the office, away from the action, but today he seemed a bit distant. As if he had something on his mind. The fight with his brothers? Or was he beginning to tire from this relationship? Worry nagged at her, so Morgan eased back and put space between them. He let her.

"Handling some phone calls and contracts. Finalizing

some invoices Tristan didn't get to yet. Sounds like you have everything in control for today."

The warning bells clanged louder. "Sure. Sydney and I are going out tonight," she said casually.

"Good." He glanced down at the stack of papers on the desk, obviously distracted. "You'll have fun."

Sometimes he asked her to stop by after dinner to see him. Sometimes he growled in her ear about missing out on her delectable body but encouraged her to have some girl time.

Not today.

Morgan ignored the dread creeping over her and gave him a tight smile. "You look busy. I'm going to head out. I'll talk to you tomorrow."

He'd already dismissed her, sitting back down and staring down at the desk. "Great. Have fun."

She walked out on leaden feet and stopped by Sydney's desk. "What time should I pick you up?" she asked. Morgan kept her tone light and frothy.

"Seven's good." Sydney peered at her, concern showing in her green eyes. "You sure you want to go out? It's okay if you made plans with Cal."

Sydney knew they were dating, and Morgan had recently confessed they were sleeping together. She'd learned to trust Sydney and her confidence. "Nope, we have nothing going on. I better get going. See you tonight."

The rest of the day crawled by. It was as if she were seeing the world through a distorted lens. Did Cal need a bit of distance? They'd been spending an awful lot of time together. Maybe he just needed his space. Men got weird when things got too intense.

She went over their time together and told herself to just back off a bit. He'd been sweet and given her a hug. Sure, he seemed distant, but maybe a few evenings off to let things simmer would be helpful. He was dealing with family stress and the terms of the will. She didn't need to see him all the time. Going out tonight with Sydney would be good for them.

Morgan ignored the emptiness and got back to work.

Cal drove his pickup blindly outside the busy city limits and toward the edge of town. The music was loud, but he only heard a dim buzzing. His head was full of images and his stomach—or his heart—was filled with emotion. Wherever those damn things came from.

He finally pulled into the old pub that had been bought and reopened, the place Morgan had been arrested for prostitution. No one would look for him here. He'd already turned off his phone so he wouldn't be bothered by thoughtful calls or texts from friends. Morgan was out with Sydney and safe. Tonight he was finally alone with the only person he wanted to be with.

Mr. Jack Daniel.

He pushed his way into the tavern, noticing the wide-open space and interesting decor that had been added. The bar was still massive but crumbling from the foundation. He made a mental note to tell the owner it needed some refurbishing, then slid his ass onto the stool and waited for the bartender.

A woman in leather pants and a low-cut black top with fringes floated over to him. There was a detailed tat on her right shoulder, climbing down her arm, of a sword with droplets of scattered blood. Interesting. Her hair was long and wild and black as a raven's. She screamed sex and fierceness, but there wasn't even a stirring in his pants. Nope, give him his silvery-haired, petite, polite, sassy Southerner any day and his dick couldn't be tamed. He was in a lot more trouble than he thought. "What can I get you?"

He slapped a few bills on the bar. "Bottle of Jack."

Her brow climbed. She looked him over with a narrowed gaze, as if trying to decide if he was worth giving the bottle to. "Why?"

Cal snorted. "Because I said so. Do I have to talk to the owner to get my drink of choice?"

She crossed her arms in front of her chest and scowled. "I am the owner. I serve who I want, when I want. If you wanna get plastered and make a scene in my bar, I'll make sure you can't walk in the morning, and it won't be from the alcohol."

If he'd been in a better mood, he would've laughed. Right now he needed only one thing, and the fastest way to get it was honesty. Bartenders were like priests. They didn't give a crap what you did and always took your apology. If he was sincere, she'd give him the bottle for his sins instead of a rosary. "I need to forget. Today is a bad day, and the only way to get to midnight is to be drunk enough where I don't care."

She jerked back, her dark eyes reflecting a shock of pure pain that stalled him. Then it was gone like a flash of light, and she nodded. "Give me your keys."

He slid them to her, and they jangled as she dropped them into a large glass jar by the cash register. Then plucked a bottle of amber liquid and set it beside him with a shot glass. "Go slow and pace yourself. I agree with you."

He poured two fingers into the glass. "About what?"

"Today is a shit day."

She turned back to her customers. He stared at the liquid in the glass for a while. The memory came rushing back in all its violent, gory form.

Cal had taken the call.

He'd been in the kitchen cooking a late-night dinner and wondering why his mother wasn't around. Cal had been working late at the job site and entered an empty house. She usually had a plate ready for him when he returned home, but lately he'd noticed she missed dinner a few times per week, citing mysterious errands.

The voice on the line iced his blood. They couldn't reach his father. His mother had been involved in an accident. He needed to come now.

Fighting back panic, he'd driven frantically to the hospital, telling himself she would be okay, because shit like this only happened to other people or in the movies. He wasn't going to lose his mother at twenty-six years old. He was going to marry Felicia, give his mom a bunch of grandchildren, and watch her grow old. That's the way things were done. That's the way life was supposed to be.

But Cal learned life made its own rules.

She died before she could get to the ICU. Limbs crushed from crumpled metal and skin peeled off from the fire. They tried to keep him away, but he went apeshit so they finally left him alone. Cal wept at her bedside before they could take her away and hide her under a sheet. He held her charred hand before they could stick her in a coffin and plaster makeup on her and pretend she was okay.

His father came, with Dalton and Tristan trailing behind. The horror hit full force when they all realized the fight was already over before it had even been fought. Mom was really gone.

When the police told them the driver had also been killed, Cal remembered the confusion that struck them all. When they discovered it was a man's name they weren't familiar with, even his father reacted with disgust and denial.

Until they learned it wasn't a mistake.

That there were two fully packed suitcases in the trunk. And two tickets to Paris booked in his mother's name and the stranger's.

It was then that Cal learned life wasn't done with them yet. Caught in a tangled soap opera, they found his mother's closet halfway bare. The damning evidence kept building, but Cal knew the truth the moment they discovered the small shell-like box she'd always treasured, zipped up in a protective pink pouch in her suitcase.

Her sons' baby teeth. She treasured each tooth fairy visit with an open joy that was part of who she was, collecting each one like gold on a pirate hunt. She labeled each one with their names and kept them all in a box Tristan had given her one Christmas. Cal used to tease her about the creep factor of keeping teeth, but she always insisted having a part of them with her all the time soothed her. It was a way she could let go as they grew up.

Cal realized she'd never been planning to come back.

Somehow the mother he loved and adored had had a secret life. She'd left her sons and her husband behind, never realizing an ignored red light would be the turning point in all of their lives. They'd never be able to talk to her, get any explanations, or find a way to understand the horrific betrayal.

After that, Christian Pierce became so cold, Cal wondered if real blood actually ran through his veins. All of them died a bit that night. They never seemed able to recover once the light of their lives flickered out.

Six years. How had six years gone by so quick? How had six years gone by so slow? Pain clawed at him. Cal lifted the glass in silent salute to the Fates and tipped it back. The fiery liquid burned his throat and warmed his belly. It would take a long time to wipe out the images, though. But the bartender was right.

Cal needed to pace himself.

Morgan touched up her lipstick, ready for her night out, when her iPhone beeped. Sydney's voice echoed on the other end. "Morgan, it's me. I'm so sorry about this, but I have to cancel tonight."

"Are you okay?" she asked.

"Yes. Becca just has a low-grade fever, and I don't want to risk it. I hate that it's last-minute, but I'd be worried about her all night."

"Oh, my goodness, of course! I understand completely; she needs some fine chicken soup and her mama."

Sydney laughed. "That sounds like the perfect combination."

"No worries. I'll snuggle up with a good book tonight and order in."

"Good." She paused. "Have you spoken to Cal?"

Morgan stiffened. She didn't want to think of Cal and his odd detachment. "Not since I saw him at the office. Why?"

The pause was longer this time. "Did he seem like he wanted to see you tonight? Or act differently?"

"He definitely didn't want to see me tonight," she said. "He seemed fine. What's going on, Sydney? I feel like I'm missing something."

A sigh poured over the line. "Normally, I'd mind my own business, but Cal's changed since you both started dating. He's happier than I've ever seen him, but he's not the type to reach out and ask for help. I think he needs you."

"I don't think so," she said softly. Her throat tightened. "He was very . . . distant."

"Morgan, today is the sixth anniversary of his mother's death," Sydney said quietly. "She died in a horrific car accident."

Morgan sucked in her breath. "I didn't know."

"Cal doesn't like to talk about it. The thing is, they found out she was running away with another man. They both died in the crash. Cal and Dalton and Tristan never got over the betrayal."

Her mind spun. The way Cal seemed tired and disengaged today. The raw emotion whenever he spoke about his mother, and his refusal to discuss the circumstances of her death. The pieces clicked together, and emotion surged. Morgan had been so focused on herself, she'd never noticed the ache in his eyes. "Is he with his brothers?"

"I don't know. They've been separated for five years, so I'm not sure if they'll be together tonight."

"Do you have any idea where he'd be?"

"No. Maybe at home. Or some bar. He wouldn't want to see anyone he knows."

"I'll call and then go to his house first. Thanks for telling me, Sydney."

"You're welcome. You're good for him, Morgan. He seems . . . whole with you."

They hung up, and Morgan immediately shot him a text. Then a call that went straight to voice mail. Grabbing her purse and her keys, she decided to head to his house first.

She had to find him.

chapter eighteen

D ude, what are you doing here?"

Cal looked up. The Jack was finally doing its job, and a delicious fog softened all the hard edges. He squinted and focused on the familiar figure next to him. A short bark of laughter escaped his lips. "Hey, little brother. Fancy seeing you here."

Dalton slid onto the bar stool next to him. He shook his head and picked up the half-empty bottle. "Started without me, huh?" His wavy hair was twisted back in a ridiculous man bun, and his face looked a bit haggard. "Well, I guess I better catch up."

Cal dragged his bottle back across the bar. "Get your own bottle."

Dalton shook his head and lifted his hand to motion to the bartender. She came strolling over with pure disdain, like he was an annoyance for wanting a drink. Yeah, he was beginning to like her.

"I'll have a matching bottle," Dalton said. His youngest brother flicked his gaze over the hot girl. "Nice tat. What's your name, gorgeous? Mine's Dalton."

Her scowl grew deeper. "None of your business. You re-lated to him?" She jerked a thumb at Cal.

"Yep. He's my brother. But you'll like me better."

Cal smothered a snort at Dalton's smooth lines. His charm was epic, but this woman only looked annoyed. "I don't like either of you. Keys."

Surprise shot over his face. Dalton wasn't used to women ignoring him. Cal raised his glass in another salute to Hot Girl's prickly attitude. "She don't like you, Dalton. Deal with it."

Dalton handed over his keys and smirked. "Give me some time, dude."

The bartender slid over a bottle and a shot glass, then poured them both a glass of water. "No attitude or puking in my bar," she warned. Then floated over to her other custom-ers while Dalton watched her like a wolf on a starvation diet.

Cal rolled his eyes. "Really? Do you have to bang every girl you ever meet?"

Dalton poured a shot and tipped it back. "Nah, just ninety-five percent."

"How'd you find me?"

Dalton shook his head. Some of the sarcasm drifted away. "Wasn't trying. Just needed a place to drink and get through the rest of the night."

"Yeah, me too." They sat in silence for a while, listening to the soothing sounds of a bar crowd. "It never gets easier. Does it?"

"Nope."

"Is it worse being here? Where it happened?"

Dalton peered into his shot glass like it held the answers.

"Nope. I was halfway across the country, and I still kept seeing her face in that fucking coffin, while Dad pretended he didn't give a shit she was gone."

"Yeah."

They drank. Cal admitted the presence of his brother next to him eased the tightness a little. Usually it was only him and the demons. Having somebody who understood gave some comfort.

"Where do you think Tristan went tonight?" Dalton asked.

A voice rang out. "Right here with you boneheads."

Cal swiveled his head around. Tristan stood by the door, glaring at them as if they'd taken his own personal bar space. He shook his head in pure disgust and sat down on the third stool. "Out of all the bars in all the world, you have to be in mine."

"This is kinda weird," Dalton announced. "Did you know we'd be here?"

Tristan snorted. "No, I thought I was being smart by coming here. Thought I wouldn't see anyone. I'm in a shit mood."

"Join the Jack club," Cal said.

Hot Girl came over and wrinkled her nose in disdain. "Don't even tell me you know these two."

Tristan gave a polite smile. "They're my brothers. I'll have what they're having."

The bartender scowled. "I don't have another bottle of Jack. You'll have to share." She slid a shot glass over and put out her hand. "I need your keys."

"I don't drive intoxicated," Tristan said.

"And I don't care. Give me your keys."

Dalton grinned. "You are really hot."

"And you're not."

Cal and Tristan gave a hoot of laughter. The keys dropped in her outstretched hand and she added them to her famous glass jar. "Your brothers will tell you the rules." She turned and dismissed them with a shake of her long hair.

Tristan leaned over. "What rules?"

"No fighting or puking," Cal said. "Or she'll kick our asses."

Dalton stared at her. "That would be one delicious ass kicking."

Tristan poured himself a shot glass and sipped.

"Thought you were more of a vino guy," Cal commented.

Tristan turned. His amber eyes brimmed with emotion and demons. "Not today."

They all nodded in agreement. And drank.

Cal wasn't sure how much time passed before the silence was broken. It was as if by sharing the evening together, and the memories, the brick barrier between them began to soften and liquify. It also helped that they began to pass tipsy and hit the outside barrier of intoxication.

"Do you really think I'm like Dad?" Cal asked.

His brothers shared a meaningful look. Tristan finally spoke up. "Dad understood you best, Cal. It was harder for Dalton and me to break into the secret club, and it seemed to get worse. Are you like Dad in a lot of ways? Yes. But you're not cold. You're a pain in the ass but not an asshole. Make sense?"

Actually, it did. Cal rolled the words over in his head. "I think you two were Mom's favorites," he said. "Dalton was the baby she doted on. And you, Tristan? She was always talking about how you reminded her of Great-Grandpa. Said you have vision and think outside the box."

Dalton rolled his eyes. "Don't tell me this is gonna become a whinefest of who Mom loved more."

Cal pushed his fingers through his hair. "Nah, I'm just telling the truth. No whining."

Tristan shook his head. "You weren't around when she was constantly telling me to be more like you. From your stupid grades to your work ethic. Drove me nuts."

"Yeah?"

"Yeah."

Cal let the information settle into a good place. He hadn't known that.

"I didn't fuck Felicia," Dalton announced.

Tristan groaned and took another sip. "Really, dude? Do we have to get into that again now?"

Dalton stared at him with pure stubbornness. "I know I deserved shit from Cal. I know I did it in the wrong way, too, but you never wanted to listen to my explanation."

Cal let out a breath. "Fine. Go ahead. I've got a bottle of Jack and I can't run away. Just tell me."

"I caught Felicia with Jeff. They were making out in the woods."

"Jeff Pallatin? My buddy from high school?"

Dalton nodded. "I freaked out, and when I confronted them, they swore to God it was a fluke and it would never happen again. She begged me not to tell you. Cried hysterically that you were the love of her life and one mistake shouldn't destroy everything. The wedding was only a month away, and I didn't know what to do."

"You never told me about that," Cal accused. "Why would you keep that from me?"

Dalton clenched his jaw. "I didn't know whether to believe her! I was worried about you, and I thought if I could prove she was a cheater, I'd go to you with the information. I told her I'd keep her secret. I began to flirt with her, watching to see if she'd become uncomfortable or back off, but she came right at me, Cal. That night you walked in on us was the first time I kissed her. I needed to know she'd cheat before the wedding, with your own brother. I planned to go right to you and tell the truth, but you walked in on us and I never got to explain."

Cal gritted his teeth and tried to sort through his rioting emotions. He'd been so hot for so long about his brother betraying him, it was hard to try to understand where Dalton had been coming from. Deep inside, hadn't he worried Felicia wouldn't be happy with one man? Mom said she liked her, but Cal spotted the worry in her gaze. Felicia was a glittering peacock who adored attention. She loved all the trappings Cal could give her. It had never really gone beyond the lust for money and the zeal of youth.

Dalton rubbed his head. "It was such a stupid idea. But I was only twenty-two, Cal. You rushed into the marriage after Mom died, and I was all fucked-up, thinking I was gonna be this hero and save you."

Tristan cleared his throat. "I believe him, Cal," he said quietly. "Dalton's always been a man whore, but he wouldn't cross that line. He's also stupid enough to think that type of plan could work."

Dalton groaned. "Thanks for nothing, bro. But it's true. Looking back, I know I should've just told you straight up when I saw her kissing Jeff. Instead, I built this whole PI scenario and screwed everything up."

How strange, after all these years of refusing to talk about the incident, that it was finally revealed in a dingy bar on the anniversary of his mother's death. The wound that had festered for years broke open and oozed clean. The truth rang out in his brother's voice. For the first time, Cal accepted the reality and realized though he'd screwed up, Dalton had never set out to seduce his fiancée. It was almost as if he could feel his mother's presence wrapping around them, desperately trying to get them to listen to one another.

"I'm sorry, Cal. I really am."

The apology struck home. Emotion clogged his throat, so he just nodded. His voice came out gruff. "Apology accepted."

And then they sat awhile longer, not talking.

Morgan slammed the car door and trudged toward My Place. The sight of it made her shudder with bad memories, but she'd been all over Harrington and was running out of places. Her texts and calls went unanswered, and she couldn't get ahold of Dalton or Tristan, either. Maybe Cal had sought haven in a bar more outside of the main town.

She pushed open the door and stopped short. And stared at the sight before her.

Cal, Tristan, and Dalton sat on stools by the bar with two empty bottles of liquor. They were laughing. Tristan had his arm loosely wrapped around Dalton's neck in a man hug, and Cal was scrunched forward close to his brothers, a huge grin curving his lips.

Without giving away her presence, Morgan stepped to the side and watched the amazing scene before her.

"They belong to you?" Raven motioned toward the men. Humor glinted in her dark eyes. "'Cause if so, you're driving them home. They're trashed, and I confiscated all their keys."

Morgan smiled. Warmth flowed as Dalton gave Cal a noogie on the head. It was as if through their mutual pain, they had found each other again. "Yeah, I got them covered. What is it about men drowning their demons in alcohol?"

Raven shrugged. "Fastest way to silence them." Her face hardened. Seems she had big secrets, too. "You're not a hooker."

The statement caused a flush to darken her skin. "No, I'm definitely not a hooker," she retorted. "I'm hoping we can put that whole scene behind us and never bring it up again."

"Already done. I knew the cop was an ass. Anyone could see you're as proper as they come."

Morgan sighed. "Yeah, I know. Boring, right?"

Raven smiled. "You? Don't think so. I have stellar instincts, and you've got more hidden layers than an onion, as Shrek would say."

"Thanks." Somehow the comment from such an interesting woman spiked her ego. "I do."

"Which one's yours?"

A glow settled over her. "The one on the right."

Raven nodded with approval. "Good choice. Stay away from the one in the center. That man's a heartbreaker."

"Came on to you, huh?"

"Darling, he probably comes on to anyone with a vagina."

She smothered a giggle at the accurate description. "Thanks for taking care of them."

"Part of my job."

Morgan headed over to the men. Heart pounding, she hoped they wouldn't feel as if she was intruding on their private time. The need to check and make sure Cal was okay won over her nervousness, so she stopped beside them and laid a hand on his broad shoulder.

"Cal?"

He looked up. Those charcoal eyes lit up with pleasure, and without a word he reached up, tangled his hands in her hair, and kissed her.

The dim hoot from his brothers singed her ears, but she didn't care. She kissed him back in full public view in the bar she'd gotten arrested in. And she loved every moment.

"Hey, baby," he drawled. The slight slur told her he'd been drinking awhile. "What are you doing here?"

"My plans with Sydney got canceled. I wanted to come see you. Give you a ride home. Hi, Tristan. Dalton."

Dalton treated her to a sloppy grin. "Morgan! Wanna drink with us?"

Tristan raised his glass. "Another bottle of Jack!"

She laughed. "No, thanks. Just think of me as your designated driver. Are you ready to go home yet?"

She had no problem letting them have their time with one another. As long as they were together, she'd wait till closing time to drive them home, so at least she knew they'd be safe. Raven strolled over and leaned her elbows on the bar.

"I'm out of Jack, gentlemen, so I'd advise taking the lady up on her offer."

Tristan looked mournfully at the bottle. "It's all gone."

Cal nodded. "We drank it all."

Morgan pressed her lips together. "You certainly did. I'm impressed."

"Sh'okay. I'm ready to go." He stumbled a bit getting up, but for a man who had downed a whole bottle, he was pretty steady on his feet. Tristan and Dalton got up carefully, swaying just a bit. "It worked."

"What did?" she asked.

Cal gave her a beautiful smile. "I feel better. You're pretty."

Morgan linked his hand with hers and squeezed. "So are you."

Dalton grinned at Raven. "You're pretty, too," he said. Raven laughed. "I'll be back for my keys tomorrow, and maybe you'll even give me your name. My name is Dalton. Dalton Pierce."

Raven jerked back. Her mouth made a tiny little O, and shock filled her eyes. "Pierce?" she whispered. "Your name is Pierce?"

Dalton didn't seem to notice her reaction. He slapped his hand on the bar. "Yes, sirree. This is Cal and Tristan. We own Pierce Brothers Construction. You're pretty. I'd like to take you out."

Morgan would've laughed, but Raven suddenly looked like she'd seen a ghost. She pressed her hand against her trembling mouth and gazed at each of them, a frantic look on her face. What had just happened?

"Raven? Are you okay?"

Raven backed away from the bar. Her voice turned to ice. "Get out of my bar."

Morgan blinked. "But—"

She couldn't finish because Raven turned and disappeared.

Dalton gave a longing sigh. "I don't think she likes me."

Morgan made a note to check on Raven later in the week. She didn't know what had happened, but she didn't have time to figure it out now. She led the men out of the bar and into her tiny sports car. Tristan's head bumped against the roof, and Cal groaned as he folded his long legs up so his chin almost rested on his knees.

"Open the windows," Dalton croaked. "All I smell is Tristan's breath."

Morgan hit the button and the roof rolled open. They breathed a sigh of relief. She smiled and drove.

The stars streaked overhead, and the wind was warm as it whipped against her face and lifted her hair. She loved driving a convertible and the small sense of freedom it gave. Finally she pulled up to the mansion and helped them inside the house.

Balin and Gandalf leaped up, knocking down Tristan and unleashing an array of curses from Dalton as he fended off paws and licking tongues.

"They need obedience school, dude," Dalton said.

Cal surrendered to the affection. "They flunked out twice. I don't know what else to do. Someone's gotta give them water. And walk them."

"I'll do it," Morgan said. "Just tell me what to do."

Dalton groaned. "I gotta go to bed. Night, guys."

Tristan stumbled to the stairs, fingers pressing against his head. "Me too. I'm too old for this shit."

"Night," she called to them. She placed her hands on her hips. "Okay, what do I do for the dogs? How do I walk them?"

"You don't. They'll trample you. Just let them go potty down the path toward the woods."

"Do I watch them? Or would they rather have privacy?"

He grinned. "Just let them do their thing. Then give them fresh water. I gotta sit."

She led him to the couch and brought him a glass of water. "Here, drink this." Once she was sure he wasn't going to get sick, Morgan faced the dogs. Shaking with enthusiasm at the thought of a different routine, they waited. "Okay, pups. Let's do this." She opened the door and they bounded out with her, following her down the woodsy path they'd taken to get to the shed earlier.

Morgan dragged in a deep breath as the darkness closed over her, but the sound of paws in the brush and panting breath soothed her. Gandalf and Balin wouldn't let anything happen to her. Gandalf squatted, then gave her a sidelong look of concern, so she turned her back and let him go without an audience. Balin kept sniffing and running ahead, leading her in a bit deeper.

"Okay, guys, let's head back," she called.

They gave her a joyous look. Then disappeared into the brush.

Her heart pounded faster. Something brushed against her leg, and she jerked back, frantically shaking her foot. This was creepy. Where'd they go? The sound of bushes moving and a low whimpering echoed. Oh, my God, what if a bear got them? No, there weren't any bears out here, but could a gopher hurt them? A deer?

"Gandalf! Balin! Get over here now!" she whispered fiercely.

A low bark. A rustling. Oh, hell, what was that? She took a few steps back, eyes trained on the shaking bush in front. "Doggies?" Caught in the middle of a horror film, she moaned, wondering if she should run back to the house and get Cal's help, or stay and fight.

A small black-and-white furry thing raced in front of her. Skunk!

Morgan began to turn and get out of the danger zone, but suddenly both dogs leaped out of the bush, and a scream broke from her lips. She fell back on her ass in the brush, and then the dogs were on her, thinking it was a fabulous game of hide-and-go-seek that they had won.

As she fought them off and scrambled to her feet, the smell hit her first. The stench was so bad, she gagged, pressing her hand over her nose to try to ward it off. She had to get away from the skunk's spray, so Morgan began running out of the woods, and the dogs followed, barking wildly.

Finally she reached the house and breathed in a sigh of relief. Then gagged again.

Oh, no.

The stink of skunk was everywhere. As the dogs circled her, their fur gave off waves of scent, and when she lifted her shirt up and sniffed, Morgan stumbled back.

Oh, no.

They'd gotten sprayed by a skunk. All of them. Her first official walk with the dogs and she came back like this. Cal was going to kill her.

"Stay here," she warned them. "You can't go in the house. Goodness gracious, what am I going to do now?" she moaned.

Morgan went inside and stayed back in the foyer. "Umm, Cal?"

"Everything go okay? I'm starting to feel better."

"I had a little problem."

He quirked his brow and stared at her. "Why are you all the way over there?"

"Because I can't get too close to you. We, umm, encountered an animal."

"We have tons of deer here, baby. Nothing to worry about. You can let the dogs back in."

Morgan sighed. "Actually, it was a skunk."

His eyes widened. "You gotta be kidding me."

"I'm sorry, Cal. They wandered into the woods and I couldn't stop them and suddenly there was this skunk that jumped out at me and it was too late."

Cal shook his head and stood. "Okay, that happens sometimes. I got an outdoor shower to give them a bath. Let's make sure they don't come in the house. It's hard to get the smell out."

"Then I'd better take a shower with them."

The knowledge dawned on him at the same time he smelled her. Cal stopped midway, his face crumpling up to protect himself from the stench. "You got sprayed?"

She nodded miserably. "'Fraid so. I smell bad, Cal."

He studied her for a moment in silence. Then burst into laughter. "Poor baby. Come on. Let's get everyone cleaned up. I think I have a few cans of tomato juice left."

Oh, hell no.

chapter nineteen

Cal waited outside the bathroom door, listening to the sounds of the shower. His hand closed around the knob, and he bowed his head, thinking, considering. But there really was no other choice. He'd never wanted Morgan Raines as badly as he wanted her right now.

They'd managed to clean up the dogs, fighting to wash the wriggling skunk-sprayed furballs with tomato juice. Finally, after two rounds, the stench had faded, and after an extensive drying session, they were let back into the house. The entire process had gotten them both wet, sweaty, and smelly, so he waited for Morgan to rinse herself off and shampoo her hair. Once the initial wash down was done, she was safe enough to send into his master bathroom for a steam shower, and he went into one of the other bathrooms to cleanse himself.

Most of the hard liquor had worn off after a few glasses of water, and though he still felt a bit woozy, he wasn't going to be sick. As he headed into his room to bring extra towels, the full impact of the night hit him full force.

Somehow, someway, he'd broken down some barriers with his brothers on the worst day of the year.

And for the rest of his life, some of the most painful memories would be replaced with Morgan. The way she hunted him down at the bar. The way she took care of him. The way she'd looked when telling him about the skunks, and the way she laughed when they were stuck in the shower with two smelly dogs. She'd managed to replace so many bad images with ones that made him smile. And just like that, Cal knew his mother's anniversary would have a whole new meaning.

He caught the low strains of off-key singing, and he didn't hesitate a second longer.

Cal opened the door and went in.

Steam curled in thick clouds, hovering in the air. He caught the outline of her naked body through the fogged-up door, her Southern twang adding extra zest to the popular Rob Thomas song. Cal quickly stripped off his clothes and joined her.

Her gasp was accompanied by the instinctual raising of her arms to cover herself. He grinned, his gaze raking over her wet curves, from her gorgeous plump breasts peeking out from her fingers to her round hips and soft thighs, all the way to her pretty pink-painted toes.

"What are you doing?"

He put the condom on the shelf and grabbed the bottle of liquid gel that smelled like coconut. "Making sure you don't miss a spot." He squeezed a dollop in his hand. "Can't have you in bed smelling of skunk."

She dropped her gaze deliberately to his heavy erection. "Why don't I believe that's your only motivation?"

He stalked over to her and pulled her hands from her breasts. Raw want licked at his nerve endings, fogged his brain, thickened his dick. Everything about this woman made him want to howl at the moon and mark her as his. "You came to find me. Why?"

He soaped up her breasts, rubbing his palms in circles, dragging them across the tight peach tips. A moan escaped her lips. She arched back into the caress. "I was worried about you. Sydney told me what happened."

He paused. "I'm not sure how I feel about that."

Her hands covered his. "Don't be mad at her, Cal. She was worried about you. And I—I thought your reaction in the conference room meant you needed some space. From me."

His brows snapped into a frown. "What the hell would give you that impression?"

Morgan bit down on her lower lip. "You seemed distant. I don't know, I just thought maybe you were feeling pressure because we've been together a lot, so I figured I'd back off."

Anger pumped through him. He grasped her upper arms and lifted her to her toes. "Next time you try and jump to conclusions, ask me. I won't lie to you, and I won't play games. And I'm far from done with you, Morgan Raines. In fact, I just started."

His mouth slammed over hers, punishing and demanding. She thrust her fingers in his hair and gave herself to the kiss, wildly pumping her hips against his throbbing dick and biting down on his lower lip. He pushed her against the slick tiled wall and lifted her right thigh high in the air so she was open to him.

"Tell me you'll never do that shit again," he growled. He nipped at the vulnerable curve of her neck and caught her shudder.

"I won't."

"Tell me again why you came after me tonight."

Her face reflected the truth. Her voice was a whisper of sound. "Because I didn't want you to hurt. Because the idea of you in pain broke my heart. Because you mean something to me."

Fierce satisfaction slammed through him. "Good. That's exactly how I feel about you. Now I'm going to fuck you until you know I'm not going anywhere."

He donned the condom in record time and pushed between her thighs. His eyes rolled back in his head as her tight, wet heat clenched around his dick in a silken vise. Keeping her legs spread and her back pinned against the wall, he rolled his hips and took her hard with short, violent thrusts. She gripped his shoulders, her fingers curling and her nails sinking into his flesh, crying his name over and over in a chant that urged him on. Faster, harder, he claimed her as his and felt the spasms clutch her body as she fell into climax. A low, guttural moan ripped from her throat. He swallowed it whole, fucking her mouth as fully as her body, and captured every glorious convulsion that wracked her.

His kiss gentled as she came down from her orgasm. He was still hard inside her, so he lifted her up so her head slumped over his shoulder and her legs wrapped tight around his hips. Cal carried her out of the shower and to the bed, laying her down on the satin quilt without breaking contact.

Her eyes drowsily opened. An ocean of blue trapped his gaze. "I thought you couldn't have sex when you were drunk. I thought it didn't work."

God, she was adorable. He pressed a kiss to her swollen

lips. "False. In fact, you're in for a hell of a night. I have whiskey dick."

She blinked. "Sounds serious."

He nipped at her earlobe, then soothed it with his tongue. "It is. Means I can go for hours without coming. Means I intend to devour you inch by inch and make you come so many times, you beg me to stop."

Pure lust dilated her pupils. She tightened her muscles around him and dragged out a groan. "Bring it."

And right then and there, Cal dove out of the plane in a free fall that stole his breath and pumped him full of adrenaline.

He fell in love with Morgan Raines.

With a savage groan, he took her lips and plumbed the sweet treasure while his fingers tweaked her hard nipples. She twisted underneath him and ran her hands over his body, stroking his ass and hips, digging her fingers into his thighs as she asked for more of him.

Cal pulled out, ignoring her broken protests, and slid down her body. Kissing her stomach, nibbling at her belly button, he used his thumbs to part her swollen lips and gazed at the pretty pink folds glistening for him. Using his tongue, he licked her, swirling just enough pressure around her clit to bring her to the edge and keep her there. Adding two fingers, he pumped in and out in slow strokes until she pushed up for more, grabbing his head to force him to give her more pressure. He chuckled and scraped his teeth against her clit, never slowing his motions. Finally he felt her body tighten and shudder in delicious torment. Curling his fingers, he hit her sweet spot and sucked hard on her clit.

She came in his mouth.

Feeling like a conqueror, he drank in the very last of her climax until she collapsed against the mattress, breathing hard.

"Cal, oh, my God. Cal, I can't take any more. It's too good."

He looked up at her sweet, naked body and slowly smiled. "Not done."

He flipped her over. Placed her on her knees. And plunged into her pussy.

Her scream was heaven to his ears. Grasping her hips, he pumped in and out, holding her at an angle where her G-spot was stimulated. Sensitive from her last two orgasms, she shook beneath him, pleasure and pain twisting together to give her the sweet edge he wanted, and with one final buck, he owned her final orgasm.

This time Cal let himself go over with her. Body stiff, he threw his head back and let go, spilling his seed and giving himself up to the raw tendrils of satisfaction seeping through him. He collapsed on top of her, catching his breath, and managed to roll to the side to avoid crushing her.

She buried herself into his arms, limbs entangled with his, cheek resting on his chest.

Finally she spoke in a dazed slur.

"Anytime you want to go drinking, feel free. The benefits are amazing."

He laughed and hugged her close.

"I need aspirin."

"I need more coffee. Why'd you drink the last cup?"

"Dude, I gave you the bigger mug. My head is throbbing, and all I could find is Tylenol. I need something stronger."

Tristan tried to snort but ended up rubbing his temple. "Maybe if you didn't drink your coffee with all that froufrou cream you like, you'd get more of an effect."

Dalton glared from across the island. "Really? You're gonna try and pick a fight with me over cream in my coffee? And you call me immature."

Morgan tamped down a chuckle and slapped down two pills in front of Dalton. "Take these. They work." Dalton quickly chugged them down with water. "I'll make pancakes and bacon. There's another pot of coffee brewing."

"Yes!" Dalton softly cheered. "No eggs, though—I'll puke."

"Can I have my bacon extra crispy?" Tristan piped up.

"Yes, but you both have to clean up the kitchen. I hate dishes."

"Deal," they both agreed.

Morgan found the frying pan and set out the ingredients. Humming under her breath, she maneuvered around the kitchen in bare feet, yoga pants, and a pink T-shirt. A few weeks ago, she had begun stuffing some extra clothes in the top drawer of the bedroom bureau. Just in case. She tried not to think too much of it, but slowly realized the spare outfit had been joined by bras, panties, and pj's. After all, Morgan never knew when Cal's brothers would be around. She refused to be caught in the walk of shame. Balin and Gandalf lay in front of her, hoping to catch a crumb or two. She'd already let them out and fed them breakfast.

"I can't believe you got skunked," Dalton said. "Is it

wrong to tell you I'm glad I went to bed before that incident? Washing those mutts is a nightmare."

"It wasn't a highlight of my life," she said. "And I don't think I'll ever look at tomato juice the same."

Tristan shuddered. "You're a trooper, Morgan. Thanks for driving us home last night, too."

"I'm glad I can help. I'll take you both over so you can pick up your cars this morning."

Dalton lit up. "Nice. Maybe the bartender will be there."

"Her name is Raven. She's the owner. Sydney and I met her a few weeks ago. She also makes a mean cocktail."

"Just my type of woman."

Tristan shook his head. "As long as she's not involved in building any houses or selling real estate, go for it."

Morgan wondered if she should tell them about her strange reaction once she heard their name, but Cal entered the kitchen and wiped out any other thought in her brain. Struck mute, she took in his rock-hard abs and his low-slung sweats that only emphasized every delicious muscle on his body. He caught her looking and gave her a slow, smug smile. Morgan turned back to her skillet, ignoring his knowing laugh. "Morning." He grabbed a mug and filled it with coffee. "How you ladies feeling today?"

"We'll live," Dalton muttered. "Let's just say I won't be friends with Jack for a while."

Tristan laughed, then winced. "Morgan's taken pity on us. She's cooking some breakfast."

"Thank God. You two bozos need to learn to cook."

Dalton rolled his eyes. "I can grill and put cold cuts on bread. I'm good."

"Hey, I cook," Tristan said. "I happened to take a course at the culinary arts school last year on French food. But I need to feel inspired."

Cal muttered something into his mug. "French food to go with fancy French wine, bro? Next thing you'll be crooking your pinkie finger while you drink your tea."

"Fuck you," Tristan said mildly.

Morgan fought a giggle and began sliding pancakes onto a plate. "First stack's ready. Bacon's almost done. And if you don't leave one last mug of coffee for me, you'll never get this again."

The guys began munching, and Morgan enjoyed the scene before her, warmth buzzing through her veins. God, it felt good to be with these men. She cared about them, on and off the job site, and wanted them to be close again. She'd never had this before. After she left her parents, she'd been a bit of a nomad, chasing the next job and next location. Being in their kitchen, cooking breakfast, laughing at their banter—all of it struck her with a sense of rightness.

What was happening to her?

She poured the batter onto the hot pan and studied the bubbles popping up. Things had shifted between them. It wasn't just the sex. It was almost as if by admitting she'd been afraid of him pulling back, she strengthened the bond between them. Emotion was now involved, and she was caught up in the intricate web of pure want and need for Caleb Pierce. Her heart had galloped ahead and caught up with her body. She was falling hard, and she had to make a decision.

To tell him the truth.

Time was ticking, and they had only three months to complete and deliver the Rosenthals' house.

He deserved to know she couldn't have children. He needed to know how important her job was, and the demands of constant travel. He was owed the right to choose the life he wanted, and it might not include her.

The word *love* had not passed between them, but it was there. It seethed beneath the surface, waiting for the time to spill from their lips.

She shook off her thoughts at the smell of burning batter and slid the last stack of pancakes onto a plate along with the bacon. They were talking business. "Paint is scheduled to be here tomorrow," Tristan noted, cutting his pancakes into perfect bite-size pieces. "Sod is ordered for the landscaping, and I've got Brian coming in with the trees and bushes. The rock wall should be done by then, too, and then we just need to finish the covered deck."

Cal shoved a few pieces in his mouth at once. "Thank God we don't have to deal with the pool problem. The sauna and hot tub will keep them happy, and if they're still here in the spring, we can do a quick install."

"Smart," Dalton commented. He ate with more casualness, stopping often to nibble on bacon or take a swig of coffee. "Did you put that in the contract, Morgan?"

"Damn right I did. Pierce owes us a pool if we decide on it. No reason to take that on now, and the Rosenthals agreed."

"Appliances should be installed by end of the week. When are the movie screen and chairs coming?" Tristan asked.

"I'm putting in the call to check today," Morgan noted,

finally sliding her own pancake onto a plate. "But I need those red velvet cushions and tapestries here. Tell me they're not back-ordered. Please."

Tristan waved his hand in the air. "I took care of it."

"I love you."

"Hey!" Cal swung his gaze and gave a mock glare at his brother. "Don't mess with my woman."

Morgan couldn't help the silly grin that curved her lips. "Neanderthal," she whispered teasingly.

He winked.

She finished eating and scooped up her cell phone. "I have to make some calls, y'all. Oh, Dalton, I need you to look at that grandfather clock I bought from your shed. I want to restore it and carve in the Rosenthals' initials for the numbers."

"Nice. Cal made you pay for that stuff?" He turned and shot his brother a look. "You couldn't even give it to her for free, dude?"

Cal shrugged. "It's business."

Morgan laughed and walked out of the kitchen. "Wouldn't want it any other way," she called out.

She strolled out with a light heart and a promise to come clean with Cal.

Soon.

Cal took his coffee out to the front porch and sat down in his favorite wicker rocker. The dogs dropped by his feet, their heads resting on each ankle, and he gazed out over the sprawling acres of lawn spreading as far as he could see.

He was in love with her.

Should've probably told her. He'd been a bit caught up in the sex and the need to mark her. Then she collapsed into sleep so fast, he didn't feel like it was the right time. He'd tell her, though. She needed to know. Cal wasn't sure if she was ready to say the words back to him. The woman kept her emotions tight, but the way she had looked at him last night and confessed she didn't want him to hurt gave him a clue.

He had three months left. To build a house. To make her stay. To get her to fall in love with him.

"She's cool." Tristan dropped in the chair next to him with a matching mug. Some of the tension had eased between them since last night.

Cal nodded. "Yep."

"Did you tell her why we were at the bar last night?"

"Yep."

"Things good between you both?"

"Yep."

"Thanks for the heart-to-heart, bro."

Tristan started to get up, but Cal shot his arm out and grabbed his brother's. He let out an aggravated breath. He wasn't used to sharing, but it was time he got used to having his brothers back in his world. "I'm in love with her."

Tristan jerked back. "Didn't expect that. She feel the same?"

"Not sure. I haven't told her yet. I'm afraid she'll make things more complicated than it is."

"She's a woman for a reason, dude. It's her job."

They shared a grin, and Tristan leaned back in the rocker. They sat in a comfortable silence that men understood and women bitched about. Within the silence, emotions worked their way out. "You really gonna try to take the company from me?" Cal finally asked.

Tristan waited awhile before answering. Just sipped his coffee and considered. "I'm not doing it to hurt you. I just feel it's best for the company to incorporate flipping houses and real estate. I think it's smart to have Dalton run the woodworking part, even though he sometimes goes nuts with his creative crap and pisses customers off. He's still the best."

"He is one talented son of a bitch."

"Makes his ego even bigger than it should be," Tristan said. "At first I didn't want to stay here. I had my own life in New York, and I liked it. But being back in Harrington, building houses again, working in the company, things started to stir. Now I want to stay. This is my home, but I can't continue as a lackey, Cal. I can't be ignored. And if I have to fight you to take control of the company to make my voice heard, I will."

Cal listened to the calm explanation and waited for the rage to hit. But it never came. He actually understood what his brother was saying. Oh, hell, he didn't like it, and he intended to make his own points known, but Tristan had never gotten the shot he always craved. His father had refused to let him have his dream. And the company was called Pierce Brothers. Founded by his mother for all three sons.

Not just Cal.

The acceptance was hard. He knew it wouldn't be easy, and there'd be a mess of pitfalls and stumbles, but Cal wanted to try. Because last night in the bar, with his brothers, he'd found a happiness he hadn't experienced in a long time.

"I'll try."

Tristan gave him an assessing look. "Don't patronize me."

"I'm not. When Dad refused to listen, and you took off to New York, I was sick. I felt like I had let you down. I told myself I was doing what was best for all of us, but the bottom line is I never fought for you. I don't think I wanted to. I liked being the one to call the shots. And even though Dad was hard to work with, there was a payoff being the only Pierce brother here. Makes me feel like shit, but I'm being honest. Maybe it's time we try again."

"You're open to letting me flip and do real estate?"

Cal nodded slowly. "We have to go slow. And we have to do everything possible to make sure Morgan gets her perfect house and we turn a profit by end of year. After that, yes, I'll work with you."

Tristan gazed at him for a look time. "You've said this before and things didn't change."

"I want to try again. Give me another shot."

His brother sipped his coffee. "Okay."

It was the best they were gonna get. Cal was satisfied. Nothing was guaranteed, and their promise could explode before they even got close, but steps had finally been taken.

For the first time, Cal felt like they had a true chance.

chapter twenty

L et's cancel the party. Stay home alone. In bed."

Morgan ducked as Cal dove for her, throwing her hands up to ward him off. The sexy gleam of mischief in his eyes told her he'd hunt her down and ravish her. "No!" she said. "It's been a few weeks since we've all been in the same room together. It'll be fun."

"I see my brothers enough, thank you very much. They just want a home-cooked meal. They're spoiled."

"Brady and Sydney are coming, too, along with Becca. Behave."

"But you like it when I don't." Her gaze dropped to his straining jeans, and Morgan had to fight her own impulse to have a quickie before everyone showed up. Goodness, she was becoming quite a sexual harlot. It seemed every time they were in the same room together, they couldn't keep their hands off each other. Restraining themselves on the job site only added to the delicious excitement and tension, until they fell into bed together and made love for hours.

She blocked him by shoving a cutting board and fat

tomato at him. "Later. I want to get the appetizers ready before they come."

Cal let out a breath and dropped them on the counter. "Fine. But my brothers live here, for God's sake. Why do they get special treatment? They should be helping in the kitchen."

"Because it's nice to do things for family."

"I'm nice. I keep Dalton stocked in Hershey bars. And I ordered that ridiculous French wine Tristan drinks like water. Cost me a fortune."

Her face softened as she gazed at him. Sexy as hell, dressed in jeans and a white button-down shirt left open to expose his muscled chest, he took her breath away. Hair damp from his shower spilling messily over his forehead, he stood in bare feet cutting up tomatoes, his musky, masculine scent filling her nostrils like the sweetest perfume. His outer gruffness hid a mushy heart that she was falling for more every day.

"You're a good brother," she said quietly. "You're a good man."

He looked up. His gaze devoured her whole, leaving nothing behind she hadn't already given him. "You bring out the best in me."

Her throat tightened. Morgan opened her mouth, desperate in that one moment to tell him how much he meant to her, but the sound of his brothers' voices filling the hallway stopped her.

"Tomato and mozz! Awesome," Dalton said, grabbing a fat piece of tomato.

Cal slapped at his hands. "We didn't even put the oil and

basil on! Hands off. Better yet, get your ass to work. Sydney and Brady are going to be here soon."

"What's cooking?" Tristan asked, peering into the super-sized Wolf oven.

"Spiral ham. Shrimp with grits. Zucchini and carrots. Biscuits and gravy."

"Damn, this is better than I thought. How'd you get to be such a good cook when you're stuck in hotels most of the time?" Tristan asked.

Morgan smiled and handed Dalton a stack of fancy china plates. "Here, set the table. My mama is Southern born and raised, so I learned to cook when I was young. Y'all don't understand a woman is nothing if she can't put a solid meal on the table and serve in three-inch heels."

"I'd love to meet your mother," Cal said, mixing up a bowl of oil, garlic, and basil. "Does she look like you?"

"Yep. Many say we look more like sisters than mama and daughter."

"A dangerous combo for your daddy, I bet," Tristan commented. "No siblings?"

"No, just me."

"Does she ever fly in to see your final projects?" Cal asked. "I'm sure she's proud of the work you do."

Morgan carried a crystal vase filled with pink roses into the dining room. "She tells me all the time how proud she is. I'm lucky to have her. And yes, sometimes she's able to come see me at the end of a project. Not this one, though. They're having the floral parade in Charleston, and she's booked solid through fall."

"Then maybe we'll have to go see her," Cal said.

She stumbled slightly and cut him a look. He winked and got back to chopping. It was the first time he'd mentioned a future after the house was completed. They'd grown closer the last two months, falling into a routine that soothed her soul. Morgan knew they needed to have a serious talk and see where they were willing to take their relationship. If he wanted to. Her heart leaped, but she was careful not to get her hopes up. She needed to concentrate on finishing up the Rosenthals' home and then deal with her burgeoning emotions for Caleb Pierce.

They worked in a steady rhythm until the doorbell rang.

Sydney and Brady stood on the step with Becca. Her bright red hair was curly, reminding Morgan a bit of Little Orphan Annie. Her white skin, freckles, and sea-green eyes could have landed her a movie role. She was all Sydney. Morgan gave Sydney and Brady a quick hug before kneeling down in front of Becca. "Hi, Becca. I'm so glad you could come tonight."

Becca grinned, popping out matching dimples, and Morgan's heart was fully captured. "Thank you for inviting me. Mama said you can come over again to watch *Inside Out*. I like Sadness the best, even though Joy is supposed to be the star."

"I'd love to see that movie. I made a big dinner. I hope you're hungry."

Becca nodded. "I like to eat a lot of things but not brussels sprouts. You're not cooking those, are you?" she asked in a worried tone.

"Becca," Sydney warned. "We'll eat whatever Morgan cooked for us."

Morgan laughed and offered her hand to the little girl. "No brussels sprouts. I don't like them, either."

Brady tugged on the girl's curls and tickled the back of her neck. "Neither does Uncle Brady. Yuck!"

Becca giggled, and they made their way into the kitchen. Dalton greeted them in his usual relaxed way, but Tristan seemed more formal. His gaze studied her with a bold curiosity, and he nodded quickly to Sydney, obviously uncomfortable in her presence.

Interesting.

"Watch out—the hounds are coming!" Cal called out.

Balin and Gandalf had been tucked in the back room while they prepped dinner, and now the scrambling of paws on the floor hit her ears. They came whirling around the corner, lost footing, and skidded right in front of Becca and Sydney. Morgan went to grab them in case the gentle giants scared Becca, but the little girl opened her arms in sheer joy and hugged them both at once.

They could have easily knocked her over with their tails or greeting, but instead they plopped themselves down in front of her, as if recognizing she was a child and they needed to be gentle. Balin moaned in ecstasy as Becca rubbed his fur, and Gandalf bumped his nose against her leg, urging her to do the same to him.

Sydney laughed and rubbed Gandalf's belly. "You guys are getting better," she said. "Did you finally graduate obedience school?"

Cal snorted. "Heck, no. I tried getting them re-registered and was told the class is full for the next year. I think they're lying."

Brady shook his head and handed off a bakery box with a bottle of wine. "I told you, Cal, they need a firm hand. Animals respond to discipline. Same thing in relationships."

Sydney and Morgan stared at him. "What did you just say?" they asked in unison.

Brady held up his hands in defense. "Let's be honest, ladies. A weak-willed, waffling man is not attractive."

Becca looked up from the dogs, a thoughtful expression on her face. "I like nice men," she announced. "They're the best."

Cal laughed. "Argument settled. Becca wins. Now let's go eat before Sydney and Morgan gang up on you, Brady."

They drank cocktails, nibbled on appetizers, and watched Becca run around with the dogs. By the time they sat down for dinner, everyone was laughing amid the brothers' bantering and teasing of Brady about his archaic views on women. Seemed the architect liked the old-fashioned Latin ways, where final decisions were made by men, and women's job was support. Morgan mentally hoped he'd find someone to challenge those views and teach him a few things. With his dark good looks and quiet intensity, she doubted he lacked for many women dying for the opportunity to tame him.

"Uncle Cal, I'm still waiting for my tree house. You said you'd build one for me. Sally Peters has a big one, and she has tea parties in there for special guests like Disney princesses." Her pout was pure genius and adorable. "I wish I had one."

"Becca, Uncle Cal is very busy," Sydney interrupted. "He has to build a lot of houses first before he can work on your tree house."

Cal faced the little girl with a serious expression. "I'm sorry, Becca, you're right. I did promise. Tell you what. I'm going to order the wood and supplies, and on the weekend we'll build it together."

Her eyes bugged out in shock. "Me? I get to build it with you?"

Cal nodded. "Yes. I need an assistant, and you need to learn the business. We need more women in our employment."

Becca clapped her hands. "Thanks, Uncle Cal. I'll do a great job!"

"I know you will, sweetheart."

Morgan smiled at the exchange. Sydney seemed choked up, but instead of gazing at her daughter or Cal, she stared straight at Tristan. A mingle of sadness and longing gleamed from her green eyes, but Tristan had ducked his head and missed the look. Suddenly he pushed his chair back. "Excuse me," he said roughly. "We need more wine."

Sydney turned away.

Dalton laughed, unaware of the sudden tension. "Always knew you'd make the best father out of us, Cal. Seemed to always attract animals and children like the Pied Piper."

"Do you have any children, Uncle Cal?" Becca asked innocently.

Cal grinned. "Not yet. But one day, I plan to have at least six."

Sydney winced. "Back off, buddy. Your woman may have a problem with that."

"Fine. I'll settle for five. There's something about a big, chaotic household that intrigues me. I think it would be fun."

Sydney gave a snort. "Sure. Not sleeping for a year due to colic or teething is fun. Worrying about every step you take until you're a nervous wreck is fun. Balancing work with day care and household tasks and watching *Barney* or *SpongeBob* instead of CNN is fun."

"We love to watch *SpongeBob* together," Becca said seriously.

"Yes, we do, sweetheart," Sydney said. "The reality is sometimes not what you think it is."

"But you got her," Cal said. "That's worth it all, right?"

Sydney suddenly blinked away tears. "Yeah. It is. You're right, Cal, it is fun."

Becca smiled sweetly, not caring that the conversation didn't make sense.

And right then and there, Morgan's heart sunk.

Cal wanted a big family. Somehow she suspected it, but she'd been holding out hope that maybe he wouldn't want children. The image of Elias leaving her after finding out what she couldn't give him slammed into her mind. Her fingers trembled around her fork. She had to tell him. Things were getting too serious, and she fell harder for him every day.

Brady interrupted her thoughts and dragged her back to the present. "So, Morgan, when is the Hollywood power couple flying in to see their house?" he asked. "We're still on schedule?"

She forced herself to focus. "We're nearing the end. The next few weeks are design oriented and final finishes. Each room has to be completed and decorated. Dalton's cabinetry turned out exquisite, and the exterior and landscaping are almost done. I have various tapestries and rugs arriving, along with the furniture. We're in excellent shape."

"What's your next job, Morgan?" Dalton asked. "Going somewhere more exotic than Harrington?"

Morgan shifted in her seat. Usually she lined up her next gig way before the one she was working on ended. She had a vast supply of contacts and a potential client list that would keep her busy for a long time. This time, though, she hadn't committed to her next job. She told herself she liked keeping her options open, especially since a lot hinged on the Rosenthals' opinion of the house she created for them. But deep down she knew the real reason.

It was Cal.

She hated the thought of leaving him behind.

Morgan felt his gaze probing, but she kept her attention on her plate. "Not sure," she said lightly. "I have many options. Right now I just want to concentrate on delivery."

"I hear you," Sydney said. "I'm sure they'll be pleased. The last time I visited I couldn't believe how gorgeous it is. They'd be crazy not to love it."

Tristan returned and refilled his wineglass. "I've cleared my schedule to help you with the decor. Managed to snag a few pieces in SoHo you'll go crazy for," he said. "Oh, and we do have something to celebrate." His eyes sparkled with triumph. "Pierce Brothers is now the new owner of two properties."

"The farmhouse on Balance Street I told you about?" Morgan asked.

He nodded. "That was an amazing tip. I also scooped up the other one on the block they were renting out to tenants. I'm going to convert it into a two-family house."

"So, you solved your issue with Sandy Harper?" Dalton's eyes glinted with mischief. "Thought her father hated my work on the deck."

Tristan sighed. "You were right. He loved the red maple and sang your praises."

"A little louder, please?"

"That's all you're getting, bro."

Dalton laughed and raised his glass. "Well done. Here's to making buckets of money and taking on the Property Brothers."

Tristan rolled his eyes and picked up his glass, then swung his gaze to Cal.

Morgan held her breath. Cal kept his face expressionless but slowly raised his glass. "To Pierce Brothers," he said quietly.

They shared a small smile, and Morgan finished her dinner with a goofy grin of satisfaction on her face.

A few hours later, the dishes were piled up to the cabinets, the garbage cans were full, and company had left. Tristan and Dalton snuck out before Cal could ream them about helping clean up, then sniped about his cleaning woman wanting to quit since his brothers moved in.

"Screw it," Cal said, looking at the disaster. "I'll make them deal with it tomorrow. Imagine how surprised they'll be when they figure out we didn't clean up for them."

Morgan nibbled her lip in concern. "Yes, but the party was my idea."

"You cooked and set up. They clean. We're going to bed."

"But—"

He stopped any further protest by scooping her up in his

arms and carrying her to his bedroom. As hard as she tried to be affronted by the caveman behavior, she was already wet with need for him. That commanding streak in him turned her on. He placed her on the bed, then took a few steps back. Eyes hot and hungry, he studied her, then sat down in the oversize leather chair in the corner of his room and hooked one foot over his ankle in a relaxed pose.

She blinked. "Aren't you coming over here?"

His slow grin was wicked and made her belly twist. "I want you to strip for me."

She sucked in a breath. Hesitated. He waited her out, and suddenly her inner temptress stood up and took over. There was something about the way this man made her feel that urged her to do things she never would have thought of. She felt like his own personal goddess: a sexy, powerful woman with nothing to hide. Morgan loved the way he made her own her sexuality without apology.

Without answering, she climbed off the bed and stood before him. She was dressed in simple cream pants and a lilac blouse. But she'd put on her new bra and panty set today, knowing he'd take it off. Even buying it made her feel deliciously wicked.

She began to unbutton her blouse, going slow and steady, then dragged the silk material down over her shoulders, hooking it on her elbows. He ate her up with those charcoal eyes, taking in the delicate plum lace of her bra. "Went shopping, huh?"

"Yes."

"I highly approve." He cleared his throat. "Continue."

She smiled with pure naughtiness and dropped the

blouse on the floor, then slowly removed her bra as well. Running her fingers lightly over her breasts and tweaking her nipples, a low moan escaped her lips. He shifted in the chair, his erection straining his jeans. Dragging her palms down her belly, she stroked the edge of her waistband, then snagged her thumbs underneath. Paused. And slowly dragged the pants down.

"Fuck. You're beautiful."

The matching plum thong showed off her freshly shaved pussy and stubble-free legs. She kicked the pants off her feet and waited.

"Finish for me, baby. You're killing me."

She caressed her outer thighs and grasped the sides of her panties. Pulled them off. And stood before him naked.

He drank her in, and she reveled in the glory of being the woman he wanted. She straightened up so her breasts thrust out proudly. Let him take his time. She waited for him to come to her.

"What are you reading now?"

Her mouth fell half open. What had he asked? Her brain was a bit foggy, and it was obvious he was aroused, but had he just questioned her on her reading material? "Huh?"

Cal got up from the chair and walked to the bureau. "I was thinking about our conversation regarding books. Reading. You said you enjoyed Austen, Dickens. Fitzgerald. You know, boring old classics, dusty with age." Opening a drawer, he took out a few condoms and laid them on the table. "Is that what you're still reading?"

She watched him reach inside the drawer, sifting around for something. What the heck was going on? Morgan fought for sanity. "Umm, I wasn't expecting a literary discussion right now, but yes, I told you. I like the classics."

"Interesting. Did you finish up the story on the inn? You know, the one in Boonsboro?"

Uh-oh.

Morgan stared at him with suspicion. "Yes. Why are you so interested?"

His fingers closed around the object he'd been looking for, and he pulled it out of the drawer. A bright, silky red tie and a pair of fuzzy handcuffs were laid next to the condoms. The roaring in her ears grew to epic proportions, and her blood flowed thick and hot in her veins. A small moan broke from her lips. He knew. Oh, God, he knew.

"Nora Roberts is a popular author," he said conversationally. His fingers stroked the bright tie in a loving caress. Wetness dripped down her thigh. "She certainly doesn't write dry history books. Seems you're a bit of a romantic, Morgan Raines. And from your newest read, a very naughty, naughty little girl."

She tried to speak, couldn't, then tried again. "You read my Kindle."

"Yep. I grabbed it to check something on the Internet quickly. Imagine my surprise when I discovered the current scene with Amy and Brad. Quite hot." He clucked his tongue and faced her. The full force of his masculine presence whipped around her. His eyes glazed with lust and a determination that wracked shivers from her body. "I took the liberty of checking out your library to see what else I was missing. There wasn't a Dickens in the bunch."

"Cal—"

"I'm going to do very bad things to you tonight, Morgan Raines. You won't need a safe word."

"Cal—"

"'Cause all you have to do is say yes."

He stopped in front of her. His thumb pressed against her lips, dragging them open. Her tongue flicked out to taste him. He leaned in, and his breath struck her with each deliberate word. "I'm going to make some of your fantasies come true tonight, baby. What's your answer?"

The floodgates broke open and she reached for him, tangling her fingers in his thick hair and offering her naked body up to every filthy thing he wanted to do to her.

"Yes."

His mouth came down on hers, and he delivered on his promise.

Hours later, Cal listened to her breathing in the silence. Stroking her back, he relaxed in the tangle of damp sheets and held her. Her leg was thrown over his thigh and hooked around his knee. Her silvery hair spilled over his arm and caught slivers of moonlight that leaked through the half-open window.

He couldn't let her go.

When Dalton had brought up her next job, his gut clenched and he fought to keep his shit together. She seemed to hesitate, as if she struggled with her decision to leave again as much as he was struggling to see if she'd stay. He didn't have the answers, but Cal knew he'd do anything to make it work. She completed him. Oh, God, he was channeling stupid Jerry Maguire, but it was damn true. He liked the man he was around Morgan Raines. He saw a bright future that was completely cliché and wonderful. Dogs, children, chaos, having fights, making up, making love, building houses. He wanted it all. He wanted it with her.

"Morgan?"

"Yeah?" Her voice was tinged with the thread of sleep. Her warmth seeped into his skin.

"I love you."

She stiffened. His heart banged against his chest, and dizziness threatened. Cal hadn't said those words to anyone besides Felicia. Oh, crap, he was so stupid. Women didn't want to hear that type of declaration after sex. They wanted it in the daylight, in a romantic setting, with more of an explanation of why he loved her. He'd screwed up. Could he take it back and tell her later? No, it was done. Ruined. He squeezed his eyes shut and trapped an aggravated groan. This was bad.

"I love you, too."

The words hit his ears and his heart at the same time. A quiet joy settled into him, found a home, and stayed. She loved him. And they'd work out the rest later.

She didn't say anything else after that. She didn't have to.

Cal held her tight and they lay together in the dark.

chapter twenty-one

Yes, I'll expect you here tomorrow afternoon," Morgan said briskly. "I'll pick you up from the airport and take you straight to Harrington . . . No, everything's in order, and you'll be ready to spend the first night in your new house . . . Good. Call me if there's any questions or issues. Safe travels."

She clicked off the phone and dragged in a breath.

It was almost showtime.

They'd worked tirelessly and nonstop over the last weeks as all the final details pulled together to create a livable home. Morgan stood on the newly paved path, looking up at the gorgeous blending of brick and stone, the two giant columns that set off a wraparound porch. Two smaller decks were strategically placed above the porch so an onlooker's eye would be drawn to the center and caught in the impression of sheer power and grace. Each precious curve and piece of wood had been lovingly picked and it seemed to show in the aristocratic lines of the house.

Purple plums, rosebushes, African grass, pear trees, and an array of distinctive landscaping swirled through rainbow rock to a private deck with a hot tub and a gorgeous cedar-built sauna and outdoor shower. Elegant French doors opened up to the back of the house and led to a private circular staircase connected to the master bedroom. The Rosenthals could easily leave their own oasis in secret and be straight at the hot tub without walking through the house.

Morgan pressed the remote in her hands and watched windows and doors slide open on command with just a whisper of sound. The alarm had finally been installed and the cable company had spent days working on having everything wireless—not a cord in sight.

She walked through the heavily carved mahogany door inspired by Cal's home and looked around in the hushed space. The grand staircase and floating balcony overlooked the open kitchen, which was a dream for any type of cook. Gorgeous precious-metal pendants lit up the marble countertops in a huge horseshoe, with a built-in stove top and cabinets shimmering with the richness of cedarwood. Cushioned stools lined the countertops, and Dalton had constructed a table with special carvings in the legs and matching benches. The golds, tans, and muted wine color blended together to soothe the eye but also startle as bursts of vivid orange and sunny yellow showed within the accents, from the mix of sculptures and four-foot vases filled with exotic florals.

Her gaze assessed the subtle green walls, cocktail tables, and vintage coffee table Dalton had restored. Beveled crystal glass mirrors shimmered, and muted oriental carpets were thrown carelessly in seemingly random patterns that set off the artsy chairs she'd lovingly reupholstered in lipstick red. The punch of color was needed to pull together the aesthetics of the open brick fireplace, wood, and neutrals.

A smile curved her lips as she took in the grandfather clock on the far wall. It was the true centerpiece of the room, with the Rosenthals' initials stenciled in place of the numbers. The soothing ticktock brought a life to the room that would've made it more of an art show. Morgan had made sure each room had a particular item that carried the decor. For the main living room where people would gather, it was the clock, representing the passing of time, the preciousness of moments that tick by, and the reminder to spend them well.

As Morgan toured the rest of the house, a strange worry and restlessness coursed through her blood. This was her client's house, but so much of herself beat through the soul of every room. How many times had she struggled not to cross the line of what she envisioned this house to be and what the Rosenthals expected? She'd never had that problem before. Morgan followed the rules. But this one time she'd taken a bit of a gamble. From the herb garden on the back patio, to the stark white lounge chair that was both comfortable and stunning, to the jewelry armoire lined with velvet and embossed gold knobs, she'd picked every piece of furniture and accent that would add to the spirit and beauty of the house.

It had to work. She'd done what Cal had urged and gone with her gut. Surely her years of experience and knowledge would shine through. The Rosenthals would see what she saw in this house and fall in love. Then she'd score another large client and move on to the next house.

Morgan stopped as the thought held her. Was she going to leave? Maybe she could stay in Harrington for a while. Take a mini vacation to recharge, and see if they could build a life here. It was possible. Anything was possible.

He loved her.

She hugged the knowledge to her heart. That night, his simple words had buried deep inside her and claimed her forever. He wasn't a man to give love easily. But once he did, Morgan knew she'd be his own personal queen, because that was the way he made her feel every day and every time he looked at her.

"Morgan? Are you up there, baby?"

His voice echoed through the house. She climbed the stairs and looked into his beloved face. His dark tan had lost some of its color from the turning of fall but was still a golden brown. Tiny lines bracketed his eyes and mouth, confirming his nonstop schedule and little sleep gotten within the past weeks. His T-shirt was dusty, and his jeans had a hole in the knee.

"We alone?" he asked.

"Yeah."

"Good." Cal reached out and snagged her around the waist, dragging her into his arms. His lips feasted on hers with a raw hunger that still held an edge, as if he'd never get enough of her. She clung to his hard strength, enjoying the scent of male sweat and spice that drifted from his skin. She kissed him back with open enthusiasm that ripped a growl from his mouth.

"We doing dinner tonight?" he asked.

"Yes. I told your brothers they could join us."

He groaned and nipped at the curve of her neck. She shivered. "Princess, I'm sick of those bozos eating with us all the time. I have a great idea. Let's go back to your hotel and order room service. Let them fend for themselves."

She laughed. Funny, she was rarely at the Hilton anymore. Her nights were spent over at Cal's, along with weekends when they could catch a few hours of downtime. They'd gotten in a routine, including his family, that made her soul happy. "I promised. The Rosenthals come in to-morrow, so tonight is our last dinner for a while. I'll be tied up with them finalizing details, completing paperwork, and making sure they're settled in Harrington."

He blew out a breath. "Fine. But I'm kicking them out early."

"Fair enough." They gazed at one another for a moment, and she caught an odd light in his eye. "What's the matter? Is something wrong?"

Cal cocked his head, as if wondering if he should say something. "Yeah. I don't want you to go when this project is over, Morgan. I want you to stay with me. Do you want that, too?"

Her heart surged at the same time that guilt struck her. She remembered his words to Sydney. He wanted a big fam-ily. He was owed the truth before they promised each other anything. "Yes. I'm in love with you, Cal. I want to work something out, because everything about us feels good and right."

He tried to pull her back into his arms, but she backed off. Wrapping her arms around her chest, Morgan gathered her courage to tell him her story. "What's the matter, baby?

You don't look happy. Are you worried about work? I don't intend to tell you to stop doing something you love. Look at this house. It's amazing, and you put your whole heart and soul into it. It's not just a house anymore. You actually made it a home without one person living in it yet."

She blinked back the sting of tears. Damn the man. "Thank you for that. No, I have to tell you something I've been holding back. It never seemed like the right time, and I wasn't sure what would happen between us. I never expected to fall in love with you." She gave a half laugh, trying to gather her thoughts. "I don't want you to think I deliberately kept this from you for any other reason than I just wasn't ready."

"Okay. I'm listening."

Morgan dragged in a breath. "I can't have any children, Cal."

A frown creased his brow. He scratched his head and probed her face with his gaze. "Baby, of course you don't want children now. Did I scare you when I told Sydney I wanted a football team?" He grinned. "I'm sorry, I was talking about the future. Way in the future. Nothing to worry about now, I swear."

"No, you don't understand." She fought her nerves and pushed forward. "I *can't* have children. I'm not able to have children; I'm infertile."

He shook his head as if trying to make sense of her declaration. "Okay. I've heard of this before. When it's the right time and we decide we want to try and get pregnant, we can go to fertility experts. We'll look into options together."

"I had a hysterectomy, Cal. When I was eighteen, I was

diagnosed with cervical cancer. It spread fast, and my only option was the operation. I will never have your children."

He jerked back. Shock filled his eyes, and she watched him try to process. "Wait. You were sick? You had cancer?"

She nodded. "It was a long battle, but I'm healthy and strong, and my regular checkups have been clean. There are no guarantees, but the doctors feel positive."

"God, Morgan. I wish you'd told me sooner. That must have been such a horrible experience for you."

"It was hard, but I got through it. I'm stronger now, and I learned a lot of valuable lessons along the way."

Respect glinted in his eyes. But there was something more. A distance and worry that hadn't been there before. Like he was unsure what his reaction should be to her news. "I'm not surprised. Another reason you're incredible. I watch people give up every damn day. You? You're a fighter."

"I look at every day as a gift," she said softly. "But I still lost something precious that I'll never get back."

"You think not being able to have children changes the fact that I love you?" Temper flickered over his face. "You think I'm that type of man?"

She grasped herself tighter. "No. I knew you'd try to understand and support me. I know you still love me. But my question is this: Are you willing to give up your dreams of a family forever? Because I can't do this with you unless you're sure. I can't give my heart and soul to a man who's one day going to realize he needs to have a family to be complete."

"Has someone hurt you like that before?" he demanded.

"Yes, that's the real reason my ex dumped me."

"That's what you meant by a serious issue," he muttered. He turned and paced. She waited while he gathered his thoughts. "I don't like you comparing me to that asshole, Morgan. Dammit, I'm not the type of man to run at the first challenge we get thrown. I thought you believed in me more."

"I do believe in you," she whispered. "I just know this has high stakes for me. I'm being realistic about what I can give you. I've made my peace with this a while ago, Cal. Sure, sometimes I get angry or feel depressed, but mostly I love my life. I don't need my own children to be complete, but I understand if you do. That's not a terrible thing, it's just a fact. Have you really thought about what I can offer you?"

"We can adopt."

"Yes. If we both want to. But adoption is a long process. It's hard, and we have to be willing to love another child like our own."

"I can do that."

Something began withering deep inside at his stubbornness. He didn't want to think of himself as selfish or a man who'd run out on a relationship when problems arose. But this was bigger than an everyday problem. This was an important life choice, and politeness wasn't what she needed right now.

She needed the truth.

Morgan gathered her courage and crossed the room to him. She reached out and grasped his hands within hers. Jaw clenched, simmering emotions flickering over his face, he looked like a man who was haunted. And that wasn't fair to either of them.

"Cal, listen to me. You have to be brutally honest. You owe it to yourself, and you damn well owe it to me. This has nothing to do with being a good person, or nice, or standing by your woman. This is about a life you need to choose. Are you ready to give up on ever having a child of your own? Or will you regret that choice for the rest of your life because you were too proud to admit it?"

The silence seemed to shatter like broken glass. He jerked, turning his face from hers for long precious seconds that told Morgan exactly what she needed to know.

"I don't know."

The words dropped between them. Coldness seeped into her skin and her soul. She couldn't blame him. She couldn't even be mad. Morgan had held on to the last moment, but he'd already made his choice. And though she understood, there was still a part deep down that felt betrayed because he didn't love her enough.

"Morgan—"

She bit her lip hard and forced a wavering smile. "No, don't. You think I don't understand? I do. I don't blame you, either. I just—I just need to be alone right now."

"I don't want to leave like this."

She backed away from him, needing the distance. "We both need some time apart, Cal. It's been a hell of a week, and I need to organize for the Rosenthals' arrival. I'll take a rain check on dinner. Can you explain to Tristan and Dalton?"

"Yes. I still think we should—"

"I have to go." Morgan hurried out of the house like ghosts were chasing her. And they were. The ghosts of the past, and the ghosts of regrets. But Morgan had learned early not to play that game, and damned if she was going to begin thinking less of herself just because Cal couldn't handle it.

She was worth more than that.

Still, she cried all the way to the hotel.

Cal fumbled for his good bottle of bourbon and poured a quarter of a glass. Considered. Then poured more till it hit the halfway line.

He needed every drop.

Gandalf and Balin danced around, waiting for their treat, so he got two out but didn't have the heart to wait till Gandalf played dead. It reminded him too much of Morgan. The dogs whimpered a bit as he headed outside but then dragged their treats to their beds. Hunger always trumped playtime with canines.

He carried his drink out to the front porch and slumped in the rocker. He felt like shit. Worse than shit. He'd been so eager to spend the night with her and plan a future. Dreams of a life with Morgan spun in his head like fluffy cotton candy, fogging reality and a hard truth he needed to figure out.

He'd just left her. She'd shared this shattering news with him about her illness and losing her chance to bear children. She'd told him with her chin up and a glittering resolve in her ocean-blue eyes. God, she was so strong and brave and beautiful. And he'd walked away because in one flash of a moment, he'd been terrified she might be right.

Cal never thought about the future with a woman because he was too busy. When he did, it was misty fragments of a general scene that every person had. A wife. Children. A house. Careers. Family. Dogs.

There were never any specifics. When Morgan came into his life, everything narrowed down to a tiny pinpoint of light. Suddenly he had a focus, because he was positive he'd be spending his life with her. A gut instinct and driving need beat through this body and soul, guiding him to his own personal true north.

But there may not be any children in that future. Was he okay making that choice? Would there be regrets?

"Hey. Where's Morgan? When's dinner?"

He glared at Dalton. "Go away. She's not here, and you're not getting dinner."

"Bad day? I'll join you; let me get a beer."

"Would rather be alone right now, thanks anyway." Dalton disappeared and returned with a Heineken, dropping into the chair beside him. "I told you I want to be alone."

"Tough shit. It's my house, too. Did you cancel because tomorrow is the big reveal?"

Cal simmered in brooding silence. He had a lot to think about and wasn't in the mood for banter with his brother.

"Uh-oh. Did you guys have a fight? You have that look on your face men get when being dissed by their woman."

Another voice joined Dalton's, and Cal groaned. "Hey, where's dinner? Where's Morgan?"

"We're out here, Tristan!" Dalton called. "Grab your wine and join us. Cal got into a fight with Morgan."

"Son of a bitch," Cal growled. "When did the words

leave me alone become code for a chat? I fucking hate heart-to-heart chats."

"Yeah, so do I, but sometimes you need them," Dalton said.

Tristan came out onto the porch and took the third seat. Swirled the burgundy liquid in his crystal glass. Then stuck his nose in the glass to take an appreciative sniff before trying a sip. The gesture annoyed the crap out of Cal. "Why do you have to engage in foreplay with your liquor? It's ridiculous."

"Not if you're a wine connoisseur," Tristan said mildly. "What was your fight about? It would probably be best if you just apologized. Then maybe we can save dinner. Morgan said she was making stuffed pork chops."

"For God's sake, this isn't an intervention. Morgan decided she had work to do to get ready for the Rosenthals and decided to get room service. No big deal. No fight. Let's move on."

Tristan and Dalton shared a glance. "Lie," Dalton announced. "You look ripped up. Just tell us, Cal. It'll make you feel better."

"Fuck. You're such a pain in my ass." Temper and frustration snapped through his body, making his fists curl. God, he wanted a fight. A bruising, exhausting, messy, bloody fistfight to get out all this aggression. "Fine. I found something out tonight that changed things. She can't have children."

Tristan frowned. "What do you mean? She's infertile? Or she doesn't want kids?"

Cal ground his teeth. "She had cervical cancer when she was eighteen. They had to give her a hysterectomy."

Dalton whistled and shook his head. "That's some bad

shit." They considered his words in silence. "She must've been through hell and back."

"Yeah," Cal muttered.

"She's special," Tristan said. "What was the fight about, then?"

"That was it. She told me the truth and asked me to make a choice. Told me she wouldn't live with my having regrets."

Tristan looked confused. "So? She can't have kids. That sucks, but there's always adoption. Or not."

Cal shifted in his chair and drank more bourbon. "She asked me straight out if I'd ever have regrets. I told her I don't know."

Dalton gave a long sigh. "And there was the fight."

"You love her, right?" Tristan asked. "Is it the long-term-I-want-to-marry-her type love? Or more like this-feels-really-good-and-I-don't-want-it-to-end-but-I-can't-commit love?"

"The forever kind," Cal admitted. "The get-down-on-bended-knee kind. I know it's fast, and you probably think I'm crazy, but that's how I feel about her. But I owe it to both of us to make sure I'm honest. I always wanted a big family."

"You already have a big family, Cal," Dalton pointed out. "You have us. And Brady and Sydney and Becca. You have Balin and Gandalf. And you may have kids down the line. But most of all, you get Morgan. Morgan becomes your family. I guess to me, there's only one choice. Her."

The words startled him. Reached deep into his gut and spread through his body like fire, warming him from the inside out. Nothing really mattered without Morgan. The idea of being with another woman was impossible. She was his soul mate, his other half. They completed each other, dammit, and he'd been stupid enough to walk away when she was most vulnerable and hurting.

"You're right," Cal said. The words tore out of his mouth. "My God, I got so freaked out, I couldn't see clearly. I choose her. I'd choose her every time, because nothing else matters."

"See," Tristan said. "We told you."

"Heart-to-hearts are good once in a while," Dalton said. "Can we go inside and watch the play-offs now? And order chicken wings so no one has to cook?"

"Sounds good to me. Let's go," Tristan said.

They got up and walked back inside the house, leaving Cal alone with his lightbulb moment and his heart pounding and the need to tell Morgan he'd never let her go.

It was late. She was probably sleeping and didn't need any revelations from him right now. He'd let her get some rest and tell her everything tomorrow.

Tomorrow, he'd set everything right.

chapter twenty-two

Morgan escorted her clients out of the limousine and stood on the pathway. Petra and Slate looked tanned and relaxed from their cruise, and both seemed excited about seeing their new home. They'd been able to take an earlier flight in, but Morgan hadn't called Cal to let him know. He thought they were meeting at the property at two p.m., but Morgan didn't want to see him yet. She could handle the reveal by herself, and then if there were any issues, they'd be able to meet with Cal later.

Morgan barely slept, her mind sifting through every word they'd exchanged. Her heart ached and she'd cried for too many hours, but she made sure that her Vera Wang tailored cream suit was flawless and that her makeup hid the dark lines under her eyes. She dressed for battle and presented a confident, experienced, professional designer who was about to rock their world.

Inside, she felt like throwing up.

Petra gasped as her gaze ran over the elegant lines of the house. "Morgan, it's stunning," she said. Genuine pleasure shone in her violet eyes, and her white teeth flashed in a smile. "Darling, I adore the columns. Take us around the property."

Slate nodded as she gave the full tour. Miles of acres spilled out on a perfectly manicured lawn, and the gorgeous reds and golds of fall were in full bloom, mixing with an aqua-blue sky shimmering over the marina. Morgan guided them through the gardens, over to the hot tub and sauna and past the covered deck.

Petra ran a finger over the thick carved beams. "What type of wood is this, darling?"

"Teak."

"Stunning. The outside is exactly what I wanted. I can't wait to go in."

Relief and satisfaction flooded her body, but she kept her face polite and impassive as she showed them the extent of using the remotes to open the doors and uncover the hot tub. Petra chattered excitedly to her husband as Morgan circled them back around to lead them through the mahogany door. She took a deep breath and stepped inside.

Peace settled over her as she gazed at the house so lovingly created. The unease in her gut settled. This was a home worthy of greatness and full of heart. There was no way the Rosenthals wouldn't love it.

Morgan launched into her speech. "You'll see the central staircase and floating balcony, so you have an open concept space for entertaining. I've worked with a green palette as a base and mixed in Tuscan neutrals to give the kitchen a cozy Italian feel, yet glamorous enough to host a huge dinner party in." Her heels clicked over the Italian tile floors as she listed the various furnishings, appliances, and decor.

Morgan led them from room to room, enthusiastically embracing the theme of each. The grandfather clock; the brass bed in the master bedroom; the gorgeous marble structure of an ancient goddess on her knees begging Zeus; the fabric chandelier in the bath; the restored pool table in the billiard room; the gold-tassled curtain in the film room. Each room had a story, and Morgan told each one, her voice filled with joy and pride as each floor was uncovered like a massive present.

When they arrived back in the central living room, Morgan finally realized they hadn't really said a word.

Petra gazed around with a puzzled look on her face. Slate's lips pressed together in a strange expression of concern and irritation. Tamping down a brief tide of panic, Morgan faced them.

"Welcome to your new home," she said simply. "I worked hard to incorporate your vision with my own expertise in design, and I truly hope you love it."

Petra bit her lip. "Where's the red and black?" she asked. "Where's the minimalist lines I specifically told you I wanted, Morgan?" Her honeyed hair swished over her shoulders as she shook her head. "Tuscan has been done to death. I'm bored with it, and so are all my friends. The brass bed is simply horrific and reminds me of Ikea."

Morgan fought not to flinch and remained impassive as her client spoke.

Slate jerked his hand toward the hallway. "The film room is way too small. And what the hell is that grandfather clock doing on that wall? It must be from the 1800s."

"The theme of the room is time," she explained patiently.

"It's been restored and is priceless. And the balcony and extra private booths give the film room a bit of the exclusive, which I thought would work better than just space."

Slate frowned, not happy with her argument. Her gut lurched. Her skin grew hot. The panic temporarily held at bay began to flow through her body like a flood, and Morgan desperately tried to fight the rising tide. Showing fear would be the end of her.

"Petra, Tuscan style is coming back in a huge way. I understood your new interest in minimalism, but I used the concept through some of the rooms to give you a taste, but honestly felt you'd grow bored too soon. Believe me, classical mingled with a bit of the wow factor will have everyone talking."

They weren't buying it.

Petra picked up a few throw pillows, then strolled around, studying the items Morgan had carefully picked out to give the room creativity and warmth. Morgan kept talking with pure boldness, knowing she needed to sell this concept as hot or fail.

She never failed.

She demonstrated the high-tech gadgets, the customized appliances, the Italian tile, the Parisian paintings, and the specialized furniture and cabinetry Dalton had worked so hard on.

Finally she stopped.

Waited.

Petra walked over to her. Gazed straight into her eyes. Morgan noticed again how perfect she was, her beauty an almost shimmering presence in the room.

"I hate it. There is absolutely no way I can live here."

Slate shook his head with banked fury and glared. "You disappoint us, Morgan. We trusted you. You're supposed to be the best. Now what the hell are we going to do?"

Morgan stood in the middle of the home she loved more than anything while her future shattered around her.

It was over.

Cal tried not to panic.

He couldn't get ahold of Morgan. He planned to go by the site before their appointment but she wouldn't answer his messages. So he'd jumped in his truck and driven there with the intent of forcing her to listen to him.

She wasn't there.

He'd checked with Sydney and his brothers. Nothing. At two p.m., he waited at the Rosenthals' new home, ready to enjoy Morgan's success when her clients saw what she'd created for them. He waited till three p.m. and no one showed up.

After another round of frantic calls, Cal headed to the Hilton and knocked on her door.

No answer.

He was just about to lose his shit and call the police when he heard a dull thud inside. "Morgan!" he yelled frantically, pounding on the door like a madman. "Are you in there? Open up, baby, I'm freaking out. I need to know you're okay."

Palm flat against the wood, he waited.

Nothing.

"Morgan, if you don't open up right now, I'm kicking it in."

The knob turned.

He knew something was wrong immediately. Her usual impeccable appearance was gone. Barefoot and clad in sweatpants and an old sweatshirt, she looked back at him with a dullness in her blue eyes that scared the crap out of him.

He stepped inside and closed the door.

"I'm sorry I didn't tell you our appointment was canceled," she said politely. Morgan walked over to the bar and poured clear liquid into the glass. Whoa, that wasn't water. Or wine. Hell, that was straight vodka over ice. "I had a bit of a problem."

Cal assessed the situation. Slowly he sat down on the couch and watched her. Something bad had happened. He kept his voice light and nonthreatening. She seemed to be a bit in shock. "Is your mom okay?"

She seemed startled by the question. Good, that dragged her out of her hell and reminded her things could be worse. "No, she's fine. I showed the Rosenthals the house."

"I was there, but no one showed."

"Their flight came in early, so I decided to take them myself."

Irritation rose, but he pushed it back down. Probably after their encounter she hadn't wanted to deal with a confrontation. He couldn't really blame her, though it was his right to stand beside her when they presented the house. "What was their reaction?"

She gave a full-out belly laugh with no humor. "They hated it! Oh, this wasn't a bit of dislike where they want to change this and that, or do some tweaking. No, they hated it. Hated my choices and furnishings. Hated the colors. Hated the grandfather clock Dalton spent hours on and the cabinetry he lovingly crafted. They hated Tuscan tile and the brass bed and the film room with the red velvet chairs we restored. They hated it."

Shock raced through him. It had never occurred to him the Rosenthals wouldn't like the house. Morgan had been ruthless regarding her choices, putting everything she had behind every nail and piece of wood and swing of the hammer. "Baby, I'm sorry. I really am. But they must be blind. You put your heart and soul into that house."

Her head swung around. Blue eyes glinted with fury. "Exactly." She lifted her glass in a mock salute. "I went wrong the moment I started choosing things I loved rather than think of my client. I built that house for me, Cal. Me. Not the Rosenthals. My ego got the best of me, and now I've failed. Not only my clients, but myself."

His voice lashed like a whip. "Don't you give me that shit," he said. "You're not a failure because you took a chance. Because you tried to create something a person would love instead of some pretty objects on a shelf an onlooker would admire. You found yourself when you were building that house, Morgan, and you found me with it."

"Don't! I'm not in the mood for false declarations, Cal. Don't push me."

He got up from the couch and stalked toward her. "Well, I'm gonna, whether you like it or not. Here's the thing. You've spent your life creating perfection for others but it never touched you. Sure, you took pride in your work, but this house was personal. It's filled with who you are, like a precious gift you tried to give. Did it work for the Rosen-thals? No. But that's their damn loss. And you did the same to me. Gave me yourself, all of you, and I walked away. I'll regret that for the rest of my life, Morgan, but it's something I'll have to live with."

"Stop." Her hand trembled around her glass. "You need to go. I don't want to hear that you're sorry we didn't work out. I don't want to hear that you loved the house we built together. I just want you to leave."

"Never. Do you hear me? I'm not leaving you, Morgan, never again. I love you. I never should've walked away last night, but I'm stupid enough to think I needed time."

Her shoulders slumped. Cal's heart sank in his chest at the defeated look on her face, a look he'd never seen before. "I understand. You needed to be honest, and it's best if we part ways. I don't belong here anymore. I need to deal with the fallout and go back to Charleston for a while. Decide what my next move is."

"Oh, no, you're not." He spun her around and forced her head up. "You're not going anywhere, not without me. This is the deal. You made a very reasonable argument last night about making sure I have no regrets. The truth is simple. If I let you go, I'll never forgive myself. It will be the biggest regret of my life. I need you, Morgan Raines. I love you. I don't give a damn about children, because you're my fam-ily. You and my crazy brothers and my goofball dogs. If we decide to adopt, great. If not, I don't care. I want you by my side every day. That's all I need to be happy."

"You said you didn't know." Her lower lip trembled. "You left."

"I came back. I needed a few hours, okay? When you find the love of your life, sometimes it takes a slap in the head to remind you not to be a jerk!"

A small laugh escaped her lips. "You are a jerk sometimes," she muttered.

"Agreed. But I'm the man who loves you. You're just going to have to forgive me. Then you're going to marry me."

"Not with a proposal like that," she grumbled.

He cupped her cheeks and tilted her face up. "God, you're sweet." He paused. "God, you're everything."

He kissed her, long and deep and slow, until she softened in his arms and clung to his shoulders and surrendered. Breathing in the scent of wildflowers, he gave her all that he was in that one kiss and promised her everything he'd ever be.

When he finally broke away, she closed her eyes and leaned against him. "I ruined my career. I built them a house they don't want. I'll never work for Hollywood again."

He closed his arms around her and pressed his lips to the top of her head. "We'll fix it," he said. "Whatever we need to do, I know it's going to be okay. One house is not going to ruin your career. You're too talented."

"This is such a mess."

"It's our mess," he said. "You just need some time to figure things out. Where are the Rosenthals?"

She gave a shuddering sigh. "Staying at the Plaza. I don't know what they're going to do. My contract is ironclad, so they can't come after me for the money, but they can certainly ruin my reputation."

"Did they like the structure? The outside? Did they give you specifics of what worked and what didn't?"

She seemed to consider his question for a while. "They loved the outside—that was a total win. The deck, the hot tub, the property. All of it worked."

"Good, that's something that's harder to change. I think we should go over everything in each room. Item by item. By listing each separate problem, we can get a handle on the possibilities."

"Cal, I don't want you to worry. You delivered on the contract and met the delivery date. Pierce Brothers gets full payment."

"I'm not worried about that now," Cal said. "Let's get the team together and construct a plan."

She pulled back and frowned. "What team?"

"Baby, Tristan and Dalton and Brady won't let you do this alone. That's what family is about. Took me a while to realize it. But as I admitted, I'm slow sometimes."

She laughed, leaned in, and hugged him tight.

chapter twenty-three

The next day, Morgan met with the Rosenthals in the conference room at Pierce Brothers. The chilly distance in the air set the tone. She didn't blame them. Morgan had sold them on herself and failed. Now it was time to make things right.

"Thank you for meeting with me," she said in greeting. Back to polished perfection in her power suit and heels, she handed them a folder that contained the proposal. "My job is to make sure you love your home, and I failed. I'm requesting you give me a short extension to fix it."

Slate narrowed his gaze. Those movie-star eyes and that masculine intensity were made to intimidate, persuade, or demolish. Morgan refused to cower beneath him. "Why should we trust you?" he challenged. "We can find ourselves in a bigger hole, and I refuse to give you any extra funds. Shooting schedule begins within the month."

Petra remained silent.

Cal squirmed beside her. She'd already been clear she didn't need him to defend her. Morgan dealt with celebrity clients on a consistent basis and prepared herself for some stinging comments. Cal was there to back her up and answer any questions. She loved him even more when she saw how he struggled not to jump and defend her honor. "I understand," Morgan said. "I take full responsibility, and I'm requesting ten days to make the necessary adjustments. Our original meetings had been clear, and I didn't listen when you informed me you had made adjustments to your vision of the house. When you mentioned minimalist, and specific colors, I assumed you didn't want me to stray from our course and tried to bring the theme in on a limited basis. I won't make that mistake again."

Petra tapped a bloodred nail against the folder, considering.

"These are my proposed changes. There will be no further cost to you. The structure and outside will remain the same. We're looking at redoing the kitchen, expanding the film room, and changing the decor to suit your tastes with a more modern spin. I've included some photos of designs I think you'd like, and already have some specific pieces lined up for you if you approve."

She waited in silence while they glanced at the new contract. Petra nibbled on her lower lip, and Slate kept a bold silence as the minutes ticked by.

"What if in ten days we're still not satisfied?" Slate demanded.

"I won't let that happen again," Morgan said simply. "I know how to fix it, and I can."

Petra stared at her. "Is it even possible to do this within the time period?" she asked.

Cal spoke up. "We have the building and design team

on standby. It is possible, and I promise you we will meet deadline."

Morgan locked gazes with Petra. Slowly the woman nodded. "Yes, I like these changes. Since we're in town, I'll be able to work with you. I'll go through your pictures and tell you what I think."

Slate turned to his wife. "Are you sure?"

Petra shrugged. "The Plaza is quite satisfactory, and I can see a few Broadway plays this week. We can manage ten more days. I think we should give Morgan another chance."

Slate nodded. "Then I'll go along with my wife. You have ten days."

"Thank you," Morgan said.

They shook hands, and she walked them out. When she returned to the conference room, Cal simmered behind the table.

"I hated the way they talked to you," he grumbled. "He'd look more manly with a black eye."

Morgan laughed. "I'm sure you've dealt with your own demanding clients. He has a right to be pissed. He's spent millions on me, and I didn't deliver."

"His opinion. Not mine."

"I know." She crossed the room and leaned in for a hug. The overwhelming demands of the next ten days should have made her want to weep. Instead, a rush of adrenaline and challenge beat in her blood. This time she knew exactly what she had to do. "Are we ready to do this?"

"Yes. Tristan and Dalton are already at the house. Sydney's making calls to suppliers, and Brady's already restructuring the measurements for the film room. I booked my team for overtime, and we'll work through the night if we have to."

She stood on tiptoe and pressed a kiss to his lips. "Thank you, Charming."

"Welcome, princess. Now let's get to work."

Eleven days later, Morgan sat in the kitchen surrounded by boys, munching on pizza. "I'm going to sleep for a week," she groaned, taking a moment to shove a piece of crust in her mouth.

Cal grabbed two Heinekens from the refrigerator and slid them across the marble countertop. "It was close, but we did it. Petra loved the new design, which made Slate less of an asshole."

Tristan laughed and poured himself a glass of wine. "The Chinese lanterns were a brilliant touch," he said. "It brought so much color to the stark red and black."

"Yeah, but taking out those cabinets felt like a crime," Dalton muttered. "I like Morgan's original vision so much better."

"I caught you crying when you used your hammer," Cal teased.

"Imagine Michelangelo destroying *David*. That's how it felt."

Tristan rolled his eyes. "You are no Michelangelo, dude."

"You were always jealous of me."

Morgan laughed. "It hurt me, too, Dalton. Thinking of all that beautiful art and wood in the shed breaks my heart."

"You'll find another use for it," Cal assured her.

"I'm going to have three houses to renovate in the next few months, so those items will save my ass."

Cal took a bite of pizza, wiped his mouth, and nodded. "Brady scored an addition job downtown, so I'll be starting on that next week."

"And Sandy Harper's dad hooked me up with the Bingo crew. A bunch of them saw his deck and want one for themselves, so that'll keep me busy awhile," Dalton said.

"The Rosenthals will be doing a spread in *Home Style* magazine, so the publicity should bring you new clients," Morgan said. "Will it be enough?"

"To turn a profit for the first year? Hopefully. We have two more months to hit it hard."

"We'll make it," Dalton said with confidence.

"What about you, Morgan?" Tristan asked. "Gonna take some time off, or do you have another client?"

She glanced at Cal. He stiffened, but there was a determination in his eyes. They were going to make it work because there was no other way. They needed each other. When Tiffany Taylor emailed her, asking if she'd complete an entire renovation on her three-million-dollar house in LA, Morgan knew Cal was right. One mix-up with the Rosenthals wouldn't have broken her. Now, with the successful redesign, she'd proved she could deliver even when there was an error, which only made her worth go up. It was a glamorous project she'd normally jump on. But last night, considering the next few months, Morgan experienced a lightbulb moment. A way to give them both what they wanted. She was just a bit nervous about bringing it up, just in case they didn't like the idea.

"Actually, I considered sticking around here for a bit." They stopped eating and stared at her. "Seems like Pierce Brothers is expanding. With all the properties Tristan wants to buy, and the renovation projects piling up, I was wondering if maybe, well, maybe you'd need some help?"

Cal grinned. Tristan and Dalton high-fived.

"Is that a yes?"

"Hell yes!" Tristan said. "Are you kidding? I'd love to work with you, and I'm looking at pushing in right on the edge of Harrington. The possibilities are endless."

"Are you sure you won't get bored?" Cal asked. "Harrington isn't glamorous. There's not a lot of celebrities hanging around, looking for million-dollar houses."

"No, I think the people in Harrington are even better." Morgan smiled. "They're real people who want a home. A beautiful home. I'd like to be a bigger part of making their world a better place."

"Welcome to Pierce Brothers," Tristan said.

Morgan stared at the men around the table. Tears stung her eyes. They had her back like she was part of the family, calling in favors and working twenty-four hours a day to make sure the Rosenthals' house was done within ten days. It had been her fault, and they could've walked away, knowing their part of the contract had been met. Instead, they refused to blame her and did everything to help, like she belonged to them.

"Thank you," she said. Her voice came out ragged. "I couldn't have done this without you."

Tristan and Dalton looked nervous, eyes filled with wariness. "Umm, Morgan, we're good. Please don't cry. We can't handle that shit," Dalton said.

She blinked furiously and gave a half laugh. "Okay. But you mean a lot to me."

"Back atcha," Tristan said. "Besides, you belong to Cal. Which means you now belong to us."

And that did it.

Tears streamed down her cheeks, and a choking sob came from her throat.

Cal groaned. "Dude, did you really have to get mushy? Look what you did."

"I'm sorry! Shit, don't cry."

She laughed and cried until Cal gave an irritated sigh and pulled her into his arms, patting her back. "It's okay. I would cry, too, if I was stuck with the three of us."

Morgan held on to Cal in the middle of his kitchen, surrounded by his brothers, and felt like she was finally home.

epilogue

"This doesn't feel kinky, Cal. It just feels creepy. Can't I take the blindfold off?"

"No. We're almost there."

She gave a long, dramatic sigh and he grinned. His truck bumped along the uneven road as they climbed a hill that was half-hidden in the trees. Finally he pulled to a stop and faced her. "We're here."

"Good. I'm getting carsick."

"Sorry, baby. Hang on."

He got out of the car, opened her door, and eased her out. Cal ignored his racing heart. It was ridiculous to be nervous. Stupid, even. She'd like it. Wouldn't she? His gut lurched, but he manned up and decided to see it through. Couldn't put her back in the car at this point anyway.

"Cal? Can I take this off now?"

"Yes. One minute. Okay, here we go."

He pulled the scarf from her eyes. She blinked in the sunlight, taking in the scene before her. The acres of land were untouched, and high weeds choked the lot. The barrier of thick woods lined the back, and a small pond lay to the right. The view from the hill gave a tantalizing view of the harbor in the distance. It reminded him of the Rosenthals' property but set further back.

"Well?" he asked impatiently. "What do you think?"

Morgan turned around to see the full plot of land. "This is beautiful, Cal. How'd you manage to buy it? Most of this property was taken. When I was looking into building for the Rosenthals, we had limited options."

"My father bought this piece of land years ago," he said. "There were three separate lots to go to each of us, with no restrictions on how we use them. We could sell the land or build on it."

"Did you get a new client?" she asked. "Are we going to build a house here?"

Cal swallowed. "Yes. We're going to build a house here. But it's not for a new client."

Morgan frowned. "I don't understand."

Cal dragged in a breath. Reached in his pocket. And dropped to one knee.

"I want to build our house here, Morgan. I want you to have the home of your dreams, inside and out. With me. You changed my life and I love you. Will you marry me?"

"Oh, my God!" She covered her mouth with both hands and shook. "Oh, my God!"

Cal snapped open the box. The two-carat solitaire was classic, pristine, and elegant. It shimmered with pure beauty. Just like his future wife.

If she said yes.

She reached out to touch the ring with a trembling finger. "Goodness gracious," she whispered. "You want to marry me? And build me a house?"

"Build us a house. Princess, my knee is getting a little tired. Are you going to give me an answer?"

"Oh! Yes! My answer is yes, yes, yes." She jumped in his arms and he fell off balance, tumbling back into the grass. She climbed on top of him, pressing kisses all over his face, and they laughed together, rolling over the land that belonged to them and held their future.

"Welcome home, baby."

Samuel Dyken clasped his hands and rested them on the mahogany conference table. A thick stack of papers lay in front of him. A glass of water rested to his right. The same gold-embossed pen lay neatly on the left. His suit was black and tailored perfectly.

Cal and his brothers sat around the table. One year. It had gone so fast. They'd met again as strangers, at odds and in pain. Now they had managed to heal the brokenness and grown stronger. They were once again brothers.

"Gentlemen, congratulations. You've achieved the goal to the exact terms of your father's will. Your profit margin was slim but impressive considering the setbacks you had on top of being forced to start at ground zero. Pierce Brothers will revert back to you in equal shares, effective immediately."

Cal shared a look with Dalton and Tristan. Pride etched their features.

"Now, it's up to you if you'd like to sell out your shares," Dyken continued. "You're no longer required to live in the family house. I'll be happy to help you with any further paperwork needed. For now, I'll let you discuss a bit. When you're done, please see Tricia, my secretary, and she'll set up an appointment. Congratulations."

They thanked Dyken, and the door closed behind him.

Dalton let out a breath. "We did it. Who would've thought?"

Tristan leaned back in the chair and grinned. "Hell, that felt good. We did this without Dad. We actually worked together. And we made a damn profit."

"I had no doubts," Cal said.

Dalton rolled his eyes. "Sure, bro."

Cal studied the polished sheen of mahogany and gathered his courage. "I guess it's time to talk about what happens next."

"What do you mean?" Tristan demanded.

Cal studied his brothers. "Well, Dalton told me he was going back to California. And, Tristan, you threatened to take the company from me."

Dalton stood up from his chair. "Are we going back to this bullshit, Cal? Now that Pierce Brothers is safe, you want to push us out?"

Tristan jabbed a finger in the air, face contorted with anger. "I thought we agreed on what we were going to do with this company! We talked about a vision. You son of a bitch, are you backing out on everything we agreed on?"

"No! I want you to stay, okay? I don't want to run this company alone anymore. I want to run it side by side with my pain-in-the-ass brothers and make it great on our terms. I want to hang out with you on weekends, and watch the ball game, and make fun of Tristan's sissy wine, and rag on Dalton about his man-whore ways. I want you to stay right here in Harrington so you can be my best men for the wedding. I want you to help me build our dream house."

Dalton's mouth dropped open. "You guys are getting married?"

"Yes. For some reason, she said yes. I have to move fast before she realizes I'm not good enough for her."

"Ain't that the truth," Tristan muttered.

"Well? What do you say? Do we do this together?"

Dalton nodded. "I'm staying."

"So am I," Tristan said.

They grinned at one another.

"This calls for a celebration, boys," Cal said. "My Place?"

"Sounds good. Hopefully Hot Girl will be there," Dalton commented.

"Let's go pick up Morgan so she can join us. Congratulations, buddy. About time someone tamed your asshole ways," Tristan teased.

Cal walked out of the conference room with his brothers at his side and a smile on his face. He knew the road ahead wouldn't be smooth. No, there'd be twisted paths and dead ends. There'd be fighting and messy emotions. But there'd also be loyalty, and trust, and joy. Love.

And home.

acknowledgments

Yeah. It takes a village. Thank goodness mine is built on a strong foundation with room to grow!

A huge thank-you to my amazing team at Gallery/Pocket who make everything better. Lauren McKenna, you are perhaps the most gifted editor in the world and you are all mine! Special thanks to Kristin Dwyer for incredible PR and nonstop laughter. Thank you to Elana Cohen for being such a wonderful assistant and always having an answer to my questions.

Kevan Lyon, agent extraordinaire, thank you as always for your tireless work and dedication and belief in my talent.

Thanks to Jessica Estep at InkSlinger, Lisa Hamel-Soldano for keeping me sane, and the Probst Posse for their consistent support and cheerleading.

And finally, to my readers. What can I say? You guys rock!

Keep reading for a sneak peek of the next book in
the Billionaire Builders series

any time and any place

Available this fall from Gallery and Pocket Books!

Fifteen-year-old Raven Bella Hawthorne watched the casket drop into the ground. The rain caused the hole to look slippery, almost like a mud hill. When she was younger, she probably would've looked at the slope as a great adventure, letting out a big war whoop while she hurled herself down the edge like it was a giant Slip 'N Slide. She'd climb out with a big grin, mud encrusted on every part of her body, and her father would shake his head and try to scold her. Meanwhile, his dark eyes would glint with laughter, and Raven would know she wasn't really in trouble.

But now her father was in the hole. She'd never again see that sparkling humor, or hear his deep belly laugh, or listen to one of his lectures in that gravelly voice that reminded her of a big papa bear.

Because her father was dead.

Aunt Penny squeezed her hand but Raven hardly felt it. The cold chill of rainwater seeped into her skin and her soul, burrowing deep inside and making a permanent home to rest in. The crew of men in black suits with bowed heads recited a prayer as the casket disappeared for good.

People threw roses into the hole. One weeping woman clutched her rosary. The priest concluded the prayer service, telling Raven and everyone else not to grieve, because Matthew Albert Hawthorne was in heaven with the angels and was finally, mercifully, at peace.

Raven stared at the priest. At her mishmash of distant relatives she barely knew, and friends who seemed more focused on the scandal surrounding her father's death than on her. No, other than Aunt Penny, she was truly alone. And she didn't feel grateful, or happy, or humbled that her father was with God.

Instead, Raven was filled with rage.

Her beloved father, who had been her entire world, was a liar and a cheat. The man who dragged her to church on Sundays and lectured her on saving her body for love, and being kind to others and always believing she'd accomplish great things in this world, had abandoned his only daughter to run away with another woman. A stranger.

If it hadn't been for the red light, her father and that woman would be in Paris, building a new life away from their children. Instead, they were both dead, lying in the cold, damp ground while she dealt with the stinging slap of betrayal. For the first time, Raven Bella Hawthorne knew what it was to hate.

She hated her father. She hated the woman who had stolen him away. She hated the three sons the woman had left behind, sons who spread evil words about Matthew luring their innocent mother away, painting him as a charming manipulator who cared nothing about the bonds of family.

Her father's once spotless reputation now lay in tatters

around her. People gossiped and stared and whispered behind raised hands about the single father who'd ruined two families by seducing the matriarch of Pierce Brothers Construction. Somehow, some way, Diane Pierce had become a martyr. Which made Matthew Hawthorne the only villain of the story.

So Raven hated and burned for revenge while she stood in the rain, nodding at well-wishers. She listened to Aunt Penny thank the endless line of people who offered food, prayers, and help in an effort to feel validated during someone else's tragedy. Finally, Raven walked to the limousine and slid onto the smooth leather seat. As they pulled away toward her new life, Raven had only one thought:

Payback was going to be a bitch.